Melissa Lucashenko is a Goorie (Aboriginal) author of Bundjalung and European heritage. Her first novel was published in 1997 and since then her work has received acclaim in many literary awards. *Mullumbimby* won the Victorian Premier's Literary Award for Indigenous Writing and the Queensland Literary Award for Fiction. It was also shortlisted for several awards and longlisted for the Miles Franklin Literary Award. Her sixth novel, *Too Much Lip*, won the 2019 Miles Franklin Literary Award and the Queensland Premier's Award for a work of State Significance. Melissa is a Walkley Award winner for her non-fiction, and a founding member of human rights organisation Sisters Inside. She writes about ordinary Australians and the extraordinary lives they lead. Her latest book is *Edenglassie*.

Book club notes are available at www.uqp.com.au

Also by Melissa Lucashenko

PRAISE FOR *MULLUMBIMBY*

'A modern tale of the clash between cultures, of the importance of belonging ... It deserves the widest readership.' ***Bookseller + Publisher*** '4-star Review/Top Pick'

'The highlight of the novel is the way it veers into a kind of indigenous magic realism and how this forces the reader to question many of their prior assumptions.' ***Weekend Australian***

'There is a lot going on around the edges of this novel that gives it depth and richness ... [an] engaging and often illuminating novel.' ***The Advertiser***

'Place is key here, and it is beautifully realised ... a warm comedy of rural and race matters.' ***Sunday Age/Sun-Herald***

'There is a strong sense of landscape in this smart, surprisingly funny and beautifully written work, which will certainly go on to become a classic of Australian literature.' ***Sunday Mail***

'The novel gives us evocative descriptions of place, believable characters and a strong and distinct voice.' ***Canberra Times***

'A humorous, heartfelt, occasionally abrasive and brave work by a writer with an acute ear for language, an eye for subtle beauty, and a nose honed to sniff bullshit at a thousand paces. This book will most likely leave you laughing and crying at the same time. As importantly, it will leave you thinking.' ***Australian Book Review***

'This is a novel perfectly cast for modern times as well as celebrating the physical beauty of the country and its deep historical and spiritual meaning ... powerful.' ***The Hoopla***

MELISSA LUCASHENKO

MULLUMBIMBY

UQP

First published 2013 by University of Queensland Press
PO Box 6042, St Lucia, Queensland 4067 Australia
Reprinted 2013, 2014 (twice), 2015, 2016, 2017, 2018, 2019 (twice), 2020 (twice), 2021, 2022

This edition published 2023

University of Queensland Press (UQP) acknowledges the Traditional Owners and their custodianship of the lands on which UQP operates. We pay our respects to their Ancestors and their descendants, who continue cultural and spiritual connections to Country. We recognise their valuable contributions to Australian and global society.

www.uqp.com.au
reception@uqp.com.au

Cover design by Jenna Lee
Author photograph by LaVonne Bobongie Photography
Typeset by Post Pre-press Group, Brisbane
Printed in Australia by McPherson's Printing Group

This project has been assisted by the Commonwealth Government through the Australia Council, its arts funding and advisory body.

A catalogue record for this book is available from the National Library of Australia.

ISBN 978 0 7022 6571 6 (pbk)
ISBN 978 0 7022 5095 8 (epdf)
ISBN 978 0 7022 5096 5 (epub)

University of Queensland Press uses papers that are natural, renewable and recyclable products made from wood grown in well-managed forests and other controlled sources. The logging and manufacturing processes conform to the environmental regulations of the country of origin.

For my teachers

'Thin love ain't love at all.'

Toni Morrison, *Beloved*

NOTE

This novel is set mainly on the Arakwal lands of the Bundjalung Nation. Like the characters, however, the specific locations of Tin Wagon Road, Piccabeen and Lake Majestic are entirely fictional. They exist only in the author's imagination.

Chapter One

It is a truth universally acknowledged, reflected Jo, that a teenager armed with a Nikko pen is a pain in the fucking neck, and if it isn't then it fucken well oughta be. For here came Timbo wandering up the hill, his tiny brown chest tagged with fat inky swirls: *No Justice, No Peace. Better pay or I ring DOCS.* And in certain parts of certain cities that would be Aboriginal art. Teach the lad to stand still, and people, we've got ourselves an installation.

Timbo beamed at Jo from beneath the number-three haircut that Kym gave all her boys until they were big enough to resist the onslaught of the clippers. What her nephew mouthed was drowned out by the roar of the Mullumbimby Council's ride-on mower.

'Hey?' Jo cupped her hand to her ear.

'I got dadoos,' Timbo yelled, his arms outstretched in demonstration.

'I can see that, darlin.' Jo grinned as she drew the Honda to a halt. She took off her hat, hung it on the cracked grey-black knob of the gearstick, and mopped her forehead with her arm. Dollops of sweat flew sideways onto the newly shaven couch grass. Pulling the boy close, she used the bottom of her damp red singlet to remove a transparent snail trail from beneath his nose. For the thousandth time she was struck by his beauty: perfectly feathered dark brows above the blackest of black eyes. Keep your pink-cheeked dugai cherubs, she thought, gimme Kym's boys any day.

'What's that tattoo say then, bub?' she asked. The child's forehead crinkled, and he traced the loud black ink of *pay me a living wage* with his slender brown index finger, as though he could take in the written word by osmosis.

'It says . . . Tim Bone Walker.'

'Ellen –' Jo yodelled towards the white metal donga that was their home. 'Stop tagging ya cousin! How many times?' The ink couldn't be doing his little immune system any good – not to mention who would have to scrub it off before his mum picked him up in an hour!

There was no reply from the donga. Ellen would be onto a different art project by now, headphones blaring hardcore rock into her thirteen-year-old head and the tedious task of babysitting her cousin sidelined, if not forgotten altogether. Jo frowned. She had lots more mowing to do, nearly all the Protestants, and maybe she could make a start on the RCs as well. She couldn't be watching Timbo while she worked. That's what she was paying Ellen six bucks for.

'You go back and see what Ellie's doing, darlin,' she encouraged Timbo, 'and later we go for a feed. Hot chippies, hey?'

'Fish n chips?' Timbo brightened. He was the Bruns Co-op's biggest fan. Jo had shown him years ago how to lie on the splintery jetty, watching the water through the narrow cracks in the pale grey timber. If you spat down a mouthful of chewed chips you could always bring up the large school of wily jalum that lived in the river. They came joyously to the clouds of food, came close enough almost to touch, but always refused to bite for any misguided jalum bira tourist who might chuck a line in. Lying prone there in the sun on the Bruns jetty was a meditation upon fish, and on temptation, and on gullibility too.

'Can we get dem little fish baits?' Timbo pleaded.

'We'll see. Aunty a bit broke this week, bub,' Jo replied, like there were weeks she wasn't. 'You go see Ellen now, darlin. And stay away from that road, orright.'

Timbo turned away. His tiny brown back beseeched her: *Wash Me.*

Laughing, Jo pulled her hat down onto her forehead, and surveyed the expanse of lawn she had yet to mow. Before her lay one hundred and fifty years of dead white Mullumbimby.

The cemetery where she worked and lived was an oasis of mature eucalypts, surrounded by thick scrub on two sides and on a third by the neat gardens of houses set well back from the quiet side street. Dappled sunlight fell through the high tree canopy, splashing the hillside with gold in the early and the late of each day. Ruined headstones lay scattered in regimental patches: RCs. Methodists. Salvation Army. Most of the memorials to white lives were old, and a few were ancient by Australian standards, mossy and unreadable except for tantalising remnants. In her first few months as grounds-keeper, Jo had often stopped to try to decipher them, wondering whether . . . *oc* . . . .*elly, b. 18. . d. 1928*, had been a man or a woman. Was *Bain . . . Mc . . . ett* lying next to his wife or his child in that double grave? These stories that had once been so important to the town, that had needed carving in granite – where were they now?

After those first months Jo let the stories be. Wherever they were, it wasn't here anymore. And there was something about the cemetery that put things into another perspective altogether. Spend enough time among the silent majority, Jo discovered, and you found your-self worrying less about tomorrow, and more about today. There are so many tomorrows, after all. How could a person possibly keep track of all of them?

She didn't have a lot of visitors at work, of course. Eeh, too many mooki there, sis, the local Goories – the Watts, the Bullockheads and the Browns – muttered in disdain, before they quickly changed the subject. It's not the mooki that worry me, Jo would reply airily, it's the living, and this was mostly true, though, if she was being totally honest, she wasn't in any great hurry to investigate odd noises once the sun slipped down behind the hospital across the way. But those noises had only happened a few times; so far it was always the Mullum kids trying hard to lose their virginity under a full moon, and who, surprised by Jo suddenly looming out from behind William Protheroe *(1910–1964)*, generally demonstrated a mastery of Anglo-Saxon nothing short of remarkable. She cack-led aloud at the memory of the last screaming pair disappearing

3

around the corner at a rate of knots, gravel flying in their bare-arsed wake.

Still grinning, Jo turned the key and brought the Honda roaring back to life. As she plunged forward beneath a row of Chinese rain trees heavy with salmon-pink blossom, she wondered whether Cecile Johanna Mallett and Thomas Edward Compton had really been close enough in life to warrant lying beside each other, there on her right-hand side, today and ever after till kingdom come. Once you were in the ground, that was it: no more rent or eviction notices, but no freedom of association either. Not that everyone in the three acres below her was dead, mind you. No siree, she wouldn't be making that amateur's mistake. Thelma Margaret Farina *(1910–1971)*, for example, was *Only Sleeping*, and she was a pretty fucking sound sleeper at that, since Thelma Margaret hadn't noticeably stirred in the fifteen months that Jo had been mowing around her granite monument with a six-horsepower mower that needed its muffler replacing, if Trev at Farmcare could ever get around to ordering the bloody part.

And if that's my biggest problem, Jo told herself, revving the mower up the incline, then I could be doing a whole lot worse. The Goories might shy away and suck their teeth at ghosts, but a modest life of mowing and brush-cutting and keeping an eye on which flowers needed chucking in the compost, it suited Jo. She had her sister in Brisbane, a few mates in Ocean Shores and Bruns, and Ellen was as happy as any clever, artistic kid was going to get in a one-horse country town. If Jo missed the excitement of the band, well, all good things come to an end. It wasn't as if she'd played a lot of gigs the past few years anyway, not with Paul around being Eeyore and dragging her into his tight white world as much as he possibly could. The hectic days of jam sessions and after-parties and joints as fat as your thumb were a whimsical memory now, as though they'd happened to some distant relative and not to her at all.

Jo slowed the Honda to a loud yammering crawl. She could see, but not hear, Ellen emerging from the donga at the base of the hill

4

to unchain their two ecstatic mutts, check the fireplace, and lay a few more dry tallowwood branches across the embers that were smouldering from breakfast. Jo checked her watch. Four o'clock in mid April, and Timbo still running about with no shirt and a runny nose. Jo sent a loud cooee echoing down the slope.

'Shirt – putta shirt on him,' she yelled through cupped hands. Ellen looked up, fat black earphones sitting on her head like they were bolted on, and cast her arms in the air. Jo tugged at her shirt, pointing at Timbo. Ellen nodded. As a fresh plume of white rose from the firepit, Jo got moving again, wondering about her chances of Ellen cooking some dinner if she kept stubbornly mowing for another hour. Slim to nonexistent, she told herself, especially since Timbo would surely have reported the likely prospect of hot fish 'n' chips. *Arniejo said so.*

Jo narrowed her eyes and pursed her lips in a sudden recognition of tactical defeat. That would have been the entire point of sending the lad up to bother her, of course. Ellen was too fucken smart for her own good, and understood people in a way her mother never would. Jo sighed. Horses and dogs were the people for her; her favourite humans all lived in the pages of novels. She racked her memory till some lines of Whitman bubbled up:

> *I think I could turn and live with animals,*
> *They are so placid and self-contained*
> *I stand and look at them long and long . . .*
> *Not one kneels to another,*
> *Nor to his kind that lived thousands of years ago,*
> *Not one is respectable or industrious over the entire earth.*

Yeah, the old poofter genius was on her wavelength, alright. Jo could stand and look at horses long and long, because yarraman were proper easy. Probably it was no coincidence, Jo mused, that the people she worked with were all dead.

She put her foot down and steered carefully around Kathleen

Mary Watson *(1866–1943)*, drifting back, as she did so, to the year Kathleen had been born. What would the Mullum cemetery have looked like in 1866? No narrow bitumen track splitting the hill for one thing. The graveyard for the brand-new hamlet of Mullumbimby Grass would have been too tiny to need any real road. Here on the hill everything would probably have been forest. At the bottom of the slope a dirt track made by bullock drays might have trailed into a clearing, but no more than that.

Jo shrank the cemetery in her mind, lopping off three quarters of the plots, and replacing the headstones with tall strangler figs and silky oaks drooping with lawyer vine. The Big Scrub would have towered where the Mills and the Garrards now lay under green mottled marble, the rainforest still healthy and filled with animals and birdlife, not yet doomed by the axes of men who – months or years from anything they thought of as home – had tried to slash and log and burn their way into freedom here. A funeral back then would have been a big effort, she thought, seeing the mourners sweating and slapping at mozzies as they forged their way through Bundjalung mud to a six-foot hole in the good red earth.

Who had cleared that first dugai gravesite for the mortal remains of William John Collins, and what had been here before him? Had the Bundjalung watched his muddy funeral from the forest edge, or even from among the crowd? Had the Mullum hospital always been just a little to the south, and was this spot the distance that a full coffin could be carried from there by a few strong men? Or was this clearing simply the pragmatic distance that meant no funereal stench could make its way back into the main part of town?

Uncle Freddy Humbug would have an opinion on this, Jo mused, for despite his madness and his painful coterie of hippy admirers, the old man often made sense, especially in off-pay week. Uncle Humbug, yeah. Aunty Sally Watt, too, if Jo could catch her between meetings. Wondering what the elders might have secreted in their memories about the history of the cemetery, Jo decided to mow just the Protestant half of the hill for now, and let the Micks enjoy their peace and quiet a bit longer. She was starting to taste those hot fish bites with vinegar herself.

'Time to get our own place, now. I've had just about fucken enough of being Trailer Trash,' Jo told her sister across the coal fire. She popped a chip in her mouth and licked tomato sauce off her fingers, looking at the black half-moons that were revealed. She wondered yet again where the nail clippers might turn up. It was a constant mystery, how she and Ellen could live on top of each other in an eighteen-foot metal box and still things managed to get lost. *Sardine Dreaming.*

Kym looked at the headstones and shuddered.

'I dunno how youse do it, living ere,' she said, wrapping the last remnants of burnt chip ends back into the butcher's paper and chucking them on the coals where they immediately burst into brilliant orange flame.

'The dogs woulda eaten them, Aunty.' Ellen said, disapproving of the waste.

'Don't be fucken myall,' Jo told Kym. 'Mooki not gonna hurt ya unless you've done something really wrong. Nah, the big problem here is worrying what to tell Basho if Daisy and Warrigal start excavating and run up to someone at a funeral with a bloody great shin bone in their mouth.' The women cackled.

'They never started digging, eh?' Kym asked, glancing at the dogs, who lay just inside the firelight, mouths open, enjoying the warmth as well as the human company and the prospect of greasy chip crumbs.

'Nah. Course they're tied up most of the day. Prisoners, arncha, Dais?'

Daisy wagged a red cattle dog tail at the sound of her name, while Warrigal just kept scratching.

'He needs a wash,' Ellen observed redundantly.

'He's allergic.' Jo frowned. 'To everything.'

'Got fleas too,' Ellen told her.

7

'Yeah, well, put it on your list,' Jo responded brightly, 'cos mine's looking a bit bloody full. You can wash them both first thing tomorrow, alright?' There was no reply. Ellen started pulling fleas off Warrigal and bloodily crushing them between her black-inked fingernails. That Nikko pen had had a workout lately and no mistake.

'Alright?' Jo repeated in a harder voice.

'Yeah, I said!' Ellen snapped.

'Geez Louise . . .' Jo rolled her eyes.

'You looking forward to the Blues Fest, Ellie?' Kym intervened with a warning look at her sister.

'Yeah. There's a grade twelve kid I know playing, Nat Bowden. He's a really good singer–songwriter.'

Jo wondered in sudden alarm if Ellen had a crush on this boy.

'Be a good line-up this year.'

Ellen brightened. 'Yeah, it'll be awesome.'

'Not if those dogs don't get washed,' Jo threatened. 'It'll be awesome minus one thirteen-year-old.'

Ellen scowled sideways and Kym sighed, her good work undone.

'I looked after Timbo today, didn't I?' Ellen replied sourly, before stalking into the donga to work some voodoo on her mother.

'Yeah, for about five minutes,' Jo retorted as the door didn't quite slam. 'I wouldn't stop her really, the bloody ticket cost me a fortune,' she whispered to her sister. 'No freebies for me this year. I musta walked under a Chinaman's ladder carrying a black cat or something.'

'Gonna give us a song?' Kym asked without much hope.

'Nah, the gits all got busted strings,' Jo told her.

'Ah, gammon, busted strings.' Kym said.

But Jo swore it was the truth.

'So what's going on with the settlement?' Kym asked when they finally rose from the fire, brushing off salt grains. 'Heard anything?'

'Any day now.' Jo shifted remnants of burning wood around with the toe of her runner, which had had its tongue sliced off and been retired to mowing duties. Smoking timber broke to ashes beneath her feet. 'Coral Avenue already sold. I can thank Paul that I didn't get a crack at it, the stupid prick,' Jo said quietly so Ellen wouldn't hear.

'You'd think he'd want it settled too,' Kym wondered.

'Oh, he's still fully got the shits, eh,' Jo replied, alluding to the brief but spectacularly destructive affair that had ended her marriage. 'It was two years ago, for Chrissake. But the solicitor reckons he can't delay settlement again without going to court. I don't reckon he'll go that far.'

'Men, eh,' was all Kym could say. The sisters erupted in laughter that spoke of too much testosterone-poisoning over the years.

Jo pulled at Daisy's soft ears. Giant brown puppy eyes gazed up at her in adoration. Dogs and horses, thought Jo, that was the go, warrigal and yarraman. Comet was worth ten of any men she'd seen lately – And you are beginning to sound, she interrupted herself, like a pickled old dugai propping up the bar at the Billi pub, saying, 'Aaarggh, women, they're all the fucken same . . .'

'No such thing as a painless divorce, my sister.' Kym's eyes crinkled kindly, knowing all about it from her own first marriage, which had given her a blond, blue-eyed son and years of misery before meeting Jason at the Brisbane NAIDOC Ball.

'Nah, specially when you hook up with a *dickhead*. He marries a black muso from the sticks and then decides he wants a white city accountant for a wife. Anyone who marries outside their own culture wants their fucken head read, onetime,' Jo observed tartly – 'Me included.'

'Seeya later Timbo mah man,' she cried, leaping upon her nephew and tickling his ribs till he squealed. Then she picked his little body up and threaded him headfirst through the window into the front seat of the Pajero.

Kym pointed at Timbo's seatbelt.

'Use safety belt, countryman,' she instructed, going all retro on his five-year-old ass.

Timbo sighed and strapped himself in, the ghost remnants of his tattoos still visible on his narrow little forearms. Jo twisted her mouth in wry amusement. What other thirteen-year-old kid in Byron Shire would know what a living wage was, for Chrissake? Her daughter absorbed information like a sponge. An angry Aboriginal sponge, demanding knowledge from every quarter. Speaking of which.

Ellen's head popped out of the donga.

'Seeya, Timbo,' she called to her cousin, who promptly made squashed faces against the car window at her. In return, Ellen stuck her tongue out and finger-dragged a gargoyle grimace.

'Thanks for having him, hey, preciate that.' Kym gave a wave and drove crunchily away over the gravel.

As the dust from the Pajero's wheels settled, floating oh-so-slowly back to earth under a three-quarter moon, Jo stood and stared into the glowing coals, remembering. Her biceps were hard, yeah, but her fingertips were soft as butter now, and inside her chest there wasn't a flicker of whatever it was that made you stand in front of a mob of punters and see them wild for your song. She doubted any of her guitars were even in tune, those that did have six strings. No, she was no musician, no more, no more, I ain't gonna sing no more, she chanted aloud to the fire. The music had left her as quickly and mysteriously as it had arrived in her teens, and there wasn't a lot anyone could do about that.

Jo glanced over at the headstones.

'You mob might try and help a woman,' she told them matter-of-factly. 'Sling a bit of inspiration this way, eh?' But nothing happened. Jo went inside and closed the metal door. She shut out the mooki and the winter chill; she even managed to push down the annoying, unanswerable, and ever-more-present question worming away in her brain: If you aren't a musician after all, Jo Breen, then who the hell are you? And what exactly do you think you're doing here?

'I'm going to town,' Jo told Ellen the next morning. 'Need anything?'

'Free money,' said Ellen, absorbed in a charcoal drawing of a woman's face. It was completely realistic except for the faint suggestion of horns nestled underneath the curls.

'No wurries, I'll stock up on gold bullion while I'm at it, eh?' Jo tilted her head at her daughter.

'Dog food and some chocolate.'

'Got it. Wotcha drawing?'

'Fifty dollar notes.'

'I dunno how I ended up with the only raging capitalist in the whole Bundjalung nation –' Jo shook her head – 'but you may as well draw some for me while you're at it. I thought you were going up the paddock?'

'Sore leg. I'll go up with you later on.'

Jo swung into Burringbar Street with the radio blaring Country Sweethearts, the best thing about any Saturday morning in Mullum. She liked to drive *slow as* through town, checking out the locals. Just to drive slow was relaxing in itself, she was fond of telling all and sundry, no need to hurry everybloodywhere, now was there? Just stick ya elbow out the window and putter along nice and easy. Muttika therapy. Let the tourists fang it over the dodgy backroads; Jo wasn't burning any extra juice for anyone, not with The Waifs on the radio and the April sun so pretty in a blue sky – you'd swear you lived in paradise, for all that you worked hard for a crust and made yer yumba in a tin can.

Jo pulled into the car park opposite the Which Bank, where the lilli pillis had finished fruiting months before. Walking past, Jo greeted them. 'Jingawahlu baugal jali jali,' she whispered, touching the trunks with a soft hand. No call to ignore someone just cos they don't have a feed for you. Respect is a fulltime job, twenty-four seven. The way to behave in the world so that nobody's pride gets trampled, so that anger doesn't get a chance to ripen into disaster. Aunty Barb had shown her that: noticing that Jo had binung and mil that worked from time to time, she had taken Jo aside for instruction, not long before the accident. *You are a blackfella 101.* A lot of it forgotten now, or pushed aside in the daily grind of paying bills, but, ah, some things remained. Some things remained.

Jo fingered the delicate pink new growth on the trees, marvelling at their softness. The leaves gleamed in the bright morning sun: British Racing Green for the older growth, palest whitish-pink and bronze for the new. When the berries on these particular trees arrived again in September they'd be the intense hot pink that said they were tasty and soft, worth stopping for. This is the world you live in, Jo told herself, so look at it. Sit, and look, and listen, them things that lie at the heart of being proper blackfella. Dadirri. Sit still long enough and you see everything clear, bub, Aunty Barb had promised, a fishing line welded to her aged hand. Sit until the superficial bullshit falls away – but, ah, sit still long enough, you make yourself a target at the same time. That dadirri be a two-edged sword, my aunt.

As Jo stood looking at the ads in the real estate window, a ruined white Econovan drove past, beeping madly, with a barking black collie hanging out the passenger window and shedding dog hair down the length of town. Jo grinned and yelled back as the woman rounded the corner opposite the Middle B too fast, almost cleaning up a redhaired teenager with his face in a pie – sweet Jesus, that's not a magical zebra crossing, lad, Jo winced, look where ya going. Chris swerved around the kid and braked, horn blaring some more.

'Where ya going, ya mad gin?' Jo yelled through megaphone hands.

'Got to get to the library before twelve! I'll come and see ya later on.'

Jo gave Chris the thumbs up. She was better, then. What had it been this time, two weeks holed up in the backblocks of Tin Wagon Road? Three? The Mullum hills were full of mental health stories, and Chris with her depression was one of them. When she was well, she was a normal, happy, vital woman, and then when the illness struck it was like someone had sucked the soul from her body. Chris was constantly hopping between naturopaths and snake oil salesmen with different theories to peddle. Hurling her tiny sickness pension away on miracle cures and dodgy diagnoses ... but right now Jo's mate was well: she was out and driving around, enjoying the end-of-April sunshine and the spectacle of Mullum doing its Saturday shopping. All the people – the town and the country, young and old, beautiful and otherwise – on display in their autumn clothes, heading for the markets to stock up on fresh vegies and Stokers Siding honey and chili jam and –

Jo stopped dead in her tracks.

– and speaking of the beautiful people, she goggled, who was this coming out of the bookstore twenty metres away, looking very fine and very fit? The dreadlocked man was a footy player or such by the look of him, considerably darker than she was herself and very obviously a blackfella, and fuck me *sideways* he's carrying a book – and he's not a local, and how can I find out his name and nation and marital status and sexual preference *right now*, Jo was thinking, with a kind of bemused astonishment at her own interest, which had gone seriously AWOL ever since her divorce. Was he here for the Blues Fest? A tourist just passing through? Or a new arrival in town, joining every other bastard on the east coast for the sea change they thought they had to have?

The Koori man glanced down the street towards Jo, developed a sparkling cheeky grin as if to say Here I Am and There You Are Sistergirl, and Ain't Life Grand? and then carried himself and his new book down towards Mullum Medical, where he promptly disappeared. Jo literally rubbed her eyes. It was an apparition, right? She had hallucinated herself a spunky blackfella because now, after nearly two years of celibacy, she was ready to find another bloke ... that was all *this* was. Except she knew better; she had her fair share of madnesses to draw on, and then some, but visual hallucinations weren't one of her party tricks.

For a moment Jo contemplated going into the bookstore and asking Denise what the man had bought, hoping – please, oh please – that it wasn't Armistead Maupin, but she couldn't bring herself to do it. Get a grip, Jo, she ordered herself, you're thirty-five, don't you know better? Aren't the flash-looking ones always trouble? Cos for sure he'll be married up or have a good reason not to be. Back in the car she turned up Morcheeba to push gorgeous

13

black men out of her head, while she tried to remember what she needed to get off that miserable, fat Italian bastard Tony at the co-op.

'Halters and leads.'
   'Check.'
   'Lunge rope.'
   'Check.'
   'Chaff.'
   'Check.'
   'Let's be wenting, Cisco.'

At the agistment paddock at Main Arm, Jo stood and watched as Oliver repeatedly trotted a handsome chestnut filly and then turned her into the rail in a cloud of grey dust. He was teaching the horse how to gather her haunches beneath her, pursuant to spinning on a dime when she started campdrafting. The trainer was an ugly battered gnome who looked and sounded like an evil troll, but with horses he knew how to be supple, if not soft, and he rode like he'd been stitched into the saddle. Jo made several unflattering mental comparisons of his skill with hers, before remembering to interrupt her self-loathing. The man spends eight hours a day on a horse, she told herself, and I'd be lucky to spend eight hours a month lately. She focused on the filly's movements. Excellence of any kind was enchantment, and she could ignore, if not actually forgive, Oliver's bright red neck when he was working a stockhorse.

Impatient for her attention, Comet nickered over the steel railing, raising a front hoof at the prospect of a feed. Handsomest yarraman. His black-tipped ears were sharply pricked in her direction, looking for the chaff.

'I detect cupboard love,' she answered him. 'But you'll work for ya tucker today.' She slipped a halter on him, and tested his mood with a fingertip instruction to shift sideways. Hmm. Not bad. The horse was learning to listen to her intently. Her: the herd leader, the Boss Mare. The one who really did the work and kept the show on the road, while the stallion galloped around, tossing his mane, looking important and strong and sexy. Making babies and looking for fights. Ha.

'See ya,' said Ellen from on top of Athena, Comet's mother. 'I'm going up to Holly's.'

'Okay, watch out for that bull,' said Jo, assessing her daughter's posture on the horse and giving it a giant mental tick. 'I wish you'd use a bloody saddle but.'

Ellen made a loud fart with her lips at this, and Comet startled sideways against Jo, his eyes wide in alarm. They laughed.

'He's never heard a human fart before,' said Jo.

'I find that *very* hard to believe,' answered Ellen, grasping a handful of Athena's black mane and cantering away.

'Smart-arse!' her mother yelled. 'Be careful!' And don't come running to me when you break your neck.

She picked up the lunge. Coiled the long flat cotton rope in her left hand and swung the other end in a circle from her right fist. Comet's left ear tilted inward, conceding to her authority.

Walk on.

The colt stepped forward instantly, his packed brown rump forcing the clean-boned legs forward, and his back hoofs overreaching the marks left by his front ones.

Baugul yarraman . . .

Can you jump? Jo wondered. And if you can, does that mean you'll buck under saddle? Her right hand swung the end of the lead a little faster.

Trot on.

If I had the money, my friend, Jo told him silently, you'd win royal sashes, but who's got a horse float? Not me, boyo, not me. So we'll just ride these hills and, once Ellen leaves home, we'll hit the National Trail and really have us a time . . . She frowned and increased the tension on Comet's halter.

Git up there! None of that . . .

The colt was snaking his neck towards the ground, testing to see how serious Jo was about this trotting in circles nonsense. She gave the lunge a sharp snap. His head dipped low again and his back heels flicked up in irritation at having to follow orders. I know that feeling, bunji, Jo told him, but you're outta luck. The whole point of lunging the horse was not to exercise him, but to teach him to yield to her authority, her voice, her rope, and her fingers. If she worked well enough, the colt would eventually obey directions made with a mere flick of her eyes. She had seen Oliver do it. Whether she had his skill and patience was another matter altogether, but it was something to aim for. A second sharp tug saw Comet return obediently to the circle, blowing loudly out of flared nostrils and steadily trotting with his neck arched, inside ear pricked to the Boss, patient now with this rounded business that the human creature found so important.

Goooood booooy . . . baugul yarraman . . . Woah.

She halted the colt, worked him in the other direction, threw a few tarps around to get him used to the noise, and then left him tied to the railing to teach him about the waiting game.

Oliver was still spinning his magic with the now foam-flecked chestnut. She wandered over to watch.

'I'll chuck a saddle on that colt next week if you want.' Oliver spoke out of the side of his mouth.

'Does the pope shit in the woods?'

'What?'

'Nothing, bad joke. That'd be great.'

'Will he draft, do ya reckon?' she asked.

'He's been watching my cattle, so I'd say so. Could probably do just about anything, that colt.' Oliver halted the chestnut merely by shifting his weight backwards in the saddle, leaving his reins untouched. Jo beamed. He thinks Comet is good enough to draft. I done good. I bred him – yeah that's right, me, Jo Breen. Ah am the Greatest –

'But he's too good for you,' Oliver added.

Jo stopped beaming onetime. Rude old redneck fucker.

'You wanna sell him on to a pro like Annie Beaumont,' he advised, dismounting.

16

'That horse is not for sale!' Jo said. 'Even to Annie. I'm doing the National Trail on him.'

'Well, I better ride him next week then.' Oliver led the chestnut away and left Jo steaming in his wake.

'How'd the old girl go?' Jo asked when Ellen rode in the gate twenty minutes later.

'Good.'

'Holly home?'

'Yeah. She had homework, so I didn't stay.'

Ellen was an oddball in many ways, but a typical Goorie in at least one: she spoke around half as much as a white child her age. Learn by watching and listening, using your mil and binung, was the centuries-old habit, and not by asking bloody silly questions all the time.

Jo couldn't help it. Oliver was going to ride Comet *next week*. Her face and her heart opened, she grinned fit to beat the band, and for once her freckled, green-eyed daughter softened and smiled back.

Baugul jahjam.

JAGAN

LAND

Chapter Two

The sun was creeping above the slash pines, and its early slanting rays bathed the twenty acres with a brilliant golden sheen. To her left, Bottlebrush Hill gazed benignly down over the old farmhouse and paddocks. To her right, the heavily forested ridgeline made a thick green barrier between her and the rest of the world. Few trees stood out distinctly on that high ground, but in one thinly wooded eastern section, Jo saw, a large eucalypt – a mountain ash perhaps – raised its curiously heart-shaped canopy in outline against the lightening sky. She slowly breathed out a stream of cold white breath and contemplated an astonishing fact: from where she stood in the middle of the big paddock, she could take off running in any direction and be winded before she'd left her own land.

That was something for a Goorie woman to think about; something to hold onto and savour.

The bottom dam was hazy with mist. White wisps lingered among the dark knotty pines beside it. The morning felt miraculous, as though this was the First Day after some tremendous upheaval which had somehow left Jo standing unscathed. It seemed to her, facing the dawn, that anything might be possible now, and as if the day – *this* morning, *this* sun upon *these* hills – called for a kind of reverence that she could barely express. She kicked off her dirty runners and let her bare feet meet the earth. The grass she stood on was moist with autumn dew. The cold of night still lingered in the soil beneath, especially here in the shadow of the enormous tallowwood tree. Jo stepped away, out into open pasture where the sun could fall directly on her skin, and, as its warmth reached her face and chest, she lifted her arms high in supplication. *Black Old Sun*. Oh I musta done something right, someday, somewhere, to be still standing up alive here on Bundjalung land. She turned in a slow circle, arms still high, watching the ridgeline. Here I am, my budgeree jagan. Here I am. Know me for who I am, a Goorie jalgani, jinungalehla here, poor and ignorant though I might be, I'm here at last. Jo closed her eyes and saw Aunty Barb perched on the rotting veranda at South Golden in a canvas deck chair, fishing line in the canal and a durrie in the ashtray wisping smoke around her creased brown face.

Sit ning and listen, JoJo. Gotta hear the world around you, bub. You just sit ning and you'll soon work things out.

Jo's face suddenly felt cold as something came unexpectedly between her and the heat of the sun. When she opened her eyes she laughed aloud in astonishment. No more than twenty metres overhead, level with the top of the tallowwood, a wedgetail was circling with its enormous dark eye cocked to observe her movements. Jo could clearly see the precise curve of the bird's killing talons, and the blackness of its diamond-shaped tail. The eagle's motion was silent, other than the occasional slow flap of its giant wings. Transfixed, she let her arms drop and watched the bird watching her. The sun had made it right over the top of the pines now, and as the dew on the grass dried and her feet lost their chill, Jo realised that she was being ringed by two distinct but joined circles: that of the bird in the air, and the one its shadow was making on the earth below. An unfamiliar sense of great peace descended upon her as she remembered:

Circles protect you if you let them, girl. But you gotta let em. Gotta not get in their way.

'That you, Aunty Barb?' Jo asked the eagle, hearing the waver in her own voice.

The eagle gave one harsh cry – of dissent, Jo thought – and rose swiftly in the air, soon becoming a tiny black dot above the ridgeline.

Couldn't be, anyway. Aunty Barb's meat was that slowpoke tree-dweller, boribi – koala. Couldn't get much further from boribi than a wedgetail. It was just one of those things, one of those odd and striking visitations of nature, Jo decided, as she dragged her runners back on. Still, the feeling of having been seen by the eagle stayed with her. Her arrival on the farm had been witnessed, Jo felt. She had asked for a sign, and a messenger had welcomed her. She was Home.

As the mourners turned to leave the mound of red earth covering the late Mrs Lacosta, Jo found herself face to face with Cheery Dan, Fat Tony's offsider at the rural co-op. His permanent grin had been muted to a half-smile in deference to the occasion and, Jo now realised, he was standing alongside the same bloke who had driven past her farm in a yellow ute that morning.

Yellow Ute Man was fit from outdoor work and he had a hard face, Jo thought, a hard face with intelligent grey eyes that wouldn't easily look away from a fight. A bit of a dangerous character, perhaps. Then, as Dan introduced her, she amended this: it's not so much a hard face, maybe just tough. Tough I can live with, she thought. Tough I like, in men and women both . . . Even if he hadn't stopped when she tried to wave him down.

'G'day,' she greeted him. 'You drove past me an hour ago when I was looking at that cow on Tin Wagon Road.'

'Oh. Yeah. Rob Starr,' the man said, putting out a rough square hand for her to shake. His skin was freckled, and the hair on his muscled arm shone copper in the hot sun. 'Yeah, I knew that heifer was already dead, otherwise I would have come down and shot it meself.'

Starr made it sound as though Jo was a long-time resident who had been lumbered with the shooting of a sick beast.

'I wasn't – ah, I didn't know how to make sure it was dead,' Jo confessed. Starr raised his eyebrows, as if this was information hard-wired into all humans.

'If you can't see any breathing going on, you just touch the eyeball, see if it jumps at that,' Starr said.

'And if you're still not sure, give it a kick in the guts and see what happens,' Cheery Dan added.

Yeah right, thought Jo, wincing at the idea of kicking a dying animal anywhere.

'Well, I haven't got a rifle anyway, so it wouldn't have mattered much.'

'You might want to get yerself one,' Rob Starr said mildly, looking to Cheery Dan for agreement. 'There's a fair few wild dogs in them hills up the back of your place.'

'Oh.'

This was news to Jo. *Wild dogs.* Did he mean dingoes? And how did he already know where she lived?

'They're getting real bloody cheeky, too. Darren Ferrier lost a good bull calf last month –' Cheery Dan was on the same assassinating wavelength as Starr, it seemed.

'Well, don't go shooting any dingoes with collars on, will you?' Jo interrupted these dugai histrionics. 'If it's got a collar on it's our yellow dog.'

'Any yella dog comes onto my place it takes its chances.' Starr replied, deadpan. He shook a cigarette out of its packet, and felt in his jeans pocket for a light.

They weren't long on diplomacy in Tin Wagon Road, then.

Jo nodded slowly and pursed her lips, jutting them out as though for the life of her she was trying, and failing, to see eye to eye with him. If anyone shot Warrigal, she didn't know what she'd do. Poison their waterholes, probably. Steal their children. It was at moments like this that she understood the old Goories refusing to walk behind the dugais when they travelled together in the forests. Just in case the temptation to sink an axe into their ignorant European skulls became altogether too overwhelming.

Rob Starr angled out a cloud of smoke. It faded into nothingness as the first of the mourners' cars began to drive away to the Middle B to get on the hops.

'So which is your place then?' Jo asked him. A neutral response.

24

Don't start anything at a funeral, she told herself. She heard Therese: *Remember to breathe, Josephine.*

'Right at the end of the valley, where the ridge loops back on itself.' He gestured north-east. 'I back onto the World Heritage. Our places meet up near the old abandoned banana winch – the corners meet, or near enough. Old Jim Mooney's kids used to walk through my place to get to the Pocket school, years ago.'

'Run cattle, do you?'

'Brahmins.'

'Rightio, well, I better get cracking.'

Cradling a bowl of Weetbix the next morning, Jo looked out to where a shiny Land Cruiser troopie had pulled up in her driveway. Daisy and Warrigal were sniffing around the wheels, lifting their legs and issuing a few tentative barks, still unsure of the rules on the new place. A fiftyish blond bloke sporting an akubra and permanent sunburn had his elbow sticking out of the Cruiser window. He was looking down at the dogs.

'You're right, mate, they won't bite,' Jo called from the yard. The man didn't get out. He cast his gaze around at the ongoing work in the paddocks, the ute full of junk and the smoking rubbish pile, then came back to Jo.

'G'day. You got a teenage girl here that rides horses?' he asked, pushing his hat up to show more of a face that had drinker written all over it.

'Yeah, my daughter.' Jo took a sustaining sip of good sweet coffee, and kicked a dry dog turd off the lawn and into the dust under the house. 'Why?'

'The name's Darren Ferrier. I live up on the last bend before Nudgel there, place with the stockyards. Anyway, me neighbour reckons he seen a girl riding my horses there, round about dawn the last couple of mornings. You know anything about that?'

'Riding *your* horses?' Jo said, astonished.

'Yep. Bareback, he reckoned.' Darren Ferrier looked a lot less than pleased.

'I dunno . . . she can ride, but –' Jo stopped. Wouldn't put it past the little bugger. '– we've got our own horses. I dunno why she'd go and do that.'

'Well, it only started last week, when you moved in and Mooneys moved out.'

'Are they quiet?' Jo asked abruptly.

'They're broken in,' he replied. 'Blood horses, too. But that doesn't mean I want them ridden. Specially not by some kid I don't know. Put yerself in my position.'

'Nah, well, I'll have a word with her,' Jo said slowly. 'But I can't see it really. No one else around here it could be?'

Darren Ferrier shook his head. His expression said that he was pretty damn sure who had been mucking around with his stock, and he wanted something done about it, pronto.

'Kids'll be kids,' he said, softening an iota. 'But I can't cop it, hey? If she fell off and got hurt, or whatever . . . Or if my horses got hurt. Plus the whole trespassing thing.'

'Yeah, well,' Jo told him, 'I'll get onto her about it, don't worry.' The word *trespassing* out of a dugai mouth didn't sit happily with her. But Ellen hadn't left her in much of a position to begin an argument with Darren Ferrier, horseman, Longbeach smoker, and offended new neighbour. Jo paused, wondering how to get the truth out of Ellen.

'You've been doing a fair bit of yakka here.' Ferrier complimented. Understatement of the fucken year. Everywhere she looked was hard work done, or hard work still waiting to be finished.

'There's a bit more to do yet,' Jo said drily. 'But we'll get there –'

'It's always the way on a farm, eh, it never ends. What was your name?' Ferrier asked belatedly as he stubbed out his cigarette in the ashtray of the Toyota. Jo gave him her name and took the hand he proffered through the window, shook it hard, the way whitefellas liked to.

'Where are ya from, anyway?' Why are you brown of skin and hair and eyes? he meant. Why don't you look like me?

'Brisbane. I grew up in South Golden as a kid, though.'

Ferrier was nonplussed, but Jo didn't relent in the pause that followed.

'Oh. Okay. Well, I'll let this horse business slide, if you manage to knock it on the head.' Ferrier advised her. He started up then reversed out past the hibiscus bushes onto the narrow bitumen of the road, he raised a forefinger in farewell, and roared off.

The dogs erupted noisily – and suddenly old Granny Wotsername appeared from nowhere, cycling down Tin Wagon Road at a rate of knots. Her dark legs pumped up and down, peddling hard, nearing the front gate where the Goorie flag hung in dewy folds of red, black and yellow. The old girl would never see seventy again, and she wore the sort of clothes that said she shopped exclusively at St Vinnies and Lifeline. Her hair was a cap of short tight grey curls, and while Granny was solid around the middle she still had the slender limbs and the rounded features of a Bundjalung showing beneath a paisley head-scarf. She rode a thirty-year-old sit-up-and-beg bike, and was dressed in a poor woman's clothes, but nothing poor showed in Granny's bearing: her back was straight, and her face took the world square on, saying quite clearly that she was nobody's fool, thank you kindly.

Jo grabbed two dog collars quickly, and brain-scrabbled for her name – Granny what now? Granny Nunn kept coming to mind but that wasn't right.

Granny's eyes met Jo's for a moment as the old woman drew level with the gateway. A pair of blue fairy-wrens that lived there had a lot to say about intruders so close to their bottlebrush tree, flitting up and down in brief alarmed parabolas and giving their high-pitched ratcheting call. Jo let go of Daisy just long enough to give a quick wave, but Granny had a fair pace going and she didn't slow down. Nor did she wave. There was a brief formal nod from her, that was all. Barely even a nod, and then she was past the pine trees, halfway to where the road dipped for the creek crossing.

Jo straightened up and scratched at her cheek, wondering whether to be offended. Had she just been snubbed? Hard to tell with somebody of that vintage. Jo knew that she'd been introduced to the old girl years ago at a function. Granny hadn't been too friendly then, either, come to think. But to give her the benefit of the doubt, maybe the woman was just shy, or absentminded, or even half-blind, nodding to shadowy indistinguishable figures all day long.

According to Chris there weren't any other Goories living on the road, hadn't been for twenty years or more. Still, Jo couldn't help feeling affronted. Had the old lady failed, despite the flag hanging right there in front of her, to realise that Jo was a blackfella? Or was she just not very friendly, period? Social complications seemed to be multiplying by the minute. The cemetery had been a very simple place to live, Jo reflected. You knew where you stood, with the dead, since for all their failings they had that sterling virtue of consistency that others so frequently lacked.

Jo drained her coffee cup and went inside to bang on Ellen's door. Bloody teenagers. Just when you think you've got em sussed, they turn around and get you all over again. Riding the neighbour's horses! Bareback! After a week!

'We don't let it bother us,' Chris said later that week, stirring Tyagarah honey into her cup of tea. 'The few rednecks on the road. Not when it's this beautiful.' She gestured at the African tulip tree flourishing beside Jo's garden shed. Three king parrots, a male and two females, bobbed in their gorgeous bright crimson and green plumage. The male stood on a narrow branch in front of one of the females, dipping his head first to the left and then the right. It must have meant something to the hen-parrot, because after he completed the ritual, she let him nibble briefly at the back of her neck.

Jo was struck afresh by her friend's ability to be grateful to life when she had enormous buckets and shitloads of Nothing. Nothing except long black curly hair and money problems, that is. Chris lived in a caravan high on the ridge that overshadowed Tin Wagon Road, three creek crossings up among the rainforest. Leech country, and ticks. And a cranky white neighbour who regarded the long-established dirt track up to her home through his front paddock as a personal favour he was doing her and her father, allowing him to dictate everything from when Chris's nephew could ride his motorbike to refusing them the use of the prettiest little bogie hole for fifty miles around.

'So tell us about Rob Starr.'

Jo related the conversation she had had at the funeral with her new neighbour. Chris looked pensively at Warrigal sprawled on the veranda.

'Oh, Warrigal, ya better look out, lad.'

'I couldn't believe it, eh?' Jo continued. 'No beating around the bush, just if I see any yella dogs on my place I'll shoot em. I felt like saying, yeah and if I see you in my paddock I'll shoot you too, ya dugai prick . . . Only I'd already said I don't have a gun, so it would have lacked a certain something,' she added lamely.

'Geez, it don't take long, eh? A week on the Road and already you want to shoot the whitefellas.' Chris went off in a fit of laughter, and Jo joined in. They both knew Jo was about as likely to shoot Rob Starr as she was to run off and join the National Party.

'Come to Bruns tomorrow night and see the full moon with us,' Chris proposed.

'It's not full already!' Jo said. She swivelled in her seat looking for the pale disc in the afternoon sky. *No way* was it full moon already.

'Time flies when you're having fun!' Chris looked meaningfully at the paddock in front of them.

Four sagging strands of rusty barbed wire fence framed a view of thistles, billygoat weed, dismantled sheets of corrugated iron, lantana thickets and other assorted old farm junk. Jo's ute was parked at an angle to the house. Its tray overflowed with pieces of nail-riddled timber destined to go on the fire, and rusted metal junk for the skip that was yet to arrive from Bangalow. A doorless fridge stood squarely beside the twin tyre tracks to the front gate. Its open mouth gaped at the passers-by; on the grass around it were scattered a collection of various-sized fuel drums, big lumps of broken concrete with rusted wire sticking dangerously out of them, anonymous car parts, and what seemed like a never-ending supply of empty beer bottles found beneath the house, the trees, the grass, the car bodies – everywhere. A makeshift fire circle beyond the ute was smoking a billowing white cloud into the sky, telling them that the prevailing breeze was headed south-east towards Ocean Shores. The fire had been burning non-stop for the past week, and Jo wasn't about to run out of fuel for it any time soon.

Fun, Jo considered, picking at a long morse code of scabs on her left forearm. Was it fun? She decided that yes, despite her aching muscles, shredded hands and yawningly empty bank account, it actually was. Except that it was so much more than fun. This was *her farm*. Unbelievably, she and her brother Stevo had together bought back a patch of Bundjalung land, reclaimed a fragment of their country. It wasn't so much fun as a deep, solid vein of primal satisfaction that flooded through her day and night whenever she gazed about her in wonder at the paddocks and trees and mountain. Dawn on the bottom dam made her catch her breath; the evening light along the ridge brought tears to her eyes. *Her* paddocks. *Her* trees. *Her* mountain. My country, right or wrong.

'Well, it sure don't feel like work,' she said. 'Not on your own land.' Chris nodded in agreement, and Jo continued.

'I'm cleaning this endless shit up for us mob. Making somewhere for me and Ellen, and Stevo when he comes home – and Kym and Jase and the boys eventually, I hope. Get the place in order and look after it the right way. Keep the old people happy.'

'Yeah. That's right. You're doing it for the family. And the old people. *And* you're a workaholic,' Chris teased.

'*And* I'm a workaholic,' Jo agreed cheerfully. Then made a snarling face to tell Chris that she was getting a bit too bloody cheeky. 'Aaagh, you're just jealous cos you're never gonna be able to buy back any Gadigal land,' Jo told her.

Chris laughed. 'God, would I want to? All the womba dugai

down there – anyways, I'm officially Bundjalung now. Aunty Sally told me at Wollumbin Dreaming that they're claiming me. I've been here long enough now after thirty years, she reckons. So how about you knock off busting ya hole and come down to Bruns?'

'Can't, tidda,' said Jo. 'Can't get the horses here till I replace that fucking horrible excuse for a fence. Congratulations on joining the tribe, though.'

'Ah, the work'll still be here next week. Full moon won't,' Chris urged.

'Christ. Alright . . . what time?'

'I thought head down just before black o'clock hey, and watch the sunset at the rock wall.'

'Yeah, orright. Pick us up on the way through.' They stood and Jo stretched a weary, weary back. There were a couple more hours of daylight, and several more decades of Mooney junk to be chucked, stored, burned or recycled. She stuck her hat on as they went outside. Once more into the breach, dear friends. Then a sudden thought occurred to her as Chris was leaving.

'Hey, who's that old aunty round here who rides a pushie? I can't think of her name.'

'Might be old Granny Nurrung,' Chris said, after a moment's thought. 'Sam's Nanna. She's got a treadly that she rides to church in Ocean Shores.' Ah, that's it, breathed Jo as the name brought back a flood of vaguely unpleasant memories. Unsmiling Granny Nurrung, she now recalled, had that extremely upright back because the Good Lord Jesus was walking approvingly by her side with every step she took.

'Yeah, that'll be her,' she called. 'Seeya when the work's finished! I wish.'

'No rest for the wicked, darl,' Chris replied, heading in the opposite direction to chauffeur Uncle Pat to the doctor.

'Ellen,' Jo turned and yelled at the house, 'I didn't say you could knock off yet, where the bloody hell are ya?'

★

'Guess what?' Therese's almond eyes peered through the kitchen window a couple of days later. She heeled her gumboots off onto the bare veranda boards that Jo intended to paint once the two hundred more important jobs – building yards, slashing, lopping, burning, dismantling, poisoning where unavoidable, replanting, digging, mulching, weeding, fertilising – had been completed.

'You're mad and I'm not?' Jo responded, putting the kettle on.

Therese plonked down at the kitchen table, her body just as grimy as Jo's.

'That's not news,' Therese answered, tapping on the kitchen table, impatient to deliver her gossip.

'You've decided to ditch Amanda and come be my fulltime unpaid farmhand and cook?' Jo's face glowed with enthusiasm for this excellent idea.

'That's it!' said Therese. 'And I'll chuck in aaall my good advice for free while I'm at it. She reckons she's sick to death of me farting in bed, anyway.'

'Deal,' said Jo, plonking her cup on the table and sinking into a well-deserved rest. The two women had just made short work of another two hundred metres of decrepit barbed wire. A score of uprooted fenceposts lay beside the fireplace, ready for a bonfire. 'And I won't even charge you for cuppas,' she added.

'Seriously, but,' said Therese, 'about these new blackfellas I met on Monday.'

'Oh, yeah?' Jo feigned indifference. This was something to be hearing. One would have to be the Spunk from the bookstore, surely. Jo slowly turned her tea mug in front of her, making a wet ring on the speckled laminex.

'New in town from where?' she asked, pausing in the turning long enough to spoon three sugars in.

'Got enough diabetes there, luv?' Therese asked. When Jo didn't bite, Therese went on. The Goories were down from Brisbane, and not only new in town, but claiming native title over Tin Wagon Road and the surrounding valley. Twoboy and his brother Lazarus were here to prove their claim with books and family trees and law-yers and argument by any means necessary.

Hooley dooley. Hundreds of acres of previously uncontested coun-try. The goonah around here was going to hit the fan and then some.

'Did he crack onto you?' Jo wanted to know.

'There was a hint of that,' Therese smiled, 'till I put him straight about Amanda. I'm all in favour of a light refreshing male between serious relationships, but I told him we're together for the long haul, and he took it alright.' Well, well, well, thought Jo. A liberal blackfella her own age, single, gorgeous, and in her town. Unfuckingbelievable. She briefly scanned the horizon for flying pigs.

'So how'd you meet em?' Jo said, lifting her aching, grimy feet up onto the kitchen table and not caring if it was rude cos it was Therese and she was as much a sister to her as Kym was, and non-judgemental with it, as a good Buddhist should be. And plus, anyway, she shoulda asked her along to this meeting on Monday morning. It was altogether too cheeky not to. Therese wasn't even a blackfella and here she was knowing the good goss before Jo. Came of being a teacher – she heard everything off the kids. Talk about wikileaks, they had nothing on Ocean Shores Primary.

'Oh, someone told Laz that Amanda's good with websites, and he wanted some help with theirs,' Therese said. 'She's gonna do it up for them on Saturday. We were thinking of offering them the spare room for a bit, actually.'

Jo sucked air through her teeth in alarm.

'What?' Therese reacted.

'I hope you know what you're getting into. Sticking your oar in.'

'It's just a website,' Therese waved Jo's anxiety away. 'Anyway, what's the point of talking up Goorie rights if ya won't actually get involved?'

'Yeah, and there could be a fucken huge war between all the black-fellas around here for the next fifty years, too, while they work the native title out,' said Jo. 'Do you really want to be *involved* in that?' Therese had no idea what went down between blackfellas when land was at stake. Think Gaza, she warned her. Think Custer's Last Stand.

'Ah, you worry too much,' Therese laughed.

'Bullshit, I do,' Jo retorted.

Several days later, the horses were installed in their brand-new paddock. Straightaway Jo threw her right leg over Athena, and eased down onto the smooth brown leather of her favourite old stock saddle. Her feet found the stirrups and her body remembered, for the ten thousandth time, the feeling of a horse between her knees. The mare fought against the bit, though, wanting to get free to scratch her foreleg. Jo let the leather reins slide through her fingers so that Athena could stretch and use her teeth on the offending itch. But afterwards the horse began swishing her tail in irritation, sidestepping away from the gate to Tin Wagon Road. Jo shortened the reins, bridging them on the mare's mane, and dug her heels in. *You will do as I say and not what you feel like.* Athena tossed her head in dissent, her tail going like a semaphore. A hind leg lashed out in anger, striking nothing but air.

'Whattya you been doing with this yarraman?' Jo asked Ellen, who was standing beside the bathtub that now held the horses' drinking water. The kid had a list of Saturday jobs a mile long to get through before she could escape back to her room. Ellen was morose as she wove the end of the hose through five strands of barbed wire so that the slow drip would fill the tub.

'Riding her.' Duh.

'Well, she's got the manners of a frigging racehorse all of a sudden,' Jo snapped, finally getting the gate open and riding through. 'Bugger off, you idiot,' she said, clapping loudly at Comet who was approaching the half-open gate with interest. The colt propped and snorted, and paused long enough for Jo to lean sideways, far out of the saddle, and slide the chain end over its silver knob, securing the paddock. Comet was altogether puzzled to suddenly find the steel gate between himself and his mother.

As Jo rode away along the fenceline, he began to trot in agitated circles, tossing his nose at the sky. He neighed a frantic neigh, unsure of himself in his new paddock, and hating to be left alone there. Bloody herd bound, Jo cursed, what a pain in the neck that could turn out to be. Then Athena shied beneath her, pretending to see snakes in the long grass under the lowest strand of fence wire, and Jo grabbed the left rein, digging her heels in and wheeling the mare in tight circles as punishment.

'Don't leave that hose running too long, alright? We're not on town water anymore,' Jo ordered over her shoulder.

'I'd forgotten. It's been at least five minutes since ya told me,' Ellen called back with a face like thunder.

'If you weren't binung goonj I might not have to tell you things a thousand times,' Jo retorted. 'And if you rode this flaming horse properly I wouldn't have to re-educate her every three weeks.'

Ellen stiffened.

'She went fine for me at Oliver's,' she yelled. 'Maybe it's you that needs to ride her "properly" and not be so mean to her.'

'Yeah?' Jo reacted. 'Well, if I'm "mean" to her it's because she needs to know who's in charge – not her. Same as you're not. Goddit?'

There was no reply from Ellen, who was now stalking back towards the house with her fists clenched at her sides. Jo fumed and bellowed at this insubordination, swinging the horse around.

'Ellen! Don't you walk away from me! Have you been riding this bloody mare the way you're supposed to, or not?'

The girl stopped and stood stock-still without turning around or acknowledging her mother's question. Her thin body radiated displeasure and tension. *Fuck you.*

'Cos I had a visit last week from a neighbour who reckons you've been riding his horses up the bloody road. Without asking.' Jo was horrified to hear this come out of her mouth. She'd meant to broach it tactfully, over hamburgers or something, when Ellen was in a mood to open up. But she was aching all over from fixing the farm – had been aching all over for a fortnight – and now Athena was being a mongrel, and Ellen had turned her back on her, which you just don't do to your mother. Not if you don't want attention, you don't. Real quick attention upside of the head, same as she got as a kid with far less provocation than this.

'Well?'

'Yes. I've been riding her!' Ellen turned to face Jo. They both knew it was only half an answer.

'Just bloody watch yaself, alright? We're always gonna be easy targets around here.' Jo's voice was hard, but she didn't know what else to do. She had a mighty job on her hands. Keep the locals onside, keep Ellen in line *and* talking to her, not a silent hating teenager like so many of them seemed to be, keep the cops well away so that disaster in a uniform didn't have a chance to find them, keep the animals healthy and alive, get the farm cleaned up, get to work on time five days a week and keep Basho happy, especially now there was a mortgage to consider.

'Is anything I say to you sinking in?' she asked, at last allowing Athena to come to a breathless halt. Ellen shrugged. 'Well, is there anything you want to tell me?' Jo asked in exasperation.

Ellen suddenly spoke the truth. 'I miss my town friends. And I'm sick of all the work here. I never wanted to move here in the first place, it was your idea to buy a farm. Not mine.'

The girl stood with her arms folded in the shadow of the Piccabeen palms hanging over the bathtub. Jo sighed, and hauled Athena's head up from the paspalum patch she'd just found. Hadn't she spent night after night explaining to Ellen what it meant to have their own place? To have the horses right outside the back door, and much more important, to be owners again of some Bundjalung land? To take back even a tiny fraction of what had been lost? She thought Ellen had wanted it, too, as badly as she did.

Comet neighed and half-reared, his anxiety growing with every minute his mother was on the other side of the fence.

'Well, look at it like this,' Jo told Ellen shortly: 'You're gonna spend about six billion years turning back to dust in that bloody cemetery once ya dead, so take this as a very short enforced holiday away from the place, okay?'

'Oh, you've got what you want, and I'll just put up and shut up. Fine!' Ellen stormed away into the house muttering curses under her breath that she wasn't foolish enough to say to her mother's face. Jo heeled Athena into a canter and left the latest drama of motherhood behind, as Comet took to his heels too, rocketing up the length of the paddock, bucking wildly and protesting his abandonment all the way.

Chapter Three

'Whaddya waiting for, hotpants, a written invitation?' came a familiar merry cry from the the side veranda. Jo peered into the dimly lit space where Therese, Amanda, and two other figures were perched on the deck. She wandered over, wrinkling her nose in disdain. *Hotpants.*

Drawing nearer, Jo saw in horror that one of the men was the blackfella from the bookstore, looking as good up close as he had from half a street away. The weathered dreadlocks which cascaded down his broad back were tied together with a yellow cord that ended in a tassel of cockatoo feathers. A narrow leather bracelet beaded in red, black and yellow circled one wrist. From close quarters she saw now that his very dark skin wasn't down to Islander blood. A few strands of loose hair that had escaped his dreads had no kink to them, and his features were too Aboriginal to evoke the islands of the north, or of the Pacific either.

Ambushed, she leaned on a veranda post, glared at Therese, and felt her internal defences fall into place, unbidden. Slam, slam, slam. They slid sideways and they slid vertical, like the doors on 'Get Smart'. All of these doors were solid, locked, and smoothly impenetrable. All of them had emblazoned on them the same simple and undeniable message:

Good-looking men are nothing but trouble.

'Fellas – this is Jo Breen, our mate, the one with the farm I've been telling you about.'

Therese affectionately threw a crooked arm around Amanda's neck, crossed her legs and flashed a look at Jo that said *Well?* Jo gave her one straight back that read: Did I even say I was looking for a man, you cheeky slag with your 'meet us at the pub' and your 'wear that red t-shirt', ooh, your arse is so grass my friend, your arse is so fucken grass.

The man grinned, giving Jo the little chin lift that signalled acknowledgement and he didn't look away. Then he didn't look away some more. Jo, transitioning at warp speed from wary to transfixed, was sideswiped with lust from behind her slammed-shut doors. Oh for Chrissake, she snarled at herself, you're not fourteen. Get a fucking grip, girl.

'Which way?' said the man, still not breaking their eye lock, his smile broadening.

'Same way,' said Jo. Her pulse surged in her throat, and she was frightened to say more in case she jabbered rubbish. She stuck her hands in her jeans pockets and bunched them into fists.

Good-looking men are nothing but trouble.

At that moment, Basho lumbered past, his cumbersome pot belly banging the edge of their long wooden table. Apologising, he had to say 'g'day Jo' twice before his voice even registered. Rob Starr wandering through to the servery covered in engine grease and red mud didn't rate any kind of attention at all. Then Amanda finally leaned over, breaking the spell; she pulled Jo onto the pine bench seat beside her.

'Hey spunky, you scrub up alright, don't ya? Jo – this is Twoboy and Laz. The Jackson Brothers – straight outta Compton. Compton Road, Woodridge, that is.'

'The Jackson two,' Jo said, relieved to have regained the power of speech.

'That's it,' Laz agreed from the opposite side of the table, a slightly heavier, younger Twoboy without the dreads or the juice.

The gelded version, Jo thought, then mentally smacked her hand for thinking it.

'Your shout, moll,' Jo told Therese.

'Stevo turn up yet?' Amanda asked.

'Two guesses,' Jo answered, wincing with the strain in her aching legs as she stretched them beneath the table.

'My little brother,' she explained to the Jacksons. 'We're fencing this weekend. Guess who hasn't shown.'

'Fencing's hard yakka,' Twoboy answered knowingly. 'You'll feel that the next day.'

'Last time we done any real fencing was out round Canungra as young blokes, eh?' Laz chipped in. 'Must be a good, what, fifteen years since I sunk any posts.'

'Well, anytime you feel like rediscovering the lost art, brother, just say the word,' Jo replied. Like Twoboy, Laz was tall and well-built. He looked like he could shift a fair bit of timber without too much effort. But Laz simply laughed. No fucken way, his gap-toothed smile said.

'So, you fellas been round town long?' Jo asked, as Therese handed her a beer.

'We drove down from Brissie with our old Mum a couple of weeks ago,' Laz answered. 'She gone home to the grannies in Logan now, but we're staying put. We got a nation to rebuild.' And it will take a nation of millions to hold us back, Jo thought automatically.

'True. So you're Bundjalung then?' Jo replied with a faint hint of suspicion. You're pretty dark for Bundjalung boys. *Where the hell are you from?* Are we related, or enemies by default, thanks to some long ago war that our relatives fought with each other? Or so distantly connected that we might be what dugais call strangers?

The temperature at the table dropped a couple of degrees. Laz grew still, and the gap between his front teeth went into hiding. It was Twoboy who replied, with ice just beneath the calm surface of his voice.

'Too right we're Bundjalung. This is our great-grandfather's country we're sitting on here.' Twoboy palmed the air in demonstration, Tupperware style. 'This pub's on our land. Nudgel. Tin Wagon Road. All the way up to Crabbes Creek. Us Jacksons are claiming the lot, onetime.'

Jo could just about hear Uncle Oscar Bullockhead in Piccabeen having a heart attack from where she sat. *These two black bastards waltz into town and start chucking their weight around, telling lies about whose country this is . . .*

Twoboy waited for some sign of assent or approval, but Jo found she had no words. What was Uncle Oscar going to do when he heard about this declaration of war? And Aunty Sally Watt? The silence at the table grew taut as Jo imagined the firepower of the Bullockhead and Watt families coming up against the two Jackson brothers.

'So you're dead set slapping a claim over the valley then?' she asked.

Her grin made this something between an innocent query and an outright challenge. The silence at the table expanded, bulging at the seams with unspoken tension.

Twoboy put his stubby back down and then laced his fingers together behind his head. Slowly he leaned backward and gazed across at Jo. His tongue found the inside of his top lip and pushed it out. Anxiety burned all the watching faces. With his hands behind his head, Twoboy's biceps had flexed into dark sinewy peaks half-showing beneath his snug black t-shirt sleeves. Jo wondered if he knew how gorgeous he looked, and thought that yes, he was a smart bloke and he probably did. But when Twoboy finally spoke, there was no flirtation left in his voice or his eyes. What he was lusting after, Jo suddenly saw, was not a woman for a night or a week, but for his country. The man spoke with utter certainty and great emphasis.

'That's it, sis. I'm the eldest and that makes me the one true blackfella for this place la. Our great-grandfather, Tommy Jackson, he knew this valley back to front and inside out, and he knew who he was too, a Bundjalung man robbed of his rights by the land-grabbers. Fred Wheeler kidnapped him into the Native Police in 1864 –'

When she heard the words Native Police, Jo gave a tiny involuntary flinch sideways. Twoboy noticed, but he continued in a strong, level voice.

'– and the first chance grandad Tommy had – after about a week – he shot that booliman over him. He took off running and didn't stop till he got past Rocky.'

Ah.

'He didn't have any interest in murdering Goories for the benefit of white men and their bullang. He didn't like that idea one bit, so he grabbed a station girl from the north, and they travelled all over the Top End together. Laying low his whole life with a false name cos of that dead sergeant. But he knew where he really belonged, made sure all our family knew it too. I got his name, and I got his meat. And now we're back to collect what's ours. Humble Pies n all.'

The silence returned as Jo and the others digested this.

'Black Power Pies,' joked Laz, raising a semi-ironic fist.

'Bloody oath,' agreed Therese amiably, holding her stubby to the light to assess its state, which was nearly empty. 'Sounds like a plan.'

In the next three seconds, Jo came speedily to certain conclusions. These were that (a) native title over the Billinudgel valley generally, and the Jackson family genealogy in particular, was really none of her business; (b) that getting involved in the looming shitfight between Jacksons and Bullockheads and Watts was asking for way, waaay more trouble than she had stomach for; and (c) above all else, her daughter and her farm with its title deed sitting in her kitchen drawer were the only things that really mattered. She had her twenty acres and her version of culture safely tucked in her back pocket. There's no chokecherry tree on my back, she reminded herself. I'm a free enterprise, freehold blackfella, beholden to nobody except my own family and my own conscience. She'd circled right around the hideous politics of colonial fallout, and bought back the ancestral land herself.

Cash on the stump, you fuckers. *Game over.*

'Well, just don't go claiming my farm,' she told Twoboy, 'or it'll be pistols at dawn, brother.'

The tension broke with this tacit consent to the Jackson's wider claim, and everybody breathed out, grinning broadly.

'I don't fight women,' Twoboy answered. 'Only Mr Pitiful does that.'

'You're a lover, not a fighter, is that it?' Therese flirted as though she wasn't a dyed-in-the-wool dyke from the year dot. Jo and Amanda rolled their eyes and groaned. Oh, puh-lease. No, insisted Twoboy, ignoring the flirting and groaning, he was a lover *and* a fighter. Only these days we fight with lawyers, not with guns. So long as the Native Title Tribunal came to the party anyway. If they didn't, then he'd be on the phone to Al Qaeda mob, onetime.

'Eh, knock off!' Lazarus chimed in with a frown. 'Start talking like that some dickhead'll have us in the paddy wagon before ya know it. CIA'll turn up in Wilfred Street.'

Jo shouted with laughter, and talked into where her wristwatch would be if she owned one.

'Radical blackfellas at two o'clock. Book em Danno.'

'That might be just what it takes, eh,' Twoboy twinkled at the three women sitting opposite. Jo hoped the brother was joking. There had to be a middle path didn't there? Something between the white man's table crumbs and the Taliban? Else we're all fucked.

'Uh, there's no twin towers round here, in case you hadn't noticed,' she suggested, gesturing at the one-horse town that was Billinudgel.

'No twin towers!' Twoboy said in mock-horror, half-rising from his seat and looking about him at the weed-infested railway line and the tennis court with its torn and rusted wire mesh hanging lazily from the poles, testament to a thousand bored pub brats using it as a bouncy castle. 'You mean we *aren't* in downtown Manhattan?' He turned to Laz.

'This is another fine mess you've gotten us into, Pocahontas!'

Jo found herself warming to Twoboy.

'Not to tell you your business or anything,' she said drily, 'but you might wanna get your continents straight before claiming them land rights, bala. This is Australia, y'know? Dead Heart. Meat Pies. Holden Cars. Racists.'

Twoboy put an index finger to his pursed lips, thinking hard.

'And – waaait – it's *America* with the Statue of Liberty, and the Lincoln Memorial?'

'I believe so, yes,' Jo answered, grinning.

He winced and smacked his forehead, making the yellow feathers on the end of his dreadlocks do a little dance. Then he beamed at Jo, who was laughing in disbelief. Spunky. Educated. Smart as a whip. *And funny*.

The workmen in the front bar roared as someone in another city scored a try.

'Titans,' said Laz to Therese, ignoring Twoboy's performance. 'Titans and Rabbitohs.'

'What's the score?' asked Amanda, but nobody knew.

'I've been missing those land rights, you know,' Twoboy said softly to Jo. 'They really tied the room together.'

And just like that, Jo felt the hard carapace of her resistance begin to flake and crumble away. Years worth of armour fell from her tender heart. Great slabs of steel and granite hit the wooden floorboards and shattered into fragments there. Jo sat, wondering, among the shards. This isn't happening. A black prince rocking up at the Billi on a Friday night, quoting the Coens at her.

'Well, The Dude abides,' she murmured in disbelief.

'He certainly fucking does.' Twoboy grinned, untying his dreads and shaking them loose. 'But maybe not in Billinudgel,' they chorused together, laughing.

Lazarus noticed this sudden softening of Jo toward his older brother. He wondered in an abstract way whether Twoboy would fuck things up for them again. There were more important things at stake in Billinudgel than whether Twoboy got his dick wet tonight, Laz worried. Much more important things.

Twoboy drained his last long mouthful of beer and stood up to replace it.

'Well, anyways, if you're Bundjalung tidda, yorright by me. We'll let ya stay on ya farm.'

He leaned across the table and gave her shoulder a friendly squeeze as he winked. She could feel the steel of his strength even in that brief touch.

'That's bloody big of ya,' Jo retorted, tingling from his fingers on her skin and wanting more, more, more of the same. He was Goorie, and gorgeous, and her desires were endless.

If many hands make light work, Jo silently asked the paddock in front of her, then why is it that many hands always arrive just as the light is failing. Why is it that *many hands* sit around the fire drinking your piss and talking up a storm about how much work they're going to do at some pleasantly nonspecific time in the future?

Pondering this perennial question, Jo let her gaze drop from the rolling hills to the firepit. There stood Stevo warming his arse in front of the latest stack of burning fenceposts. A six-foot eucalyptus fencepost is a mighty heavy thing, even when the termites have got to it and the barbed wire that gave it a purpose has rusted into earth a dozen summers ago. Each blazing post had left a tightly knotted signature in Jo's neck. She flung her head sharply to the right, hoping to hear the bonecrack that would signal relief, but there was none. Jo *nil*; fenceposts *too many to count*.

Stevo, whose supple neck muscles held no tight memories at all, was grinning at his girlfriend Caroline.

'— old Bingo would've loved them bones!' He rocked with laughter on the heels of his near-immaculate Blundstones. The workman's boots had gotten very slightly muddy on the way from the car to the fire, Jo noted sourly. First time for fucken everything.

'That's the oldest joke in the book, my love.' said Caroline, draining a squat glass that reflected the yellow blaze of the fire. Stevo's newest conquest pushed a hank of gleaming blonde hair back, revealing the garnet earrings that Stevo had just given her for their six-month anniversary.

'Yeah, don't give up your day job.' Jo shifted the timbers further into the fire with a blackened tomato stake that she had discovered gave her a fresh sense of purpose and meaning in the world. 'Anyway, I need a shower,' she announced, stripping off her dirty suede gloves.

'What's for dinner, Horse?' asked Stevo. The setting sun was making his face glow the colour of bush honey. Jo gazed at him, speechless at his effrontery.

'Horse?' Caroline squawked in horror. The siblings laughed.

'We call her Horse sometimes,' Stevo explained. 'When she was five she really thought she was a horse, and it stuck.'

Caroline lifted one smooth eyebrow and said nothing.

'Here's an idea, Stevo – what if I stagger to the shower with my last shred of remaining energy, and *you* cook?' Jo proposed.

'Fuck off. Since when dya invite people down and then expect them to cook?' Stevo's outrage was palpable.

'Since when dya offer to help ya poor sister do some fencing and show up at five o'fuckenclock in the afternoon?' Jo asked, knowing in her mitochondrial DNA that the answer was forever.

'She's got ya there,' Ellen chipped in.

'Oh . . . it's gang up on Uncle Stevo time, is it?' But he wilted under the hard look from three women.

'And I shall be Queen of the Fire,' offered Caroline, easing herself down onto her elegant saronged haunches and picking up the blackened Tomato Stake of Authority.

Jo and Stevo walked inside to a kitchen reincarnated from their childhood. Mum's familiar array: IXL jam in fat steel tins. Gold Coast Bakery bread. Bulk rice, and Keen's Curry Powder, even now when better, fancier curry pastes filled whole supermarket shelves.

'You can find everything, eh?'

A clatter of pots and pans behind her was the answer. But Jo was already in the bathroom, can of Coke and all, ripping off her filthy paddock rags and stepping into the bliss of hot water on her screaming muscles. In the past month, she had lost several kilos, grown visible triceps, and learned the hard way about always wearing gloves when she walked out the door. She ran soapy hands down past her breasts and stomach, scratching halfheartedly at the splashes of dried mud on the back of her brown calves. Some days it felt like the only way she'd ever be really clean again was to drive to South Golden, flop in the surf all day, and then take a two-hour sauna. It hardly seemed worth scrubbing it all off when the next day would see more grime, and the next, and the next. But thinking that way lies ruin, she told herself, and walking ocelots on a rhinestone leash. Or else rolling around in the mud at Nimbin with the ferals, god bless em and their dirty little dreads.

She briskly shampooed her hair and watched the bubbles around her feet – rising in an alarming puddle. Now the flaming shower wasn't draining properly. *Beautiful.* So tomorrow she'd crawl under the house and see what she could see among the white poly pipes and dog dust and fleas. Just add it to the list, she told herself, trying for calm, think of the Glorious Ten Year Plan. You mow and spray and weed all week in Mullum for Basho so you can come home and mow, and weed, and clear away the Mooneys' shit, and plant and fence here. It'll be worth it, one day, when the place looks like somebody loves it. When the land *knows* somebody loves it, she corrected herself. Ya caring for your jagan, girl, it's gotta be more than just words.

And though her neck still had a machete stuck in it, and her back felt like it belonged to her great-great-grandmother's billygoat, it was already time to turn off the precious tankwater, no matter how good the gushing torrent was. Jo gave herself another five seconds of scorching heat on the back of her neck. Another ten. At fifteen seconds she heard her mother's voice from childhood: *I had to drink water with dead frogs floating in it.* Jo turned the taps off and reached for a worn, stripy towel as she heard Chris's dying Econovan clatter into the drive.

Early the next morning, Jo and Caro pulled on gumboots and walked across the small paddock to check on Jo's young jali jali billa. How she'd made the time to plant the small grove in her first week on the farm, Jo couldn't remember rightly, but these thirty knee-high seedlings were her special project. The effort spent digging holes in the moonlight would be well worth it.

'You wouldn't have heard of the Tree of Knowledge, I suppose – ' Caro said, with only half a question mark at the end of the sentence. This was exactly half a question mark too little for Jo's liking, and she felt her face stiffen.

'Ah, Tree of Knowledge, umm, no . . .' she answered. Caroline was about to speak again, when Jo interrupted.

'Unless, oh, hang on – do you mean the Tree of Knowledge in Barcaldine, where the modern Labor Party grew out of the iconic shearers' strike of 1897?' *Don't patronise me, luv.*

'Oh, you've been there?' Caroline asked in surprise.

'Just a lucky guess,' Jo said, shortly.

'Oh.'

'Degree in Australian history and comparative literature, actually.'

'Ah. Woops.'

Caroline went bright pink, and balled her fists inside her trouser pockets. Fucken hell, dugais are hard work, thought Jo.

'It's okay. We've got special trees here too, you know,' she said, pointing around the paddock.

'Oh, which ones?'

Caroline grasped at this new thread in transparent relief. Jo pointed her lips at the neighbouring cattle property.

'Well . . . see that big wattle starting to flower there over the road, no the big one further to the right, that one without so much blossom on it. Well, round here we call that the Tree of Children's Learning.'

'Get outta here.' Caroline looked as though if she had a notebook she'd be scribbling in it.

'Yeah, true. And that young spindly sandpaper fig closer to the fence, well that's the Sapling of Self-Importance –'

Caroline glanced sideways.

'– and a bit further back, well that's the Camphor Laurel of Patronising City Folk, and just along here flourishing like billy-o we have the Groundsel of Rural and Regional Ignorance . . .'

'Okay, okay, point taken.' Caroline looked skyward as a crow flapped east. 'I apologise. I just didn't think someone who mows grass in a cemetery would have a university degree.'

'Me neither,' said Jo ruefully, twisting her mouth at this hard economic fact.

'Sorry,' Caro repeated.

'Ah, forget it. Help me with my jali jali billa.' Jo told her, as she bent to check the soil around the base of the she-oaks. She plucked at and straightened the narrow plastic bags which protected the trees, in theory, from wind and weeds and wildlife. Jo stroked the soft leaves of the seedlings, healthy and brightly thriving in British Racing Green as was proper and correct. She touched their soft scaly trunks, no thicker than pencils.

Together the women spent a half-hour peering into the protector bags, tutting or not as the situation demanded, weeding around the seedlings, and pouring buckets of dam water onto the mounded earth beneath them. The dogs lay blissfully in the morning sun, watching them work, Warrigal still scratching like it was his mission in life to wear out his skin.

'That bloody dog's going in the dam if he doesn't stop scratching,' Jo threatened. 'We've done him for fleas that many times.'

'Bit cold isn't it, the poor thing,' Caro said in his defence.

'Ah, he's a dingo, he'll cope.' Jo replied. Though maybe it was a bit cool. Both Stevo and Caro had worn jumpers the whole time they'd been at the farm, and traces of mist still lingered this morning, ghosting the big camphors in the dip. Fairy-wrens twittered like manic high-pitched machine guns in the neighbouring lantana bushes. The cold wasn't worrying them; they chittered like they were onto their fifth strong espresso. Jo smiled. She loved those little birds.

'It's like Narnia,' Caroline said as she drained her final drops onto the last bag and stood gazing. 'It's so lush, and so peaceful.'

Jo spoke then, about how time warped once you left the highway and entered Byron Shire proper. Even your blood pumped more slowly, leisurely winding its way through arteries and veins, taking its own sweet time. No rush hour here, and still not a traffic light to be found in the shire. And enough shades of green to put Ireland to shame.

'It's my idea of heaven,' Caro said, collapsing to sit cross-legged beneath the slash pines that fringed the dam.

Jo looked around. She knew that feeling. The resident kingfisher flashed past on its way back to its nest, a blurred blue rocket with something long wriggling in its mouth.

'Yeah, I still can't believe we own it, eh. I keep waiting for someone in a uniform to turn up and wave a bit of paper at me and tell me to piss off.'

'But isn't it Bundjalung land?' Caroline said in suprise. 'That's why Stevo jumped at the chance to be in on the deal.'

Jo winced and turned away to hide it. *The deal*. As if retrieving your ancestral land was some kind of a game, not the work of generations. The blueprint of your life, and the only thing worth working for.

'Yeah, but Bundjalung covers a lotta country. We know our ancestors come from somewhere around here, but not exactly where. I've resigned myself to never knowing. Some things just happened too long ago to find out.'

Caroline chewed this over.

'But the way Stevo talks sometimes, it's all that matters, getting back to the land. Mabo and all that.'

Jo sighed. Land was the lodestone, the foundation of absolutely everything in the culture. On the other hand, she hated rhetoric.

'Well he can *talk* Mabo all he wants, but they took our grand-parents and the rest of em away to assimilate our families and fuck up our connections to land. And it very nearly worked. So there's a bloody great need to compromise in families like ours. Why do you think Stevo's run overseas and stayed there?'

She gazed at Stevo's girlfriend, conscious of the chasm between them. Cos you have to be a fucked up blackfella to know what it's like, not being able to prove who you are, or where you belong. The agony of the stolen descendents, hiding in shame as if it was all their fault. Or else getting hypertension trying to fit in; to force history never to have happened simply because it shouldn't have. Jo rammed her garden fork into the ground beneath the pines. Who elected me spokesperson, she thought, as she picked up the watering buckets. End of lesson.

'I'm running off at the mouth – must be from spending so much time on my own. This valley's full of people that want to earbash ya.'

'It'd be worth it to live here. It's . . . perfect.' Caroline's face softened as the female heron Jo had christened Bluey lifted awkwardly from the dam and flapped towards the creek over the road, where it would be unmolested except by grazing bullang and the occasional wedgetail.

'You could always stay on and do that fencing.'

'Um . . . nah. The flights are booked. It'll have to wait till next time, sorry.'

Beneath her breath, unheard by Caro, Jo whispered very softly: jingawahlu mulinyin.

'Gorgeous,' Caroline reiterated, bony white hands propped on her bony white hips.

'Well, why else would I sell my soul for thirty years?' Jo said, watching the bird circle over the burbling creek then land on the opposite bank. 'I certainly wouldn't do it to live in a brick shitbox in the suburbs.'

'For sure. But don't you ever get lonely, all the way out here?'

Jo laughed, and told Caro that no, she didn't feel alone, what with Ellen and the yarraman, and the magpies singing and mulanyin flying around and the fairy-wrens talking a mile a minute, bossing everybody around with their little chittering instructions.

'Alone! Not even. Most of the time visitors make me feel like the TV's on full blast with the remote missing.'

The women both laughed, though Caro laughed louder, a woman in love.

It had been nearly two years since Jo had had anyone to hold in bed, and she was beginning to miss it something fierce as the mornings got frosty and she found an occasional grey hair among her long brown ones. Probably that was all that had happened at the pub with Twoboy the other night: sexual starvation rearing its ugly head. A woman could get enough of being alone every night, and a woman's body could realise the fact long before the woman herself did, Jo mused.

Half an hour later Caro and Stevo backed their Avis Falcon out of the drive.

In the deep quiet which fell in their wake, Jo stood beneath the mango tree and looked to the west. She glanced at the far fences sagging into the foothills of Mount Chincogan. The weak and rusting strands ended up in the high ridge, where the hills and gullies were full of old banana trees nobody had farmed for years and which had now gone wild. What else was hiding up there in the thick scrub? Rob Starr's corner boundary, for one thing, not that she was in any hurry to visit *him*.

Listening to the huge booming silence of the paddocks, the word she had denied so vigorously that morning suddenly struck Jo afresh. Maybe Caro had a point. For all that the farm was only twenty minutes from town, maybe she really was more alone than she'd recognised. Chris was regularly depressed for weeks on end and Therese spent half her free time in Brisbane getting a fix of the city lights. A flicker of doubt entered Jo's mind for the first time since she'd seen the farm in the real estate window.

Think of the Ten Year Plan, she encouraged herself. It doesn't have to all be done right now. And you might also remember, dickhead, that a woman without a man is like a fish without a bicycle – but this commonsense advice didn't cancel out the faint ember of fear that had lodged in her chest. Try as she might to ignore it, Caro's question – *Don't you get lonely out here on your own?* – reverberated all day, unwelcome, in her ears.

Chapter Four

Jo pressed the tea towel hard against her shoulder, but blood continued to seep slowly through the striped cotton in an oddly Australia-shaped blot. Shit and damn and fuck, she thought, where're the bloody doctors in this joint? Though the Mullum hospital was mere staggering distance from the cemetery, proximity wasn't much comfort if there was no bloody staff, was it. She buzzed for help again, and this time, hallefuckenlujah, a nurse popped her head out from the double glass doors of the general ward. The doctor would have to come in from town, she said, the GPs were on rotating call from their own surgeries.

Peeling away the tea towel, Jo displayed an impressive gash running horizontally across her upper arm.

'I think it might need stitches,' she said, trying not to look at the revolting scarlet drips she was leaving on the tiled floor.

'How'd you manage that?' The nurse wasn't giving anything away, least of all free sympathy. Burnt out from trying to cover for missing doctors. Or maybe she just didn't like blackfellas very much.

'I tripped and fell onto a vase,' Jo answered, wondering if the nurse assumed she was drunk. She didn't add that she'd tripped at work, nor that the vase was a jar full of fresh flowers on the grave of a little kid killed a month ago in a crash near Pottsville. Served her right, really, for stepping rudely across a grave of the newly dead instead of walking around it.

The nurse gave her arm an expert touch with her forefinger and pursed her lips.

'Is that a clean tea towel?'

'Came out of the wash today.'

'Well, keep pressing down on it, that does need stitching. You can sit in here till doctor comes.'

The nurse opened the ward door again and motioned Jo into a plastic chair just inside. Instantly she heard an unmistakable Goorie-holler from the far end of the long blue room. It was Uncle Humbug, cleaner than Jo had seen him in ages, shaved even, wearing a hospital gown with tubes running every which way out of his medium brown body. 'Take me *home*, girl,' he immediately ordered Jo, 'take me back to Bruns fer Chrissake.' The nurse – for whom Uncle Humbug was a nebulous entity somewhere between a person and a problem – shot daggers out of her eyes at this, and it quickly dawned on Jo why her own reception had been a bit on the cool side. There was Blood Pressure to think of before discharge, the nurse said starchily to Humbug. And Sugar Levels. And the Tendency of Certain Patients to think that they Knew Better than the Doctors and Fail to take their Medication until they were Admitted in Diabetic Comas in the Middle of the Night. Jo didn't give a sound to her mirth, but Uncle saw it in her eyes and took fresh hope.

'How long ya been here, Uncle?'

'Too pucken long! Take me 'ome to my house! My tidda won't come get me from Lismore, the bloody black bitch of a thing.'

'She knows very well that you're better off here where we can look after you properly.' The nurse was implacable, having seen it all before from any number of patients.

'I'll have an 'eart attack if ya don't lemme go – that'll show yez. Kidnapping a man! I'll have the law on yez! I'm an Indigenous elder, and this the way yez treat me!' Uncle Humbug was breathless with outrage at the way he had been shanghaied once again into the hands of authority, for it was the longstanding story of his life.

'Is that the same law that brought you in unconscious two nights ago, with a full bottle of unopened medication in your bag?' the nurse countered, adjusting something on Humbug's drip.

Uncle Humbug heaved an angry sigh. 'I know my rights,' he muttered. 'You mob just wanna steal blackfellas, that's all it is.'

'Nobody wants to steal you, Mr Milbung,' the nurse assured him with some feeling.

'Take me 'ome to my house, girl!' This last exhortation was for Jo. House, she thought, what *house*? Uncle Humbug lived in a sixth-hand rusty van wedged deeply in the bush at the back of the Bruns park. How he managed to persuade council not to evict him was an enduring mystery of the shire. Maybe he knew where Basho's skeletons were buried, Jo mused. Regardless, anybody who stood long in his vicinity would soon discover that Humbug was not only the owner of the unregistered rust bucket, but also the self-appointed manager, groundskeeper and caretaker of the Bruns park and all the wildlife in it. Most particularly, Humbug was the custodian of and brother to Slim, an enormous carpet python which lived a charmed life beneath the old Bruns bridge.

'Ah, better not risk it, Uncle,' Jo warily avoided the old man's ordering and beseeching. Take him home and he carks it she knew who'd get the blame from a suddenly devoted family. It would probably do him some good to have three feeds a day for a while anyway. The old man was very thin underneath his hippy trousers, multiple coloured necklaces and woven bracelets. His hands were so meatless that they resembled great huntsman spiders flopping loosely against the bedcovers.

'Ah, risk what? Better than risking being bored to fucken death in this bastard dugai joint!'

Uncle Humbug grumbled on to himself from beneath wild silver eyebrows. Poor old bugger. Well, no, not old – he probably hasn't even hit sixty yet, Jo thought. But sick as a dog, and just another statistic waiting to pile up in somebody's report, somebody's fucking thesis.

'I'm the one true blackfella for this place, and what've I got?'

Uncle Humbug spat hotly at the nurse's retreating back. 'You dugai bastards sitting on a gold mine ere in Mullum! Everybody cept Humbug making the biggest dollar from this place!'

'Yes, of course you are,' the nurse patronised him over her shoulder, 'and that's why we need to keep you here to get you healthy, Mr Milbung.'

Jo stared at the old man. *The one true blackfella.* Those were the words Twoboy had used the other night at the pub. Were the two men related – or had Uncle Humbug in his madness simply picked up a convenient phrase floating around the zeitgeist?

Stung with guilt at not busting him out, and filled, too, with curiosity about his claim (for she had always thought of him as a Koori and a southerner) Jo promised that she would call in after work and see about taking him home. Hardly appeased, Uncle Humbug watched as Doctor Michelle put six stitches in Jo's upper arm.

'You come get me when you knock orf work, girl,' he dictated, as she went to leave.

A hand flung in the air from the other side of the double glass doors was her only answer; giving Uncle a lift home was going to wipe half an hour at least off the time she had available for riding Comet. Humbug took the provision of lifts and food and tithes as his natural born right. Jo was not only youngish and a Goorie, but she was female and therefore, in Frederick J. Milbung's eyes, entirely subject to his constant demands. Could you get any further from aloof Granny Nurrung with her straight back riding her treadly to church, Jo wondered. And where, she thought in added irritation, were Uncle's legions of white hippie girlfriends when he needed them? Normally there was at least one dreadlocked drama queen hanging on his every solemn pronouncement and feeling she was all-but-Aboriginal after rooting Humbug for two weeks in the back of his decrepit van.

'You coming to the beach?' Jo asked her daughter a few nights later, hoping Ellen might have something going on with friends.

Ellen shook her head, picked up a toasted sandwich and headed silently back to her room. Jo watched that narrow disappearing back. At what point, she wondered, do you start to worry? At what point does ordinary teenage angst start to look like depression, and isolation, and looming disaster?

'Well, the dogs are fed. And if I'm not home, I'll be at Therese's,' she called out as she grabbed her keys. 'Love you!'

In the South Golden car park Jo could hear the sounds of merry-making from beyond the dunes, and see sparks flying up from a driftwood fire. Somebody had brought a guitar, and two or three somebodies were singing 'Flame Trees', with a mouth organ wailing along for good measure. An old white couple wandered back to the car park through the banksias, their grey hair still dripping from the ocean, and half-zipped wetsuits draped around their hips. Bit bloody late in the year for swimming isn't it, she thought. *Respect.*

'They're getting pretty happy down there,' the man warned her with a grin.

An alcohol-fuelled cheer rose as Jo crested the narrow track. Below the timber lookout platform, Therese sat cross-legged in the sand, a cheap new Chinese ukelele in her lap, smiling broadly and sampling the joint that was doing the rounds of the fire. Drawing closer, Jo could see Therese's niece and nephew, Amanda's stepsister from Tweed, Therese's next-door neighbour Trinity, and a few strays Jo knew by face but not by name.

'Happy Birthday, ya old bag,' Jo said, hugging Therese and giving her the only present she could afford this month, a five-dollar scratchie from the Billinudgel newsagent. 'That's from Ellen, too. Now, are you turning sixty or seventy? I couldn't remember.'

'Ah. That would be down to my air of timeless oriental wisdom, grasshopper,' Therese replied, steepling her fingers in front of her and adopting a Fu Manchu expression.

'You came!' Twoboy was suddenly there, rising to his feet. 'I've been hanging out to see this gorgeous chick from Billinudgel! How lucky am I? Wanna cold one?'

Jo accepted a stubby of Heineken. *What an Extremely Bad Idea you'll doubtless turn out to be.*

'I thought it might be too good to be true,' Twoboy said, his gleaming black eyes hooking her in and holding her spellbound. When he put his hand on her right shoulder and leaned in to kiss her hello on the cheek, an electric thrill rocketed up and down the length of Jo's body. A faint whiff of marijuana came along with the kiss, perfuming the air between them.

She looked at the jewel-green glass of the stubby she was holding, and spoke like someone who had full control of their limbs and faculties.

'Heineken! You win the lotto, didja?'

'Why not Heineken? You deserve the best. We all do,' Twoboy said, holding his sculpted arms wide. The straight women around the fire were checking him out, but Twoboy was unfazed by their attention.

'Is that right?' Jo grinned.

'Fucken oath, sis. My family never signed any contract agreeing to live happily in poverty all our born days. While I'm breathing, I'm gonna grab the good life with both hands.'

'Come and give us a song,' beseeched Amanda from the fire, but Jo ignored her, and the guitar passed safely to Trinity.

'Do you always talk such shite at parties?' Jo asked Twoboy, glad of the yarndi she could smell because it was something she could use to dismiss him. A safety valve for her heart.

'Talk shit? Me? Never. Well – maybe if I'm really sparked up,' Twoboy grinned. 'Or when I'm just about to fall madly in love.'

'So you'd be pretty sparked up then, eh?' Jo asked. If the bloke got any more relaxed it looked like he'd subside into a big black puddle of gorgeousness beside the fire.

'Not at all, Jo,' he said, much more quietly. 'Not even close.'

Jo looked away from this imminent and fascinating danger, down to the waves slapping the beach over and over again. The stars burned magnificently overhead. A few fishermen were trying their luck up the beach closer to New Brighton, but otherwise the horizon was empty. Jo took herself away from the fire. She meandered to the water's edge in search of firmer ground, and stood there with her head craned skywards. The huge Njuruyn of the Milky Way lay across the heavens. Jo breathed out deliberately, remembering how long it had taken her to see it: sitting not far from here on the Bruns rockwall with Aunty Barb, peering into the sky night after night, until it finally crashed into her under-standing all of a sudden, just before her twelfth birthday. Having seen the Emu once, Jo now saw it every time without difficulty. She realised with a small shock that Ellen was already past the age she had been that night, and a stab of regret pierced her. If only Aunty Barb had still been here to show Ellen, but the old girl was long gone into the Piccabeen cemetery beside Mum and Dad, poor darling, and the job of teaching Ellen was down to her.

With a jolt, Jo became aware of Twoboy standing in the dark behind her.

'Deadliest sky, eh?' Jo said, swivelling on her heel. Come on, she silently invited the man, patronise me. Tell me about the Njuruyn hidden in the stars. Offer to show it to me. To open my eyes.

'Yeah, she's a beautiful night,' Twoboy answered, his gaze high and his lips slightly apart. 'Them emus be laying yet, you reckon?'

Nonplussed, Jo turned back around and let her eyes drop to the surf endlessly curling over itself onto the sand. Back at the fire someone was drumming on a beer carton with a driftwood stick. These are the same sounds the ancestors heard, thought Jo. Waves. Drumming. Human voices, and laughter around a wirringin fire.

'Nah, June they sit on the nest, eh,' she replied.

'Hard to keep up sometimes. There's a bit of an emu shortage in Woodridge.' Twoboy smiled wryly.

'At least she's still there.' Jo gestured skyward with her stubby. 'She's not going anywhere in a hurry.' They both gazed up at the Emu, conscious of a mutual urge to retain their old people's knowledge.

'I've grown up in the culture,' Twoboy said quietly, lowering his gaze to the water, hunching his broad shoulders and pocketing his hands away from the cool night air, 'and I've had some bloody good teachers, but I still sometimes feel like I know fuck all, eh.'

'Ah, we all know fuck all really,' Jo agreed, feeling a tension she hadn't been aware of instantly drain away, 'us young ones. My aunty, not my blood aunty, other way, she had the names for the constellations, the whole bloody lot, in two or three different languages. And she could tell you exactly where every single star was – in the *day-time*. But she went and died before I was old enough to really listen.'

Twoboy glanced at Jo, his eyes soft.

'You still miss her, eh?'

'Every day. Her. And what she had to teach.'

Twoboy drew close, and they both stood silently, looking at the waves and listening to the night. Jo could feel the heat of the man's body close by her side. Something odd was happening to her breathing, and her legs wouldn't stop trembling. Jo was intensely aware of the narrowness of the space between them, and the distinct possibility of that space vanishing at any moment.

'Come and have a dorrie from up the top.' Twoboy urged. 'From the deck.'

There was nothing to be seen from the surf lookout that couldn't be seen from the shore, Jo knew. What was waiting up there was privacy, a wooden space three metres square that was invisible to the birthday party and to anyone else walking or jalum bira on the beach. Which was, of course, the entire point.

I'm sober, Jo told herself with a glance at her barely touched stubby, completely stone-cold sober. So why is my arm burning coals where he brushed me; why is it so hard to walk? Why is it impossible to think of anything except grabbing Twoboy, unbuttoning that shirt, tracing with my fingers and mouth some new pathways all over his fine dark body. Why is it that stepping up the gritty wooden steps onto the platform, with the man first grasping my right hand to help me up and then lifting that hand to his mouth, turning that same hand over and kissing it on the palm, and then pulling me into him, holding my face between his hands and leaning down to – oh! – kiss me – turning me yes (oh yes I will) into Molly Bloom, oh yes – why is it . . .

And yet this question and all the questions Jo had ever had became lost, suddenly, in a sweet medley of hands and lips and tongues and bellies pressed against each other in the darker imprint of the night, and a very clear and overwhelming urgency to be at Therese's house, on a bed, closer and closer and ever closer to this man, Twoboy, to be held inside his embrace, touching his face, his chest, his jun, his mouth, his everything, yes everything, oh, this is what's been missing all this long long lonely time, this long lonely two years of untouching, this, oh yes. This. This. This.

CHAPTER FIVE

Jo sat in a cane chair, soaking up the brilliant deep blue of the Bruns river and the way its shining health made her feel strong inside. She knew that if she got up and stood on the footbridge just beyond the park, she would likely see a family of stingrays hovering in the shallow current, sheltered by the little cluster of mangroves growing there. If she sat on the concrete steps below the footbridge and dangled her jinung in the current, tiny translucent prawns would come out hungrily from among the rocks. They would eventually surround her feet in an omnivorous cloud, nipping at her toes and forcing her to retreat.

Just this side of the jahjam's playground, a flock of ibis waited to harass anyone foolish enough to reveal their paper parcels of fish and chips. *Mura-kurahr*, Jo thought automatically, straight after she thought *ibis*: Big Nose. There was a time the ugly critters were on the local menu. A rare hungry time, it must have been, those months when the jalum and tailor weren't thick in the water, and the wallabies and geeyahn unusually scarce.

Jo turned back to the cafe. The weekend papers had already been snapped up by other, earlier, birds, so she amused herself by playing But Really I Am A Millionaire. Perusing the menu: I can order anything I bloody well want. The world's biggest cappuccino, as big as my head. Or I can have the *Monster Brekkie* with eggs, toast, baked beans, mushrooms. Not in the mood for minya? The vego option, then, no problemo. And if I happen to fancy a smoked salmon omelette for breakfast, then I have simply to ask. Nothing to it. I don't even have to wear shoes to this cafe if I don't choose to, since the entire town, nay, the whole bloody shire, knows that the streets I walk on are showered with gold dust. I'm like Steinbeck, rich enough to dress that bad. I'm Bob Marley, I'm Oprah, I'm Obama in drag, baby.

Jo smoothed her imaginary raw silk dress with freshly manicured nails. But no – and here she put a thoughtful millionaire's finger to her bottom lip – no, perhaps I'll exercise restraint. I'll just have a coffee, for now. I don't want to be too bloated when I have my full body massage later this morning at the Jade Tortoise, after all, and there is that reception in Newrybar that my private charity is throwing tonight –

'Yufla got ten dollar?' croaked Uncle Humbug, looming large on the other side of the laminated menu. Jo startled back into the real world onetime.

'Holy crap! You scared the living bejesus outta me, Uncle!' Jo said, catching her breath and grinning at his ambit claim. Uncle's wild hair and sparse teeth drew close; the pungent reek of his tobacco and campfire-infused wardrobe reached her. Combined with his brown skin, woolly locks and madly unconventional wardrobe, it advertised his status to anyone within a hundred yards: Keeper of the Park. Wild Man. Snake Spirit Brother. And most of all, Law unto Mybloodyself and Mind Ya Own Bloody Business Ya Dugai Wankers. 'Ya wanna drain me for smoke price, do ya?'

'Not after smoke price. I got juhm, but I'se proper hungry, my girl.' The skinny old man had been out of hospital for several days. 'And I hear you a big landowner round these parts, now,' he added pointedly, observing that Jo was going to put up something of a fight.

Uncle thumped the footpath with his carved eucalyptus walking stick to add emphasis to his plight. Jo winced. By sitting in full view at the Dolphin Cafe with tourist prices on the menu, she may as well have hung a sign around her neck saying, 'Payday today, all local blackfellas welcome, roll up, roll up!' The dugai at nearby tables were paying close attention to their little tableau. And in truth, Uncle Humbug was a sight to behold. Above his white-stubbled cheeks and crafty brown eyes, a snakeskin headband decorated his frayed straw cowboy hat. Said hat was crammed firmly on top of Humbug's red, black and yellow land rights beanie, which never left his skull, winter or summer. The old man wore his favourite black tracksuit pants, ripped at the left knee to display a hairy brown patella. A large blue flannelette shirt hung off his bony frame, reaching almost to his thighs, and Humbug's pipe-cleaner legs disappeared into a pair of brand-new Nike runners that Jo had noticed sitting trustingly on a local veranda just a day or two before.

This mob'll be snapping photos soon, Jo predicted, looking out the corner of her eye at the fascinated tourists. They'll be lining up to have their picture taken with an Authentic Aboriginal Elder.

'You wanna eat that kubbil of yours,' she proposed facetiously, glaring at the old man, 'plenty minya there sitting under the bridge.' Humbug drew himself up to his full five feet ten inches, and glared back. Slim was his brother. *You don't eat family. What do I look like — a fucken savage?*

'I'se terrible ungry, my girl,' he repeated, turning up the dial on the pathos. 'I dunno the last time I hadda decent feed.' Jo could just about hear the tourist binung zeroing in. They'd be crying in a minute. Howling for poor old Uncle Humbug. Fuck me.

Jo sighed an entirely Aboriginal sigh.

'Siddown, Uncle,' she capitulated, 'but I only got —' and here she scrabbled in her purse — 'seven dollar fitty. And if I don't get coffee soon someone's gonna die, so you want toast or what?'

What Humbug really wanted was lashings of ham, bacon and eggs sluiced down with a gallon of hot sweet tea, followed by a free ride to Byron Bay, but if absolutely necessary (a fact he wasn't yet ready to concede), he was prepared to settle for Jo's toast. The young backpacker waitress arrived to take the order and, though she'd developed a surprised expression, she made no fuss about the apparition that had appeared beside Jo. Uncle Humbug looked at the girl and his bloodshot eyes lit up.

'Us mob proper starving, girlie!' he declaimed loudly. The waitress looked to Jo for help interpreting this cryptic announcement, but Jo was discovering in the *Echo* classifieds how to have her aura cleansed. The tourists at the neighbouring tables had now abandoned their knives and forks and were paying rapt attention to Humbug's performance. A forty-something woman was giving out an air of irrepressible concern from behind her Dolce and Gabbana sunnies.

'I'm sorry?' The waitress was German. Six months out of high school on the other side of the world, and here she was with Humbug to contend with. Resolute, Jo shook the *Echo* out with a firm crack and hid inside it. A local poetry competition had been announced, she read on page fifteen.

'Goorie too hungry,' Humbug explained as though to a moron, rubbing his stomach, 'got no minya, no tucker back at camp.' The girl stood, gesturing helplessly that she didn't understand her role in this conversation at all. The sentiment radiating from the tourists was palpable.

'Vould you like to order, sir?' she began again, louder this time, and with an optimistic Teutonic pencil poised over her pad. *Sir*, thought Jo, biting down hard on her bottom lip, nice touch.

'Sree fried eggs. With toes, and bacon,' Uncle Humbug instructed even more loudly, 'and a carbadee and –' Jo slammed the *Echo* down hard on the table.

'Uncle!' she hissed loudly. 'I haven't got enough bungoo! What you *doing*?' Humbug's eyes flicked at Dolce and Gabbana so fast Jo wasn't sure at first that she'd seen anything at all. Then she sat back heavily in her seat.

'You know, mah girl,' Uncle informed the entire cafe via the waitress, one index finger raised and describing a slow trajectory from the river to Chincogan, 'I bin really lovin this Country. This Bundjalung Country e blong me proper way . . .'

Jo swore violently under her breath. Less than five minutes ago she'd been Oprah living her best life. Now she was rapidly sinking into unmanageable cafe debt and still hadn't had her caffeine fix. Then she heaved a pragmatic sigh. A smart woman knew when she was beat.

'I'm really sorry,' she explained to the waitress, 'but my uncle can't read, you see. The menu doesn't mean anything to him, and he doesn't really understand whitefella money. Cancel what he said. We've only got enough for –' here Jo conspicuously tipped every last cent of bungoo onto the tabletop and raked through the coins at a glacial pace – 'toast and jam, and maybe *one* coffee.' She peered at Humbug as though the *one* had been for his benefit.

'I'm sorry, my uncle,' she hammed it up with a stage whisper, 'I'm hungry too, but we just haven't got enough.'

'Just wanna good ol carbadee . . . and a decent feed . . . on my own true country . . .' A faint, saintlike expression fixed on Humbug's face as he gazed about him at the tourists. And then, suddenly developing the ability to speak standard English, 'Hello! Good morning to you, ladies.'

'Oh! Oh, please,' Dolce and Gabbana was undone. 'I couldn't help overhearing – would you – I don't mean to be rude, but I'd like to buy your, ah, uncle some breakfast, and if – would you like . . . ?'

Jo smiled and thanked the woman graciously, wondering if there were any circumstances in which she might possibly stump up enough for a contract killing on Humbug, who had shoved his straw hat backwards on his head (what, you Brad Pitt now?), and was launching into his favourite saga, The Manifest Failings of White Society, Part One.

Pretty soon, Humbug would be on his way to the Byron Bay Cash Converters where a longed-for yidaki with his name on it was waiting for his breathless new lady friend to discover.

In the park across the road, the ibis were muttering to each other in Bundjalung, green with envy for Humbug's accomplishments.

'You on proper Goorie time, eh?' Jo said mildly to Twoboy as he pulled a chair up, late and bare-chested from the surf, in front of

Humbug's plate still sitting there with Humbug's egg smears and Humbug's bacon rinds on it. Twoboy saw but made no comment on the plate. Instead, his face drawn down with worry, he told her: Laz's boy, the one who had had his stomach pumped out twice last year, had been missing for a day and a night after breaking up with his girlfriend. This morning his parents had found him tossing a rope over a tree at Zillmere – just in time, thank God, after the twenty-four hours from hell.

Twoboy had been on the phone to Brisbane for most of the last hour.

'Daw, poor things. Laz okay?' Jo asked in a very different voice. 'And Rhonda?'

'They got him home.' Twoboy rubbed his salty face with his palms. 'Got him home in one piece.'

Jo nodded. It was the mantra all grassroots parents knew. Keep the child alive and hope remains. Overdose, car accident, feuds, expelled from school, trouble with police, juvey, ripping family off, knives, drugs, gangs. Just keep the child alive long enough to come out the other side. Keep fighting every hour, every day. Refuse to let go. Get help from anywhere. Try everything. Anything. Just keep the jahjam breathing and hope remains.

'I dunno. He's very athletic, that kid, but he's real angry, always has been,' Twoboy said to the table in a weary voice that Jo hadn't heard before.

Jo put her hand on his arm.

'Gunaan gunaan . . . but he's home safe with family now, eh. How was the surf?' she asked softly. Cos *ya gotta acc-en-tu-ate the positive*, or we'd all be in intensive care – Twoboy himself said it all the time.

He brightened a fraction.

'Yeah, five-foot swells – storm coming in from Vanuatu. It was pumpin, but after the first few I could feel something wasn't right, so I came back in. All the boys thought I was womba. But you can't tell whitefellas anything, eh?' They shared a wry look: Goories knew what they knew – the rational approach was all very well

67

but sometimes you just knew shit without any rhyme or reason. You just *knew*.

'So ya going up home then?' Jo asked, realising that the day they'd planned — surf, cafe, markets — was history.

'Yeah, I'll head up dreckly. We got the fucking Tribunal tomorrow too, on top of all this — Laz and Mum were at the State Library with Kylie and Rhonda when the news came . . . Anyway, I could leave my board and stuff at your place, instead of in Mullum — that's okay isn't it?' He smiled nervously. A raucous night in the sack at Therese's, and now leaving his gear at her place. That amounted to a marriage proposal in some people's books.

'Sure.' Jo knew that Twoboy would want to hit the highway. There was no time to waste driving up to the room he'd rented in Mullum to dump his shit.

Then his mobile rang with the sounds of The Herd, and he glanced at the number.

'Laz again,' he said. 'Sorry, darlin, I better cruise. Call ya later, eh.' He stood and kissed Jo quick and deep, his wet dreads falling across them both, leaving saltwater drips sliding golden down her neck into her cleavage. Then he was gone across the street, cradling the phone to his ear as he shifted the board one-handed from the back seat of the Commode into the Hilux.

'Oh,' said the waitress, appearing with a jug of iced water, two glasses, and an application of fresh lipstick, 'he's gone.' She looked mournfully across the road.

'Yep,' Jo said as she folded the *Echo* and stood up.

'He's very good-looking . . .'

Jo mentally rolled her eyes. Yes, yes he is. Thanks for that update, luv.

'He's gay,' she lied suddenly, 'as camp as a row of tents!'

The waitress deflated like a stuck balloon.

'Gay?'

'He lives with his boyfriend.'

The waitress pouted.

'They're getting married in Hawaii next year,' Jo added maliciously, as she went inside to pay for her second coffee.

One afternoon later that week, an odd noise took Jo's attention away from the spuds and carrots that Ellen had flatly refused to peel for dinner.

'Check this out' Jo called to her insubordinate daughter, who was on the laptop in the lounge, erupting every few minutes with complaints about the glacial slowness of their connection. Every time it rained the phone line went bung; the initial thrill of having any internet at all had worn off after the first week. Ellen was threatening long and loud to set up a site called 'I Hate Telstra dot com'.

Supremely oblivious to the digital divide, Comet stood at the back screen door, his ears pricked as he watched Jo's movements in the house. He nudged the screen door hard with his nose. Because the door was held in place with a gammon arrangement made from an old ocky strap, it clattered loudly back and forth but didn't actually open. Comet was rather impressed with the racket he'd just made. In his world, noise in the vicinity of humans very often meant food. With the normal curiosity of any young animal, he nosed the door again.

Amused by his cheek, Jo stepped over to the sink, and rattled the pots and pans soaking there. The horse whickered in approval. To Comet, this building was simply another stable, possibly one with extra tucker inside for the likes of him, and the pots and pans the magical containers of chaff and pellets.

There was no reply from Ellen. Par for the bloody course.

Jo went to the back door, blowing her breath through the wire insect screen onto Comet's extended muzzle. He blew gently back through soft, black, grimy nostrils. Well, at least *you* talk to me, Jo thought. My beautiful boy. We'll have a little ride when I've done these spuds, we can work on your lateral flexion in the paddock, before the rain hits.

Then it dawned on her that Comet was still wearing his halter from when she let him into the backyard to graze an hour ago. He looked quite calm, despite the greenish storm clouds that were now clustering heavily over the back ridge, threatening hail. Would it be too silly to . . .

Jo smiled wickedly.

She took a piece of decaying Mooney string from the nearby bathroom cupboard, and tied the screen door back to an unused washing machine outlet. The way into the house was now clear. The horse whickered and took a tentative step up the concrete ramp, bringing his head into the timber-lined passageway which led to the kitchen. He goggled at the whirring fridge, blowing his breath out to let it know of his presence.

'Ellen,' Jo called again, offering the colt the top crust from her devon and salad sandwich. His mobile lips explored it briefly, and then he seized it between his teeth, flipping his head up and down as he manoeuvred the bread into position in his mouth.

Enjoying the treat, Comet dared to take another wide-eyed step inside, to who-knew-what further goodies. His wide brown hips brushed lightly against the sides of the passageway. Two more steps, Jo thought, and then we're really committed. At least until we get you into the lounge and have room to turn you around.

The Bedouin live with their horses in their tents, don't they?

She quickly grabbed a towel from the bathroom and laid it on the floor, to muffle the sound of his hooves on the old lino. Cos if the mountain won't come to Mohammed. She crammed the remaining devon and lettuce into her mouth, and sacrificed her second slice of bread, to occupy Comet for a few seconds while she swiftly moved kitchen chairs out of the way.

Ellen was just visible from the far side of the kitchen, sitting on the lounge with her dark hair falling around her face. Lost in cyber land, she hadn't heard a thing.

Jo wished she could wrap Comet's hooves in clothing to muffle the sound, but he would probably freak if she tried, and the smallish interior of a 1950s fibro and timber farmhouse was not the place to teach him. She suddenly envisaged salad bowls flying through the air, and the half-peeled vegies airborne, too, and Comet's muscular neck and head smashing through the glass front of the kitchen cabinet as he tried to escape the clutching monsters that were grabbing at his feet. When you thought about it, Jo gulped, there was quite a difference, really, between a Bedouin tent surrounded by thousands of miles of sandy desert, and an Australian farmhouse with copious amounts of glass and easily-shattered fibro.

But it was literally too late to back out, for all of Comet was now filling the kitchen. And the top of his head was exactly on a level with the bare, hanging light bulb –

A few more cautious steps on hastily rearranged towels. Jo stroked the horse's neck with a sweating hand. 'Atta boy,' she whispered. 'Nothing to it. Just another sort of stable. You can do it.'

Comet peered with great interest into the lounge. Is that where the food is, his eyes and ears asked. Shaking with repressed laughter that was half terror of what would happen if the horse panicked, Jo hid herself behind the wall that divided kitchen from lounge.

'Ellen,' Jo said, in a Here's Another Chore for You monotone, knowing that she would be ignored.

'Mmm.'

'Give us a hand getting the washing in, please.'

'Mmm.'

'Now, eh, before it rains.'

'Mmm. In a minute.'

'No, now,' as she jabbed Comet in the rump with a forefinger, pushing him forward the last few steps to where Ellen was slaying Dark Knights. The horse lowered his nose to the feedbin that the young human was holding. A high-pitched scream. And simultaneously, a crash. Comet whirled 180 degrees in front of the TV, his tail swishing in alarm. His rear hoof stepped backward and missed the fallen laptop by a centimetre.

Outside, Athena whinnied in concern for her absent child.

Comet neighed loudly, too, prancing with nerves but unclear how to return to his mother and safety. Athena screamed in relief: Here I am, my son, here, here! Come to me!

'What the *fuck!*' Ellen shouted, her hands flailing and her eyes wide. 'What's *Comet* doing in the house?'

Jo moved smoothly in and seized Comet by the halter, rocking with laughter.

'Did he give you a fright?' she asked innocently, before doubling over in mirth. Comet's nostrils flared, and he swung his head around, looking for escape routes. Jo clung to his halter with difficulty. He neighed again to Athena, who was now running frantically up and down the fenceline beyond the mango.

'You're insane!' Ellen screeched, moving closer to the endangered computer.

Comet raised his glossy black tail and deposited a gleaming green pile of manure onto Ellen's bare feet. Jo lost the ability to speak.

Ellen yelped as she leapt away from the richly scented pile. Jo was staggering now, clutching her guts and gesturing weakly for her daughter to grab the horse. Oh, to have a camera. Oh. Can't breathe. Face leaking. Guts aching . . . Oh, oh . . .

'Do you know –' gasp '– how long it took me to teach him to do that?'

'I'm adopted,' Ellen announced in a deathly voice, raising and examining – but not touching – one foot and then the other.

'Yes, yes, my adopted daughter, but *your face!*'

'I can't wait to leave home. Then you can marry your bloody horse, and be happy here, just the two of ya,' Ellen retorted.

'You know where the door is.' Jo clutched at her stomach as she clung to Comet.

'You can both live together inside in a big pile of horseshit and rusty old barbed wire and lantana. That'd be your idea of heaven, wouldn't it? That'd be just fricken tickety-boo.'

Tears of silent laughter rolled down Jo's face. She could tell that Ellen was thinking of picking up some steaming horseshit and hurling it at her.

'I hate you . . . Oh, I hate you So Much.' Ellen's lips pursed and her green eyes narrowed to slits.

'I love you,' Jo wheezed, 'I'll even pick that manure up.'

Tremendously jollified, still giggling, Jo led the horse safely out of the kitchen and through the back door. At the top of the concrete ramp, she heard Twoboy's Redfern whistle, just as he came loping around the corner, laptop in one hand and his Uni of Melbourne backpack slung over his shoulder.

'Aaay, Goorie,' Jo greeted him with a wide smile, walking Comet down the ramp. As the decrepit Mooney string gave way and the back door slammed behind them, she led the horse across to the small side paddock.

Rain finally began to fall and – what's that? of course the horse had been inside, he liked to watch that 'Letters and Numbers' show on SBS in the afternoons, what about it?

'So tell me something,' Jo said to Twoboy, who was lying beside her, with the roast vegies all consumed and Ellen disappeared into her room. She was using her right index finger to trace an intricate pattern on Twoboy's almost hairless dark chest, and remembering the waitress at the cafe. 'Tell me how come a *good-looking* –' she lightly kissed his left nipple – 'and *hejimicated* –' his right nipple – 'and occasionally even *charming* –' the point on his stomach equidistant from both nipples – 'blackfella like yerself manages to stay single?' She leaned back onto her left elbow, and waited to see what his response would be.

Outside the bedroom window, the storm had arrived in earnest. Rain cascaded over the top of the drooping gutter and formed a room-length silver curtain between the lovers and the rest of the world. An enormous green tree frog, resident in the downpipe closest to the bed, was making a helluva racket reporting on the weather, while Jo and Twoboy lay enclosed by water and sound. At that moment, neither of them cared one iota about what lay outside.

'Hard to believe, I know,' Twoboy responded cheerfully to the bedroom ceiling, both hands folded behind his head and his skinny black ankles crossed. Just yesterday, the Tribunal had accepted the Jacksons' application to be counterclaimants over a substantial northern slab of the greater Brunswick valley. Like Mum Jackson, Laz, Rhonda, and Uncles Cheezel and Rory, Twoboy was in an exceptionally buoyant mood.

'And yet?' Jo slapped him lightly on his delightfully S-shaped upper arm.

'Well, truth be told, you snagged me in the five-second gap between supermodels.'

Jo groaned and rolled her eyes, though the uncomfortable truth was that, in public, a female commotion followed, apparently permanently, in his wake. And it wasn't like he was unaware of it, either, she warned herself. *Good-looking men. Trouble. You do the math, Jo.*

'Yeah, yeah, yeah. So what happened to the last supermodel?'

'The last one . . . well, the last one that meant anything is my kids' mum, in Melbourne,' he said. 'Sam.'

'That was years ago, wasn't it?' Jo was suspicious of this lengthy gap.

'Four years. Justice was six and Yabra had just turned five, the poor little darlin.' He'd shown Jo the photos of his kids on his phone and in his wallet. Cuties, the both of them, curly-haired and cocoa-coloured; their mother Sam was a Wurundjeri woman burdened and blessed with skin as milky-pale as any whitefella.

'Four years is a helluva long time between drinks,' Jo probed.

'Oh, there've been *women*.' Twoboy laughed a little awkwardly. 'I'm not a monk. But I went a bit beserk as a young bloke, as Laz and Mum will no doubt delight in telling you. Christ knows why I haven't got twenty kids instead of two. So when we split, I made a decision to slow down. I hooked up with a Tamil activist for a bit down in Melbourne. And when I moved back up here there was a proppa womba one in Ipswich, but she was a fucken nightmare, and so here I am, girlfriend. Ripe for the picking.' He spread his arms wide, inviting Jo to get the goodies on offer.

'Ah, you got tickets on yaself or what?' Jo scoffed, noting carefully at the same time that Twoboy expected her to be talking with his mother. And there was also that phrase that had popped out: 'you snagged me'. What did *that* mean?

'I could ask you the same question, anyways,' he said, rolling onto his own elbow so that their eyes and mouths were level and yet not quite touching. Twoboy took Jo's tracing index finger and bit it gently, nibbling down her forearm until the hair on the back of her neck stiffened and she goosepimpled down both arms. Twoboy laughed and warned her that he just might be a cannibal like his father's ancestors in the north.

'Whether I got tickets on myself?' Jo asked, noticing absently that her legs were toned right up from all the extra farm work and riding she'd done lately. Her quads and hamstrings were clearly defined hillocks of muscle beneath golden skin. Pity about the farm-fixing marks and bruises that dotted every limb. On her upper right arm the horizontal scar from the broken vase was barely healed, the stitches not yet out.

'No, how come you're single, doofus? Gorgeous thing like you . . .' Now he was kissing her neck, working his way down to her left breast, bringing his spare hand to her hip, and –

'Who sez I'm single?' Jo joked, as desire flared. 'My man gets back next Wednesday.'

'I knew it was too good to be true,' Twoboy murmured.

'Gammon. We split two years ago. I'm only just recovering. Ah. Ooh.'

'Want some help with that recovery process?' Twoboy asked, smoothly rolling over so that Jo was beneath him. She could feel her nipples hardening, the weight of the man pressing onto her hips and thighs. He wore the sun in his eyes, the surging strength of the ocean in his body. Jo caught hold of a handful of dreads and brought Twoboy's face down to hers, let her lips and tongue answer him in that old, old language that has no need of words.

★

75

Next morning, Bottlebrush Hill was shrouded in mist and cloud. Both of the dogs had helpfully left trails of muddy paw prints all over the veranda, in their canine version of a weather report.

'More rain coming,' declaimed Jo as she put three hot cups on the kitchen table, 'how bout we make fences while the sun shines, people?'

'I don't roll on Shabbos!' Twoboy called from the bathroom.

'Pass,' added Ellen hastily through a mouthful of toast and Vegemite, 'I've got an assignment to finish and then I'm going up to Holly's.'

'But who shall help me *eat* the loaf of bread, cried the little red hen?' Jo pouted as she sipped her first coffee of the day.

Twoboy looked at Jo's large brown eyes, and at her sculpted mouth, which he had not yet done with kissing.

'Okay, I'm in,' he said, winning a huge smile from the other side of the table. 'But how about we ring up for reinforcements?'

'More the merrier,' Jo said, 'but we've only got an hour clear I reckon by the look of that sky. It's gonna piss down by the time anyone gets here.'

'Fair enough,' said Twoboy, 'and hey, whose guitar's that in the spare room?'

From beneath her fringe Ellen shot her mother a look that spoke volumes.

'Oh, Ellen mucks around with it a bit,' said Jo, giving the look back to her daughter with interest. She told Twoboy she didn't mind if he had a play with it, hoping this didn't mean a morning spent playing music and no work done on the fence. The man came back to the kitchen and eased himself down with the Maton comfortably positioned against his broad chest like a ukelele. A few chords to test the tuning, a bit of finger picking.

'This isn't a cheap guitar,' he noted with approval.

'Ellen's dad bought it,' Jo said, allowing him to think it was a gift from father to daughter. Technically, Paul had bought it – when she was still married to him.

'I woulda killed for a Maton when I was thirteen,' Twoboy told Ellen, his eyebrows raised at how easy she had it.

'Don't put ideas into her head,' joked Jo. 'She's already sallying forth and taking up the neighbour's bloodstock.'

Twoboy lowered the guitar into a normal playing position and began to sing 'Redemption Song'.

His voice was strong, and he played pretty well for an amateur, Jo assessed. Good song, too. Oh pirates, yes, they rob us mob, alright. But the likelihood of Ellen outing her as a muso made her uneasy. She headed to the veranda the instant the song was over.

Jo didn't know why it mattered that this part of her remained private. There was no easy answer, except perhaps that the bloke was already very much at home here. Some part of her needed to remain off limits. To her intense annoyance, Jo was thinking about Twoboy at odd hours of the day and night; dreaming about him; smiling goofy smiles as she remembered moments they had spent together. Wondering, even, how long it was going to last, for Chrissake.

Twoboy looked at Jo through the window, as she unceremoniously pulled her dirty gumboots on.

'So, I guess the show's over then,' he said. 'You're a hard one to impress, Jo Breen.'

'The way to my heart is through a kilometre of fencing wire,' she answered, 'and if I want music I can turn on the radio.'

'And here's me thinking I found the way to your heart last night,' Twoboy smirked.

'Oh, way *way* too much information,' wailed Ellen, jamming her fingers into her ears and fleeing, both from Twoboy and from the imminent danger of being asked to wash up, 'lalalalalalalala!'

'Do you have to?' Jo asked, pretending parental concern to banish any lingering idea that Twoboy had ever had – or would ever have – anything to do with her heart. Perish the thought.

★

Half an hour later, Twoboy gestured to Jo, who was standing a hundred metres uphill holding a piece of string. A few spots of rain dotted her hoodie, but the full onslaught of the low black clouds was yet to hit.

'Left! No, back the other way a bit. Bit more. That's it.' Twoboy gave her the thumbs up and Jo used the head of the sledgehammer, grasped sideways, to bash the tall star picket easily into the soft ground. A long row of pickets now guarded the hill, from the house to up near the big tallowwood, passing the top dam on their way.

'What's the idea here, anyway?' Twoboy wanted to know. Jo explained that this line was the first of four sides of a horse paddock, replacing the damp Small Paddock where Comet was being held isolated from his mother and the steers. Once it was built, he'd be visible to Jo from the back door of the house, and dryer as well, less prone to footrot and greasy heel disease.

'He's stuck in solitary, poorfella,' Twoboy observed.

'Well, he'll be out on good behaviour dreckly,' Jo answered. 'But for now he needs to be away from his mother, to bond with me.'

'We done a good job here. It must be just about smoko time, eh?' suggested Twoboy, looking at the blur that was the sun and then clapping Jo firmly on the arse. She ignored both provocations and began methodically snipping foot-long lengths of plain wire to attach the barbed wire to the pickets.

'Nope, not even close.'

'Shit, speaking of smoko.' Twoboy thrust a hand into his black-and-grey camo trouser pocket, and checked for mobile coverage. A relentlessly blank screen looked back. He shook his head.

'Not even a bar. How do you like living in the Pleistocene era?'

'I like it very bloody much,' Jo grunted as she picked up the heavy roll of barbed wire by its protruding wooden handles. 'It's a –' gasp – 'piece of –' gasp – 'piss. And –' gasp – 'if you was a real –' gasp – 'black –' gasp – 'fella, you wouldn't even worry about –' gasp – 'shit like that.' She carried the awkward wire to the top of their fenceline, and then fed the loose end downhill so it passed each of the twenty stakes they'd just banged in.

Twoboy pretended affront.

'The reason I need coverage, madam,' he retorted, 'is so I can get onto Uncle Cheezel and get him down to town to testify for us next week. Otherwise Oscar Bullockhead and his pack of lying black dog southern cunt rellos are gonna do me out of my land. *Our* land.'

His and Laz's land, Jo knew he meant, and Mum Jackson's, and that of Justice and Yabra in Melbourne, and the small horde of nieces and nephews and cousins who were scattered the length and breadth of the east coast. Jo couldn't prove a damn thing about her family, which meant that she – and Stevo, and Ellen – would find no place in any Native Title tribunal in the land. The Breens were, and would likely remain, the acknowledged traditional owners of three-quarters of nine-tenths of sweet fuck all.

'Give it here,' Jo said, heaving for breath, her hand outstretched. 'No, put the message in first –'

'What's the point?'

Jo swivelled her hand and made an impatient face, until Twoboy, sighing, entered the text and passed the phone over. She then instructed him to turn and face the house. The man folded his arms, tilted his head and gave her a deeply sceptical glance. *Now come on.*

'Humour me,' Jo insisted.

Twoboy rolled his eyes, but reluctantly obeyed.

'Can I turn around yet?' he nagged after ten seconds.

'Not yet. Wait . . . Okay – now.'

'And?' he said.

'I've sent it.' Jo told him. 'It's gone to Uncle Cheezel.'

'*Bull*shit.'

Twoboy scrolled down to Sent Items and discovered that Jo was telling the truth. Yet there were still no bars showing. He squinted and carefully tightened the rubber band holding his dreads back. Then he rubbed his mouth slowly with the back of his hand, torn between a strict cultural imperative never to betray surprise, and an overwhelming urge to know how she'd done it.

Jo cracked up at his quandary.

'Did I forget to mention I'm a cleverwoman?' she teased.

Twoboy stared at her in deep alarm, as though she really might be, and *then* what would he have gotten himself into?

Jo laughed even harder, and held her hand out again for the phone.

'Better see if he's answered, eh. Oh look – no bars. So sad.'

She held the screen up so he could see the ongoing absence of bars. Twoboy pursed his lips. He resented being the butt of whatever joke Jo was pulling.

'Can we just finish the bloody fence?' he said.

'But don't you want to know if he's answered it?' Jo taunted, waggling the phone beside her ear. 'Isn't he your star witness next week?'

'If we can do it without all this fucking around, yeah.' Twoboy folded his arms.

Jo grinned, enjoying her power. *Sure we can.*

'Watch and learn, grasshopper.'

She tossed the mobile, end over end, high into the air, spinning it fast, four, five, six metres straight up, and then catching it silently in two careful hands when it fell. She repeated this, then on its third flight the phone beeped shrilly from the top of its orbit.

Airily, Jo flipped the phone back to Twoboy, who nodded in grudging admiration as he checked the inbox.

'He's still on for Wednesday. Ya had me going for a minute there,' Twoboy admitted as he pocketed the phone.

'I really am a deadly cleverwoman, but,' Jo insisted with a grin. 'And don't you forget it.'

'Yeah, and I'm the Dalai Llama's underpants,' Twoboy answered through a mouthful of wire ties.

Soon they had two full-length strands of wire fastened tautly to all twenty pickets.

'You know what Amanda said to me the other day?' Jo asked him quietly. An insect fluttered in her belly.

'Yeah, cos I'm psychic,' Twoboy grunted, tying more wire.

'She goes, Are you sure that bloke isn't just chasing after you for your farm?'

'That's it – she's onto me! I wanna marry the cockie's daughter . . .'

Twoboy hooted with laughter and wound his forearm around Jo's waist, pulling her in close to him. Then he seized her by the shoulders and kissed her full and enthusiastically on the mouth.

'Ouch, shit, careful!' His hand had clamped on her wounded arm.

Hastily he let go, sorry, sorry, and then drew up close again, this time more careful, his hands resting each side of her head and neck. Glossy dark brown curls spilled beneath his fingers. He gently nosed her forehead. Jo felt herself melting.

'You don't trust me. Well, why should you?' he murmured.

'It's just . . . I dunno.' Jo's farm wasn't Crown Land, but there was more than one way to skin a cat – Amanda's suggestion had sent chills down her spine.

'Newsflash, darlin – dugais don't get it,' Twoboy said. 'Whitefellas always think any little gammon bitta land's good enough for Goories. Not that it isn't beautiful here,' he hastily amended, seeing Jo's face cloud over with insult. 'But for fuck's sake, I don't just want a hobby farm. I want the recognition we never had growing up without two fucken cents to rub together – *useless boongs*. Laz n me didn't leave our good jobs to claim your twenty acres, Jo. We moved back here for the whole bloody lot, and to live like blackfellas should – on Grandad Tommy's country, and practising his Law.'

'Well that's good to hear. Cos this little black duck does want a little farm – and now I've finally got one,' Jo told the man, kissing him fiercely before picking up the fencing tools. Her heart was hammering from Twoboy's touch, and from getting up the nerve to raise Amanda's question, too. 'And if you fenced like you talked, Lawman, we'd be done by now,' she added, handing him the lengths of plain wire for attaching the third strand.

'I do fence like I talk,' he replied, walking down the slope and gesturing at Bottlebrush with a soft upward flick of his fingers. 'Straight and true. Cos the old people are watching us. Watching to see we get it right.'

'Yeah, yeah, yeah.' Jo glanced around at her paddocks, which according to Twoboy were crawling with spirits: good, bad and indifferent. 'Well, I hope them old people like looking at camphor laurels and crofton weed. That moll at the real estate told me this place had so many weeds on it cos it was close to organic certification. What a crock.'

'Well,' Twoboy said cheerfully, taking hold of the third strand of wire. 'Remember what Goebbels said – if ya gonna tell a lie, make it a big one.'

The world was nothing but water in the air and water in the streams, water in the swelling dams, and the narrow black snake that was Tin Wagon Road awash with a thin transparent skin of water feeding into the brown, churning, rising creek. The harsh roar of rain hammered on the tin roof, drowning out all other sound except for the thunder of the frogs. It rains here, thought Jo, entranced by the spectacle, as if the gods are trying to wash away some terrible story, wash away the blood in the rivers, wash away the names of the true owners of this place. Maybe that's why our connections are so weak, so tenuous, me and Kym and Stevo. They took our ancestors away, and it's pissed down so hard ever since then that the floods have washed away all their footsteps, washed away half our belonging. That's me – a *washed-up* blackfella. She stared at her sodden paddocks. It was one thing – and a bloody big thing – to buy your country back off the landgrabbers. But how do you buy back a tribe? Where do you shop for a mob to call your own?

'Gotta cruise,' said Twoboy over Jo's shoulder, frowning at the downpour and making an unhappy mouth. 'I can't get stuck here, my darlin. That judge'll be giving me country away to Oscar Bullockhead, to anyone with a black face and a lovely yarn to spin em, if I'm not there with Mum and Laz on Wednesday.'

'Off you go then.' Jo was shivering on the veranda in wet clothes. She had just returned from fixing the water pump which delivered her water out of Stoney Creek across the road. The neighbour's cattle regularly knocked the cover off, exposing the pump to the elements. No cover, no working pump. No pump, no water in the tanks for showers or washing. And so every time rain threatened it was a sprint across the road to undo the Brahmins' endless mischief. And that would continue to be the story until Jo found time to move the pump and hook its black plastic pipes up to her own top dam instead of to the cleaner running water of Stoney Creek. It was just another of the many tasks that seemed to multiply while she was at work, and only got remembered in the early hours before dawn when Jo would lie awake in the dark, worrying about them.

She unceremoniously shooed Twoboy away. *On ya bike.*

'You think I want to go, eh?' Twoboy raised his eyebrows in amusement, feet planted squarely on the boards of the veranda.

'How the fuck would I know what you want?' Jo put one hand on her hip as the wind whipped the rain in under the roof, making the dogs cower against the kitchen wall, daw, poorfellas. 'Just go if ya going. No need to make a song and dance about it, is there?' And what a dugai expression that is, Jo realised, even as her shooing hand flicked him towards Tin Wagon Road and the tribunal in Brisbane that would decide his family's future.

'What I want –' Twoboy grabbed Jo's dismissive rain-wet hand and held it pressed hard up against his heart – 'is to stay here with you for a *very, very* long time. But if I'm not there for the hearing it'll put us about three years behind the bloody eight ball. And you know how these creeks come up.'

Jo didn't, in fact, know the nature of 'these creeks', having grown up in the shady backwater of South Golden Beach, where the sludgy canal was a lot slower to react to storms than the streams that fed off Bottlebrush and Chincogan.

'Well, I'm learning.'

But it was no good, words were no good. Par for the course, once they were touching each other – even just rain-cold hands – nothing but their touching mattered. Twoboy was in her orbit again and she was kissing him, wrapping herself in him, lost in a universe of his dreads, and his mouth, and his warm chest, a universe of mutual desire and urgency. He reached lower and lifted her up onto him, both of them fully clothed and neither of them dry; rain pummelling the ground just beyond the veranda and the spray off the outside boards reaching them as fine mist. She clasped her heels into his wet back, kissing him and smiling at the same time, wanting this never to end.

'Why would I *want* to leave,' Twoboy whispered, 'are you insane?'

'My ex-husband thinks so. Told me on a regular basis.'

'He's a prize fuckwit.'

'Mm-hmm.'

Jo slid back down to earth and they stumbled inside, half-running to the bedroom, as the rain hammered even more heavily on the tin roof. Jo kicked the door shut, knowing that Ellen would hardly hear it bang over the torrents flooding down. When Twoboy lifted her wet shirt off and began to kiss her belly, she tilted his chin up with one finger.

'Hey – you have to go, remember? Very important tribunal business in Brisbane? And the creeks all coming up like there's no tomorrow?'

'I'm gone.' Kissing her smooth golden belly. 'I'm not here. Must be someone else doing this.' Twoboy smiled.

Jo closed her eyes as he moved his kisses slowly, oh so slowly towards her hips, her thighs, her junoo.

'Definitely not here.'

'Ah.'

'Or here.'

'Ah.'

'Or here.'

'I don't care where you are. Just keep doing what you're – *ah* – doing.'

'Nice way to talk.'

'I'm single, I can talk how I like. Oh, *yeah*, do that.'

'You sure about that?'

'Very.'

★

'I don't just want to stay a bit longer today – I want to be with you,' Twoboy told Jo when she was lying floppily against him beneath the blanket, rain thrumming on the roof. 'And I don't want to share. Very greedy I am. I want everything all to myself, no exceptions.'

'Well, you do have a penis,' Jo teased, 'so that kind of goes without saying.'

Twoboy looked out the window. The wind was lashing the white cedar tree in the paddock.

'Be serious. I want to be *with* you,' he whispered beneath the pounding rain. 'The goddamm paterfamilias.'

'You *are* with me,' Jo protested, avoiding his meaning.

'Not just like this, I mean *really* with you. I mean I've –'

Jo pulled the blanket higher, covering her heart. 'Don't say it,' she cut in, tightly. 'Not unless you mean it. Actually, don't even say it if you do mean it.'

A cool silence ensued.

'I don't like that rule much,' Twoboy told her then. There was genuine hurt in his dark eyes.

'My house, my rules. And anyway, didn't you have to be gone half an hour ago?'

'Yep. Yep, I did.' Twoboy got up and dressed faster than usual. There was a new wound in him now. The man didn't so much as glance at Jo as he searched the room for his runners.

She lay and grimaced at the ceiling. It was never easy. *Nothing* was allowed to be easy. You had to be building granite fortress walls to protect yourself – that, or be the one getting boiling oil poured on your head from above.

'Don't rush me,' she told Twoboy as he brusquely kissed her goodbye. 'I've *heard* how much men love me too many times in my life, that's all. And I have to think of Ellen, too.'

'Believe it or don't believe it,' he told her without the usual smile lighting up his face. 'It's the truth.'

CHAPTER SIX

Jo pulled the ripcord, and the whipper snipper roared satisfactorily into life first go, sending vibrations coursing up her forearms and into her braced elbows. She reefed her earmuffs down – as if she wasn't half binung goonj already from the band days – and headed over towards the cemetery's memorial wall. Lowering the machine head, she began to tidy up the only signs on this earth that various Mullumites had ever existed. Mullumites? Mullumbimbians? Mullumbimbos – yeah, she decided with a grin. Mullumbimbos. As the sweeping motion of the work gradually took hold, her mind drifted away from the cemetery. Grass spewed sideways from the spinning head with its lashing plastic string, but in her daydreams Jo saw only Twoboy's smile, Twoboy's mesmerising black eyes, Twoboy's dark arms reaching for her in bed yesterday. And that was okay, no problemo. What she *saw* was fine. It was what she then remembered coming out of his mouth that troubled her.

I want to be with you, really with you. And: *I don't want to share.*

Jo felt a deep primal alarm in her gut as she remembered these words. She'd thought she could make marriage work with Ellen's father, of course, but that illusion had been disastrous. During her divorce, Jo had decided that she was too damaged to love anyone except Ellen. Mum and Dad had done their best, but flogging her and Kym and Stevo into compliance was all they could think of to protect their coffee-skinned kids from the dangerous world of dugai power and dugai hypocrisy. Hide from trouble, don't fight it. Be Quiet. Be

Obedient. Be White. At thirteen, when the car accident killed her parents and took her world away, Jo had already had it with their strategy for living. She'd fled South Golden and, despite the hard yakka put in by Aunty Barb, it didn't take long for trouble to find her. She'd had to climb a long way up from the floor of the pub toilet since then.

And here I am now, a parent myself, Jo thought, with me and Ellen all on our lonesome ownsome – except then Twoboy arrives chucking declarations of love around like confetti. Coming in to fuck everything up, just when I've got my freedom, a job I can tolerate, the best horse I could ever hope to breed, and the farm I always dreamed about. Sweet Christ Jesus.

How did that Dylan song go? *I gave you my heart but you wanted my soul.* Jo had never really understood the difference. Giving her heart away felt exactly the same as giving up her soul. She wasn't ready to gamble on Twoboy, wasn't nearly ready to sign up for the swings and roundabouts of being only the half of something. No, she was already the whole of something else – something completely different. And there was Ellen to think of, too.

As Jo worked her way around the edge of the memorial wall, digesting these problems beneath the comforting, muffled, white noise of the whipper snipper, a sharp quartz pebble rocketed up, flung by the plastic string of the machine. It pinged loudly against a metal name plate before ricocheting back onto her shin.

Jo took her finger off the trigger. Silence fell.

Her shoulders and forearms ached from the effort of keeping everything looking nice, and she became aware that she'd been frowning as she worked. She read the bronze memorial plaque on the wall while she rubbed her stinging leg:

Anne-Maree Gascoigne. 09-05-1958 – 10-03-1984. Sadly Missed By Her Husband and Daughters. RIP.

Rolling up her jeans Jo discovered a small boomerang of a bruise already decorating her shin. Should she, she wondered, take this stinging quartz pebble, this tiny attack of the universe upon her person, as evidence that life was short, that any love is good love, and a clear enough indication that she should dive headlong into the deep, dangerous territory of Twoboy Jackson and his unreliable professions of fidelity? Or should it rather be read as a message that real love is worth waiting for – that husbands and daughters who will grieve for you are not thick upon the ground, and that she should look long and hard before she leapt?

As she considered this concept – sorrowful husbands and daughters – everything, suddenly, was too much for Jo. Her eyes welled up, surprising her with tears for her lost marriage; for her tightly held dream of a family. The dream she had fucked up all on her own with her cold anger and her rages and her disappearing to gigs; her refusal to let Paul in; her immense self-loathing that told her constantly that whatever she had was never, never enough. That she was bad, and if anyone dared to love her, it was simply evidence that they, too, were deeply and irrevocably flawed.

Frustrated at her welling tears, Jo smacked the side of her head so hard that she floated momentarily, located somewhere between the pain in her shin and the stinging of her reddened right ear.

Ellen's dad wasn't coming back. She didn't want him to. They were so badly matched she must have been insane to ever conceive a child with him. So why this ache, this never-ending burden she carried in her gut? The craving for the dream of a real family, a Mob. Belonging. A couple of dozen people who hung together and shared and laughed, who were all on the same team. Her team.

Terrifyingly, this was what Twoboy had whispered the possibility of, beneath the pounding Bundjalung rain. This was his implicit offer, his solution to her desperate, unspoken, unacknowledged loneliness. But Jo wasn't sure she was brave enough. She felt hollowed out by life, feared that she was useless for anybody who wanted a complete human being to love. Ellen had the best of her, and there was bugger all left over. Twoboy thought there was enough for him to love as well, but Twoboy was just plain wrong.

Jo started the whipper snipper up again with a savage yank, and laid into the setaria threatening the appearance of the dead all over the hillside. She massacred the clumps of lime-green grass, flayed them, ground them so low that Basho would beam with pleasure at her meticulousness, unaware that really Jo was killing the past. Murdering the final lacerating months of her marriage. Assassinating the pain of Paul finally walking away, having had enough. And not least, flaying the dugais for what they'd done long before Paul came along to try and live with the half-crazed consequences.

After an hour of this frenzied attack Jo halted, sweating and defeated. The cemetery was immaculate, but she was a mess. And worse, far worse, she was just playing silly buggers, going round and round in circles in her own mind. There was no way she could say no to Twoboy. She knew she was already in too deep with that dreadlocked fella, and no matter what he was selling with his handsomeness and his smiling declarations of fidelity, the price could never be too high.

'You gotta come over right now!' Therese insisted down the phone on Friday afternoon, knock-off time or near enough. Jo's lip curled automatically at being told what to do, even by her best friend.

'*Why* do I gotta? What's up?'

'Just get your arse here straight away – I got something you and Ellen need to see.' There was an excited burbling in Therese's tone, a lightness and a promise of good times that did the trick. Jo scratched her scalp, and decided that it wouldn't kill the horses to be fed after dark for once.

'Okay, seeya in ten.'

She turned to Ellen, and gave her the news. Ellen moaned a familiar mantra: the world against her; powerless; trapped into going home with her mother instead of catching the long and winding bus down Main Arm Road. And now it would be an extra hour, probably, until she was safely inside the cocoon of her own locked room with the adult world kept at bay for another night. A spasm of irritation shot through Jo at these complaints, but she contained herself. Show some self-discipline, she thought, and have a bit of patience with the child. For she is just a child, though where last year's joyful twelve-year-old had gone was one of life's little mysteries. Maybe Ellen was getting her first period? Lordy, that was gonna be fun. Not.

'What's she want?' Ellen asked, texting somebody her misery.

'Got good news, she reckons. She wouldn't say what.'

Ellen stopped texting, closed her eyes, and let her head rest briefly against the glass of the passenger window. Did she already know what good news was coming?

'What's up?'

'Noth-ing.' Ellen sighed. Like she didn't want to spoil the surprise.

Jo shuffled left-handed among scores of CDs, and picked a Spearhead track to bounce them down the Tunnel Road to the beach. She cranked it up and sang loudly to Ellen, to the birds, the camphors and the banyan trees. Oh yeah, baby. Music was the solution, nine times out of ten, to any of life's littler woes and trifling problems . . . and that was definitely worth making a song and dance about, truegod.

Pulling in at Therese and Amanda's place, Jo found Trinity's RAV4 was also parked on the footpath. Even Chris's last-legs Econovan was putting in an appearance. Jo raised her eyebrows. A part-ay, it looked like. But why, and why unheralded till an hour ago?

They drew close, and Kasey Chambers pounded out of the kitchen window, along with shrieks of laughter and the sound of bottles being uncorked. The kettle was screaming its whistle along for good measure. Fat-bellied Buddha sat on his wooden stand beside the stairs, wearing a new plastic hibiscus lei. 'Bit bloody noisy round here,' Jo told him, but Buddha simply smiled serenely back at her. Must like Kasey, old fat belly. And why wouldn't he? Buddha was cool, even if he was two thousand years old.

Jo saluted the statue, then slid open the glass door to Therese's lounge – where a motley assortment of family and friends were clustered together having their photo taken. As she stepped inside everybody erupted into laughter and bewildering screams which evolved into 'For She's a Jolly Good Fellow'. Therese and Amanda both threw themselves at Jo and Ellen, hugging them like they'd last seen them three months ago, not three days.

'Come here, you good thing, rub some of that Virgo magic off onto me!' Trinity fell upon Ellen in a cloud of patchouli and tie-dyed cheesecloth. Ellen grinned and sucked it up, for what Trinity lacked in sanity she made up for with a heart the size of Sydney Harbour.

'Look!' Amanda flapped wildly at them, waving something in the air and cackling. Jo put down her keys and mobile and seized the bit of shiny paper. On three of the jagged scratched panels she read, *$10 000*.

'Well fuck me dead and bury me pregnant,' Jo said to Therese, gazing at the scratchie and shaking her head, 'for once in me life I got something right.'

'For you,' Therese yelled later that night over the hubbub, holding out Jo's mobile – 'Twoboy.'

Jo took the phone down the hall away from the chaos, giving Therese's hip-thrusting action the middle finger as she went. Cheeky yellow slag.

'Hey you.' Jo smiled to hear her lover's voice.

'You never said there was a party!'

Jo laughed and told him about Therese and Amanda's good luck. Twoboy gave a low whistle.

'They chucking any your way?' he asked.

'Not that I heard,' Jo answered. 'Grog and pizza for everyone tonight, and Therese slung Ellen a hundred cos she picked out the scratchie.'

'Huh,' Twoboy grunted. Jo could tell what he was thinking – that despite her Japanese father Therese was still a typical tightarse dugai.

'So when ya taking me surfing?' Jo asked, partly to change the subject and partly to make up for the hurt of last weekend.

'Anytime. I didn't know you wanted to.'

'Yeah, you gotta teach me to stand up,' she said. 'Can I use your board?'

'Mmm ... we might hafta find you a slower one, I reckon ...' Twoboy sounded as if he was seeing Jo wiped out bigtime and his prized McCoy board snapping in two.

'Well, let's do it this weekend, hey?' she said with a surge of excitement.

'Okay,' agreed Twoboy, 'you borrow a big, slow Mal and I'll teach ya. In our spare time,' he added ironically.

'I'll make time if you do,' Jo told him, and then rang off before he could get all lovey-dovey on her. *Whoo hoo*. She struck a surfer's pose in front of Therese's bathroom mirror, and sang the 'Hawaii Five-O' song to her reflection.

And somewhere between the pizzas being delivered from Ocean, and the bolt at nine o'clock to the Billi for another slab of Tooheys Old, Jo was reluctantly prodded to pick up a guitar, for the first time in three years, and give Kasey a run for her money.

The more Jo drank the better she played, until, her fingers flying over the frets during 'Me and Bobby McGee', she looked over to see Ellen riveted.

'Why?' her daughter asked in the car on the way home. 'Why did you ever stop, when you can play like that?'

'Ecclesiastes,' answered Jo drily. 'Ecclesiastes, and a crying baby girl.'

Jo woke as Saturday's dawn poured in her bedroom window, and was instantly buoyed as she remembered yesterday. Therese and Amanda both worked fulltime jobs but they – like most people – had no safety net, no savings. They lived week to week, much as she did. But now her mates had something to put aside. *Sometimes* things pan out for the good people, Jo thought happily, sometimes. And it's a sunny morning, too, hallelujah, crisp, and not so windy you'd be taking your life in your hands to ride a young stockhorse up the western ridge, she decided.

She gulped a coffee down, threw on jeans and riding boots, and in ten minutes had Comet saddled in the backyard. Once she was on board though, Jo realised that she'd forgotten to leave a note for Ellen saying where she was headed, just in case of the black snake striking. The horse rearing on top of her. The hoof in the rabbit hole and the snapping of the front leg. The girth that didn't hold. The branch that slammed you off and left you concussed, high on the remote ridgetop. Or any other of the thousand disasters that awaited you when you saddled up and put your life in the hands of a half-ton prey animal with a mind of its own. She took her right foot out of the stirrup, then hesitated, and thought: *fuck it*. Although today was definitely not a good day to die – no day is a good day for that, are you fucking kidding me – if it had to be today, then so be it. Her phone was in her pocket, not that there would be any coverage, and the sun was shining, and God was in his heaven according to some, all was right with the world according to others, and she was not getting off Comet and being sensible like she knew she should, not for anything, no siree.

Instead, she footed the stirrup, gathered up her reins, and wheeled the colt around into the Big Paddock, heading for the back corner where the farm met the fire trail bordering the World Heritage. As Comet stepped out beneath her with his mother's big thoroughbred stride, Jo looked at her flourishing stands of camphors that needed poisoning, and at the Big Paddock that needed slashing with a tractor she didn't own, and would have to hire with money she definitely didn't have. These jobs, lingered on, normally drove her to distraction, but this morning she felt something close to detachment. Heaven is the breeze between a good horse's ears, the Arabs reckon. True dat, she thought, as Comet plunged through the knee-high paspalum, eager to be cantering, while Athena stood at the dam with the fattening steers, her head raised, calmly watching where her son and the human were off to this time.

Past the makeshift wire gate and inside the World Heritage,

Comet trod a narrow kangaroo trail through high, white-trunked eucalypts and the ever-present camphors, climbing, climbing all the while as the farmhouse shrank behind them and the calls of pigeons and whipbirds replaced the sounds of cattle and the rushing creek. Civilisation faded and the ground grew steep on both sides of the track as they climbed. The red soil of the gully Jo rode through was moistly lush, sprouting dozens of tree ferns. This high country harboured tribes of lizards and birds and other slithering critters which rustled away through the leaf litter in alarm at her intrusion.

Halfway to the top, Jo noticed a light green plant-protector marring the jungled slope on her left. Curious, she pulled Comet up. When she dismounted and clambered over to it through the lantana thickets, she discovered a healthy marijuana seedling happily thriving inside the little, open-topped plastic tent. It's not my land, she told herself, and so it's not my problem, unlike the dozen or so plants the Mooneys had left dotting the margins of the farm. Plants that Jo had pulled up and thrown unceremoniously on the fire pile, while making sure that Ellen saw, and noticed. The kid knew very well that her mother considered yarndi just another tool of the landgrabbers. *Leave it alone. Stay away from the snake. Addiction is no revolution.*

Leaving this plant unmolested behind her, Jo rode on through dappled sunlight. Comet was sweating now, but still steady and sure-footed beneath her. The kangaroo trail broadened out, branching to the right and turning into a clear cattle path as they climbed above the thick scrubby country into more open land. Now there was an occasional glimpse of the ocean. Far below were the houses on Tin Wagon Road, and the cattle yards where the old dip used to be – and here was a family of four bounding wallabies making Comet shy and prance, half unseating Jo and making her swear and wonder about the whole idea of riding alone on a young, green horse in remote hill country.

She heaved herself back into position in the saddle, shaken and breathing hard. Then came some cloven cattle tracks, and a motorbike tyre print in soft mud, strange, it looks quite fresh and yet I've heard nothing, Jo thought: even if the breeze is from the other direction, you'd normally hear a trail bike, wouldn't you? And here is some country that's had a bit of a fire through recently, and here's some tall lantana to avoid so as not to be sandpapered by it as the horse goes past, and here, suddenly, is a fallen eucalypt log a metre high blocking the bloody trail, and the ground on either side far too steep and too soft to ride around –

Bugger.

Jo sat still, contemplating the situation. On the other end of the reins Comet snatched a few mouthfuls of grass. The tree trunk lying in front of them was smooth and barkless, exactly like the white gums she'd ridden through for the past half-hour. If she'd been on Athena it would have been an easy decision to back up a few metres and then trust the clever old mare to make the jump, since the track on the other side was clear and open. But jumping Comet? The colt was barely used to having her on his back, let alone leaping fallen trees on high, narrow bush tracks with nobody around to help if things went wrong. Jo screwed her mouth sideways, considering the risks. The smart thing to do, she knew, would be just to turn around and go home. Mosey on back to the ranch, cowgirl.

Finally, she reached a decision, and dismounted. She unclipped one side of the rein from the bit, and pushed Comet back with a stern finger on his nose. Obediently the horse reversed in a straight line, until there was ten clear metres of path between him and the tree. Jo geed him up, and then she ran on foot directly at the trunk, the double-length of rein clutched in her left hand and Comet trotting willingly behind her. In a fluid motion Jo leapt onto the trunk – willing Comet to jump, too, and for her riding boots not to slip and fail her.

After the tiniest of hesitations, Comet lifted his forelegs and curved himself easily over the tree, landing on the other side with room to spare. Then he kept going – with enough speed to snatch the single rein unwittingly out of Jo's hand.

Jerked forward by the horse's momentum, Jo stumbled. She fell hard against a protruding branch of the fallen eucalypt, *shit and bugger and fuck* as the muddy ground whirled up to meet her head, very *very* much the wrong way.

Jo sat, blowing, coughing, and spitting several times onto the bushfire-blackened ground beside the track.

When her breath eventually returned to normal, she cursed her empty left hand and rubbed at her bruised ribcage. Comet had disappeared around the bend, rein flapping merrily in the breeze of his departure.

'Comet,' Jo called hopefully. 'Comet, come back boy.'

As if. That never happened. Horses didn't backtrack, given a choice. He'd be halfway to Mullum by now, if he could find a trail through. Probably hightail it back to his old paddock at Oliver's. Jo cursed a final curse, and cautiously began to haul herself up to her feet by the offending branch, which promptly snapped and sent her back to earth once more, arse up. Streaks of pain radiated up and down her left side from the rib that was really caning her now. This time Jo's swearing was of a rare quality: she lay face-up in the mud cursing the malice of the tree, her own stupidity, the dugai who had so rightly created a World Heritage park and then so wrongly failed to maintain the tracks (and what were cattle doing up in the World Heritage anyway?), her bruised ribs, the unknown and unheard motorbike rider for not being here to rescue her, and even poor innocent Comet who could hardly be expected to know he was meant to stop beside her once the trunk had been successfully negotiated.

Jo lay in the red mud a good while, gazing up at the clear blue of the sky, wondering what the lesson was here. Not to overreach the abilities of young horses, probably, though Aunty Barb would have said she was stood on ground that didn't want her there, and to listen to that ground, pay attention to it or else pay the price.

Listen to country, girl, it's been here a damn sight longer than you have.

Jo sighed heavily and felt the pain in her side afresh. Okay, Aunty Barb, you win. She lay and pricked her binung and deliberately let in the bush sounds that she had been keeping out with her swearing and her incessant thinking. Shuttup, Jo, and just *listen*. Where am I?

What lives here, who lived here? What's gone, and what remains? Jo's breathing gradually eased to slowness, and she at last really began to hear. Birds. Insects. A humming in the far distance. The trail bike rider. Or no, perhaps not a bike. A plane? No, not that either. Superman, she laughed to herself, as the humming continued.

The sun warmed Jo's face where she lay, and as her hurt rib stopped complaining she became almost comfortable. Her limbs relaxed, and her jaw softened. The smell of the earth's rich humus entered her nostrils. A magpie sang a little further down the slope. *Listen to that koruhmburuhn talga*. Just slow down and listen. Aunty Barb's dry cackle echoed in her mind – 'It's always a good time for dadirri, unless a Brahmin bull's after you that is!' No Brahmins here, Aunt, not many even down on the road a good half-hour walk away as the crow flies, but still the humming of a motor continuing, on and on. The koruhmburuhn warbled again, and was answered now by a bellbird medley. A chainsaw, maybe? No. Water pump, then. No. The sound had a human quality to it that ruled all these out. And it was at the instant that this thought came into Jo's mind – a human quality – that the humming became much louder and much clearer. And then, goosepimpling all over, Jo finally heard the humming for what it really was. It wasn't a motor at all. What she was hearing was voices. Ancient human voices.

Chanting.

The hills were singing to her.

Jo's bowels shrank where she lay. Oh Jesus, oh sweet fucking Jesus Christ. She froze as though utter stillness could stop the terror, could save her. How she wished, now, that she'd never gotten on Comet, never ridden through the wire fence into the World Heritage, and, above all, had taken seriously the blind freddy message of a felled tree directly in her path. How stupid am I, she wondered, how fucking blind? Just like the dugai, blundering into God knows what danger for God knows what insane reason.

On and on the chant hummed, now rising and now falling. Like wind in high treetops. Like waves slapping a shoreline over and over.

The words were indistinct. Although Jo was far from fluent in language, she thought she could pick out some words. *Jagun* – *land* – and *mibun* – *eagle* – among them. And *jalgani* too – *woman*. The voices, she realised after a minute of horrified gut-clenched listening, were male and female both. Jo breathed out then, a tiny hesitant breath, since women's voices meant it was unlikely she'd stumbled – stupidly, ignorantly, unbelievably unwittingly – onto sacred men's ground. Breathing lightly now, her heart racing still. Good one, Aunty Barb, so what do I do now? Dadirri is one thing, but what the hell do you do with *this*?

Is a Brahmin bull after you? Aunty Barb asked sharply from the Piccabeen cemetery. No, Aunt, Jo replied testily, obviously not. Well then, Aunty Barb retorted, *it's always a good time for dadirri*.

And so Jo reluctantly lay still and listened some more. Two minutes of chanting passed. Three minutes. She heard the words for Land. Eagle. Woman. Water. The Southern Cross. And could have sworn she'd even heard *yarraman* and something that sounded a lot like *Tin Wagon*, too.

Maybe, she suddenly felt, maybe it's not a warning at all, but some other kind of message. Not a sign to stop on pain of death – No Trespassing – perhaps instead, the tree was just a means to slow her down, stop her mad rushing about, to get through to her? Wait here a while, girl. Stop with us.

Heartened by this thought, Jo slowly winched her way to the vertical, using the branch stub. She sat and looked about her. There was nobody visible, from this century or any other. The talga belonged to the trees, the wind, the earth, the charcoaled ground where fire had passed through, the lantana thickets and the tree ferns that clustered at the base of the strangling figs and camphors. And was the chant fading now? Growing fainter?

Struck with longing to hear it continue, in fact for it never to end, Jo felt tears rise up in her eyes. Don't go! she wanted to cry out to the singers, but didn't. Instead she snatched her phone, hit the record button, held her Nokia up to the Bundjalung talga echoing off the ridge around her. Played it back, and found miraculously that centuries could talk to one another after all. I've got it, she marvelled, as the chant faded away to nothing, a mere whispering of leaves and the return of birds chirping and calling, I've got it in my pocket. She replayed the song three times, amazed and fearful and wondering. Why me, why now? What for? And above all else, what's Twoboy gonna make of this?

'Hey, you two,' Jo called from where she stood pegging clothes one-handed onto the line, her ribs still nipping at her each time she lifted her arm. On the veranda, Twoboy was finger picking the Maton, trying to bring back old chord patterns and long-lost Archie Roach lyrics.

'Hmmm?'

'Whaddya reckon's up there? In the hills?' She gestured with her lips and chin to the high country. The singing country.

Twoboy glanced up at the ridgeline and then at Chris, who was flicking through the paper. Chris shrugged. Not really her country, despite what Aunt Sally had said, and despite living on the oppo-site ridgeline below Bottlebrush for nearly fifteen years. Her shrug deferred to Twoboy as a real Bundjalung.

'Jiraman. Snake, possum.' Twoboy said.

'Plus the Beast of Billinudgel,' Chris grinned. 'And a bitta yarndi.'

'*Lotta* yarndi,' Twoboy chimed in with a wry smile.

'Yeah, not that. I mean old stuff.' Jo turned around from the clothes line, her basket empty on her hip.

'Oh.' A pause. 'Be heaps, probably.' Twoboy was close-lipped, wary of the question. Having Chris sitting there didn't help much either, but Jo pushed on nevertheless.

'Cos you know how I rode up there this morning –'

Twoboy stopped fingering chords as Jo came over and sat with her back up against the veranda post, legs straight in front of her. She stared at the knees of her jeans, which were thinning, just about to break through the visible white strands of remaining denim into actual holes. Time for a visit to Vinnies.

'I got up past the thick scrub, to where it thins out . . .'

'Yeah.' Twoboy put the guitar aside.

'And something pretty weird happened.' Jo stopped. She didn't want to sound womba. She didn't want to *be* womba. Twoboy and Chris waited patiently for her to elaborate.

'I fell off, like I said, and I was lying in the mud up there, I was sorta catching my breath, see, and I heard this buzzing noise. At first I thought it was a trail bike or something . . . but it wasn't.' Jo halted again.

Worried, Chris folded the newspaper in half and put it on the veranda.

'Did you hit your head?' she asked.

'Nah, just bruised my ribs is all. I was thinking alright,' Jo explained. 'You know that old bush saying about when you get lost you siddown and have a cuppa tea before you do anything else? Well, I figured doing dadirri was the best thing to do after Comet buggered off. And lying quiet way, there on the track, I heard this trail bike. Only it wasn't a trail bike.'

Jo hesitated, then threw herself off the brink.

'It was chanting.' She whispered. 'Chanting in language. I'm positive it was.'

Well, *that's* captured their attention, Jo thought. Both Chris and Twoboy were staring now, and four dark arms were goosepimpling. Six if you counted hers; she had spooked herself, remembering. On the other side of the house, one of the horses, unseen, blew breath noisily out of its nostrils, and was answered by the other. Cattle two properties away made long bovine complaints about being yarded. And across the Big Paddock, level with Jo's eyeline, the heron flapped her way from the top dam across to Stoney Creek. Her harsh croaking punctuated the afternoon. 'Jingawahlu mulanyin,' Jo called softly, and wondered about the timing. What you telling me this time, my bird?

Hearing chanting in the hills, a wide-eyed Chris agreed, was very fucking full-on.

'I caught it on my phone,' Jo added, growing bolder. 'Listen.'

She hit the play button and all three of them leaned in to the phone, listening with utmost attention. Nothing happened. Four more attempts to find the talga failed, and Jo sat back in exasperation.

'It was definitely saved – I played it back a couple of times when I was still up there.'

'Let me try.' Twoboy had a go, but he was no more successful than Jo had been, and he finally handed the phone back in disgust.

'Maybe it's only going to work when you're up there,' Chris suggested. 'If that's where the song belongs –'

Uncharacteristically, Twoboy interrupted Chris. 'Did you understand any of it? How did it go?'

The man's face was clouded over with frustration. Jo easily hummed the tune, and described the few words of lingo she'd been able to pick out. Headshaking, Twoboy swore one long ferocious swear, then abruptly got up from the veranda and stalked off into the Big Paddock.

'What's his problem?' Chris asked with a wrinkled brow.

Jo shrugged, her eyes still on the man. Jealous, maybe. Everyone wanted the culture back, mobs all over the country were trawling in dugai libraries and dugai archives retrieving little bits of songs, stories, dances. Those fragments that had been recorded or written down while elders lived. And yeah, theirs was a living language, true, but only barely, and this talga might be a completely unknown song for a little understood patch of country.

Together the women watched the tall outline of Twoboy stride the length of the farm and finally reach the World Heritage corner. To Jo's surprise, he stopped at the wire gate as though that dugai boundary meant something to him. Twoboy stood a long while facing the hills, an upright black exclamation mark upon the green page of the farm. Jo imagined that he was talking to the old people using what language he knew, asking them to share with him the song that they'd let her hear. Pleading his case. What mood would he return to the house in, she worried, picking up the Maton to put it back in its hard protective case. As she lifted the guitar, it swung sideways and its body hit the side of the farmhouse, making a loud expensive clang. Jo hissed anxiously through her teeth and examined the treasured instrument for chips. It looked okay, luckily, but she was a great deal more careful as she laid it down and locked it away safely inside its red-velvet resting place.

'I'm so gonna win this next year,' said Jo confidently, as Kym and the kids clustered around the Australian Stockman's Challenge website. Jo could picture it now. Herself and Comet, galloping past the finishing post to victory with a red, black and yellow saddlecloth, sticking it to all the dugai cattle farmers who rubbished the blacks who built their empires for them. Nine-year-old Jarvis asked hopefully if he could enter the challenge, too. Jo smiled. No fear, that kid, and no idea that some things might be way out of his reach.

'Yeah, course ya can, bub. When you've learn to ride but, eh?' Jo grinned at his innocent ambition, wondering if Kym would allow the lad's Little Athletics legs anywhere near a yarraman.

'You go girl,' Kym encouraged her sister while Ellen blew a loud raspberry. 'You wish you were gonna win it,' the teenager snorted, the polar opposite of her aunt.

'You'll see,' Jo retorted, 'and no need to come looking for part of the prize bungoo, either. Me 'n' Aunty Kym'll grab it and have us a holiday, eh.'

'Yeah,' Kym agreed. 'We can go up north in a troopie, go to Laura.' The kids and adults were all enthused by this idea, the kids in the mistaken belief that it might mean time off school. Jo and Kym began to formulate a real plan, one that involved Therese and Amanda and their newly acquired ten grand, and a hire car, and borrowed swags. Then Kym remembered that the festival clashed with the zone finals.

'Can't they skip it one year at least? For their culture?' Jo probed. A withering look from Kym told her that the answer was no.

'Comet's going fantastic, eh,' Jo said later as they collapsed in front of the TV, red wines in hand. Kym raised her eyebrows.

'You got how many busted ribs now?' she asked.

'Bruised, not busted,' argued Jo.

'Yer mad, ya unit,' Kym replied amiably.

Jo paused, and wondered if she could to talk to her sister about the chanting without sounding like she was indeed completely off her head. The song had never come back onto her mobile. It was gone for good, despite Twoboy taking the phone apart umpteen dozen times as well as haunting the ridgeline most of last weekend. Jo took another sip of wine and decided the time wasn't right. Kym was one of the few people who knew about her being slung in the PA psych ward at sixteen, and Jo didn't feel like dredging that old shame and horror up, thanks very much.

'Is Comet as good as Athena?' Kym asked, the old mare her single point of equine reference. Jo nodded. To her, Comet was so much more than his mother was, but unhorsy Kym wasn't about to grasp that difference. Dog, cat, horse – they were all just pets to Kym. Not *family*.

'Better. He's better balanced, and he's smart as all get out, too. But nice natured. A lot of smart, athletic horses are arseholes, but he's sweet, and he actually likes people.' She glanced over at the screensaver which showed Comet beneath the mango tree and Jo standing beside the colt with her arm flung over his neck, grinning at Twoboy as he took the shot.

'Well, just don't come running to me when you break your leg,' Kym parroted their mother's classic expression. 'Actually, don't come running to me any time, I've got me hands full with this lot. Talk about smart athletic arseholes, we see em every weekend when the boys flog em. They come and congratulate us through gritted teeth.' Kym demonstrated the gammon, pained smile of the other athletes, and both women laughed. 'Ah, it's worth it when they do good,' Kym added happily. 'Even if it does mean I live on the road.'

'Mum's taxi's what you get for having so many jahjams, luv,' Jo told her sister, secretly a bit jealous of the happy brood that Kym took so much for granted. Maybe she should have done what her sister had done, grabbed the first decent black man who asked her out, and had a clutch of youngsters with him.

Her sister grinned ruefully.

'They don't tell you when you sign em up at six that you're gonna be driving them to meets all over the state for the next ten years,' she moaned, not really minding cos Kai could run the pants off a kangaroo and, more importantly, off just about any other kid black or white in the south-east region. His half of the dresser he shared with Jarvis bulged with gold statuettes. Kym and Jason had last year refused a meeting with Athletics Australia on the grounds that, no, their jahjams were far too young at ten and nine to be talking pre-sponsorship deals with anyone. Lettem be kids for Chrissake.

'Give us a look at ya, bub,' Jo swung back to where Kai, Jarvis and Ellen were mucking around on the laptop.

'Stand against the wall, eh.'

Kai stood, his neck stretched as high as possible, and Jo scanned him while she marked his height on the door jamb that was mouldy white from the weeks of rain. The boy was as lean and brown as an ironbark sapling. He had her own long-jawed face, and his Waka Waka father's dark body, all muscle and sinew. Yet despite his good looks and the many trophies, Kai showed none of the attitude she'd noticed in the other Little A kids over the years.

'Ya lookin fit there, lad,' she praised him up. Accentuate the positive.

'I train hard,' Kai shrugged.

'Only every day,' Kym said drily, 'in the car at 6.30 five mornings a week, and meets every weekend.'

'Me too, eh,' added Jarvis in his high-pitched voice, pushing in with his crewcut and a grin that could melt any heart. 'I'm lookin fit too, eh, Aunty Jo,' flexing his nine-year-old biceps beneath a Titans guernsey, busting to be noticed, for someone to look at him for once and not at his star older brother.

Jo grabbed her nephew and hugged him to her chest. 'Yes, darling, you looking fit too, you'll be giving budda a run for his money soon . . .' And that was all it took – him and Kai and even Timbo were off, hurtling around the circuit between kitchen and lounge, flat strap, heads down, legs pumping.

'Youse two wanna knock orf, ya moogle lot!' Kym yelled, thinking of tomorrow's meet in Coffs Harbour. 'I didn't take three days off work so youse could pull hammies mucking around here. Save it for the track!'

'Wait for me, wait for me!' screamed Timbo as the older boys lapped him, but they had selective deafness and paid him no mind, hurtling one-armed around the doorways, leaping the Wii console and shoving each other back roughly, as though there were sheep farms at stake.

'Aunty Jo, makem wait up for me!' Timbo ordered as he slowed, tears brimming and five-year-old lip all aquiver.

'Ah gawd, competitive sport,' Jo muttered, 'c'mere, my darlin.' Her arms were a wide-open haven, and Timbo was heading happily towards them when Jarvis casually cuffed the back of his brother's head with an open palm on the way through. Timbo flipped in an instant from sooky to homicidal. Jaw thrust out, he hurled himself back into the fray, charging after the older boys with one arm straight out in front, index finger extended.

'I'm gonna powerpoint you, Jarvis! You better lookout, man, my powerpoint's gonna smash you onetime!'

'What's he on about?' Jo puzzled.

'He saw it on SBS the other night,' Kym explained with a snort of laughter. 'Pointing the bone, he means.' Jo smiled uneasily. That stuff was a little bit too strong to be mucked about with. Not when there were already ancient songs in the hills giving her messages she couldn't begin to fathom or talk about.

'What?' Kym asked, pulling Timbo out of the fray and onto her lap for a cuddle.

'Nothing. Just . . .' Jo winced. Where did you start?

'You're not getting all superstitious in yer old age, are you?' Kym wondered. '*You?*'

'I just don't like mucking around with that stuff,' Jo muttered.

'Ah, chillax. He's just playing – he's only five years old,' Kym reassured her.

'Yeah,' Jo agreed finally. 'I'm just a bit on edge cos of this claim. Twoboy takes it all super serious,' she explained. 'Must be rubbing off.'

Before falling asleep that night Jo noted in her bedside diary: *Comet came home by himself last Saturday, after I fell on the ridge.* AND THIS TIME NEXT YEAR, she wrote in precise red capitals, *I'm entering the Northern Rivers Stockman's Challenge on him. To win.*

It was very dark; it was the middle of the night. There was a doona, and the air was winter-sharp, and no other body beside her. Jo struggled up through several layers of consciousness to realise that one of the kids was crying. Probably Timbo having a nightmare. Then the last shreds of sleep left her and she got up, shivering with cold, to investigate. As she opened her bedroom door Jo realised it wasn't a boy's voice at all, but Ellen sobbing to herself beneath the thrumming of yet more rain overhead. A thread of alarm wound through Jo as she walked the dark corridor to her daughter's room. Hadn't she been vigilant enough, kept the sickos of the world at bay? What had happened to give her girl nightmares?

'What's up, Ell?' Jo sat on the single bed and shook Ellen awake. 'It's okay, bub, wake up.' Ellen's pale face was streaked with tears when she woke, and her eyes had tripwires in them. Say the wrong thing, thought Jo in fear, and she'll snap shut. I'll never get to the bottom of it. Whatever 'it' is.

'Poor ting, you were crying in your sleep,' Jo told her, carefully not grilling the girl for answers. She opened her arms, wondering if Ellen would be too old to take comfort there, but the kid collapsed into her embrace. Jo lay down beside her and stroked the back of her head, Ellen's dark curls so much like her own.

'Something's wrong,' the girl said to the wall through tears and sniffles.

'Hmmm?' Jo responded, eggshells all the way.

'Someone's in trouble.'

Jo's gut tightened. Christ. Like Aunty Barb, Ellen had the second sight, and if she said someone was in trouble, then she would be proved right. Didn't normally come in dreams, though, normally it came while Ellen was wide awake in ordinary life. Kaboom – a message from the Otherverse. Or the Dreaming. Twoboy said it was from the old people. Ellen simply knew: periodically she got messages she didn't ask for, about disasters that nobody wanted to know about.

'Is it you, darlin? Has anyone hurt you?' Jo asked. *I'll gut em where they stand.*

But Ellen shook her head.

'Do you know who? Or where?' Jo thought of Twoboy, forever driving tired on the slick road between Mullum and the Brisbane tribunal. Or Chris and her wheelchair-bound dad up the road, no doubt flooded in, by the sound of that rain.

Ellen's dark curls shook negatively again, and Jo squeezed her even closer, using a forefinger to position her daughter's hair behind the pale shell of her pink ear.

'Well, darling, you're okay and I'm okay, and Kym and the boys are all here,' she pointed out, knowing all the while it was futile. 'And the phone's not ringing yet.'

It could be Ellen's dad, of course; that would shatter Ellen, if he was hurt or dead.

'I think it's someone around here,' Ellen whispered miserably. Jo held her tight a while longer, then got up and made two big cups of cocoa. An hour later they were both tucked up in Jo's bed.

Ellen faded back to sleep fast while Jo stared at the red numerals of the clock and waited for the unhappy phone call to come.

GWONG

RAIN

CHAPTER SEVEN

Jo woke unrested at dawn, burdened with knowledge: today was going to bring terrible shit down on someone she knew.

After an uneasy half-hour listening to the gwong pound the tin roof, she rang Chris. On the ninth ring her bowels began to slacken with fear. But before the phone could peal again, Uncle Pat picked it up. Chris, he reported, was basically alright, but down, sunk in another of her Hill-dweller's Depressions. Ah Christ Jesus. She wouldn't be leaving the house for weeks, Uncle Pat yawned glumly, would in fact barely be leaving the island of safety which was her bed, even if they hadn't been flooded in since dinnertime last night.

Jo commiserated with the old man on both counts and hung up. The catastrophe didn't belong to Chris, then.

And not to Kym, clearly, and not the boys either who, power-pointed or not, had survived the night and were now filling their faces with Weetbix, hoeing into the sugar big time and complaining loud and long about Jo's low-fat milk which they claimed came from infe-rior and anorexic New South Wales cows – them are *gammon bulang*, Aunty Jo. She made a mental note to remind them at some length that they were Bundjalung as well as their father's Waka Waka, once this much more urgent business of who was headed for trouble got sorted.

Therese and Amanda were altogether unimpressed at being called so early. Jo put the receiver down – sorry, sorry – with a grin of relief. Okay, well, if not them, then who? Who?

Jason had facebooked that he was running late for the airport and good luck to the littlies in Coffs, so Ellen's midnight tears were not for him. The sisters looked blankly at each other across the kitchen, uncertain quite what course to take next.

'We can just wait,' Jo said finally, crossing her arms. 'I mean why go ringing around *looking* for a shit sandwich for breakfast? It's not like grief's ever had any bloody trouble finding us before.'

'You rung Twoboy, eh?' Kym checked. But Jo was afraid to. Of everyone she knew, Twoboy was the most likely to have bad news. Laz's boy Billy, in particular, lived on a razor's edge of cones, pills, stupid-arse street fights and suicidal mood swings. To call Twoboy and tell him that Ellen had predicted Trouble coming, Jo told her sister, would be like poking a caged tiger with a stick.

Above them the clock on the wall had somehow crept around to 7.15. About time I was getting ready for work, Jo realised, as she tried unsuccessfully to undo the hard-knotted laces of Jarvis's running spike with her teeth. Kym swung around from where she was scraping Weetbix into the compost.

'He's not getting bloody fist-happy with ya is he?' Kym had a blunt older-sister tone in her repertoire that she wasn't afraid to haul out and use. 'Cos if he is I'll be gettin Jase and his brothers to flog the piss and shit outta him, I swear ta—'

'God, no. He's a big pussycat. He's just a bit cranky with the Native Title stuff,' Jo blurted hastily. 'Or not even cranky. Just stressed. He's not violent,' she reiterated. Twoboy's fathers had taught him how to pick his battles. How to walk away when that was the smart thing to do. No, it wasn't an eruption of random violence that Jo was concerned about, but the loading onto the man's Bundjalung shoulders of even more problems than he already had to cope with. Every day that he and Laz and their mum spent in court saw new lies that needed countering; the money from the Native Title Tribunal for lawyers was running out fast, and the legal arguments went around and around in ever-expanding circles as Mum Jackson and Uncle Cheezel grew older, and more frail, and ever less equipped to keep on top of the whole bullshit saga of proving who they were and where they belonged, to the satisfaction of the dugai judge.

'You sure?' asked Kym in a been-there-done-that voice.

'*Yes*. I swear ta God.'

Then the phone rang on the kitchen wall. *Tragedy*, it said, with its first long single peal.

Yours, Jo pointed with the running spike. Kym took a wary half-step in the other direction. Then Ellen appeared. On her way through the kitchen to go julabai she glanced at the phone, and then at her mother and aunt. Her eyes developed a protective blankness.

'You'd better answer it. It's not going to change what's happened,' Ellen advised over her shoulder.

'She's right,' chimed in Kym, nodding at the sinister beige plastic handset.

Jo reluctantly picked it up – and discovered that Twoboy was fine, that he, Laz, Rhonda and their grown kids had all been at the Browns Plains RSL till midnight, and Billy had picked up fifty bucks clear profit on the pokies.

'Nobody hurt then, no dramas?' she queried.

Not as far as Twoboy knew, and he'd most likely be down tomorrow night for some more good loving, babe –

'Is something the matter?' he asked, hearing worry in Jo's voice.

'No,' she lied, 'it's all good here. Kym's off to Coffs with the boys in a minute, Kai reckons his hamstring's come good. And if it ever stops fucken raining I'll get you to help me spray those camphors next time you're . . . Yeah, nah she'll get out alright in the Pajero, Chris's already flooded in, but. Those creek crossings on the way to her place aren't up to shit. And you wanna hope this gwong stops pissing down by tomorrow, but, or there won't be any good loving for ya, it'll be owner-operator all the way, bunji . . .'

Still laughing with relief, Jo sculled the last mouthful of her coffee. Then she hugged Kym goodbye, exhorting her to drive slow and careful on the bloody wet road. More hugs, and you make sure you stick it to the competition now, for the older boys. She kissed and tickled Timbo until he squealed for mercy, and then could delay her chores no longer.

Leaving them packing up inside the house, she dragged on her raincoat and akubra, bracing herself to go into the weather. 'Tain't fit out there for man nor beast,' she muttered under her breath.

Comet and Athena were on a schedule. They would both stand at the fences and wait pointedly for an hour or more if she didn't pour a few handfuls of pellets into their dark green plastic feed bins. It was good discipline to have them come in for feed twice a day; it kept them in a routine, especially important for a youngster like Comet who would soon revert to wildness and mischief if he was left to his own devices.

So Jo lurched out the door, swearing as she bent into the torrential rain. At the small garden shed beneath the African tulip she ladled a couple of containers of pellets and chaff into a bucket, tipped half the mixture out for a rain-slick, whinnying Athena – time I started rugging you for winter, old girl – and then noticed a gap in Comet's usual spot beneath the mango in the Small Paddock. The mud, scraped and indented from his habitual waiting there, was blank. A horse-shaped hole in Jo's morning.

Here was something out of the ordinary. Here was something definitely amiss in the world of the farm.

Jo scanned the Small Paddock a second time, and a third. There was no sign of the colt. He wasn't standing among the pines, nor was he in the distance among the furthest lychee trees. She didn't think he'd escaped into the Big Paddock, since the fences all looked to be intact. From the dry veranda, the dogs were gazing out at her with unusual stillness.

Rain blew onto the back of Jo's neck and into her ears. She shivered and hoiked the raincoat higher, half over her head. Between the gumboots and the glistening yellow plastic hem of the coat her legs were bare and wet. She shivered again. Bloody yarraman. A person'd be womba to have horses, wouldn't she?

Gwong was pelting heavily now, dripping off the wire of the

fences, streaming off the mango leaves, and falling straight from the sky into the feed bucket, forming tiny rivulets among the pellets. That didn't matter, horses could eat wet feed with impunity. Her glistening wet neck didn't matter, nor did her cold legs, and neither did the growing dampness inside her squelching gumboots. But where the hell was her Comet? A sick anxiety began to develop inside Jo's chest. Nothing good could come from this odd development. It was inexplicable, unless . . . had he been stolen? Some local farmers locked their gates, but it had never occurred to Jo that this was anything more than another expression of the ridiculous anal tendencies of the dugai world.

She glanced behind her. Through the rain she could faintly hear Kym gathering the boys and their gear, and the slamming of Pajero doors from the far side of the house. The pump was throbbing beneath the house – Ellen was having her shower – and the school bus would be hissing to a halt right outside the driveway in under ten minutes. Jo knew that if Comet was to be found before work – and he had to be found before work, because you didn't leave valuable young animals lost and wandering loose all day to get hit by cars, especially not in weather like this – she would have to track him down all on her Pat Malone. Shit and damn and fuck the ways of stockhorses all to hell, Jo told the sodden earth. She contemplated giving Ellen the day off school to look for him. Ah, better not. School might be all a crock, according to Twoboy, but Jo knew Ellen didn't need any more excuses to hate the place. Jo would continue to act as though school mattered, just in case one day it did.

Time was ticking away and Jo was growing ever wetter and later for work. She put the feed bucket down at the base of the mango, where it would have some protection from the rain, and plunged into the long grass. There was only one place on the farm that Comet could possibly be – in the far corner of the Small Paddock, invisible until you got well past the pine grove. If the creek had come right up, Jo reasoned, then the colt might have become stranded on the fire trail on the far side; the narrow strip of land there was high enough that it would never flood this side of Armageddon. He might have wandered up there before the creek started to swell, and then gotten stuck, afraid to risk the ever-rising waters to come back over to the level ground where he normally grazed. She winced, imagining young, terrified Comet stuck all night in the driving rain as the creek swelled and plunged and roared beneath him. He would be freezing by now, shaking with cold and hungry, as well.

Guilt lashed at her. Walking faster, she asked herself why she hadn't simply left him in the Big Paddock with Athena and the cattle. It wasn't as though he was hard to catch. No, it was just her pathetic desire to control him that little bit more; to have him ready at her fingertips on this small, soggy patch of the earth instead of roaming the hills of the Big Paddock as he should have been, with his mother. I'm no better than the bloody missionaries, Jo thought. Berating herself further, she began to list the illnesses that a horse could develop from exposure: Pneumonia – often fatal in horses. Colic, brought on by the stress, ditto. Rain scald. Greasy heel. A hundred other ailments she didn't even know about. Oh fer Chrissake, shuttup, she told herself. You don't even know that he'll be on the bloody hillside. He could be in the back of a horsefloat on his way to a Sydney horse sale by now.

Another couple of minutes passed, all muddy traipsing and sliding through the tussocks of paspalum and rhodes grass. Jo failed to notice Kym's departure, or the school bus carrying Ellen and the rest of the kids away to Mullum. Finally she reached the edge of the pine grove, and paused on the spongy carpet of light tan pine needles. A host of camphor laurel seedlings, six inches high, erupted at regular intervals from this carpet; they all needed pulling out before they reached the knee-high stage when pulling got too difficult and spraying became unavoidable. Jo reached down and ripped several of the weeds out automatically, but impetus kept her going beyond the pines.

When she stood in the clearing facing the fire trail, the uprooted camphor seedlings dangling from her right hand, a fierce debate began between Jo's eyes and Jo's brain.

She gazed east at the corner of the Small Paddock which was now revealed. *There*, her eyes said with horrible chilling accuracy. See there – see that extraordinary dark lump, lying wetly half-in, half-out of the swollen creek at the base of the hill. That lump which is approximately horse-sized. Horse-shaped. And see, too, how the fenceline at that spot is different, the star pickets ripped from the wet ground, and the strands of wire pointing tautly into the water and failing to form a set of pleasing horizontal lines as they normally would. See the vee of that fence which, in fact, doesn't even belong there – the brand-new barbed wire fence, which is where a fence shouldn't be and never was before this day. This is what Jo's eyes saw.

And Jo's brain answered with its own rigid authority: No. No, no, no. We won't look, we won't walk over there. I refuse.

And Jo's eyes said ah but you must, and Jo's legs said we will keep walking towards the new part of this story until you tell us otherwise and Jo's eyes said here: look some more. Here we are, you see, a yarraman – and it is, after all, a yarraman you are seeking – Comet, or what had been Comet – lying large and brown and sodden, and his poor sorry head sunk beneath the muddied torrent that the hills had delivered to this lower ground. His neck was extended into the swirling dirty water so that his soft darling black nose must be pointing, beneath the murky current, the way to the ocean, floodwater washing his beautiful, long black mane away from the muscle of his neck, streaming the thick hair out like seaweed or seagrass or, no, because seaweed and seagrass grow in saltwater and this is a freshwater story and it's a story that now contains the new wrongwire of a nonsense wrongfence that shouldn't be here, a hideous unwanted barbed wire fence *that doesn't belong here* wrapped tightly around her colt's front legs and around his neck, making hideous red gashes in the brown hide, and tricking him and trapping him and murdering him, yes, murdering and it can't be, it *just cannot be* but oh God oh God, Comet it is. It is.

Jo stood for a long time. This sight. This unknown fence. This disaster and this result that had ceased to be Comet, lying wet and muddy half in a creek that was not a babbling brook any longer but a hostile murderous brown snake of fatal water, twisting and writhing its way through her innocent green farm.

Jo saw what remained of the horse, his mound of perfect muscle and skin and hair lying there lifeless, as her mind slowly and unavoidably caught up with her eyes. Then with a cry she spun away, revolted.

She fell to her hands and knees in the mud, vomiting as though she could expel the terrible truth with physical effort. The idea had suddenly lodged in her that if she just tried hard enough – retched violently enough and worked strenuously enough with the screaming muscles of her throat and gut and neck – then Comet would not be lying here in a tangle of wrongfence and wrongwire that had no place on her farm. That her beautiful colt would instead be standing as usual beneath the mango tree, insisting on hurrying his breakfast along with his interested ears and exploring lips on the bucket as she tipped it. Still heaving, Jo pressed her palms down hard into the mud until it oozed up between her fingers, reddening them. She spewed all of herself out onto the earth. Here, take it, take it. Take all of me. She spat vomit, bile, breath, tears. Anything I have, I'll offer. I'll empty myself completely. Just give him back.

She sobbed and retched until she couldn't pretend that there was anything left inside her but air. Air, and the tiny droplets of rain that she was breathing in through an anguished open mouth.

When she was finally too exhausted to even cry, she collapsed, and lay still. Then she used her shirt to wipe her face of bile and snot and got unsteadily to her feet, muddy and sodden.

She turned back around to face the creek and a whimper escaped her.

Weak and nauseated, Jo looked down again at Comet's body, at his lovely head swaying just beneath the surface of the current. An enormous rage rose in her that his head was still submerged. *The fucking arseholes.* It seemed to her to be the worst insult of all: to be drowned and then to have your head left there all night, bobbing underwater, as if nodding in placid acquiescence to your fate. *Fucking doghole murderers.* Ignoring the danger – the creek flowing high and fast, the bank a glassy wall of mud, and nobody in earshot – Jo went to his muddied corpse, and tugged hard on Comet's hocks.

Her efforts were futile.

No matter how much she bent her knees or strained her shoulders and back, no matter how many times she slipped against the mud and got up again and again and again, using her fingers as rigid hooks in the bank, it was impossible to shift him. Jo weighed seventy kilos, and Comet closer to five hundred, plus the weight of the water that was now lodged in his lungs for eternity.

Jo stepped back, breathing raggedly, and sweating beneath her plastic raincoat. She noticed with fresh horror that the creek was continuing to creep higher. The deep prints her gumboots had made on the low bank minutes earlier were already being lapped by swirling water.

In the wattle tree on the other side of the creek a trio of rank wet crows was looking on. She snatched a handful of sticky red mud and hurled it at the birds. *Fuck off! Fuck off!* She threw more dirt, threw sticks and looked for rocks, pebbles, pine cones to hurl and hurt the insolent creatures, sitting there with their beady black eyes wanting to feast on her Comet. Wanting to observe her misfortune without taking any part in it, other than stripping the remains. *'Fucking parasites,'* she screamed at them. When a particularly well-aimed rock made their branch shudder, the crows finally flapped away with harsh *carks.* *'Fucking mongrel arseholes,'* Jo yelled at their tails as they disappeared, then drew her arm across her face again for the tears and snot.

She saw again her boot prints disappearing beneath the rising water. This galvanised her; she had to move Comet before it was too late. And to move him, she had to get the wire off him, because it was the wire fence – wherever the *fuck* it had come from, anyway – which was holding him underwater, that was drowning him. *Get the wire off,* Jo thought wildly, standing there with her smeared, dirt-reddened hands, and things will be able to return to normal. It's the wire that is standing in the way of things being the way they should be. But not if the creek rises too far, floats him away! Then it will be too late! She hastily threw off her boots and raincoat, knowing that if she slipped into the creek the boots might fill and drag her to her death.

Jo's blue t-shirt soaked through in seconds as she crouched down, tearing at the metal strands which shone silver in the downpour. She struggled, managing to loosen the wire that had cut into Comet's jugular vein, at the base of his neck. She pulled it away from his swollen wound with its protruding blood vessels, slicing her hand open in the process, not caring, not caring – I don't care, so what – and then moved on to the other strand of wire, the one that had caught his front legs together in a horrible parody of a hobble. This one had bitten deeper into horseflesh though, flesh that had been in the water for at least half the night, and was, in any case, wrapped several times around his finely formed pasterns and fetlocks. As Jo twisted and worked frantically at the bone-tight wire, and as her fingers slipped and jerked time and again onto the metal barbs with no result – other than her own blood streaming out and decorating Comet's body – she gradually realised she was moaning. She knew she was failing, and she collapsed once again in exhaustion, this time on top of Comet's cold, wet body.

She lay there, breathing harshly, breathing hard enough for the two of them, yet it was only her whose body moved, only her lungs which heaved for air, pulling it in and expelling it, that lifelong dance which tied her to the cosmos. As she lay wetly defeated, sheltering Comet's young body from the horror of the world with hers, feeling the chill and stillness of his flank, the chill and stillness of death where she had only ever before known a hotly breathing, living yarraman, a yarraman that walked and cantered and neighed and shied and bucked, a yarraman who daily knew the world through all his myriad senses, Jo fell still and silent. She finally surrendered; her face crumpled like a child's.

With an anguished groan, she knew that wherever Comet's head was lying, underwater or on the land, and whether the creek rose, or whether it fell, and whether she got the murdering wire off his legs, or whether it stayed there, forever rusting in the grave with him, she understood: it didn't matter. This horror in the red earth, on her own baugal jagan – this was the trouble of Ellen's dream made manifest. And it didn't matter one bit what she now did or failed to do. Comet could never be alright again, because Comet was no longer here.

Jo stumbled into the kitchen and sagged against the sink, smearing the edge of the laminex benchtop with her muddied shirt. She ran the cold tap, rinsing clean the wounds on her hands and arms and letting the red water swirl away down the plughole. She needed some sort of antiseptic and serious bandaging. A tetanus shot, probably.

The clock on the wall had stopped at 7:49. Jo gazed at it dully. She registered that the hands were no longer moving, and that the mechanism had failed. But her brain didn't manage to make the further step, to knowing that the time on display was therefore wrong. *Still enough time to get to work by 8:30.* On autopilot, Jo boiled the kettle, made herself a cup of tea, ladled in four sugars, and drank it as she changed out of her sodden gear into dry clothes. Bloodless ones which lacked any recent history.

Outside, the rain had eased at last. Athena was wandering the Big Paddock now in distress, whinnying over and over again for her missing youngster. Jo tried to block the sound out as she got into the ute, but the awful keening followed her most of the way to Mullum. She drove over the range in silence. Spearhead couldn't fix what was wrong with today.

She left the tunnel road and was about to drive across the river next to St John's when, noticing blood still trickling down her forearms, it suddenly occurred to Jo: it might be a good idea to ring someone. Chris. No. Chris was depressed in bed, was no good to her today, no good even to herself. Therese's mobile was out of range, because half of South Golden was a mobile black hole, and Jo wasn't about to drag her out of the classroom anyway, shame. Twoboy then, in Brisbane. Still parked beside the river, Jo hit speed-dial and a moment later his warm voice was with her, a balm to her misery. His concern turned quickly to outrage.

'A barbed wire fence – on your place!' he exclaimed in disbelief.

'And Comet was all wrapped up in it, all tangled up, and he's drowned in the creek,' Jo wailed, bursting into hot angry tears again.

'Oh, I'm sorry, darling. Christ, I wish I was there with ya. Hey, hey, pull over, pull over, you can't be driving like this,' Twoboy ordered in alarm. Jo was shaking with emotion now that someone was right there on the phone, and it was finally safe to feel helpless. She told him that Kym was well away to Coffs with the boys, and Chris was down sick. Twoboy grimaced. Jo's parents were dead; vulnerability wasn't particularly high on any blackfella list of survival traits, and Jo's list of safe people to call was even shorter than his own.

'God, I wish I was there with you, darlin,' he told Jo. 'But I've gotta be in court till at least four-thirty – I can come down after that –'

'No,' Jo told him, wiping her eyes and realising that her fresh shirt was now bloodied, too. 'It's okay. It's not like it'll bring him back. If you miss court. Stay there, and come down tomorrow.'

'Okay, I'll call you the minute it's over okay,' he told her, then risked ending with, 'love ya, babe'. Click. Jo had hung up and Twoboy was left standing at court, all styled up in a charcoal grey suit, not knowing if she'd heard his last three words or not.

Jo found herself still sitting at the steering wheel. She steadied herself and dried her swollen face for the umpteenth time that morning, then noticed with horror that the car clock said 9.13. What? *Shit.* Basho was going to be ropable. She checked her phone. Sure enough, the time was correct and she'd missed three calls from him in the deadzone between home and Mullum. Jo was supposed to meet her boss at the Co-op at 8.45, to organise an order for the next six months' supplies of trees, mulch, and fertiliser.

Now she clashed the gears ferociously and pulled out and onto the bridge.

'Ah, look what the cat's dragged in. Good afternoon, madam.' Basho greeted her airily, one elbow on the counter yarning to Fat Tony. He was in a good mood by the look of it, thank Christ. 'Get flooded in, did ya?'

'Sorry boss. Nope, I had a dead colt in my paddock this morning,' Jo explained, gulping back tears and hoping she actually looked as shitty and grief-struck as she felt. The bloody lacerations on her arms would have to help with that. Fat Tony's eyes widened at Jo's words but Basho didn't understand the import of them at all, and ploughed on regardless.

'Did you try and ride it here – is that why you're late?' he joked, before he saw Jo's eyes well up and her lip quiver. He instantly turned his attention to the order for the cemetery, and together with Fat Tony started picking trees out of the seedling trays. Basho had the dugai allergy to any female emotion, and Fat Tony wasn't much better, although he at least had the mitigating factor of his mother's recent death. Jo stayed outside and, filled with shame at not being able to harden the fuck up in public, in front of *blokes*, in front of her *boss*, she leant her forehead against the green colorbond wall of the Co-op, and cried.

It wasn't long before Cheery Dan wandered around the corner in his Billabong cap and flannie.

'You right there, are ya, matey?' he asked, with a kind, boyish smile, redeeming an entire generation of male Mullumbimbos.

'Oh . . . I will be,' Jo replied through streaming tears. 'My colt died this morning. Drowned in the creek.'

'Jesus!' He frowned. 'That sucks. Severely.' He stood beside Jo, chewing on a stalk of lucerne. Jo told him the story of the mystery wire fence, then rubbed her face hard and extracted a leafy stalk of her own to chew, from the shedded bales stacked just inside the roller door.

Dan grabbed a large fistful of the tasty legume and held it out to her like a bouquet. Jo snorted a damp snort, and took it from him gratefully.

'You wanna cuppa tea, mate? Or an ... an icecream or something?' Dan asked, throwing a hand uselessly towards the ice-cream freezer that brought the high school kids swarming over the road at lunchtime. Jo smiled a watery smile. Bloody hell, she thought. With young blokes like you I think we might be alright. For all that the planet's killing us back these days, and there are wars everywhere you look. Not to mention some fucking arsehole erecting barbed wire fences on my land. Jo gazed at Dan and wondered if she wanted to kiss him on his nineteen-year-old mouth. Nah. But geez, the relief of having a human being notice that you were dying inside, and actually bothering to care. She dried her eyes on her sleeve and privately decided to declare Cheery Dan an honorary Bundjalung.

'I'll be right, Dan. But thanks. And thanks for –' and here Jo lifted and waggled the lucerne bouquet.

'No worries. You know what they say – if you've got live ones, you'll have dead ones.' He touched her arm in sympathy.

Jo put her hand on top of his for a moment, and noticed the glint of his stainless-steel eyebrow ring as the sun slipped briefly out from the clouds. If it stays clear I can go for a ride on Comet after work, she thought automatically – before realising that no, she couldn't.

'Wanna marry me, Dan?' Jo asked through red-lidded eyes. 'Get us a bunch of shitty-arsed kids and a huge mortgage?'

'Fuck, yeah. Tomorrow?'

'Deal.' Jo managed a wan smile. From the corner of her eye she glimpsed Basho and Fat Tony in the shed, turning away in relief.

'Well ... I hope ya get to the bottom of that fence business, hey,' Dan said, pulling his cap down tight over his forehead, and climbing into the forklift. 'Actually –' and here he paused in middle of the forklift's whining reversal, wondering whether or not to speak.

Jo stiffened. 'What?'

'Rob Starr bought a whole heap of pickets and some high-tension wire about three days ago.' Dan looked at Jo doubtfully. Her eyes had narrowed to savage slits, and Dan was hoping that she still didn't own a firearm.

I'll fucken kill him. I'll tie him up with wire and chuck him off Federation Bridge. He wants to see the creek run with our mob blood, well then, let the river run with his –

'It might just be a coincidence,' Dan added hastily.

'Yeah,' said Jo very slowly, 'yeah, it might be a coincidence.' But she was gonna make it her business to find out. And if it wasn't, well. Heads were gonna roll, onetime. She threw the lucerne bouquet in the back of the ute, and went inside with a stony face to sort out the order with Basho.

'Yeah, we put that bit of fence up just the other day. Friday it woulda been.' Rob Starr watched Jo warily, his right foot resting on the bottom rung of his five-bar front gate. The Hilux engine was still ticking; the screech of its tyres braking on the gravel road lingered in both their ears, and the slam of the driver's door.

Jo had knocked off early and covered the ten kays from Mullum to Middle Pocket in record time. Now Starr's dark sunglasses prevented her from beaming her hatred directly into his optic nerves, searing him with her rage.

'Did it occur to you to maybe ask me before you put up a fence on *my land*?' Jo spat in fury. Stay angry, she told herself, remember to stay proper bloody wild and then you won't cry. She'd had quite enough of crying in front of white men for one day.

'On your land?' Starr answered with genuine surprise. 'Where'd you get that idea?'

'Oh, maybe cos my pedigree stockhorse colt's lying dead tangled up in it,' Jo oozed sarcasm. 'Maybe cos I've got two eyes and a brain, and they both fucking work.' She could feel her heart hammering as she spoke. She ached to make an angry fist in the air, but if she did Jo thought she might just use it on him.

Rob Starr paused and touched the back of his hand to his nose before blowing air audibly through his lips. Buying time. That shut ya up, didn't it, thought Jo with a tiny shred of satisfaction. When he answered, his tone had softened, and most of the wariness had been replaced with insight, now that he knew why a crazy woman was at his front gate spewing gravel and spitting chips.

'Well. Well, I'm real sorry if you've lost your colt, but I still say that fence isn't on your land. I've got a survey map of the valley in the house. I'll show ya . . . if ya like.'

No, Jo didn't want to see the survey, much less to set even one toe on his poisonous farm. She wanted the fence not to exist, for Comet not to have drowned, for her not to be put in the position of arguing uselessly with a middle-aged man – and a middle-aged dugai man at that – about far-and-away the worst thing to happen since her divorce. Starr stood there implacable in his old worn jeans and a cheap sky-blue pullover from Target, but the muddied boot resting on the bar of the gate was an R.M. Williams. Landed fucken gentry. How could she even begin to argue with someone who spent one of her weekly mortgage payments on working boots?

'Well, if it's not on my land –' she snarled, 'and I'm not saying it isn't – then it'd have to be on the fucking fire trail and that's illegal too. Probably more bloody illegal than trespassing on my property. What if the ridge caught fire? Hey? How would anyone get up there to put a bushfire out?'

Starr glanced up at the sodden ridge which lay between their two properties. The idea of it catching fire seemed very far-fetched at the moment. From where they were standing, Jo could see rivulets streaming down between the old rows of neglected bananas. These narrow streams were stained by topsoil, and the country looked like it was bleeding. She could see the profile of the eucalyptus with a heart-shaped canopy that she'd noticed that first morning. Starr had a distant view of the same tree on the same ridgeline, but of course his house and front paddocks faced it from the opposite side. Same same but different, Jo thought. Very bloody different.

When Starr answered, his voice remained infuriatingly mild.

'Every fire truck I've ever seen had the universal key on it, as stock standard. And it's only a picket fence anyway. A truck could drive straight through it in an emergency. Same as every other picket fence on my place – or on yours for that matter.'

Jo was further enraged by the lack of bite in the man. If horses were to be murdered, if land was to be trespassed on, if illegal fences were to be erected, then wouldn't you think that a bit of fire and brimstone would be involved? But with no opposing force to match her anger, Jo found herself quickly becoming marooned in the sea of Rob Starr's equanimity.

The man's hands were clasped firmly over the top rail of his steel gate. Like hers, they were scarred with the recent evidence of unhappy meetings with barbed wire, though Jo's deeply cut right hand was bandaged and Starr's fingers, which were a mass of shallow scratches, were not. They'd had iodine put on them by someone. Yellow smears stained the red marks, reminding Jo of Ellen's pots of watercolour paint and her bottles full of brushes – which now lived in the back bedroom at the farm.

Jo lifted her eyes from the many cuts and stared at Rob Starr's sunglasses in contempt. Her distorted reflection looked back at her. The prick appeared to have no shame at all, was not backing down, not even bothering to argue about who was right or wrong. Just calmly agreeing that he'd erected a fence, probably on public land. Admitting that her beautiful Comet was dead and gone, sorry about it even – and for what?

Killer.

'I'm sorry about your colt,' he repeated steadily, flexing his damaged fingers on the gate, 'but that fence is definitely not on your land. I haven't lived here forty-five years for nothing, I know where the boundaries are along these roads, and I just wouldn't do that. But if you need any help sorting out the carcass –'

'No!' Jo turned away, bile rising up in her mouth at the word *carcass*. 'The day I need your help . . .' But there was no point in even insulting the man.

127

She walked away from his steel five-bar gate and his view of the Heart Tree and his R.M. Williams boots, shaking her head. They just can't stop taking, can they? They just wouldn't know how.

'Hang on, I'll get in,' Therese said, stopping Jo. She took Jo's shovel and placed it across the top of the hole. Then she crouched, and swung with muddied hands off the long wooden handle. Therese discovered that when she stood upright in the hole, only her head and neck protruded. Gazing directly at eye-level across the paddock at the newly tarped body of Comet, she gave an involuntary shudder. Amanda and Jo glanced at each other.

'You okay?' Jo asked doubtfully, through sheeting light rain. *Kipper gwong.* What a fucking horrible day it had been, and now her best mate was standing in a grave.

'Yeah, it's just a bit . . . you know.' Therese made a face. Standing in a grave, even a horse's grave, gave her the willies. She stepped squelchily backward, to give herself some room to dig.

'I should be doing this, not you,' Jo told her. She was mortified, really, even to need any help, but once Twoboy had rung them there was no stopping Therese and Amanda from arriving after school in a borrowed 4WD. They had forded the flooded road just outside Nudgel and turned up at the farm to find Jo and Ellen standing in the paddock, weeping and close to exhaustion. The wet grave was only three feet deep after a solid hour of digging.

Ellen was gently despatched to bring hot drinks from the kitchen, and the two dykes had set about finishing the hole.

'Shuttup and pass me that short-handled shovel,' Therese answered. 'Youse can both spell me in a minute.'

She dug and dug, and then she dug some more. Red earth, red mud really, steadily emerged from the hole, until after twenty minutes only the crown of Therese's head was visible. Jo could hear her gasping for breath, even over the rushing of the creek. The bloody creek, the murdering water. She would never swim there again, Jo vowed, and would never look at its winding course through her land with anything like pleasure either.

'My turn,' she tried, but it was to Amanda that the short-handled shovel went next, and it was Amanda whose wet Levis were now bright with mud from sliding down the sides of the grave. Jo stood helplessly watching as, centimetre by centimetre, air replaced solid earth in the hole. The heap of extracted dirt was a startling red against the green grass and the silver-grey of the rain. *Coochin*. The colour of blood, almost, and the colour of war, too, in the old days. She had a vision of herself, daubed liberally with the dirt, reappearing at Rob Starr's gate but this time bearing weapons, raising her tommyhawk high above her ochred head and –

'Got that axe there?' Amanda asked, reaching behind her.

Jo came speeding back to the present, and handed the axe to Amanda to chop through another pine root.

In a year, Jo told Therese, those roots will regrow, but this time through Comet's bones. They'll wind in and out of his ribcage, until it softens into soil itself. She blinked at the suddenness of death, and the permanence of it. This time yesterday her yarraman had been grazing, perfectly healthy, in this very same place. She could have leapt onto him bareback, given enough nerve, and galloped him all the way to the waves of South Golden. Now the flies clustered around his eyes, where they could get in under the edge of the tarp. His muscles had already begun to soften and rot. In the Big Paddock, Athena continued to whinny for Comet every quarter hour. The sound was lacerating.

'I'm really sorry, mate,' Therese hugged her very briefly, winding her tattooed carp and mermaids around Jo's sodden shoulders. 'He was a beautiful horse.' From behind them, Ellen, red-eyed but silent ever since hearing the awful news as she stepped off the school bus, wrapped her pale arms around her mother's waist, resting her sharp chin onto Jo's right shoulder. Jo allowed this for a moment, then found that she had to pull away. Not even Ellen was allowed close at a sorry time like this.

Watching Amanda's progress in the hole, Jo missed the tightening of her daughter's mouth when she loosened her fingers and pushed her narrow forearms aside.

The kipper gwong continued to fall as they worked steadily. As the blurred pale disc of the sun fell onto the ridgeline, the earth was finally ready to take the body. Therese positioned Johnno's 4WD, and ropes were tied from its bullbar to the horse's fetlocks. Then, with the knobbly tyres of the vehicle spinning, spraying mud out and up at every angle, the women heaved and groaned and somehow managed to drag Comet's body closer, and then, momentum building, to tumble him into the grave. Jo heaved a great sigh of relief that was as much a sob: she'd feared leaving his body out all night for the dingos and lizards to get at. He would be spared that indignity, at least.

'Do you want this tarp, or will I leave it?' Therese needed to know. Jo paused. She did indeed want the tarp. It was worth sixty bucks at the disposals store in Mullum. But she definitely didn't want dirt falling onto Comet's open eyes, or, equally horribly, into his ears. Something had to protect him from that, same as paperbark protected the old people when they went into the ground. She stood, unable to decide, and half-heartedly looked around for an oodgeroo tree to strip.

'You'll never use it again,' said Therese softly, and Jo realised she was right. It belonged in the ground with Comet. She nodded silently.

'Is it time?' Therese checked. Jo nodded again, tears rolling down her cheeks. She blew her nose on the bottom of her t-shirt.

Therese and Amanda began to cover Comet's tarp with red soil, shovelful by shovelful, as Jo stood and watched with her arms folded, shaking in grief. This time Ellen kept her distance. Ten metres away, she leaned on a pine trunk at the edge of the grove, the fairy-wrens chittering in protest above her, diving in and out of their lantana thicket, despite the rain.

'You want to finish it?' Therese held her shovel out, her wet dark hair plastered against her face, neck and chest. Orange rivulets ran down the face of the blade.

This is friendship, thought Jo shakily, as she took it and plunged it into what remained of the pile of extracted dirt, this is something real. Friendship isn't just swims at South Golden or a few beers of a weekend. No. It's driving through floodwater in a borrowed truck, to somewhere you'd rather not be on a cold July afternoon, and digging a fucking great hole in the pouring rain. That's real mates for you. She looked up at Therese and Amanda, who had clustered wetly beside Ellen, beneath the pines. The rain was intensifying again now; the three of them were shifting on their feet, wanting to get inside and cleaned-up and warm.

'I couldn't have better sisters than you two,' Jo told Therese and Amanda, after she'd used the blade of the shovel to flatten the earth on top of the grave. She stood and straightened, and held the shovel over her shoulders like an old-fashioned water yoke. Her sad hands dangled loosely over the handle, and she widened her stance, form-ing, she realised, an enormous distorted X in front of the grave. X *marks the spot.*

'I won't forget this in a hurry.' Jo told them as she walked away from the humped mound, her brain dull with death. Ellen looked over at the bare patch of the world that they had made together. She touched her forearms where Jo had shoved them carelessly aside, and closed her eyes. Something was building inside her eyelids, pressing against them.

'What – ya reckon we're gonna let you forget?' Amanda retorted, bending over to retrieve the empty tea and coffee mugs that already held a centimetre of rain. 'Geez, dream on, sister!'

'The invoice'll be in the mail tonight,' Therese added, grinning. With her full-sleeve tattoos, red smears of dirt on her shirt and up each denimed leg, and the axe hoisted over her muscular shoulder, she looked like she'd eat Hannibal Lecter for breakfast.

'Yeah, stupid me, eh,' Jo managed a feeble smile.

'Atta girl,' Therese told her with a wink. 'Let's go inside, I'm bloody starving.' She stopped herself just in the nick of time from saying what she could eat.

'You lot go get cleaned up,' Jo informed the others, 'I'm gonna take a minute here.'

Therese hesitated, and looked over to Ellen, whose thin shoulders had sagged at Jo's statement.

'Get cracking, bub,' Jo said to Ellen, walking back to the grave alone.

CHAPTER EIGHT

In the days and weeks after Comet's death – in what she came to think of as A.C. time – Jo started to examine closely things around her that she'd barely noticed before. As she drove from the farm into Mullum each morning, she ruminated on the clear fact that the country roads she travelled were lined with fences, boundaries, impenetrable borders. She saw with fresh eyes the road signs and their host of admonitions to slow, to stop, to give way. Where previously she had seen paddocks and house lots (and admired or dismissed the fences around them), now she saw mainly the fences themselves. Even many of the individual saplings on the properties that she drove past were surrounded by wire tree guards, which, of course, were nothing but mini-fences. Everything in the world, she began to see, was bordered. Almost everything was locked up and claimed by other people. The dugai had come and had planted that bloody flag of theirs at Botany Bay, and in the intervening centuries had taken it upon themselves to lace the country tight, using bitumen and wire and timber to bind their gift of a continent to themselves.

Jo obsessed over this inclination of the dugai to take things – normal, natural things like earth and creeks and trees – and tie them up in their endless clever ways. She spent hours looking at detailed topo maps of the shire, discovering in the process that Rob Starr was telling the truth; that the fence beyond the creek which had killed Comet wasn't technically on her farm at all. She rediscovered, too, that every small part of the ridge, and each acre of the low-lying land along Stoney Creek, each field and paddock and roadside had not simply been named and claimed by the whitefellas. The taking of the land had been more absolute and thorough than she'd realised. Jo found that the pieces of land, dismembered each from the other, the orphaned parts of a now-dissolved whole, were to be found on the maps all *numbered* in the way that the graves at the Mullum cemetery were numbered in her groundkeeper's register. The way that convicts – rapists and murderers – were numbered in prison. Jo found this numbering deeply disturbing.

At the same time, she was occasionally aware that all was perhaps not quite right in her head. The fences had been along Tin Wagon Road long before she had arrived. There was nothing new, either, in seeing tree guards, or stop signs, and in fact her own casuarinas had plastic protectors around them which were clearly a milder, cheaper version of tree guards. She had seen a lot number on her contract when she'd bought the farm, though the significance of it had escaped her then. The newness, the terrible insult she felt at the dividing of her budheram jagan, and at the anonymous authority of the road signs, the horror of the never-ending fences and of the numbering, some subterranean part of her realised, was in herself, not in the world. Jo swung helplessly between these two sets of knowledge: that the universe she inhabited was very clearly being bound and strangled with white people's ruler-straight lines and fences, and that the very fact of not being able to get over this meant that maybe – *maybe* – she was losing the plot.

And running beneath both these strands was another, complicating impulse that was unmistakable and constant: she needed to travel west, had to go towards the setting sun, in the direction of Mullum, and Piccabeen, and Lismore. She had no idea why.

'Do you even *know* anyone in Piccabeen or Lismore?' Twoboy asked two weeks later from the hammock that swung on the veranda.

An earmarked copy of a lengthy Native Title document lay face down on his chest, and Jo knew he was looking for any chance to avoid it.

'I thought you had to make notes?' she lectured.

Twoboy waved the document at her and curled his lip.

'I keep hoping old fatguts'll have that third heart attack and join these imaginary ancestors of his. We'd be right then. I can talk sense to Sally.'

'All cos he called you a boy?' Jo asked, recalling the incident outside the New Brighton store a week ago. Oscar and his three grown nephews had sneered from a departing car, telling Twoboy to yanbillilla over the border, onetime, if he didn't want his head caved in. Raucous laughter. Screeching of tyres. And a ton of staircase wit in Twoboy's mouth for the next three days.

Boy.

If Laz had been standing beside him, Twoboy had said in quiet fury, he would have ripped his brother's shirt open on the spot to show Uncle Oscar the scarring that said, Here is a man made by men, and that Twoboy was simply waiting his turn patiently in that ancient queue. But they had been caught off guard, and alone, with only a surfboard and their anger to defend them.

'That lying black dogfucker is gonna learn that I'm no fool, and that I'm no child either. And revenge is a dish I'm prepared to eat frozen –' Twoboy added – 'if I have to.'

Jo looked at the creek and decided to take the path of least resistance.

'I don't know anyone in Piccabeen except for a couple of people I went to primary school with in the Goldie.'

'You got another man waiting over there, eh?' Twoboy teased. 'Gonna go play up on me?'

'Hah, that's all I need,' Jo answered. There was nothing like a death to flatten your libido. A.C. was turning into After Sex as well.

'It's Mardi Grass this weekend, we could drive over there through Lismore, if you want,' Twoboy offered, pretending to roll and smoke a big fat spliff.

'You got petrol?' Jo asked. Between the two of them there was usually at least one car with the fuel light showing. But the ute was about fifteen thousand kays overdue for its service. With the rates due in a fortnight, it wasn't about to get it.

'Full tank. I busked in town the other day,' Twoboy told her. Jo raised her eyebrows. She'd noticed a yidaki in the Commode but hadn't yet heard Twoboy use it.

'How much?'

'Eighty bucks in a coupla hours. Woulda been double that, but I kept me gear on.'

Jo spluttered and choked on her cordial, before agreeing that if Twoboy was making that sort of money off the tourists then he could definitely afford to drive her to Mardi Grass. The hippies and their yarndi worship didn't interest her except as sociology made flesh, but they could go through Lismore and she might find out why the hell she needed to be over that way. Maybe shut up the voice that echoed day and night with the nagging imperative to go west, young woman, go west. And Twoboy was right. She did need her mind taken away from the farm, and from the bare red patch in the Small Paddock that she visited morning and night. The low cairn of her offering stones there already reached halfway to her knees.

And there was a third reason to go to Nimbin, too. Apart from anything else, there were fewer fucking fences over there.

The noise was unbearable. A symphony of alarms squealed from all sides. In the midst of the Ocean Shores Bi-Lo, Uncle Humbug pressed his palms hard against his ears and grimaced. Around him shoppers were looking at each other in bewilderment, before reluctantly abandoning their trolleys and streaming out of the centre. Some mothers of small children did this at a run, craning their necks to find out what the awful commotion was about. They expected to see flames crackling at the back of Maria's fruit shop or smoke billowing out from the hairdresser's. A small boy wailed to his grandmother about terrorists. The shoppers formed clumps of concern on the concrete apron of the shopping centre, while the drone of the Bruns fire-engine could be heard tuning up from across the river. Two thousand bats in the riverside colony squawked and flapped on their branches at this aural disturbance, as though they felt obliged to do their bit to add to the cacophony.

Uncle Humbug set his face grimly and continued to stand in the deli section with his palms jammed hard against his binung. They would come for him any moment. Knowing this, he acted lightning fast and slipped a block of Mersey Valley cheese into the pocket of his jacket. Sure enough, here came that young manager fella, the dugai with the comb marks in his hair and a red rope around his neck that he called a tie. The noise grew even more overwhelming, if that was possible.

'Mr Milbung!' the dugai cried, his mouth moving silently beneath the sirens. 'I'm going to have to ask you to leave the building, sir!' *Ask*, his mouth said, but *tell* was what the iron grip on Uncle Humbug's upper arm delivered. Humbug protested all the way to the glass doors, invoking human rights, Indigenous rights, land rights, citizenship rights and any other rights he could think of, but to no avail.

When Humbug had been emphatically evicted, the young dugai made a phone call to security, and the sirens abruptly cut off. The silence which followed had a peculiar quality of stark contrast to what had gone before. The shoppers standing in the carpark became aware that their ears had actually been physically hurting. They rubbed at their heads, and began joking in relief with each other.

'People!' the manager told the crowd. 'There's no problem! False alarm! Please resume your shopping. The technical problem has been –' and here he glanced meaningfully at Uncle Humbug who was scowling at the world, smoking a durrie with the skinny Scottish music teacher who had donated it – 'the problem has been rectified.' The shoppers hoisted their handbags onto their shoulders and prepared to re-enter the building.

'Who you calling a rectum?' Humbug spluttered suddenly,

forgetting for a moment that he had a kilo of stolen cheese on his person. The manager swung around. He was twenty-four years old, with a brand-new business degree, moderate acne, and a burning desire to get in the pants of Natasha on register four.

'Mr Milbung, I don't think it's going to do anyone any –'

'You the rectum!' Humbug cried. 'All I want's one jugi jugi! Once a fucken payday, is that too much to ask! Truegod, where's the respect for the black man in this country!'

A murmur of confused support ran through parts of the crowd.

'Dis fella always calling me bad names!' Humbug told the onlookers, shaking his head. 'And he reckons I can't even go in his shop! Never! Not one time!'

'Shame,' said the grandmother of the frightened boy to her neighbour. A loud boo erupted from one of the hippies at the back.

'Talk about bloody apartheid' said his music teacher friend, loudly.

The manager was young but he wasn't stupid; he made another call to security. He then spoke in a low voice to Humbug, who eventually nodded and delicately produced some coinage from beneath the illicit cheese. The manager looked at the meagre coins, and then at the crowd, where four or five locals were organising themselves into the Humbug Defence Fund.

'Roast chooks are nine ninety-nine, Mr Milbung,' said the manager, suddenly aware of Natasha watching from beside the ATM.

'Well, let me go gettim. I can put him on my card,' bluffed Humbug, who had rejected plastic money in 1988, chucking it into the rubbish bin along with Vatican Two and the fanciful concept of paying any rent whatsoever to dugai land-grabbers. He took a large step towards the glass doors. The manager immediately took a larger one, blocking his way.

The Humbug Defence Fund bristled.

'You can't go in there!' the manager blurted, knowing all too well that the smoke alarms would start screaming again the instant Humbug got within five metres of the sensors.

'You gonna stop me?' Humbug wanted to know, his eyes alight

with the knowledge that the crowd was drifting onto his side. Then, under his breath, 'You want me to come back this arvo? And tomorrow? And the day after that? Could be a veeery exciting week at Ocean Shores shops . . .' Humbug took a long drag on his durrie, and waited. He owned no watch, no phone, no clock; he had all the time in the world to wage a campaign of terror upon the Bi-Lo.

The manager smiled weakly, and shepherded Humbug to the far side of the chemist.

'No. But look. If you'll just wait here, I'll go get a hot chook for you myself. Will you wait?' Humbug agreed with this eminently sensible idea. The manager shook his head slightly and clutched Humbug's four dollars tight in his sweating palm.

'And some of that good cheese too, mate,' Humbug triumphantly inflated his order as the manager turned to go inside. 'That Mersey Valley one, eh?'

Jo looked around at the tiny festive township where everyone, Twoboy included, was having a wonderful time. Yarndi flavoured the air, drums were beating, the pub was doing a roaring trade, music was playing and old friends were catching up over cones, spliffs and hash cookies. Placards waved, declaring that the legalisation of marijuana was self-evidently a good thing, that hemp was going to save the world if only it was allowed to, and that recreational drug use was synonymous with freedom.

Above it all, over the heads of several thousands of happy revellers – dreadlocked funky hippies and the young city acidheads, the assorted Murries and Goories and the local baby boomers who'd come in the seventies and stayed – above all of these, Wollumbin sent his sacred peak soaring into a perfect winter sky. Where, thought Jo bitterly, as she looked at the shadow of the mountain's distinctive silhouette falling on the Rainbow Cafe, was this perfect weather when Comet had died? If it hadn't rained cats and dogs that week, would he have sought refuge on the high side of the creek? Gotten tangled in Rob Starr's barbed wire abomination and died there? No, he wouldn't have, and therefore the blue of the Saturday sky was pure provocation to her.

She looked up at the top of the big mountain, then quickly away. Since hearing the chanting on the ridge Jo had had a rethink about what she'd always dismissed as pure superstition. She knew Wollumbin was strong men's business, and to be avoided at all costs. She turned away from the peak, anxious to get going to some safer country.

Twoboy made his way back through the crowd holding two fish-burgers, and Jo took one gratefully. Biting into the juicy battered flake, Jo saw that the distant peak of the big mountain was clearly reflected in the shopwindow in front of her. There's no getting away from the bloody mountain in this town, she thought uneasily.

'Don't smile, ya face'll crack,' Twoboy said through red-veined eyes.

Jo didn't answer him. He'd obviously had a smoke since heading off to grab lunch. Coming to Mardi Grass first had been a mistake; they should have driven through Lismore on the way to the carnival, not postponed it until they were leaving. Now, with Twoboy thoroughly bombed, she would have to drive – and whatever mystery was drawing her to the western horizon would have to make itself known on top of the practical mental necessities of steering and navigating and not snapping at her man for getting into the yarndi that was fucking with the heads of so many blackfellas around the country. He's an adult, Jo told herself, thirty-seven years old. You're not his fucken mother. But it was bloody stupid not to have anticipated this and gone to Lismore first. Thank God Ellen had stayed behind in Mullum.

'I think we should hook it soon,' Jo proposed. 'I gotta work out who's dragging me to Lismore.' Hopefully to Lismore, she thought. Hopefully not to Kyogle, or Ku Klux Casino.

Twoboy pouted.

'The mob are having a jam . . . River's boys are there . . . and Johnny Didge . . . and that Gadigal cousin of Chris's, the fella with only one arm. Wanna come check it out?' Twoboy asked.

If only you knew, Jo thought, remembering mad twelve-hour jams in her past life.

'Nah. Like I said, I wanna get going to Lismore.'

'Well, I might go that way for a bit, then.' Twoboy had tricky alliances to build and maintain with the local traditional owners, not to mention the lure of the music itself.

'Yeah, okay, you go off and party with ya mates.' Jo hated the way she sounded, but couldn't seem to budge the anger that was burning in her since Comet died. 'And I'll go and work out this important business on me own.'

'There's more than one way back to the Dreamtime, darlin,' Twoboy told her, proffering a joint. She viewed it with withering scorn.

'Oh, what a load of crap! More than one way to the fucken psych ward, ya mean,' Jo snapped. With Laz's boy chronically suicidal from hydro, how could he even touch the stuff?

'Suit yerself. I didn't know you was such a bloody dugai,' Twoboy said, when it became obvious that Jo wasn't about to soften, and he sauntered away towards the musicians.

Yeah, you go smoke up some more, Jo told him sarcastically under her breath, and find some little white girls while yer at it who want a black souvenir of their trip to the bush. A thrill of alarm ran through her at the thought of Twoboy hooking up with some random stranger, a feeling she decided to drown at the pub.

Jo had finished one schooner and was debating whether to have a second or take the back road to Lismore alone, when a slim blonde woman appeared, silhouetted in the doorway of the bar. The woman, an attractive thirty-something, wore a short green dress with a denim jacket over the top, and was yelling drunken accusations at top note:

'Are you the fucken slut dog that wants smashing? Eh? Eh!'

As a muso, Jo had witnessed this scene a thousand times in a thousand bars. Fascinated despite herself at the drama and likely violence, she looked behind her at the other drinkers. The faces there stared back and, mystified, Jo discovered that *she* was the object of the woman's fury.

Denim Jacket had covered the ground between street and bar quickly, and was suddenly in Jo's face, breathing bourbon fumes and reeking of cones. Oh pure class, sister, pure class.

Jo slid off the bar stool and stood ready to defend herself, hands dangling loose by her side. She noted with a mixture of relief and alarm that the bar attendant had quickly removed all the nearby empty glasses. But where was the bloody bouncer? Town full to busting with cops for Mardi Grass and no law and order in the actual pub. A semicircle of interested onlookers soon coalesced around the two women.

'I *said*, is ya the fucken big hole that stole my man while I was in lockup?'

'*What?*' Jo reeled as several kinds of new information collided at once.

'You binung goonj as well, ya fucken slut?'

So you're a blackfella, thought Jo in mild surprise.

'What man? What the fuck are ya talking about?' Jo flung her arms up in consternation.

'What man?' The woman dripped with angry sarcasm, hands welded to her hips. 'Twoboy, that what man! My man! Till I gets out and find he's got some neeew woman, everyone reckons. Nevermind we sposed to go Laura next week!'

Jo stood facing the woman, paralysed with angry confusion. If only everything and everybody would go away. If only things could return to how they were before Comet died, before Twoboy arrived, before the divorce stole her real family away. If only life could be simple, and easy, and sane. But *if only* wasn't going to stop any of this. She had to actually do something, had to act before she found herself stuck permanently in the middle of a Jerry Springer episode.

The woman had a couple of mates lurking behind her; there was no way of knowing whether they were ready to step in or not. Safest to assume they would, with the bouncer still MIA. Jo was taller than the blonde woman, and a bit heavier, but she was no pub brawler. Denim Jacket, on the other hand, looked like she was in her element.

'What's your name, love?' Jo spoke as calmly as she could manage, given the surges of adrenalin pumping through her like she was hooked up to a fire hose. Don't lose it, she told herself. Do Not Lose It. This silly bloody woman's done nothing to you . . . not yet.

'Carly Wetherby, don't wear it out!' The woman was breathing from high in her chest, gulping air.

'Well, Carly Wetherby, here's the drill. If Twoboy *wants* to be your man, then you're very bloody welcome to him. He's out there yarndied up somewhere, so you go fucken talk to him about it.'

Jo flung a furious hand towards the door, then narrowed her eyes at the woman. Tried to imagine what life Carly had lived to bring her to this point, stoned and fulldrunk, about to punch on in a pub with someone she'd never met. Ready to bash a stranger and wake up back in custody with a hangover and a whole lotta nothing going on. It seemed unbelievable to Jo that Twoboy could have ever been with this person, but that was a conversation for another time and place.

'Oh, he wanna be my man, orright,' Carly spat. 'Don't you worry bout that!'

Jo indicated the open door to the street and Carly paused. Beneath the jeans and t-shirt Jo was clearly a ball of muscle waiting to be triggered into action. Carly teetered.

'I'm telling ya, he's my man – so ya better back off real fucken quick, goddit?' Carly snapped.

'You got nothing to worry about there,' Jo replied, holding her anger in with increasing difficulty, 'you're welcome to him, so why don't ya just go find him?' It occurred to her that any of the dozen wooden chairs within reach would make excellent weapons to defend herself with, if Carly decided to take things up a notch.

The cops arrived as the bouncers ran in from the back bar.

'What's up this time, Carly?' the bouncer asked, provoking another angry torrent of abuse directed at Jo. The female cop seized her by the upper arms and propelled her unceremoniously into the waiting paddy wagon. The crowd outside booed; a couple of teenagers boldly kicked at the wagon, then melted back into the masses.

'You here to make trouble too, are ya?' the male constable snarled at Jo. She turned to him with a crinkled brow and spread her hands.

'Do I look like trouble?' she asked him, a little shrill.

'You tell me,' the cop glowered, looking like he was itching to unsnap his handcuffs. He glanced at the bouncer, who gave a small headshake.

'No,' Jo said tightly, 'I don't. I'm just having a quiet beer.'

'Didn't sound very fucking quiet to me. You wanna watch yourself, alright?'

The cop looked her up and down, threw in another long blue-eyed glare for good measure, and then sauntered back outside to where, from inside the paddy wagon, Carly was leading the crowd in song.

Jo shook her head and turned to the bar for the second beer she had intended to pass up. There was a conversation to be conducted with Twoboy about Carly Wetherby, but it wasn't a conversation she was in any great hurry to have.

'You okay?' asked the nose-studded woman serving behind the bar, as she replaced the trays of empty glasses. 'She's a bit of a drama queen, our Carly.'

'Oh, yeah, you know. Never a dull moment,' Jo answered into her beer, a bit shaky on it. Not with Twoboy in my life, anyways.

'The woman's totally fucken womba,' Twoboy protested as the Commodore sped towards Murwillumbah. 'And I *told* you I had a psycho girfriend in Ipswich for a while.'

Jo narrowed her eyes at him and shifted the car into third, fish-tailing around the corner so fast that she frightened herself.

'You didn't tell me she thought you were still together!' she argued, accelerating out of the bend and spraying gravel. A family of waterhens on the verge scattered in fear of their lives.

'It didn't occur to me. I thought she had another six months to serve!' Twoboy grabbed onto the handle above the door in alarm.

'And that would have been alright, would it?' Jo asked in disbelief.

Out of sight, out of mind. How did intelligent men get off, behaving like such cretins?

Twoboy shrugged.

'I just didn't think it was an issue,' he said. 'How the fuck do I know what's going through her tiny mind? C'mon, Jo. You can't seriously think . . .'

Jo was silent as she digested Twoboy's protests. He was right about one thing. He had definitely mentioned the crazy woman, all those weeks ago. He hadn't said she was locked up though. Or what for – dealing yarndi.

'What were you even doing with her?' she asked with genuine curiosity. It seemed completely out of character.

'Horizontal folk dancing, mainly,' Twoboy joked, then pulled up at Jo's expression. 'Oh, I dunno, we hooked up at a party, and then after that she'd call me Friday nights and it was always pretty easy to go and have a drink and . . . well, you know. It wasn't anything serious.'

Not for you maybe, Casanova, reflected Jo. Cruising through life with no thought for the vulnerable women you hurt along the way.

'How long did this go on?'

'Three or four months. I was about to end it when she got busted. I was like, hasta la vista, baby.' Twoboy was looking out the window and jigging his left leg.

'So did you tell her the good news today?' Jo asked tightly. Twoboy looked at her in suprise.

'Yeah, of course! I lied and told her I was getting engaged, actually, so there'd be no room for confusion. Ya gotta be clear with these people.' Twoboy took Jo's left hand off the steering wheel and kissed it, laughing.

'Wanna get married, my darlin?' he twinkled through still slightly reddened eyes.

Jo snatched her hand back. Dickhead.

'So I suppose she's on the warpath now,' Jo muttered, picturing Carly finding her alone on the farm and setting to work with waddies.

'Nah,' said Twoboy, 'she's just working off some prison shit, that's all. She'll have a new man to harass this time next week, nothing surer. I promise.' Twoboy used his index finger to tuck Jo's hair behind her ear, and then he left his hand resting comfortably on the back of her neck, massaging it. His voice softened as he said that Carly was irrelevant – didn't Jo understand that? Today had been about meeting with some of the neighbouring traditional owners, yarning them up about the Native Title fight, and making sure that Uncle Oscar hadn't managed to undermine the Jackson position since their last meeting. The smoke around the fire had cemented the neutrality of the younger lads for the time being, and Twoboy was well pleased with his day's work.

'I hope you're right,' Jo told him, 'cos I didn't sign up for any of this psycho bullshit. She was like that woman in the Blues Brothers.' She barely slowed as the Commodore roared across a narrow one-lane bridge.

'I'm sorry, babe. Maybe I did need to talk it through with her. But it's all over now, ancient history.' Twoboy shuffled CDs. After a minute he looked up. 'Why we headed this way – I thought we were going home through Lismore?'

Jo explained in taut words of one syllable that her head was over-flowing with the day's dramas, and she didn't feel at all in tune with whatever was dragging her over to the sunset side of Bundjalung country.

It would be a waste of time to detour through Lismore in this mood. Which meant the entire trip had been a day spent off the farm when she could have been building the cattle yard, or spraying those bloody camphors, or riding Comet –

Not riding Comet.

'Hey –' Twoboy said, smiling.

Jo grunted back without taking her gaze off the road. It was hit-a-roo and wreck-the-car time, just on dusk. And why should she smile back anyway? Twoboy was a long way from her good books, now. How very typical. Stupid-arse men with their leftover relationships and their selfishness and their inevitable need to go and get stoned when she had important things to do. Well, fuck him. Putting her priorities last, and –

'Jo!'

'*What?*'

'Did we just have our first fight?' Twoboy teased, poking the now-healed scar on her upper arm. 'We did, hey? Didn't we?' His teeth gleamed very white in the fading light.

'Fuck up and let me drive, or I'll strangle you with ya own dreads.'

Twoboy gave a great bellow of laughter. Then he slid The Last Kinection inside the CD player and disappeared into the music all the way to Murwillumbah, while Jo quietly stewed behind the steering wheel.

CHAPTER NINE

'But I'm nearly an hour late already!' Ellen erupted as Jo drove up onto the footpath beside the cemetery and parked the ute.

It was Saturday afternoon. Ellen held a wrapped present and was wearing her favourite top of the moment, the one that informed the world its owner would rather be sleeping. What happens at fourteenth-birthday slumber parties these days? mused Jo. Probably not a lot of sleeping. Probably better, in fact, for a single parent not to dwell on the question too much.

'I'll be two minutes, tops,' Jo promised through the open window. Did the jahjam think she wanted to spend a second longer at work than she needed to on a Saturday, for Chrissake?

Ellen muttered darkly and hunched down in the passenger seat, oppression radiating from every pore.

Jo sprinted a few steps and scissors jumped over the weldmesh fence. She grinned broadly as she landed on the balls of her feet among the outermost headstones. That was the upside to slaving over a hot farm; she was as fit as she'd been when, at twenty, she'd jammed all week and played loud sweaty gigs every weekend.

As she slid her key into the bronze lock of the storeroom, Jo heard a small animal scuttle away from her in fright. *Rattus rattus*, no doubt, the scourge of the new world. Old world. Basho wanted her to bait the vermin, but Basho could go jump off a cliff. It was bad enough that millions of camphors had to be sprayed to stop them taking over her and every other farm in northern New South Wales. Rodents in the storeroom were a small price to pay to know that *mulanyin* wasn't hunting carcinogenic frogs in the roadside ditch; to see the parrots and fairy-wrens and butcherbirds on the farm and know that their eggs wouldn't fracture in a mess of poisoned fragments before the chicks had a chance to hatch. Long Live the Mullum Organic Rodent, Jo insisted to Basho's bafflement – although she wouldn't have said no to an occasional visit from a deadly organic cat.

'Two minutes is way up!' called Ellen, drumming her left hand urgently on the outer panel of the ute door to underscore the point. Hmm. The kid's really keen on this birthday party. Were there boys involved? Drugs? Boys *and* drugs? *Girls* and drugs?

'Yeah, rightyo, don't get ya flaps in a knot,' Jo replied, retrieving her forgotten phone from beside the sink.

As she fumbled hurriedly to lock up, Greasy Hair walked slowly past the storeroom to her habitual perch. Sundays were the usual time for families to come and visit, the day when fresh flowers appeared on the graves and weeding was done by hands other than hers. On Mondays, Jo was always interested to see if any of her silent charges had had a visit. But it was Thursdays that Greasy Hair came, as though in her isolation she was unwilling to belong even to the diffuse company of mourners. She would spend an hour sitting beside the grave of Jemima Smith, and then take herself silently away again for another seven days. Unable to contain her curiosity, Jo had asked her once if Jemima was family. No, the woman said quietly, she was my best friend, and Jo hadn't dared to ask any more questions. But now Greasy Hair had turned up on a Saturday. Jo made a mental note to check if it was Jemima's death anniversary this week.

As Jo headed back to the ute, Greasy Hair caught her eye and lifted a mournful hand in greeting. The woman's bearing spoke of an ongoing struggle to retain dignity: cheap K-mart sneakers with worn soles, old purple acne scarring on thin pale cheeks.

'G'day mate,' Jo offered, feeling unusually friendly. 'Here on Saturday this week?' That was how social interaction worked, wasn't it? You stated the bloody obvious, and then they did, and then ultimately, after endless ritualistic chitchat, someone finally said something containing information or meaning and then there was actually a point to the conversation?

'Yeah. I can't make it out this Thursday.' The woman answered, doubling her annual word total in one fell swoop. Jo nodded, encouraged by this uncharacteristic verbosity. It was tempting to offer Greasy Hair a cup of tea to enjoy while she sat by Jemima in the cool winter sun. How bereft would a person have to be to visit a grave every single week? How grief-stricken, or how lonely? Jo was on the verge of suggesting it, and going back to unlock the shed where the kettle lived, when Ellen screeched from outside the fence in indignation.

'Maarm! Can you hurry up?'

'Ah, bloody hell, no rest for the wicked. See you next time,' Jo said hastily.

'Who was that?' Ellen asked, crankily adjusting her bra strap with unnecessary force. Jo told her about Greasy Hair's Thursday visits, adding casually that she'd been tempted to offer the solitary woman a cuppa. Ellen looked daggers at her mother.

'You know I'm an hour late for my party, and you *still* want to make her a cup of tea?'

'You'll get to your party,' Jo retorted. 'God only knows what kind of life she's got.' How cruel the young are, she reflected. How selfish and hard.

'Well, thanks for thinking of your daughter first, before some complete stranger.' Ellen folded her arms and frowned at the dashboard. 'Or don't I count?'

'She's not a "complete stranger". She comes here every week.' Jo realised with a sudden small shock that this was true. She didn't know the woman's name, or her occupation, if she had one, nor did she know where she lived or with whom. She didn't even know the exact relationship of Greasy Hair to poor dead Jemima, whether *friend* was a euphemism for *lover* or not. But even with all this lack of information, Greasy Hair had still turned into something that wasn't a stranger. She was an ongoing presence in Jo's life, and now Jo felt an odd sense of unease develop, as though the woman's unspoken pain and isolation had somehow managed to insinuate itself into her own days.

'You always do this!' Ellen blazed at her mother. Hot teenage tears were building behind her eyes and she was going to yell them away. It was an old story: apparently Jo had endless time and compassion for the world, *sans* Ellen – but not for her, who had to be as stolid and tough as Jo herself was, and who had better not require affection more than once every blue moon.

'It's not fair,' howled the murderous two-year-old inside Ellen's chest. 'Not fair at all.'

'Always do bloody what?' Jo snapped, accelerating past the hospital. *Always.* Christ, teenagers. When would Ellen grow out of it and turn back into the delightful person she'd been at eleven? I at least had had the grace to run away to Aunty Barb. Ellen, on the other hand, Jo sensed, was going to stay and fight her mother's authority to the bitter death. She'd tried giving her *On the Road*, followed by *Rule of the Bone*, but no good. Things were altogether too easy for her daughter, Jo reflected, at 287 Tin Wagon Road.

'Nothin. Forget it.' Put other people first. Make me feel like an accident, an afterthought. The freak mistake that killed your music and ruined your life. Ellen turned away as the tears trembled inside her eyelids, blurring the cane paddocks along Main Arm Road into a fuzzy green waterscape.

Jo glanced at Ellen's cold narrow shoulder and at the back of her head, and gritted her teeth at both these. The gulf between them was widening each day. Sometimes she could almost feel it physically, the tearing apart of mother and child with words and looks; with deeds done and undone. A psychologist would probably say the kid was separating from her, all very normal, but whatever the reason, Ellen was rapidly turning into a royal adolescent pain in the arse. *Brattus brattus.* Time she went and had some time with her father in Sydney. Maybe Paul held the missing magical ingredient that would bring her happy curly-haired Ellen back, make those green eyes sparkle again.

'Sorry, sister, no can do,' Therese said, as she stacked her marking into a tall perilous column beside the computer. 'We're going to Brisbane Friday night. Amanda's got Mary for the weekend.'

'Again?' Jo asked. Amanda had been up to Wynumn twice in the past five weeks. Therese nodded slow exaggerated nods as she raised her eyebrows high, meaning Amanda's mother was bloody hard work, especially after a week on Special Class at Ocean Shores. She poked irritably at her marking tower, which was trembling and threatening to collapse onto the tiled floor.

'Yes, again. Mary had another fall yesterday. And of course the family think Amanda's the total bitch from hell because she won't just move up and live with her till she drops off the perch.'

Jo grimaced sympathetically. Amanda's aged mother was in that hideous limbo world where she needed a fulltime carer and had none. Because Amanda wasn't out to half her family, it seemed obvious that she, an apparently single woman with no kids, was the ideal candidate for the job.

'Serves the homophobic fuckers right if *they* end up doing it all. But daw, poor me – I'll hafta stay home and be Nigel No Friends!' Jo said, shelving her plan to go to Kym's for the weekend and snap herself out of the blues.

'Can't Chris feed the animals?' Therese proposed.

'Nah, she's been sick for a month. I really should go visit her.' But Jo knew Chris loathed visitors when she was sick; her mysterious depressions made her less welcoming of her friends, not more. 'Ah, doesn't matter much. Ellen'll be old enough to leave at home one of these days. And anyways, I can't really afford the petrol.' Jo sighed a tiny sound of despair, meant only for her ears.

Therese gave her friend a sideways look from where she'd begun emptying the dishwasher of its clean plates and glasses. She'd heard that same sigh from three of the special kids' mums this week.

'You okay, mate?'

Jo's mouth twisted sideways. She shrugged with one shoulder. Yes. No. Maybe. She regularly lay awake thinking of fences and numbers; she went to sleep the same way, tossing and turning before sleep did finally arrive with its nightmares of unpaid bills and flooding creeks. And since their abortive trip to Lismore, a nagging anxiety about Twoboy had joined the other fears swirling in her head.

Twoboy was scrupulously respectful of Jo and Ellen, but his acid response to Carly had troubled her. In her worst moments, sleepless as the early morning light arrived on the eastern horizon, Jo could imagine the same male derision being turned in her direction one day. Twoboy was quick to reassure her when they were together, but the court case was reaching determination stage, and he'd barely been out of the city for three weeks. Jo had had plenty of time on her own since Mardi Grass to imagine what she had with Twoboy warping into just another tangle of unmet needs and unvoiced accusations. She had a recurring vision of him telling some other woman in a year's time, 'Jo? Ah, she's bloody womba, I told you that. Ancient history'.

'Talk to me, girlfriend,' Therese said, hopping backwards up onto the kitchen bench and peeling a bright orange mandarin that colour-matched the carp on her forearms.

Rather than answer, Jo turned away to a brochure on the fridge. Sangsurya Buddhist Centre. *Two days of mindfulness in the beautiful Byron Bay hinterland.* A grey-haired woman with familiar brown eyes looked out from beneath the heading.

'You going to this?'

'Bloody oath, she's amazing. You should come,' Therese's voice leapt.

'Do I look like I need a fucking guru? Anyway, I'm broke, I'll just go fishing. The river's my church.' Poverty had one sole redeeming feature – it was the perfect excuse for getting out of stuff. But what was it about those eyes? Were they blackly Eurasian like Therese's? No, that wasn't it.

Therese was giving her the unrelenting look that always made Jo uneasy. To stop herself from fidgeting under the microscope of friendship, Jo folded her arms and glared back.

'So – you been getting down to the water much lately?' Therese probed.

Now Therese had one bossy hand on her hip, her lips pursed. 'You've been fishing, swimming . . . going for walks on the beach, I suppose?' Jo looked out the window. It had been countless weeks. Three months probably, since that night at Bruns beach with Chris. And even then she'd needed dragging away from the work of the farm, that early hauling and clearing and burning of old crap that had almost been forgotten now that the place was finally beginning to take shape and look like a home and not a rubbish dump.

'Well?' Therese had her head to one side, mandarin peel wadded in one hand and her cheeks bulging with the soft juicy fruit.

'I've been flat strap on the farm,' Jo said feebly, prompting a loud scornful raspberry from her friend.

'I didn't think so. What if I shout you?' said Therese on impulse. 'Go on. Do it this once, and I'll never hassle you about it again.' Her gaze didn't waver.

Jo fingered the brochure, intrigued by the clarity in the eyes of the teacher. Somebody with eyes like those might be able to see certain untellable things, Jo mused. Because nobody knew. Nobody else knew what it was like to wake in the night and be unable to get the picture of Comet drowning out of her mind, to endlessly imagine him being held underwater by the bloodied wire while the brown creek water filled his nostrils, his throat, his lungs. Nobody knew, because Jo absolutely refused to risk hearing the words: *but he was only a horse.*

Maybe going on this retreat could help her sleep again. Or make the nightmares stop.

'Whaddya got to lose?' Therese kept prodding away. 'It's two days out of an entire lifetime. My shout.'

'Ah, for fuck's sake,' Jo looked up, surprising both of them. 'Alright, I'll go.'

Athena nosed in the corners of her feed bin, making it clang against the fence rail where it hung. Jo refused to think about the blank space ten metres away where Comet used to eat. She stroked the old mare's neck instead, leaning in to the smell and feel, the absolute comfort that was warm horse. Athena had grown a fuzzy winter coat and no longer looked much like the sleek thoroughbred she'd been at Main Arm in April. Ringed at a distance by four steers with unrealistic hopes of getting their moist black noses into her breakfast, Athena flattened her ears and looked around at them, boss of the paddock. When the very last pellet had been hunted down and devoured, the mare turned to go and drink from the bathtub by the front gate.

'No you don't, wait up,' Jo told her, clinging tightly onto her black mane as Athena pulled away in protest. She wanted to ride bareback around the paddock and check the fenceline before work. It was a long-neglected job that couldn't be avoided any longer, not since the neighbour's young bull had started knocking fences down across the road, having tired of playing with the water pump cover. While part of Jo applauded him – bring it on, knock all the fucking fences down you like, pal! – the larger part of her knew that everybody's cattle in the valley needed containing and that hers were no exception. But Athena careered away, belting through the steers at an extended trot that scattered them left and right with indignant moans. The boldest came straight over to the empty feedbin and plunged its nose in. The others clustered around, begging Jo for pellets with baffled moos.

'Whadda you lot bloody looking at?' Jo snapped as she flung away a handful of Athena's mane, 'Go eat some grass.'

She traipsed back inside past a large pile of dirty washing on the laundry floor. Tension was lodged tight in her rigid neck and shoulders. It was school holidays, and Ellen had been at her father's for seven nights now. In her absence, the washing wasn't doing itself, just as the fence line remained uninspected and the car still unserviced. It can wait, it can wait, it all has to bloody wait, Jo told herself, changing into her least dirty work clothes.

As she snatched the ute keys off the kitchen wall, Jo spotted Aunty Barb's fishing rod resting unused in the corner. Jo's shoulders bunched. All the light seemed to have gone out of things. She felt as though, if one more tiny thing built up on her have-to-do or can't-afford-it lists, she would fall down in a heap right where she stood.

'Suck it up, girl,' she ordered herself sternly, 'just suck it up.' The fishing rod rested indifferently in the corner, a long strand of cobweb draped around it mimicking the line.

If she hadn't promised to go to Therese's bloody stupid Buddhist thing this weekend, she could have gone fishing instead.

'That wall's crying out for graffiti, eh.'

Jo and Twoboy were driving past the high concrete retaining barrier which separated Devine's Hill from the mangroved edge of the river. He grinned agreement, and proposed a midnight art project for Ellen sometime soon.

'She's got to do some proper art for school first, unless she already finished it at Paul's ... Hey, you got a message.' Jo picked up his phone from the console.

'Graffiti is "proper art". Who's it from?' Twoboy responded.

'Christ!' said Jo, her face changing abruptly. 'What's this shit?'

'Eh?' Twoboy replied as they passed the Burringbar exit and headed into another mobile deadzone, on their way to retrieve Ellen from Coolangatta airport.

Jo read the message aloud.

U can fool sum v da peeps sum v da time but u cant fool us ya black DOGCUNT u best be lookin behind u 24/7 cos u gonna get urs proppa wayz signed Da Real Deal.

Twoboy laughed, but not before Jo had seen it: his jaw clenched tightly shut for a brief second.

'Just Oscar and his pack of inbred rellies. That's the second one he's sent.'

'You worried?' Jo asked, hastily putting the phone back down as though it might burn with its vitriol.

Twoboy forced another laugh.

'Old fatguts couldn't fight his way out of a brown paper bag. And them boys of his aren't as tough as they think they are. Nah, Bullockhead mob come after us they'll get a real fight, don't ya worry.'

'You should go to the cops.' Jo's brow furrowed. 'Get him charged.' She spoke knowing that this would never, ever happen. The day a Goorie man took his private black business to the gunjies was the day he'd officially lost his balls, whipped them off and put them on a platter for Her Majesty to sample. It was bad enough having to submit to the bullshit and humiliation of the Native Title Tribunal.

'Maybe Bullockhead mob should go on your Buddhist retreat, eh,' Twoboy joked. 'Chill the mad fucks out a bit.'

'Did you answer the first one?'

Twoboy shook his head.

'If I don't answer, they don't know whether I've got it, see? And information is power. C'mon, darling – ya don't need to look like that. You know I'm Captain Goorie!'

Jo summoned half a smile for her very own dreadlocked super-hero. Into her guts, though, next to the insomnia and the unpaid bills, and Twoboy's response to Carly, and the never-ending memory of poor drowned Comet, a new worry now crept in and made itself a warm, comfortable nest. While she was on the retreat, Ellen would be at the farm with Twoboy in charge of her. And what if the Bullockheads really did mean business? What if they knew where to find her man, in the depths of Tin Wagon Road, and what if they stumbled upon Ellen there as well? Jo's heart hammered with potential catastrophe. She felt like buying a shotgun. Two shotguns.

Buy them with what, she didn't know, but how comforting would it be to know that a .404 was resting in the corner of the bedroom when a convoy of Bullockheads arrived in the night to dispense some homegrown justice? Tendrils of fear spiralled inside her, filling her emptiness with their poison.

Twoboy cheerfully clapped her on the thigh. *It'll be right.* Jo took his dark hand and held it tight in both of hers, wishing futilely for peace in their time. Her arms felt like they were made of boiled spaghetti, flopping uselessly as the enemy circled around her daughter. The idea of taking on the Bullockheads terrified Jo.

'You're worried about Ellen, eh?' Twoboy asked. Jo nodded, reaching a decision.

'I'm staying home with her. Bugger the retreat.' she said, making a mental inventory of the weapons on the farm – stockwhip. Pitchfork. Shovels. Star pickets. Some could be locked away and some kept close for use in an emergency. Jo pondered ringing Kym and Jason, and asking them to drive down. But no – that would just put the boys in harm's way.'

Twoboy sighed and smiled at her.

'Darlin – if you're gonna take someone out, you just do it. You don't send them texts first. Oscar's a big talker in a white man's court, but get him on the street and he's weak as piss.'

'He might bring a mob though,' she countered. Twoboy was tough and, yeah, he was big, but there was only one of him. Laz was still needed in Brisbane most weekends and had been looking after his boy when he wasn't doing research. In stark contrast, Oscar Bullockhead, who'd lived on Bundjalung country all his life, had half-a-dozen nephews to call on in Piccabeen alone.

'They only know my Mullum address,' Twoboy reassured her. 'They won't come looking for me at the farm.'

Jo hesitated. Seeing her waver, Twoboy slowed and pulled the Commodore over onto the shoulder of the highway. He turned to face Jo.

'Listen up, darlin. Them tiny words on a gammon screen mean

fuck all. Mob or no mob, anyone touches a hair on Ellen's head they'll have sixteen different kinds of shit coming down on em from me. So you go on your retreat, darling. I've got your back.'

Jo's heart swelled for a love that stood alongside her, near as fierce and protective of Ellen as her own. She wasn't alone now after all, it seemed, in keeping Ellen from a world of hate and harm. She leant over and kissed Twoboy square on the mouth, her eyes bright.

'Course, if I'm wrong, you'll have to come and bail me outta lockup. If you can *get* bail for triple homicide,' he added with a twisted grin.

'You might have to bail *me* out, pal,' Jo said, talking tough to keep down the whimpering puppy that had taken up residence in her stomach. 'I can hold me own.'

Twoboy laughed and put his hands back on the leather-covered steering wheel.

'Funny sort of Buddhist you're gonna make,' he observed, as he pulled back into the stream of traffic headed north. He took his phone and surreptitiously turned it off. The text Jo had read aloud was the fifth that day from Oscar Bullockhead, and the least vicious of the lot.

Jo wheeled her council barrow past the rainforest grove, where the leaf mould was building up nicely into a thick layer of rich pungent mulch, providing homes for beetles and bugs galore. The cemetery's resident brush turkey paused in its scratching as she passed. Its brilliant red, black and yellow colouring always struck Jo as unnecessarily lairy, the bird constantly dressed for a land rights demo. There was some purpose to it, she supposed, some natural selection that meant bright primary colours were the order of the day. What was the proper word for turkey? *Kalwun*. No, that was lyrebird. It was something like that though . . . Jo stood and puzzled for the missing word a few moments longer, before admitting defeat. Ah, fuck it.

Jingawahlu turkey.

Things could have more than one name. Things could have lots of names.

On the far side of the clustered jali jali quandong and bungwall, Jo reached the dead gum branches that she had earmarked for firewood earlier in the week. She eyed the mother gum they'd fallen from to see if another heavy branch was about to come down and crack her on the skull while she worked. Assessing that she was safe, Jo slipped her earplugs in, chainsawed the fallen branches into manageable lengths and then stacked the barrow high with enough timber for this week's cooking fires. With a sweat sheen on her face and arms despite the coolness of the day, she manoeuvred her wobbly load back towards the storeroom. She stacked the wood in the ute, then upended the barrow inside the storeroom, handles resting against the wall to save space, and cleaned the chainsaw, before flicking the kettle on and performing the increasingly useless ritual of ringing Trev.

'Any luck with that part yet, mate?' she asked, trying hard to keep a note of optimism in her voice. A weary chuckle was her reply.

'Try me again next week,' he advised her. 'The Honda rep's gone on long service leave now and there's a new one coming on Monday.'

Jo shook her head in amazement, rang off and gazed out the window that was fogging with condensation from the kettle. Muffler or not, the hill still needed mowing – the hill would always need mowing, it was a given, she was Sisyphus with earmuffs – so after lunch she would fire up the trusty Hondaroonie, hope that the neighbours could stand the racket once again and that industrial deafness wouldn't blight her old age, should she live so long. Jo made a cuppa and took it outside to the narrow wooden bench beneath the Piccabeen palms – *jali jali Piccabeen*. She opened the zen book Therese had pressed on her the other day. The ideas of the teacher were interesting, but playing insistently through Jo's mind as she read was the clear bright memory of Twoboy kissing the back of her neck as she got dressed for work that morning, his hands reaching up beneath her t-shirt to clasp her breasts, and gently insisting that she come back to bed, the warm, warm deliciousness of early morning bed, just for a little while.

Jo smiled and touched her neck, remembering. Sometimes she didn't mind being late for work.

'You coming?' Jo stood in the doorway, offering a beanie. Outside was another fabulous royal-blue day of sunshine and birdsong, and she wanted to make sure the wood box was stocked to overflowing for the freezing nights that were about to hit.

'Gimme a couple more minutes,' Twoboy answered, deep in the AIATSIS catalogue.

Jo sighed. She knew full well what a wild-goose chase he was on. Twoboy had recently rediscovered the precious recordings of an old great-great-uncle from Piccabeen and was painstakingly cross-indexing them against the brief wordlist his mother's father had left behind. Piccabeen was a bloody long way from Tin Wagon Road, true, but linguistic clues travelled far. There were words on Brisbane street maps that Goories still used every day, and a clutch of terms like *binna* and *jinung* had currency across the entire east coast. Twoboy had been told by the lawyers that he had to piece together the cultural jigsaw that had been exploded by his family's diaspora, or else accept defeat. The court wasn't interested in the gaps, only in the complete picture: songs, sites, family trees, language, ceremony. Especially songs. His case had to be watertight, strong enough to counter the automatic power that Oscar had, just from being born here and living on Bundjalung country all his fat, corrupt, deceitful life, without actually contributing anything of worth to the culture or to the Goories he claimed to lead.

'There's months of work in these bloody language lists,' Twoboy said. 'I dunno when I'm supposed to get to the Native Police records in Sydney and see if Grandad's name's there.' He raked through his dreads with his hands, scratching at his scalp in frustration.

'Well, I'm done waiting.' Jo tossed the beanie on the desk beside the computer. 'If you want us, we'll be outside, actually *working* on our country insteada *reading* about it.'

The back door banged, not quite a slam, but not far off it either. Twoboy rolled his eyes at the sound, and stayed put. He played the uncle's recorded language clips over and over, finding and comparing his transitive verbs with the murky pencilled phrases left to him in his grandfather's unschooled hand.

An hour later, Jo stood beneath the giant tallowwood holding a heavy armful of powdery-barked branches, hoping that a huntsman spider wasn't about to crawl out and start exploring her face. She staggered forward a few steps, toppled the timber into the almost-full ute, and then slapped its side twice to tell Ellen to drive on. Her daughter carefully put the car into first gear, and then kangaroo hopped over toward the beehives in the dip.

'Watch out for the bees, eh,' Jo called in alarm, imagining the mayhem if Ellen ploughed into the twenty white boxes and their savage inhabitants. The kid had only been driving the paddocks for a little while, and at nearly fourteen had as much immunity to advice on this as any other topic.

'Yeah, yeah . . .'

'One word from you and she does anything she likes, eh?' Twoboy said, appearing beside Jo, in jeans, flannie and his green woollen jumper, looking like he'd stepped out of a men's magazine.

Jo merely grunted, heading for the next lot of branches. Ellen might drive her up the wall, but nobody else was allowed to criticise her, or even to notice her flaws. The first rule of parenthood. Especially when it was her, Ellen and Therese doing all the hard yakka of harvesting wood, while Twoboy bludged on the internet, pretending to do Native Title research all afternoon when he was probably fucking around on Facebook. She stopped and toed the soft ground beneath the tallow, which was dotted with evidence of overnight digging.

'The bloody bandicoots are still going for it,' she said, changing the subject. 'You'd think the dogs'd keep em away.'

'I'll come out tonight and catch a couple for the pot, if you like,' offered Twoboy.

Jo swung around in surprise. Unlike the roos that came down regularly out of the scrub, she'd never thought of the bandicoots as food.

'You eat em?' she asked, taken aback.

'Yeah. We used to trap em in Karawatha Forest as kids. Wallaby and roof rabbit, too. What?'

'I assumed hunting bush tucker only happens, well, in the bush.'

'You assume a lot of things,' Twoboy said under his breath.

'Oh yeah, well, life's short, hey?' Jo flared. 'It saves time.'

'Not if you're wrong, it don't.'

Twoboy bent and easily picked up a large log that had been sawed years ago by some long-departed farm worker. He shouldered the timber, as Jo savagely hurled a smaller branch in the direction of the ute, now parked twenty metres away beside the camphors. Her branch fell far short; Ellen clapped sarcastically at the fail. Jo glared, showed her a lone middle finger and gestured for her to pick it up.

'Who's wrong?' asked Therese, coming up from behind them with an arm full of kindling.

'Oh, just me again, same as usual,' said Jo, still insulted. She snapped a sizable tallow branch across her left thigh and stood holding the two halves like waddies. Therese raised her eyebrows.

'So what else do I 'assume' then?' Jo asked Twoboy testily. 'Come on.'

Twoboy looked at Therese, weighing up whether or not to engage with Jo in public.

'Ah, forget it,' he muttered.

'No,' Jo insisted. 'Let's have it.'

Twoboy licked his lips and, with the heavy log balancing on his right shoulder, began counting off his left hand.

'One, you assume that I'm much like every other bloke you've met – that I only ever think with my dick,' he said bluntly. 'Two, you assume you know what the court case means to me and Mum and Laz, when you clearly don't. And three, I'm pretty bloody sure you assume that I'm gonna do the wrong thing by you, and run away just as soon as I've had my fun or won the case, whichever comes first. Shall I go on?'

Discomfited, Therese wandered away to where Ellen was gathering fallen sticks and making a game of trying to toss them unseen over her shoulder into the ute tray.

Watching Therese walk past the bees and join in Ellen's game, Jo felt winded by the man's sudden harsh commentary, not least because it was true. On some level she did expect betrayal, heartbreak and agony. Not because her lover was Twoboy, but because he was alive, and that's what living people – men, mainly – did in this world. They used you up, hurt you, took your trust and affection and betrayed you. And if they didn't, then you did it to them, often automatically, without even meaning to. Her divorce had taught her that.

But what did he mean about Native Title?

'Land means everything,' she told him. 'And how can anything mean more than everything? It means a home you can't be kicked off of. A chance for a decent life on your own country, for you and your kids.'

Twoboy gazed at her implacably and didn't answer.

'We're still here,' Ellen cried from the beehives. 'What's the hold up?'

'Wait up!' Jo yelled, as she stared back at Twoboy, standing there in his green jumper and black jeans, dreads hanging down over his shoulders and the steadily rising wind making the yellow cockatoo feathers in his hair dance a merry jig. Irritation rose in her chest at this silent interrogation. Was he playing at being a Big Man, making out there were mysteries and cultural secrets where none existed? Well, fuck him if he thought he was blacker than she was. She knew plenty of lingo, more than he did. She knew some Law too. And just as important, she really knew the country she lived and worked on. Knew it in her nostrils and in her bones, knew the feel of it under her feet seven days a week – unlike Twoboy who lived behind the wheel of the Commode, forever driving the hundred kays between Tin Wagon Road and Woodridge.

'So tell me what it means then. *Educate* me,' she taunted, ignoring the long-distance death stares she was getting from Ellen.

164

'Do you really want to know?' Twoboy asked, shifting the dead weight of the log to his left shoulder. 'Or do you just feel like having an argument, and this'll do?'

'Yes, I want to know!' Jo retorted. Christ. She stuck her hands in her armpits to guard against the chill wind. Too early this year, it couldn't wait for August to start blowing them all into their beds with double pneumonia.

Twoboy put his log down and came closer. He turned Jo around by the shoulders to face Bottlebrush Hill, put his face next to hers and pointed. High above them, the big tallowwood swayed and moaned, buffeted by gusts of wind, as the surface of the dam rippled suddenly with tiny whitecaps. When her man whispered his heart, Jo had to lean in even closer to hear it. Twoboy's gaze was fixed on Bottlebrush and the enormous trees which decorated its peak.

'Look at that hill. I dunno for sure, but I reckon Mum's old people, a lotta our old people, gotta be buried up there. And for close on two centuries now they've had to watch the dugai come in to this valley. Had to watch em cut down cedars and gums that were as thick around as six men's arms. Watch em run their horrible bloody fences over our songlines. Old Goorie law men and old Goorie law women been sitting up on that hill, dead, while the fucken cattle dip leached poison into their creek, year after year after year. Birds dying, jalum dying. Nothing them old people could do, for two hundred years, but wait for us boys to be born now, in a time when there's a chance. The tiniest chance, the tiniest little crack in the dugai law, to get a little bit of it back, and look after our budheram jagan. Heal it. Sing it. And maybe then our old people might rest easy for once. *That's* what the court case is about.'

Jo shivered, and told herself it was from the cold.

'And when we win it back –' Twoboy paused, maybe frightened to fully speak his dream aloud in case he cruelled it – 'then them old people might show us what we've lost.'

Jo reached down to the ground and pulled out one of the yellow-flowering fireweeds that dotted her paddocks. It fluttered in her hand, whipped by the wind that was tearing up the gully now. Almost everything had been lost when the dugai arrived with their guns and their axes. Which part was he talking about?

She shook loose earth off the roots of the fireweed and then tossed it aside; once dessicated by the sun and wind, the weed would quickly rot and turn into soil again. Jo was about to ask Twoboy exactly what he meant – when, with a great and sudden tearing the tallowwood, let a branch drop.

It fell lethally fast, right beside Ellen, and smashed open the closest beehive. A cloud of furious buzzing insects emerged, looking for their enemy. Ellen shrieked with her hand to her mouth, and Therese took two large unthinking leaps backwards. The tallowood groaned loudly in the wind, threatening to drop more branches.

'Holy Jesus!' Jo screamed, her feet glued in place with terror – 'Ellen!'

Twoboy ran to the girl, seized her forearm and pulled her from the drop zone, yelling at Jo to get the fuck away from the tree.

Then they bolted to the farmhouse.

With the windows firmly shut against furious bees, and cups of hot coffee in hand, they were free to imagine What If.

That night Jo made Ellen's favourite dinner, spag bol, and booted Twoboy off the computer so that the kid could have an extra half-hour on Facebook.

'If I'd lost you today,' Jo told Ellen with a rib-crunching hug, 'I wouldn't have known whether to shit or go blind, girl.'

'I love you too, Mum,' Ellen replied. Then, 'Can I get a puppy for my birthday?'

'Absolutely not.'

'A tattoo then?'

Jo peered into her daugher's face. The child was serious.

'In your dreams.'

NJANJARGALI

LIES

Chapter Ten

Winter wattle made a sensational necklace for the roads as Jo and Therese headed down the highway. Fragrant balls of blossom exploded in lemon and buttercup yellow and gold everywhere she looked, and ten thousand daw poorfellas were no doubt sneezing miserably into their indoor hankies. And ah, look. Mulanyin there, fishing for taran in the drain next to the Ocean Shores entry gates, while the traffic thundered past three metres away. Budgeree jahlela, mulanyin, good eating to you, my bird. Wish I was gonna spend the day jalum bira like you.

Therese was cheerfully gabby as she negotiated the Writers' Festival traffic, dodging a Sunnybrand truck filled with doomed chickens, and accelerating fast past a retro Kombi complete with a faded *Wilderness not Woodchips* sticker from 1987. Just how, Jo wondered idly, did Therese intend to spend a whole weekend in silence? And if there was a direct correlation between silence and enlightenment, why wasn't she herself already topped with a shining silver halo? She, who worked with the dead and lived with a monosyllabic teenager. If it wasn't for Twoboy, and his nightly phone calls when he was in Brisbane, Jo reflected, she could easily go days on end without a proper conversation. Warrigal and Daisy didn't count, not really. There's only so much you can communicate using ears and a tail.

'Don't worry,' Therese reassured her after an exhaustive rundown of what to expect on the retreat, 'if in doubt, just copy what everybody else does.'

'If you say so.' Jo cast a wistful glance at the river as they drove south through the Bruns roundabout. It was perfect weather for chucking a line in. Just her dumb luck that she'd agreed to sit inside a bloody hut with a bunch of white hippies for two entire days while the sun shone from a cloudless sky. A person must be womba, out of her tiny fucking brain. But then, as Therese had said, it was only one weekend out of a lifetime. And once it was over she would have the power, simply by lifting a cautionary forefinger, to shut Therese up on the subject of Buddhism, meditation and any other improving *modality* she felt Jo was in dire need of, ever again. That'd be worth something, Jo thought with dark satisfaction. That would be worth quite a lot. She picked up an *Echo* from beneath her feet and began leafing through it.

'That man of yours getting anywhere with his research?' Therese asked, turning into Bruns to pick up supplies. She slowed a little as they drew level with the poor womba woman who was always to be found with her thumb out, travelling between Mullum and the Bruns convenience store, continually disappointing the tourists who, in a fit of holiday-induced generosity, would stop to give her a lift, only to be met with grunts or paranoid silence.

'Oh, no, not today!' Jo hastily told Therese, and they sped up again, passing as they did young Sam Nurrung. The dark teenager was standing as proud and as straight-backed as his grandmother, thumbing a ride in the opposite direction. That jahjam likes to get around, reflected Jo. I bet he can't wait till he's old enough to get a set of wheels and hoon around like the rest of the kids.

'Yes and no. They found the exemption records online. But it's hard evidence about Great-grandad Tommy being taken away he needs. Everything else is just hearsay – his grandfather's stories about Bottlebrush, and their totems and all that. The tribunal wants to see stuff written down, not just oral history . . . and then the family trees are all so bloody complicated. When you count the northern lot, there's five John Jacksons in the last three generations alone – try sorting that lot out. Sometimes I think every blackfella in Australia is related.'

'You sure you and him aren't first cousins?' Therese asked, suddenly dubious. Jo laughed, insulted. Christ Jesus. That much at least they'd been able to work out. There'll be no raising iguanas for me, thankyou kindly.

'So no two-headed babies coming along anytime soon?' joked Therese.

'No babies of any sort, thanks. Especially not with twins in his family,' Jo answered, as if the temptation to make beautiful black babies with Twoboy had never crossed her mind.

She fell silent as they drew closer to Byron and its tourist traffic. Getting pregnant. Now, that really would be the last move, welding herself to the Jackson clan and their battle. *Exactly* what she'd warned Therese against all those months ago. She was already waist deep in the big muddy, anyway, just being with Twoboy. Last Wednesday in Mullum, Sally Watt had walked out of the council building flanked by Basho and a bunch of other bureaucrats. Horrified, Jo had been forced to flee into the library to avoid an embarassing encounter with the gracious old lady. And for all Jo knew her own name was now on the same hit list as Twoboy's in the eyes of Uncle Oscar, who had never been known to be gracious to anyone in his corrupt and contemptuous life.

She frowned and rubbed the back of her skull with her knuckles. Just because you're paranoid doesn't mean they aren't after you.

'What's up?' Therese glanced over at her.

'Native Title. Years of hard yakka and fuck all at the end of it, except a community in ruins. It's really ramping up with the Bullockheads. And it's all such bullshit.' Jo paused, and the image came to her of Humbug haunting the Dolphin Cafe that day in May, begging for his supper really, even though Uncle spun it, made it all seem like a bit of a lark. How many times a week did he go to sleep hungry? She grimaced. Native Title wasn't going to fill that old brown belly anytime soon.

'I mean take Uncle Humbug,' she said to Therese, 'he must have a Native Title claim to *somewhere*. But I can't see him fronting any tribunal, can you? He's flat out getting over to Bi-Lo on pension day.'

Therese chewed on this for a minute.

'What's Twoboy say?'

'He reckons Humbug's just another jumped-up southerner like Oscar. Not to mention having a few dozen roos loose in the top paddock, which isn't really debatable. Doesn't mean he should be left starving in the bloody park though, does it?' Jo replied.

The picture of Humbug cold and hungry nagged at Jo like a toothache. It prompted her to describe a vision she had recently developed of Tin Wagon Road: the farm with five or six houses dotted on it instead of just one, and an Aboriginal family living well in every building, thriving, healthy, prosperous.

Therese whistled. 'A nice dream, but it's pretty different to how you live now,' she pointed out. 'Like a hermit.'

Jo nodded, growing enthused.

'But that's the difference, see. It's my place, so I can do what I like on it . . . Twoboy gets proper cranky sometimes, cos he's got so much riding on the court case and I don't.'

'I can understand him being jealous of the farm,' Therese concluded. 'And here we are.' She pulled up the steep driveway of the Buddhist retreat, where huge gums framed a stunning view of Suffolk Park and Seven Mile Beach.

Jo fell silent as she reflected on how Therese's view of the world never quite matched her own. They'd been friends forever, since grade four at Billinudgel Primary, but still Therese managed constantly to fractionally misunderstand her. She sighed.

'He's not *jealous* – Native Title isn't about acreage. It's . . .' Jo struggled for the words to make Therese understand. 'It's about honour, I suppose. If he's recognised as a traditional owner, then he's a warrior who's finally made things better for his family, a tiny bit. It's about winnng a war that nobody even talked about for two hundred years,' Jo added as they got out of the car. 'And its about never giving up, *never*, no matter what.'

★

Jo was woken early on Sunday morning by a strange rattly annoyance that she didn't recognise. Were tiny elves banging on the leadlight windows of her Sangsurya cabin? She yawned and realised that she had slept through the optional six a.m. yoga that was added to the six hours of daily meditation the retreat required. No great loss there. She yawned again, then realised that for the first time in months, she had slept past dawn. Taken aback, Jo lay looking at the ceiling. Her limbs were relaxed, and her back had mysteriously lost its ache. Yesterday afternoon, during the fourth hour of sitting still and following the flow of her breath in and out, even her neck had softened. *Shit*, Jo frowned, *Therese was bloody right, the bag!* Irritated and amused in equal portions, she hauled herself out of bed and into the shower. As she dressed, she discovered that the unfamiliar tapping was the sound of fairy-wrens manically attacking their own reflections in the leadlight glass of the window above her bed. Mad little buggers, Jo thought with a shake of her head, feeling like she understood them only too well.

After breakfast, Jo joined the others in the zendo for that morning's dharma talk. Sitting on cushions along with the three dozen students, she listened as the teacher, Libby, expounded upon the causes of suffering. The possibility of an end to suffering. The illusory nature of reality, and of the self. Greed, Anger, Delusion: the causes of all our petty woes. All very well, she had commented to herself on Friday night, if you live in Paddington on macrobiotic tofu and organic beetroot juice, but not if you live on Tin Wagon Road with Oscar Bullockhead threatening to cave your boyfriend's head in any old tick of the clock.

When the first set of instructions had been given to the beginners on Saturday, it was all Jo could do to stop from busting out in cynical laughter. Sit comfortably, try not to move, and follow your breath. Or, if you prefer, concentrate on another sense – on what you're hearing, for example, or on what your body is physically touching. Jo had always imagined Buddhist meditation to be about breathing.

'It's dadirri!' she had insisted to Therese in the cabin later that night. 'It's exactly what blackfellas have been doing here for thousands and thousands of years – sitting still and listening to the world. The exact same thing. I've been meditating all my life, fuck ya!'

Therese had merely smiled and raised a finger to her lips to remind Jo that it was a totally silent retreat.

By midday Saturday, Jo had begun to re-evaluate. Sitting inside a hall on a beautiful May day was still middle class hippy crap, but perhaps, she reflected reluctantly over lunch, Libby did have some things to say that were worth hearing. But Jo grew impatient with the silence, burbling with unexpressed ideas; she itched to grill both Therese and Libby. Late on Saturday as she finished her sixth painful hour of cross-legged sitting, it had dawned on her why Libby had such familiar eyes. Their depth and their expression, for all that they were in Libby's dugai face inside a Japanese zendo at a Sufi-styled retreat, were familiar from Jo's childhood. They were, she marvelled, Aunty Barb's eyes set in a stranger's face. It had taken her six hours of sitting perfectly still to see it.

'So what's the verdict, luvvy?' Therese asked as they packed their bags on Sunday afternoon.

'There's a lot to it,' Jo admitted, swinging her bag onto her shoulder. 'But basically it's just what Goories have been doing since the year dot.'

Therese smirked.

'I knew you'd like it. Not that I reckon you mob were necessarily talking about greed, anger and delusion, back in the day.'

'I didn't say I – ouch!' Jo lifted her right foot from the floor in sudden sharp pain. 'What the hell?'

Therese apologised, and bent to show Jo what she had stepped on. It was a bird's nest that she had found in the bush outside.

Jo took the nest in her hands and marvelled. The outer layer was made entirely from old and rusted strands of barbed wire. Inside, the nest had been carefully lined with feathers, and with grey and white down that some long-dead bird had donated for the comfort of her chicks. Talk about resilience, Jo thought, as she turned the singular object around in her hands. She imagined a mother magpie bringing the strands of fence wire to a fork in a gum tree, and twisting them with her beak into a suitable place to lay her eggs.

'That's wild, eh,' Jo said softly in wonder. 'You should give it to the Sangsurya mob.'

'I offered it to them,' Therese said, 'but they told me to keep it. And it was on the ground, so the bird's not using it anymore.' She placed the nest very carefully in the top of her rucksack and zipped it inside.

It was not until they were zooming up the highway, almost back at South Golden, that Jo realised: this beautiful nest and the fence which had killed Comet were made of the same stuff. She blinked. Maybe her grief was lifting. Maybe she was starting on the way back to herself.

Humbug regarded Pete the Snakeman, and Pete the Snakeman regarded Humbug, and nothing at all passed between them. Humbug felt his lifelong sense of burning grievance double and then double again. The old story was repeating itself: a trespasser standing uninvited upon *his* land. And not content with that, the dugai world had now seen fit to add insult to injury, to deliberately send this gammon imposter – a white man who thought he knew snakes, the very idea was laughable – to evict him and his brother from where they had lately taken up residence at the RSL memorial.

Pete the Snakeman shrugged.

'Sorry, mate, just doing me job. Normal people don't want snakes in the middle of town.' Pete turned away and added under his breath, 'Or dirty old abos either.' He retrieved from his truck a long wire lasso, specially designed for extricating dangerous creatures from places they were feared or unwanted.

Humbug fumed. Until now, the Mullum RSL memorial flame had been an ideal spot from which to extract his rightful tithes from the community. The neighbourhood centre was right there next door, a handy source of hot meals, cuppas and sympathetic female attention. Public toilets no more than twenty steps away. And the razzle-dazzle itself across the road. The club was, naturally, unavailable to him with his black face, his ragged attire, and his lack of ready cash, but as a veteran Humbug found some contrary solace in the building nevertheless. And he'd discoverd it took surprisingly little effort, in the late afternoons, to walk to the park beside the river and find enough dry palm fronds to turn the symbolic memorial flame into a real, substantial fire capable of warming himself, Slim and a tribe of motley hangers-on through the length of a chill August night.

Overshadowing all these pragmatic attractions, though, was the symbolism of the war memorial. It marked a sacred site – sacred enough that even the dugai (universally milbong and binung goonj as they were) could see it, and had gone to the trouble of solidifying the fact in white marble. Humbug well recalled his most recent release from the hospital a week ago. He'd walked the length of town in search of a lift home to Bruns. Upon reaching the RSL, he had stood in front of the low chain separating the marble monument and its flame from Dalley Street. Inscribed in the dignity of bronze he had observed the legend:

**Sacred Site
Please do not sit here.**

Humbug had never learned to decode the white man's writing, but he could recognise a snake track when he saw one. Since he was of the snake totem, and Slim was, of course, a python, Humbug felt that his path was clear. Slim took a little convincing to shift home so abruptly, but Humbug had patiently sat and explained the merits of the move until his brother finally agreed to give it a try. They had hitched up from Bruns the same afternoon.

But now, this dugai. Standing here with his van and his noose. This new and intolerable outrage.

'You can't pucken touch my brother!' Humbug instructed Pete

the Snakeman hotly. His angry brown forefinger jabbed the air between them like a fang.

'Can and will. It's me job, mate. Now hop it will ya?'

'This is a *sacred site*,' Humbug insisted, as though to an obtuse child. 'Ya got no pucken business here!'

Pete the Snakeman adjusted his lasso. He moved closer to where Slim was coiled asleep in the sun at the rear of the marble monument.

'It's a sacred site for the bloody RSL, mate, not your lot. What war were you in, again?'

Humbug smiled a humourless smile that didn't reach his eyes, and allowed the contempt he felt for this imposter to show on his lips. The fool didn't realise he had been born into war. If Australia had a sole surviving battler, he was it. Humbug's mother before him had lived her entire life warring with the welfare which took seven babies off her, distributing them, apparently at random, to orphanages and foster homes throughout the land. His father's campaign against the mission superintendent and the tame blacks who did his bidding had consumed the man day and night until it killed him of sheer rage at the age of fifty-three. Humbug, stolen from his mother's arms in the hospital – or no, not *in* the hospital, out the back of the hospital in a dirty lean-to on a pile of stained chaff bags – taken from his distraught mother and gifted to the nuns down south, had likewise been at war for every single one of his forty-nine years. And now this cheeky dugai, standing there with a wire rope to twist around his brother's neck, ready and all too willing to effect another removal, wanted to know what war he'd been in?

Well.

'This one,' cried Humbug, shattering the Snakeman's nose with his hard right fist.

Outside the courthouse, Sergeant Adams stiffened, and headed for the memorial, unhooking his handcuffs. The old darkie, making trouble again. It was about time he had a tune-up.

★

When Jo arrived home from Sangsurya, Ellen and Twoboy were waiting for her in the kitchen. Ellen thrust an entry form for the art competition at her. Pleased, Jo quickly scrawled her assent on the dotted line. Art is good. We like art, for our kids and for everybody else. Then Ellen handed her a large white envelope.

'What's this?' Jo asked suspiciously, fearing some unexpected bill. Creation was good for the soul, but was she going to have to fork out for oil paints, or expensive hog-bristle brushes, or . . .

'A present.' Ellen had that brittle look on her face again. Craving approval, but ready at the drop of a hat to back away into the refuges of sarcasm and anger. Her daughter reminded Jo of the turtles that sunned themselves on the rocks in the Bangalow Creek; tentatively poking their heads out, but hard shells always at the ready if trouble should arrive.

'A *present?*'

Jo glanced over at Twoboy, who was waiting with an expectant grin for her to open the envelope. Her mouth fell open as she took out a fine ink sketch of Comet grazing beneath the distant lychee trees. Across the bottom of the drawing Ellen had written: *Comet Breen. RIP.* Jo's heart clenched tight with pain and with love. She hugged Ellen tightly to her as she told her that she loved the picture, raising her eyebrows at Twoboy over the child's shoulder.

'I dunno what you said or did to her,' she told him before releasing Ellen, 'but whatever it was, keep it up.'

'You underestimate that girl, you know,'Twoboy answered mildly.

'How about we paint the ute when Aunty Kym gets here?' Jo added as she threw a packet of frozen snags into the microwave, noting that the dogs were almost out of dry food. 'She might have some good designs. And some paint too, for that matter.' They had discussed turning the old bomb into an art car many times, but it just never seemed to happen. 'And you could talk to her about the competition, too, see if she's got any ideas.'

Ellen shot her mother a withering glance. She went to her room and when she returned a couple of minutes later, she silently handed over a large sketchpad. Jo took it in two-handed amazement. Ellen had never volunteered to show her sketchpad to anyone, ever. Something was shifting inside the child for this to happen. Jo smiled, grateful for this tiny, unheralded step into Ellen's world, as the microwave dinged behind her to say the snags were defrosted.

When she opened the sketchpad, Jo discovered a term's work that made her catch her breath and sink slowly onto a kitchen chair. Ochre handprints emerged from flying clouds of dust that suddenly became the eyes of an eagle looking down from the peak of Bottlebrush. The Milky Way – Emu in clear view – soared above a winding river of diamonds which mirrored it in the valley below. And a pencil drawing of a decayed red quandong leaf – its ribs remaining after it had been eaten out by miniscule snails (exactly as Jo had seen them lying on the banks of Stoney Creek) – which rested at the base of a grove of walking stick palms festooned with bright red berries.

Jo was lost for words. The drawings weren't just technically excellent. The kid had infused them with a real knowledge of country, and a vision that went way beyond thirteen. A shine of delight entered Ellen's eyes as Jo sat transfixed.

'Who taught you this?' she finally breathed.

'Different people. Aunty Kym mainly. What I've seen in shops. Twoboy. And DJ taught an art class at school this term. I have got eyes and ears, you know,' Ellen added slyly, 'mil *and* binung.'

'Told ya.' Twoboy ruffled Ellen's hair affectionately.

'Huh.' Jo rifled through the rest of the sketchbook, discovering that almost everything in it looked gallery quality to her. Had anyone spoken to Ellen about selling her work, she wondered, about being a professional?

'I don't mind painting the ute with Aunty Kym,' Ellen told Jo with haughty teenage dignity, 'but I don't want any help winning that prize.'

'I don't think you *need* any help,' Jo replied. 'These are really, really good. How deadly are you?' She looked up at Ellen, her dark hair falling around a pale heart-shaped face, her green eyes dancing with pleasure. *My daughter, the artist.*

'Yeah, I know, eh?' said Ellen, taking the sketchpad back and grinning.

Jo fed Aunty Barb's fishing rod backwards through the rear window of the Commode and into Chris's waiting hands. Then she hopped in the front and slapped her thighs. 'Hey-ho, let's cruise, the bream and luderick can't wait to jump on me hook today,' she said, thinking that when the moon rose over the hill tonight it would be round and fat and full. 'This arvo is gonna be my lucky day.'

'If them jalum hear you skiting,' Chris chastised the back of Jo's head, 'they'll be long gorn, yanbillilla to Tweed by the time we get there.'

Behind the wheel Twoboy offered no opinions on fishing or anything else. His mind was overflowing with tribunal depositions, State Library files, and the unwelcome lawyerly advice, offered two days ago, that their paperwork was still far too weak, lacking in hard evidence of who Grandad Tommy was or why he had left the area, let alone that his 'cultural ties and traditions' had been maintained by his descendants. As he drove past Devine's Hill into Bruns, Twoboy looked through jaundiced eyes at the country that seemed to be slipping, slowly but inevitably, from his grasp.

Clutching frozen bait and iced coffees from the Caltex, the troupe drove back over the bridge. They turned onto a narrow bush track that ended in a clearing where a small rocky peninsula jutted into the river. The three Goories got out and immediately fanned away from the car, making a slow careful circuit of the open space, gathering up the ugliness of crumpled tin cans, dirty plastic bags and loose tangles of fishing line that others had left behind to strangle the pelicans and choke the turtles. When the country had been appeased and the offenses of these nameless others amended, the time was right for jalum bira.

180

In clear view on the opposite shore, a scattering of fishermen stood next to the Co-op, reeling in and casting out in states that ranged from exaltation to misery. Most were ragged flanny-wearing pensioners from the caravan park trying to supplement their meagre government pay, but a late model Prado had disgorged a cheerful family of tourists who, Chris muttered, couldn't have caught a fish if it leapt out of the river, Free Willy style, into their waiting arms. The tourists had come well prepared in their Gap t-shirts and red tab Levis, and had brought along, for good measure, a barking beige Labrador with a comical plastic funnel around its head.

'That warrigal be picking up SBS over there, la,' noted Chris in quiet amusement.

Jo sputtered with laughter as she watched the animal take its lampshade head over and piss surreptitiously against the tourists' own esky.

The Prados stumbled about, unfolding their camping chairs, dropping brand-new handlines into the cracks between the rocks, and generally making enough noise to scare half the fish in New South Wales over the border. In a dead gum behind Twoboy, the resident brahminy kite waited for the right moment to swoop down, cross the river, and steal the Prado's bait while they weren't paying attention. Twoboy simply stared momentarily across the water at the dugai, then stalked away towards the oyster sheds, shaking his head. Colonised by wankers.

Suddenly a whoop made Jo swivel around. Upriver, Simmo, a Wiradjuri whose boy was in Ellen's grade, was steadily winding in something heavy that was fighting for its life and making her frizzy blonde halo shake with effort. Every eye on the riverbank was soon fixed on Simmo's curved green rod and the outstanding tendons of her skinny pale wrists. Her freckled face split wide open in a massive grin when a monster flattie rose to break the surface. Brilliant drops of saltwater flew as the fish twisted and writhed in the air, flashing silver. From downriver the Prado kids broke into spontaneous applause.

'Ooh, yes, my favourite!' Simmo expertly deposited the fish on the grassy river edge in triumph.

Jo called out in admiration, and discovered that Simmo was using prawns and long shank hooks, not squid and round hooks.

'But you'll pick up a nice bream with that tackle,' Simmo advised, packing up to take her trophy home for tea.

Jo strolled over to where Twoboy was baiting a handline, as far as he could get from the sight of the Prados and the other dugai fishers. Normally he would have burleyed the water first with a pointed rock, but he wasn't about to do that with every bastard in northern NSW looking on, albeit from the other side of the channel. And what Jo was doing taking advice from whitefellas on how to hunt in her own country, he couldn't fathom at all.

'Nice big flattie she got,' Jo reported.

Twoboy grunted, stood up, and made a whirring circle overhead with his line, letting it soar out till it nearly reached the small island opposite. The line fell with a satisfying plonk into the deep water where Jo remembered the sea turtles of her childhood swimming. She wondered if they still swam there. She had an idea that turtles were very long-lived. Strange to think that while she'd been travelling the continent, living far away in Brisbane and Sydney and other points north and west, the turtles she'd watched as a kid might have stayed in the same few square miles of water for decades, feeling the same currents on their leathery skins, avoiding the same sharks, eating at the same haunts. The animals, Jo reflected, they're the ones who know the country more than any of us ever will. They have no rights and yet all the deep, deep knowledge is written in their muscles and their bones. She stood watching the channel for a long time, but no turtles appeared to greet her.

With her line in the water, she eventually settled down on the flattest boulder she could find. The salt smell of the river filled her nostrils, and the afternoon sun warmed her head and shoulders. She became lost in a lasting reverie, that was only interrupted by the occasional nibble, and by Chris's success in hauling in three bream.

As the tide turned and the bites became more frequent, Twoboy's dark mood lightened. Finally he cracked open a fresh stubby of Gold, and began to yarn.

'Laz was over at the archives the other week . . .' he was telling the women by late afternoon, retrieving his line for the umpteenth time to rebait it. He shook the last piece of squid out and carefully folded the empty plastic bag into his jeans pocket.

'Yeah?' Jo encouraged, dangling her feet in the cold river water. She was bored with fishing now, lacking Chris's patience or Twoboy's killer instinct that kept them keen well into the third and fourth hours of the line-wetting.

Twoboy gave a twisted grin as he cast one last time in the wake of a passing kayaker who was headed up the inlet towards Simpson's Creek.

'He was reading about the Straddie mob, just in case something turned up about Grandad in their records,' he said. 'And – oh, true-god I laughed when he told me, eh – he found this letter in the file from Thomas Welsby –'

'Early white naturalist,' Jo chimed in for Chris's benefit, as she jigged her line and hoped to make the squid on it look alive. She wondered what Laz had stumbled across; she hadn't heard this tale before. Maybe Twoboy had been saving it for an audience. He certainly seemed pleased with himself as he told it now.

'Laz shoulda been looking for the Chief Protector reports on the Native Police, but he got sidetracked, as you do. He found this letter that Welsby wrote to the governor, complaining about the conditions on the island. Poor bloody Noonuccals, the government dumped all sorts at Dunwich back then, womba ones, lepers, murderers, you name it. And they set up the missions there, too, as if the Goories didn't have enough to worry about. So Welsby goes and writes this letter complaining that the kanakas over there were all getting around the mission holding these Christmas cards –'

Twoboy shook with fresh laughter. The two women grinned expectantly.

'– holding these Christmas cards that they'd bought off the

missionary for five shillings each – the poor bastards thought they were buying tickets into heaven!' Twoboy exploded with mirth, rocking back and forth on his boulder, dreads bouncing. Jo locked eyes with Chris, who raised her eyebrows, shook her head and looked away.

'That's not funny,' Jo retorted. 'That's fucked.'

'Five shillings,' Twoboy howled with tears rolling down his face, 'for Christmas cards!'

'You're a horrible person,' Chris told him with a sudden upward jag of her line as she felt a nibble. 'Would you be laughing if they were Noonuccals?'

'Well, they *weren't* Noonuccals,' Twoboy argued, wiping his eyes, 'Just a bunch of myall kanakas buying their tickets for heaven!' He exploded sideways again, and had to put his line down or drop it in the river.

'Can you even *talk* like that?' Jo asked, for there it was. The same worrying tone that had dismissed Carly in Nimbin. And besides, if he didn't knock off and sit ning, the fish would soon be high-tailing it away from the noise and Chris would never manage to feed them all. Jo rebaited her hook with a shred of squid that she had wisely put aside earlier, and then shifted upriver with a copy of the *Echo*. The calm ease of a lazy afternoon in the sun had evaporated, and she needed to be by herself to try and get it back. Jo threw her line in the river and found a comfy tree to lean against. Opening the paper, she discovered with an astonished snort of laughter that the poetry competition had been won, not by one of the shire's scores of angst-ridden unemployed wordsmiths, but by the lumbering and unlikely Basho. Life, she thought in wonder, is nothing if not full of suprises.

'Let's cruise over and get some chips,' Jo suggested twenty minutes later to Chris, who had decided to sacrifice a bream in the hope of a more impressive catch, and was settled now in the motionless cross-legged posture of a Buddha or serious fisherwoman.

Her friend wrinkled her nose, and kept looking into the current, reading the signs. If Simmo could catch a four-kilo flathead in this water then there was no earthly reason she couldn't as well.

'Already?' she complained, 'I'm only just warming up.'

Jo looked at Chris's two fat live bream swimming in the bucket. It wasn't really fair to expect Chris to stop now just because she, Jo, was the worst excuse for a fisherman in the Northern Rivers. She turned to Twoboy.

'How about you?' she asked hopefully.

His stomach rumbling, and not liking his chances of hooking anything, Twoboy agreed. They decided to walk across the bridge to the Co-op; Chris could drive over and meet them in an hour. Then they would chauffeur their jalum home in style, wrap them in foil, and lay them ever so gently on the glowing coals of Jo's firepit.

Jo and Twoboy padded down the quiet bush track which ran beside the river. It was in poor repair since the big rains: deep pot-holes cratered the surface every few metres. It hadn't taken long for the ground to dry out though; after a fortnight without rain the crofton weed and lantana along the low edges of the road were already caked with fine yellow dust. They walked quietly, Jo looking and listening for wrens and turkeys and other birds in the thick undergrowth which rose up the hill on their right. Twoboy listened too, harder and more intent than Jo, just in case the song of the country decided to come to him. The shadows of the trees had lengthened, and now bats began to flap by overhead, on their way out of the colony to visit the shire's banana farms and fruiting figs.

'Mum and Dad used to hunt them as kids, eh,' Twoboy told her, his head swivelling to follow the bats upriver. Jo made a face but Twoboy swore they had tasted alright, before the various viruses of the twenty-first century made them too dangerous to harvest. Jo was all for bush tucker, and for self-sufficiency too, but she thought she'd have to be mighty hungry before chowing down on anything that looked like a bloody fruit bat.

The talk of food spurred her on though, and she saw that while she wore runners, Twoboy had only thongs to protect his feet from the gravel road.

'Race you to the bridge!' she challenged as she took off. But even in thongs, Twoboy sprinted past her easily, his knees scissoring high and his dreads flying. By the time she reached the streaming traffic of the main road, he was standing waiting for her, his breathing already back to normal. Jo bent over, laughing, as she heaved for oxygen.

'You seem to forget I played for the junior Broncos,' he teased her in triumph, checking his phone for messages.

'Yeah, a million gazillion years ago when dinosaurs ruled the earth,' Jo answered scornfully, straightening.

Her pulse hammered in her neck as they made their way across the bridge. She ran her left hand along the top railing until, at the halfway point, she stopped and faced out to the Heads. She peered down the fifteen-metre drop that the local teenagers all jumped, testing their mettle in defiance of the warning signs, all summer long. It was a bloody long way down to the river; she wouldn't jump it, even if it hadn't been cold as a witch's tit now that the sun was sinking behind Chincogan. The very last rays were bronzing the water and the surrounding bush. Soon that full kibum would be rising over the ocean, dragging the fish in with it. Jo closed her eyes and breathed the rich strong mud smell of the mangroves on the southern bank. Listen, she thought. Feel. Smell. Be alive, here and now. Underneath the hum of the traffic the faint cry of gulls from the Co-op reached her, and she felt her worries sliding away with the tide. Ah girl, never forget to be grateful. You really do live in paradise, standing on this budheram jagan.

'When I go back in,' she told Twoboy, opening her eyes, 'scatter my ashes here.' She pointed to the bank of the river where the tangled trees hid a midden and other ancient stories. There was no reply.

Jo looked around to discover Twoboy standing rigid, his legs far apart and his arms folded. Stalking towards them from the southern end of the bridge were Oscar Bullockhead and his burly nephew Johnny. On the shoulder of the road a blue Falcon XR6 had screeched to a stop in a hurry, and that might be Oscar's girlfriend sitting in the passenger seat with what sounded like a crying kid on her lap.

Jo's gut clenched in alarm. Fuck me days. What now.

'Here we go. Get behind me,' Twoboy muttered, staring at the two men approaching. He handed Jo his phone.

Before Jo could answer, the enemy were upon them.

'You wanna get back to the other side of the border, cunt,' said Oscar, getting up in Twoboy's face and jerking an angry thumb towards the north bank. His nephew, a big yellow-skinned boy of about twenty-five, smirked nastily. Jo saw that he was holding a length of narrow poly pipe diagonally across his back, a hand on either end. That was the kind of people the Bullockheads were, she thought with horrified insight, the kind to carry weapons in their cars, just in case you needed to randomly smash someone.

She checked the silhouette in the distant car, almost certain it was a woman and a kid. If it was another bloke they'd be gone for sure. But of course another bloke would have gotten out, and would be standing there already beside Oscar and Johnny.

'Is that right?' Twoboy asked. He put on a show of calm Jo couldn't help but be impressed with. 'Yez gonna double-bank me now?'

'Too fucken right that's right. So take your gin and ya pretty-boy haircut, and fuck off back up where ya come from,' Oscar instructed heavily.

Gin, thought Jo, momentarily distracted from the looming danger, long time since I've been called a *gin* to my face.

Out of the corner of her eye she noticed the traffic on the bridge slowing, intrigued faces peered out of car windows trying to catch a glimpse of the drama before they whizzed past. One sedan let out an excited scream of approval as it went by. Some shithead who couldn't resist vicariously getting in on the excitement, Jo thought with a mental shake of her head, someone with no fucking boundaries at all. And us about to die.

'I don't reckon I will, ya know,' Twoboy informed Oscar lightly, as though the three men were discussing whether to go to the shop.

Johnny took a step forward, poly pipe tapping at his left palm now in a transparent indication of what Twoboy had coming if he didn't flee. A momentary flash of rage crossed Twoboy's face. Then he shut his reactions down with a deliberate, physical effort.

Did they see that shudder of his shoulders, Jo wondered? Do they really know what they're doing here? Does he?

Twoboy turned away from the muscle and danger of Johnny, and back to Oscar.

'This ere's my grandfather's country,' he informed Oscar. 'And he told me to come look after it. So I reckon I'll be stopping ere, onetime.'

'You bin told once,' Johnny taunted, pointing straight at Twoboy's face with the pipe. 'So fuck off, ya lying black cunt, and get back up ta Queensland.'

Twoboy smiled, almost but not quite managing to hide the fury in his half-lidded eyes.

'Do ya want me to take that thing off ya and show ya how to use it, Johnny?' he asked with a dangerous smile.

Jesus, thought Jo, here we fucken go. Was she supposed to step in between two blokes fighting? Was a woman an equal party in all this? Did obese old Oscar count as a combatant? She was holding Twoboy's mobile phone with all its valuable evidence of death threats, and it needed to be kept safely out of the river, too. What, she suddenly wondered, would constitute living my *best life*, right now?

Before Jo could work out a strategy for surviving the afternoon, Johnny spat a gob of phlegm close to her feet, then stepped in and swung hard and fast at Twoboy's skull. With a fluid movement, Twoboy swept towards his attacker, turned in a semicircle and somehow ended up standing where Johnny had been ten seconds earlier. A sheen of sweat glistened on his ebony forehead. Several dreads had broken loose of their leather thong and were hanging over Twoboy's face. But it was he, not Johnny, who was now holding the poly pipe.

Johnny was clearly unhappy at this reversal of fortune. He shook his right wrist hard, as though he could flick away the pain of holding the twisting pipe for several seconds too long. Despite losing his weapon, though, he stayed facing Twoboy. A stream of invective continued to pour from him.

The kid's got guts anyway, Jo thought, greatly relieved to see the pipe change hands. Then, to her horror, Twoboy tossed it over the railing into the water. Oh, that's just perfect, she thought, just bloody perfect. You idiot. What'd you do *that* for?

'We's going this way,' Twoboy told Oscar, breathing hard. He rested a hand on the bridge railing and indicated the path to the Co-op with an economical movement of the other. 'So I suggest yufla get back in ya flash car and keep going too, before I get proper cranky.'

Oscar's face darkened with rage. Twoboy had six inches and twenty years on him and was fit to boot. Oscar glanced contemptuously at his nephew.

'Well?' he asked Johnny. 'You gonna sort this gammon prick out, or what?'

Johnny swallowed. Clearly he hadn't signed up for a weaponless one-on-one fight with Twoboy, no fucking way had he signed up for that.

Jo wished futilely that retreat was an option for her man, but she knew it wasn't, and didn't waste her breath.

'Walk away, Johnny,' Twoboy advised. 'He don't care about you, man. Walk away —'

'Show this fucken dog whose land he's on!' Oscar interrupted, on the verge of smashing Twoboy himself and bugger the consequences.

Johnny stood, crucified by his uncle's giant expectations and his own pride.

When no escape route presented itself, he grimaced, shaped up, and swung a roundhouse punch at Twoboy, hard and fast. Twoboy stepped marginally sideways away from Johnny's fist as he blocked it. Then his right hand shot up.

Jo heard a loud crack and a blurred Johnny flew backwards, over the railing. A heavy splash followed, seconds later.

She rushed to peer down into the water – if Johnny was knocked out, he would drown, and Twoboy would go to jail for a long, long time. To her great relief, Jo saw Johnny begin dog paddling groggily in a crooked line to the deep mud on the southern shore. He was alive then, and conscious too, no thanks to his uncle.

'You fucken black doglicker!' Oscar shouted at Twoboy, taking off at full waddle for the path by the river, which was also conveniently the path back to his XR6. 'Ya pretty ghetto when it's an eighteen-year-old kid fronting ya, eh!' he shouted over his shoulder.

Jo shook her head in amazement. All of a sudden, the story of this encounter was being rewritten to make Twoboy the aggressor, and Johnny and Oscar the hapless victims. She'd bet good money that when it was described in the Piccabeen pub that afternoon there'd be zero mention of any poly pipe.

Twoboy was breathing hard and tying his dreads back into place, watching Oscar to make sure he wasn't coming back with another weapon or more backup. The two of them stood tall in the middle of the bridge, as Oscar flopped into the driver's seat and squealed away to retrieve Johnny from the mangroves.

'Pissweak old cunt,' Twoboy muttered, before turning to Jo with a pleased grin. 'But I bloody lifted Johnny, eh? He fucken *flew* over that railing! Must have seagull dreaming!'

Jo laughed weakly in relief, as the XR6 vanished along the road. Not so very deep down she discovered that she admired Twoboy for his flogging of Johnny. You savage, she told herself, you bloody Neanderthal.

Twoboy turned and braced both his hands on the rail of the bridge that he had just won from Johnny, fair and fucking square. My country, suckers, not yours. His bright red, black and yellow footy shirt caught the last slanting rays of the setting sun as he gazed happily downriver, where a trio of dolphins were making their way past the poly pipe, out to the ocean. The very last of the light gleamed off their smooth round backs as they looped along their ancient waterways, hunting the very same prey that Jo and Twoboy had fished for earlier.

'If it was up to me,' Twoboy said, turning back to Jo with a triumphant grin, 'That's how we'd sort Native Title out all over Australia, onetime. Behind closed doors, just between us mob, fuck the tribunal. Like the old days.'

That's all very well, thought Jo, but for one thing we aren't behind closed doors – we're in full public view and every bloody dugai that drove over the bridge in the last five minutes has seen you and Johnny brawling, shame. And second –

'Good strategy if you're young and fit,' she disagreed, 'but not if you're old.'

Twoboy shrugged dismissively. War required warriors, strong and young and ready to die. That was a given. Jo narrowed her eyes. Survival of the fittest was a dugai law, not hers.

'Well, what if it was just your Mum fighting for her land, without you boys around to help her?' Jo kept pushing.

'But she does have us.' Twoboy was unmoved. He was a street fighter. Johnny had flown over the railing like a fucking bird. It was a beautiful fight.

'Or, or, okay. Well, what about Uncle Humbug . . . what if he had a claim?'

'Humbug?' Twoboy looked at her strangely.

'He's gotta have a country somewhere . . . He told me it's here,' Jo revealed. Twoboy blew his cheeks out in contemptuous laughter.

'He wants to stick to biting tourists and talking to that fucken snake,' he responded. 'He wouldn't know what Native Title was if it come up and bit him on the arse.'

'That's what I'm talking about,' Jo argued, the heat rising in her face. 'He can't even read or write – so how's he gonna make a claim?'

'Native Title's there for the taking. And if he ain't gonna take it, then all the more for us mob, eh?' Twoboy said – before being distracted by the sight of Johnny, who was out of the river now, looking like the creature from the black lagoon.

The lad was snarling over his shoulder and dragging his sorry wet arse towards the XR6, when Twoboy gave him a Queen-like wave of condescension. Johnny erupted at this, yelling and forking the air in fury. Twoboy laughed aloud in triumph and shouted through cupped hands.

'Yeah, keep walking, Johnny, ya sorry little black cunt!'

Jo stared at her lover. If Humbug was simply a crazy old Koori in the park, a cold and hungry southerner with some mad aspirations to being a traditional owner, then there was no serious problem outside of his own grizzled head.

But.

But what if he really was a traditional owner? What if he had a legitimate claim, and nobody was listening?

All through the evening, as Jo sat beside the fire feasting on Chris's bream, listening to Twoboy replay the fight again and again, questions spun her mental wheels. Questions about Humbug, and about Oscar, and about Aunty Sally Watt. Questions about Twoboy. Troubling, answerless questions about how far her lover might go – just exactly who in the community he might be prepared to shaft – to claim the land that he insisted day and night was his great-grandfather's.

If you're gonna tell a lie, make it a big one.

CHAPTER ELEVEN

Jo stood at the counter of the Billinudgel shop with a litre of milk and a loaf of bread, hoping that the car-floor coins she held would cover it.

'Five fifty, thanks,' said the girl behind the till. Jo stared glumly at the silver in her palm, and turned to put the milk back. Ah, not to worry, eyes on the prize. She'd got the farm, and nothing else mattered, not really. Milkless tea until payday rolled around wouldn't kill her, and luckily Ellen had always preferred her Weetbix with hot water, the weirdo.

'Need a dollar, mate?' Annie asked, and Jo looked up into the soft brown eyes of the owner of the Burringbar Produce Store. She squealed with delight and hurled herself into Annie's lanky arms.

'Long time no see, girl!' Jo told the tall woman as they stepped outside. Annie propped a boot on the wooden bench, felt Warrigal's ears, and caught Jo up on the state of all her stockhorses, which were in full Ekka preparation. Jo had intended to ride around to the Burringbar Valley and visit, she told Annie, before the tragedy of Comet happened, and then it was a week before she could even as much as look at a horse. She hadn't ridden at all since that hideous day.

Annie nodded. 'I sent you a text when I heard,' she said, hooking her thumbs into her jeans belt loops and looking like a female Clint Eastwood. Annie knew all about losing horses. The year before last, her foal crop had been all colts except for one stunning black filly, and she was the one that got dysentery and couldn't be saved. The tiny curved hoof prints that had lingered in the Burringbar mud all October were enough to break anybody's heart.

'So . . . come round *this* week, and see my young stock,' she suggested in her slow country-raised accent. 'Got a real nice taffy I want to show you, she's just come up from Williamsville.' Jo smiled. Annie bred and broke and sold horses for a living. Of all the cowboys around these parts, it was Annie, with her long Kamilaroi legs, short bleached hair and horse-breaking muscles who could have pulled off carrying a six-shooter around. Jo could see it now: Annie's spurs dragging in the dust of Wilfred Street, having a noonday showdown with the local yokels. Jo pictured Darren Ferrier jerking backwards off his feet as a red cloud bloomed across his chest. Annie blew smoke off her gun barrel before holstering it. *No trespassing.*

'Shit, I got no bungoo for another horse, mate,' said Jo, 'As you might have gathered.' She lifted the milk and bread and gave a wry smile. She didn't even have enough to put Annie's stallion over Athena and try for another foal. There wasn't any point in pretending.

'I know that, geez. Come and see her anyway!' Annie sounded mildly insulted and took her foot down off the bench seat. 'There's always one of us minding shop.'

Jo promised to drop round in a few days. As Annie drove away to her Ekka preparations, Jo turned to read a poster in the shop window that had caught her eye on the way in. *Combined Schools Indigenous Art Competition: $500 Prize Money.* Three hundred big ones for first prize! Ellen was a shoo-in, Jo anticipated with a fat expectant grin – until she read the names of the judges. Two were white high school art teachers, but the third, she discovered to her horror, was *Mrs (Granny) Rosemary Nurrung.* Ah, fuck me days, Jo spat. Ellen's got Buckley's chance, not unless she decides to paint an Aboriginal Jesus hanging on the cross wearing a pained smile and carrying a bloodied bible in each of his long-suffering hands.

★

Jo banged on the kitchen wall. Does he think I'm made of hot water? Of *any* water, when every single drop needs to be pumped up from the creek, and that means fuel at two bucks a bloody litre?

'Leave some hot water for the rest of bloody New South Wales!' Jo shouted towards the bathroom as she briefly turned on the hot tap in the kitchen to underline her point. The shower continued for another three or four minutes, while she stood and fumed.

When Twoboy finally sauntered out towelling his sodden dreads she shot him a filthy look.

'I'll be sending ya the bill, ya keep these fifteen-minute showers up,' she threatened.

Twoboy immediately pointed out that it cost him fifty bucks in juice every time he turned up at Jo's farm gate, but *he* didn't go on and on about it, not being a tightarse like her; she remonstrated that he'd been driving down here for the court case long before they'd met, that she furthermore had never-fucking-ending homeowner's bills to pay already, and invited him to reassess the merits of bachelorhood anytime he liked.

Half an hour later, Twoboy was still sullen on the computer, cursing the slow connection, and giving monosyllabic answers to Jo's tentative peacemaking questions.

Finally she gave up and went and sat in front of the TV with Ellen. *This.* This was exactly what she didn't miss about being married.

Luckily a re-run of 'The Wire' was on, and she was able to distance herself from the sour figure bent over the keyboard in the next room. When the show ended, though, the tension of their disagreement lingered on. Jo got up and went to the doorway.

'I'm going to bed,' she announced, hoping to find out whether or not she would sleep alone. Twoboy looked around and up at her. Well, that's an improvement on talking to the back of his grunting head, anyway, Jo thought.

'I'll be in later,' he said tersely. 'I think Laz's onto something at the archives.'

The man clearly wanted her to ask what it was, to come over

and get all interested in the never-ending details of building the documentation, but now it was Jo's turn to grunt and retreat. Yeah. Of course he has. The case, the case, the bloody case, twenty-four hours a day seven days a fucking week. The case that's gonna save the world, bring back the culture, appease the ancestors and restore this tiny corner of the Bundjalung nation to a mighty powerful force for good and not evil. Jo stalked away, slammed the bedroom door behind her and fell face first onto the doona.

Whatever.

When Jo woke next morning, Twoboy wasn't holding her close. He wasn't even in bed.

Her heart quickly sank as she remembered last night's disagreement. Had he gone back up to Brisbane without even saying goodbye? It was Monday, and Monday through Friday was normally spent at the archives, the State Library, or at the lawyers chambers. He could have bloody said goodbye though, Jo thought miserably.

But then a clatter of cups told Jo that her lover was simply busying himself in the kitchen. Her shoulders relaxed, and she propped herself up against the bedstead with a small smile, pulling the doona around her neck for warmth.

Outside the window, Athena stood looking at the house, her hot yarraman breath showing white against the morning air. Soon, old girl, soon. Just give me a few more minutes of warm doona and a hefty shot of caffeine. Christ, there's still a fair twinge in the old back, from that whipper snippering. Maybe she should think about going back to uni, Jo mused, and find herself a white-collar job that didn't need muscle strength, before she was too decrepit to manage the cemetery on top of the farm work. If the case was successful, Twoboy reckoned, there could be National Parks and eco-tourism jobs for both of them, for the whole mob, for Laz, Rhonda, Billy. For Justice and Yabra in time to come, even for Ellen if she wanted it. Real Goorie businesses in the valley. Proper jobs that couldn't be whisked away at the whim of unseen city bosses.

Jo ran her tongue around the inside of her mouth, imagining tourists swarming over the World Heritage, toiling up the ridge, and Twoboy yarning to them about the King Parrot Dreaming. He'd love it, she thought, he'd soak up the attention of the cooing Americans and the fascinated Japanese, would pose for photos with his arms around them when they came back down picking off leeches and head over heels in love with her man to the very last one of em. It was a vision of a better future, and it all rested on the case. Without that tick from the dugai court, Twoboy had no traditional rights to enjoy in this valley, and there would be no National Parks jobs, no eco-tourism business in the World Heritage, no legal hunting and gathering, no *nothing*. He would have to go back to uni and finish his interrupted law degree. Try to get work in some city office somewhere, in a suit. Jesus.

As Jo chewed over the implications, Twoboy appeared bearing two mugs. He'd discovered a forgotten plunger stored in the spare room, and the delicious scent of real coffee filled the room. Jo sipped gratefully at the muddy infusion and decided her fella was officially forgiven for taking long showers like she was a rich dugai with money to burn. A way to a woman's heart is through her addictions, and this, oh my bunji, is mine.

'How's the surf report?' she asked, knowing full well that if it was any good Twoboy wouldn't be standing in front of her.

'Flat as a tack. I'm gonna buy you brekkie in Ocean instead!' He began massaging her neck. 'Since you've got the RDO. And listen. How about we get Kym and Jase and the boys and go up to Lake Majestic soon? Time we went bush and cleared our heads. This case is driving me round the fucken bend, and you, my darlin, are just as stressed as I am.'

Jo knew he was right. The wonderful calm of Sangsurya had worn off in a few short days. Now she was getting wild about trivia she should have laughed off. With athletics season over, and her nephews' latest clutch of medallions and trophies on display in their lounge, Kym had promised to definitely come down next weekend, cross her heart and hope to die. Maybe, Jo suggested, Chris and

Uncle Pat could come too, and how about Therese and Amanda, and if Ellen wanted to bring Holly along –

'Whoa, whoa,' Twoboy interrupted as his thumbs dug deep into her shoulders. 'Let's just keep it a bit contained, eh? Hard to hear the country sing when there's whitefellas stompin all over it and yak-yak-yakkin.'

Ah. There was an ulterior motive, Jo realised with a small stab of displeasure, a motive to do with Twoboy's real love, the bloody fucking case. If he couldn't conjure up her mystery talga by lurking on the ridge at dusk, he'd go further afield to the peaks around Lake Majestic and try there. It wouldn't be long, she mused, and he'd be sniffing around the power centre of Wollumbin itself, getting into all sorts of trouble with the TOs over on that side, and God knew what might happen if he woke up the spirit of the big mountain. Someone walked over her grave at the thought. She shuddered involuntarily, and Twoboy paused in his massaging.

'You okay?' he asked.

'Yeah,' Jo said, deciding to ignore the goosebumps.

'How about Laz though?' She threw back the doona as the coffee revived her. 'For someone who supposedly lives on country he never seems to bloody be here.'

Laz was flat out with Billy and with the research, plus he had no points left on his licence, Twoboy explained. 'He wanted to bludge my last two off me last week.'

Jo laughed and shook her head. 'Blackfellas.'

'Yeah,' Twoboy said with a knowing grin, 'and Rhonda's running on empty too, all cos of old leadfoot. He's thinking of taking Mum in to get a licence for the first time in her life, just as a backup.'

'That feels better!' Jo pushed her empty plate to the other side of the table. Her tummy was rounded and full against the denim of her jeans. The unusual feeling of having the leisure to sit still and digest her breakfast made Jo stretch her arms high with delight. She waved to the local woodwork teacher who was heading into Bi-Lo, then sat back, crossed her legs, and began to really savour a day off.

It was almost worth having to work, she reflected, just for the joy of taking your RDOs. Talk about simple pleasures: try this one – doing sweet fuck all and watching everybody else having to slave away as usual. Not to mention that supreme pleasure: quitting when the hideous saga of doing what the boss told you to do became too much to take. How many jobs had she left in her time?

Jo counted on her fingers: the car yard detailing at Tweed when she was sixteen. The bar work, the letterbox deliveries, the pizza-making in Fortitude Valley, the waitressing that turned out to be an unexpectedly satisfying vehicle for social revenge via the spillage of hot drinks and soup on arseholes who sorely needed it. The furniture factory in Nerang where she'd only lasted until the day she mentioned the word *union*. The Bundall warehouse where the boredom of filling cardboard cartons with sports clothes could have made her shrivel and die on the spot if not for the pleasure of arguing with the Jehovah's Witnesses who worked alongside her. Dozens of jobs, dozens of places. Some she'd quit and some she'd been sacked from, but none of them she regretted leaving in the slightest. Being the Mullum caretaker was the first one Jo had stuck at for more than a year, and the first straight job that she had ever found the least bit satisfactory. All that had been missing all those years, Jo mused, was a workplace where everybody but her was dead.

She looked around for Twoboy then, and discovered him propped in front of the pet shop, pursuing an ongoing project.

'Let me outta here, you cunts,' Twoboy enunciated in a low clear whisper. The parrot cast a fascinated eye over him.

'Probably trying to work out if you're a person or a tree,' Jo said as she joined him, flipping his long dreads up in the air. The parrot flapped its wings loudly inside its steel cage.

'Hello, cocky,' it said, turning its head sideways to get a better look at its visitors.

'Let me outta here, you cunts,' Twoboy repeated patiently, and was answered with another banal greeting. He pursed his lips and shook his head. He'd been trying to revolutionise the bird for ages. Was it a slow learner, or was he a bad teacher? Probably it needed lessons more often than once a week.

'We should just let it out straight up, eh,' Jo proposed, resting a fingertip on the sliding door of the cage. Bloody pet shop, caging and wiring up anything they could. Fence em in, boys, fence em in. Make everything in the world live inside a tight little metal square, so we can feel safe.

'If I was still twenty and the Angriest Black Man in the World, I would,' Twoboy replied, not taking her seriously.

Fuck it, thought Jo, as the bird's yellow crest rose in wary response to her finger. She slid the door wide open and stepped away from the cage. Let nature take its course, she thought. Let the rivers run free, and the cockies fly high.

'Christ, Jo, what are ya doing?' Twoboy slid the door back into place before the bird had a chance to react. Inside, the shop attendant had stopped fussing about with goldfish and was staring suspiciously at the two dark figures beyond the glass.

'Striking a blow for liberty!' Jo laughed an anarchist's laugh and opened the door wide a second time. 'Look at it, poor thing, sitting there like a fucken martyr to white Australian values.'

Twoboy quickly closed the cage again, then took Jo by the hand and marched her briskly around the corner of the building, to where the creek looped behind dense thickets of beach hibiscus. Jo stumbled a little, noticing, beneath her great surprise at being swept away from the caged bird, how much rubbish had been washed up against the wall of the shopping centre by the last high tide. A dozen brown iced-coffee bottles lay alongside torn plastic bags, bits of white styrofoam and old rusted Coke cans. Someone out there was missing a near new Adidas shoe as well. Jo felt a familiar sense of despair that her country was subject to such treatment.

They reached a spot well away from the shops and Twoboy stopped. When Jo was with him, he lectured, interrupting her indignant protests, she always, *always* had to be thinking of the dugai law, and the consequences of breaking it –

'Oh, for fuck's sake . . .' Jo began, pulling her hand free in irritation.

'Look at me,' Twoboy insisted, as he released her hand. He threw his arms wide in demonstration, his brow furrowed and his tone grim. 'Look at me, Jo! I'm a big, powerful, educated black man! Nobody – *nobody* – in this country, except for a few Goories, thinks that I'm a good idea. And you want to break the law when you're standing beside me? Do you think I can afford to get locked up *now*, with the case about to go before the tribunal? Christ almighty – what were ya thinking!'

Jo stood riveted by the incandescent anger in Twoboy's stance.

'But it wasn't you that opened the cage,' she argued, 'and I wouldn't let you go down for something I did.'

Twoboy laughed a short, harsh laugh and shook his head at her naiveté. It was a hell of a long time since Jo had to worry much about police, living in the liberal northern rivers with her ambiguous colour, her female good looks and a straight job that kept her off the street each day.

'As if any white gunjies are going to take a look at me and keep on going,' he told her angrily. 'I've got Cop Killer written all over me. There's any street crime within bloody cooee of me and I'll be the one responsible, Jo, come on down and smell the coffee, girl.'

Twoboy's chest heaved as he stared at Jo, assessing whether or not he was going to be safe around her.

'I just feel so sorry for him, poorfella,' Jo muttered. 'I wasn't trying to get you in any shit.'

'I know,' Twoboy said. 'And if it was up to me I'd drown the prick who invented birdcages in his own piss. But when you look like me you learn to pick your fights, Jo. Right now the only fight that matters a pinch of shit is the one with the tribunal. Everything else has to be on hold till after October, okay?'

'Okay,' said Jo in a small voice, secretly vowing to come back to the shop alone and free the bird.

'Alright then.'

Twoboy sighed and put his arm around Jo's shoulders. They walked together across the car park towards the Commodore. From its cage at the front of the pet shop, Jo saw, the cockatoo observed them weaving their way through the parked vehicles, and perhaps a new and unnameable feeling rose up in the bird's breast, for its yellow crest bounced fully forward with fresh vitality, and it spread its white wings wide –

'Let me *outta* here, you cunts!' the bird screeched, bringing the shop attendant at a dead run.

'You there?' yelled Therese the next afternoon, slamming the Astra door harder than necessary, then walking straight into a faceful of low-hanging mango blossom.

Jo had just managed to fix the busted sprayer and was about to attack the baby camphors which were flourishing in the dip. 'How'd ya be?' she asked, putting the sprayer down now. Warrigal and Daisy let out belated woofles when they noticed Therese approach. 'Yeah real good guard dogs you are,' Jo told them. Not.

Therese flung herself onto the veranda steps and lowered her head into her hands.

Jo got two beers and silently handed one over.

With stubbies cracked, the saga began: Therese was really getting divorced this time, cos she was fucken *over* it. Amanda's mother had fallen for the umpteenth time last night. Nothing broken, but Amanda had received a testy summons from the family. She had to come to Brisbane and stay with her mother for a month while the soft tissue damage healed and the others, who claimed they'd done their share and then some, got on with their busy, busy, *busy* lives –

'Do you know how sick I am of being the disgusting family secret?'

'A month,' Jo repeated doubtfully.

'I could fucken strangle Denise,' Therese added savagely, her jaw thrust forward, shaking a fist beside her ear. 'We just about had Mary agreeing to sign up for respite care a few months back, till Denise went and told her that she didn't need it. Like *she's* gonna look after her, the maggoty white fuck.' Then Therese adopted a stubborn old-lady tone: 'I keep telling you, I don't *need* any help. I just need someone to pick me up when I fall over, that's all . . .' Christ. When every day she's on the phone, complaining that she could be dead for all anyone cares, and why won't Amanda just come back to live in Wynumn and look after her?'

Therese sculled a mouthful of beer and then let loose a roar of frustration at the African tulip tree. Two king parrots feeding on its blossom bolted for their lives, flapping wildly away over the top of the house. Jo watched them go until they were dark specks over the dam, headed for Wollumbin before they slowed, at the rate they were going.

'Settle down, you're scaring the horses, mate. Why can't Denise do it, then?' Jo said, toying with the thin shoulder straps of the sprayer, testing the weight of fifteen litres of dilute glyphosate. 'Tell her she's undermining the institution of marriage,' she added with a grin.

Therese laughed bitterly. Denise was in Canberra on business for the next two weeks. 'And she never lifts a fucken finger to help anybody else if there isn't a buck in it,' she added. 'Do you know any hit men? Someone's gotta die this time.'

'I know a wog in Mooball who'll bust faces for a carton,' Jo responded, unable to mask a broadening grin. 'But I must say I'm not hearing the dharma here.'

'I'm a Buddhist, luvvy, I never said I was a fucken saint.'

'Greed. Anger. Delusion,' Jo recited piously.

'Yep, good description of Amanda's shithead family. Not to mention homophobia, racism and fucktardness.' Therese's dark eyes flashed. 'I really wanna get bombed and ring em up and tell em what I think of em, the maggots.'

'Well, before you do that, grab another beer and come and watch me spray these camphors, mate. That's the only kinda killing I want round here,' Jo ordered. Picking the sprayer up again, she wondered if Amanda would really go to Brisbane, and whether Therese would make good on last year's threats to end their relationship if she did. Ageing parents were an issue Jo herself would never need to face: a stoned driver on the wrong side of the Gold Coast Highway in 1989 had made sure of that.

As they walked up to the paddock, Therese's furious energy translated itself into action: she insisted Jo fit her with the backpack and show her how to operate the wand, then let her loose on nature. Every so often, Therese came back to where Jo was sitting beside the Top Dam with the glyphosate concentrate and a diluting bucket, and refilled the plastic reservoir of the sprayer. Waiting for the fifth refill, Therese finally cracked a smile.

'I must've been a serial killer in my previous life. I'm enjoying this,' she said, directed a final dribble from the almost-empty sprayer onto a yellow fireweed.

'Well, I hate using the shit,' Jo answered, screwing her face up, 'but camphors are camphors. Hey, leave that fireweed, it's easy to pull out by hand – the less poison on my land, the better.'

'Do you reckon Denise'd shrivel and turn brown in four days if I sprayed her with Roundup?' Therese grinned and mimed dousing her sister-in-law.

'I certainly don't think it'd do her much good,' Jo laughed, 'I always have a big shower and a couple of cups of green tea after I spray, to mop up some of the toxins. There. You're good to go. But only the camphors, eh?'

'Roger wilco,' said Therese with satisfaction, heading back to kill the exotic saplings that would take over the entire valley, given half a chance. Large, attractive, fast-growing trees that didn't drop branches, they had seemed the ideal schoolyard tree to some long-forgotten bureaucrat who had installed them in playgrounds across New South Wales. Now the hills and valleys of Bundjalung country were cloaked with the green cancer that choked out the native trees, and were pretty useless to most of the indigenous animals, too. One day, Jo had promised the land on her arrival, only indigenous trees and plants would grow on her farm. She would wipe out the camphors on her twenty acres before she died, along with the fireweed, the crofton weed and the lantana. If the task didn't kill her first, that is.

'How's the art coming?' Jo asked Ellen, ruffling her hair to show that she approved of the Miracle of the Washing Up. Ellen jerked her head away, and soaped the pan from last night's dinner, scratching hard with a scourer at the dried film of soy sauce, before placing it in the rack with their two plates, two forks, and an assortment of coffee cups.

'Alright.'

'Gonna be ready for tomorrow? Three hundred bucks, remember?' Jo pressed, hoping in vain for more information. She still didn't even know which drawing Ellen was going to submit.

Jo had decided not to say anything about the Granny Nurrung problem. Hopefully the art teachers together could overrule any god-bothering opposition, and, anyway, there wasn't any point being negative. If Twoboy had taught her anything, it was the value of enthusiasm. You Got To Accentuate the Positive, he sang down the phone line nearly every time he called, confounding her inner pessimist and putting the bloody earworm in her head till she could scream.

'No,' Ellen oozed sarcastically, 'it slipped my mind, that three hundred dollars, I mean why would *that* be something I'd remember? I've already finished, okay? Just don't ask to see it.'

Jo stuck her tongue in her top lip and gazed at Ellen. *No work of art is ever finished, only abandoned.* Who said that? She couldn't remember. Plus, this kid needs a haircut. Tight dark curls spiralled wildly over Ellen's forehead and down her shoulders. In fact –

'Is that a dread in your hair?' Jo asked, peering, and a little disturbed. Ellen stepped backwards, hand to her head.

'Maybe.'

Jo cocked her head, imagining Ellen with dreadlocks. A part of her didn't like the idea of her little girl looking like a Nimbin feral. On the other hand, Ellen would be on any hypocritical opposition to dreads like – as the Yanks said – a duck on a june bug. Whatever the hell a june bug was. What would a Bundjalung equivalent be? Like a mibun on a rabbit? Like crows on roadkill? Like a white consultant on an Aboriginal community?

'Hmm. Are you sure you want to go there?'

'No. That's why I've only got one.'

'Fair enough.' Jo paused. 'Well, what about Athena?'

Ellen shrugged.

'Can't you do it? I did the washing up.'

Big green eyes found a razor's edge between defiance and plead-ing. That jahjam is getting very freckly, Jo noted, as well as tall. Have to be onto her to use sunblock this summer.

'Mum – stop looking for excuses. It's time you got back on her. Otherwise, why even have horses?'

Jo looked away, down at a corner of the kitchen floor, knowing that Ellen had a point. Except now it was *horse*, singular, a fact which still burned in her gut. She poured and drank a glass of water at the sink, upending the glass beside the gleaming frypan. Perfect, even the stainless steel grooves of the sink were shiny and suds-free.

'Okay. I'll ride up and see Chris. Do some homework but, eh? You won't get any done this weekend if we're painting the ute.'

Jo pulled on riding boots, grabbed her akubra and heard the kitchen door slam loudly behind her. Have to buy a new latch for that door, she made a mental note, as she went to catch the old mare, pushing down the worry she felt at the idea of really acting like a horse owner, spending time with the yarraman instead of leaving her to sit in the paddock. Just as soon as the rest of the camphors are sprayed, and the cattle yard gets built, I'll be on that door latch in a jiffy. In two shakes of a lamb's tail. In anything that doesn't require a duck, a june bug, or any kind of fucking phrase that means nothing and says nothing to a Goorie woman living on her own country at the bottom of the southern hemisphere.

Under the intent supervision of the steers, Jo slid a snaffle bit into Athena's mouth and pulled the headpiece of the bridle up behind her ears, furry with thick winter hair. No carefree riding in a halter today, old girl, not when we're going out on the tarmac and you haven't felt a saddle for weeks. She swung her right leg over the nag, feeling the strain in her lower back that never really disappeared these days. Then she footed the other stirrup and rode out, away from the glaring red rates bill. Away from the still flourishing camphors along the fenceline, and the unfinished yard, away from the stony cairn that she remembered Comet by.

As the farm disappeared behind her, the slow regular clap of Athena's unshod hooves on the bitumen was as familiar to Jo as her own heartbeat, and as soothing. She relaxed into the saddle, letting Tin Wagon Road by horseback take her worries and reframe them as the minutiae they were. Jo let herself be entranced by the curl of the tree fern tips and the bright new growth on the callistemons lining the gullies which ran down off Bottlebrush; by the moist black lips of the Angus cattle chewing their cud with their forelegs folded under them; by the flitting among lantana thickets of the wrens and butcherbirds and piping yellow-eyes. A glossy black spangled drongo perched singularly on the powerline above the creek. Jo rode underneath it, admiring the perfect symmetry of its fish-like tail. Something in nature demanded that a drongo tail should have that distinctive shape, and that the wrens have their pertly upturned ones, and that the kingfisher perched there in the quandong in the neighbour's paddock should have a third sort, but what? She didn't have the faintest idea.

Ten minutes and three creek crossings later, a Mercedes coupe drove past her, two of its wheels politely leaving the road so that a wide margin separated it from horse and rider. Jo rewarded this courtesy with a brief wave. The car crawled by, both the tourists in it enthusiastically waving back. An olive-skinned woman turned around in the passenger seat, glowing with a beatific smile. You would smile, lady, Jo reflected, driving around in a car like that. Swap ya for a shitbox Toyota with an empty petrol tank, luv.

To Jo's surprise, the Mercedes stopped a hundred metres up the road, then reversed in a wobbly line until it stood beside her once again. It sat idling expensively in the middle of the bitumen. Then the woman in the passenger seat pressed a button and wound down a window. Inane pop music spilled out, and she reached to turn the volume down.

A massive square-cut diamond glinted on the woman's left hand, and Jo fantasised about turning into Captain Thunderbolt. She had a vision of whipping an old-school musket out from behind her back, demanding the ring and then galloping off into the safety of the World Heritage with it stowed in her saddlebag. *All's fair in love and war –*

'Oh! Hold still! Can I take your photo?' the woman cried suddenly, iPhone already up to her eye, and her perfect white teeth bared on display beneath it. Jo scowled at this intrusion.

No. Fuck off. You'll steal my soul.

'Go on,' she muttered. The woman promptly clicked three or four times.

'Aamaal – can we go?' the husband said, looking embarrassed.

'Oh! That's a fabulous shot!'

The woman beamed at the tiny screen and held it up for her husband's inspection. Then she wound the window back up – without speaking to Jo, let alone offering to show her the photos.

Hello? Have I dematerialised or what, she thought in astonishment.

The coupe accelerated and promptly disappeared around the next bend, leaving Jo mired in disproportionate rage. She heeled Athena forward, snorting with hostility.

A fabulous shot. Akubra, stockhorse, tan skin: yep, I'm the woman from Snowy River alright. But come home with me, Mercedes lady, come and take a photo of my unpaid rates notice stuck on the fridge. Or of the magic Toyota that runs on nothing but petrol fumes. Better yet, come up to Chris's place and frame an artful fucking shot of the tomato sauce sandwiches she's having for dinner.

Jo rode furiously, wishing that she was an old cleverwoman. She would curse the tourists and their sports car. She'd make it break down, she'd make those fuckers run out of petrol instead of waltzing around on her land with no thought for anyone except themselves. She'd make them career off the road into a nice solid gum tree, see the Mercedes explode in a fireball of plenty of petrol and plenty of money and plenty of fucking bungooed privilege that doesn't see anything past its own narcissistic arsehole –

Your anger is buried so deep, Therese had lectured her once, *you don't even know it's there.*

Jo shortened her reins and steamed as she rode on. She recalled Twoboy's jokey threat at the Billi pub the night they'd met: *I'll be on the phone to Al Qaeda mob, onetime.* For the first time in her life, Jo felt she was within touching distance of the anger that would make someone say those words and really mean them.

From the corner of her eye she suddenly noticed something watching her. Someone. It was Bluey, lifting now from one of the big bottlebrush trees beside the creek.

The heron flew towards her and landed on a fencepost not five metres away. It stood there on its scaly yellow legs and regarded her balefully. Jo pulled Athena up, the horse fidgeting and tossing her head with impatience to canter. The dogs watched with alert eyes and pricked ears.

What is it, mulanyin?

The bird didn't move, but continued staring at her. After a minute of intense avian scrutiny Jo began to feel as though she had something to atone for. She looked around. Without any word from her, the dogs had both – oddly – sat down on their haunches facing the heron, as if waiting for instructions.

What the hell?

To Jo's horror, Bluey flew down from the fencepost to land, this time on the narrow bitumen road directly in front of her, where the dogs could easily rush it. She kicked her feet from the stirrups, ready to jump down and defend her bird from the mutts. But Warrigal and Daisy continued to sit humbly and merely observe. The world's least imposing sentry, mulanyin stood there blocking her path forward on its impossibly frail legs, apparently not bothered by the dogs nor by Athena looming hugely over it.

What the fuck is this?

The heron raised its slender grey neck and released a harsh croak at Jo. Athena lowered her head almost to the road and blew her nostrils out warily at the intruder. Jo, too, breathed out in astonishment, wondering if this was a sign. Was there a disaster waiting for her if she kept going along the road? Should she turn back and go home? Was Ellen in some terrible trouble?

With a last guttural croak, Bluey lifted again and flapped its way to a nearby quandong. Jo eyed it uneasily. She felt marooned in the middle of Tin Wagon Road, warned off going forward, and yet unwilling to go back home so soon. Warrigal and Daisy stood up and turned into dogs again. Athena began to fuss and fidget beneath her, throwing her head up against the pressure of the bit, and prancing on the spot in a thoroughbred high step of impatience. Okay, okay, settle petal. Jo threw another glance at the heron, which was winging away from her now, headed towards Bottlebrush. She glanced down at the dogs, and decided to keep going, cautiously.

Five minutes later, Athena was puffing with unaccustomed effort and too much grass. Jo drew in her left rein and turned up a fire trail, almost opposite Chris's track. The mare's hooves crunched sharp gravel underfoot as they climbed the slope away from Tin Wagon Road. Jo kept a careful eye out for pointed stones that would lame Athena and mean a long walk home. After riding for a while through a heavily forested stretch, she reached flatter, more open country. The trail was lined by paddocks on both sides, and purebred grey Brahmins dotted the landscape. In this clearer country, without the trees acting as a soundbreak, Jo could suddenly hear the rushing of Stony Creek, surprisingly loud from halfway up the ridge. In front of her, rainforest clustered thickly around mossy boulders that made

Jo think of scrub turkeys and brown snakes. In the sky above the forest flamed a spectacular red and purple sunset.

As she enjoyed the spectacle – red sky at night, shepherd's delight – Jo felt the old tug in her gut return. *Go west.* There was still something waiting for her in the sunset country, something important. Things don't go away just because you ignore them, it seemed. This must be how Ellen feels, Jo thought, when she knows something's about to go wrong. Only in Jo's case, it didn't seem like bad news that waited. More like important information.

It was unsettling, though, and unwelcome, too. And what, she suddenly thought in alarm, if it has to do with that bloody talga?

With this thought Jo pulled Athena up abruptly. Twoboy was desperate to hear the voices, to get the talga down on paper for the tribunal, to prove once and for all that he owned the true song of the country, and not just his father's stories about Grandad Tommy Jackson. He had kept at Jo since the day she fell off, nagging her to return to the fallen gum with him. To Twoboy's bewilderment she had always refused. That hidden part of the culture, Jo shivered – no, he could keep it. If there were secrets in the hills, *mooki*, ancestors holding sacred knowledge and secrets, well then let them stay where they bloody well were. Life was hard enough without inviting that kind of trouble in. It wasn't as if any white tribunal was going to believe they were there anyway. Twoboy was cracked, totally bloody womba, if he thought they were.

Sitting on the big old mare as she faced the setting sun, Jo realised that her pulse was pounding hard in the side of her neck. It gradually dawned on her that, distracted first by the tourist's rudeness and then by the intervention of mulanyin, she'd turned away from Chris's gate ten minutes ago without thinking, and had – for no good reason at all – headed west when her intention had been the complete opposite. A shiver of alarm ran through her, and she quickly turned Athena around to head downhill, back where they had come from. Gravel again crunched underneath as she rode the horse forward. A few small stones dislodged and went bouncing down the steep dirt track in front of her.

To Jo's horror, after they'd gone no more than a dozen steps downhill, she heard it again. The indistinct sound of a distant motor.

Leave me the fuck alone, will you? Sing to Twoboy, who actually wants to hear it!

She gave a sharp yip of alarm, wishing that the track was wider, safe to trot or, better yet, canter down. Instead, they were forced to pick a way downhill through the gravel, at a rapid walk. The sound followed almost the whole way, finally fading as the bitumen came into view. By the time they reached the safety of the road, Jo was sweating beneath her jumper, and cranky with anxiety and confusion. She could feel the beginnings of a headache starting up at the base of her skull. It was all too much.

Bloody ignorant tourists.

Mulanyin acting like a crazy bird.

Mooki trying to sing her songs she didn't want to know about, in a place she had never meant to go.

Thoroughly spooked, Jo abandoned the idea of visiting Chris. It would be better just to get home to the safety of her own place, where mooki and mulanyin and rude-fucker dugais couldn't intrude, and where she could think in peace about what all these events might mean.

But Athena had sensed her rider's edginess and in typical horsy fashion began to share it. Agitated, and pointed towards home, the mare could see no good reason at all not to gallop at full pelt, away from the inchoate danger in the hills. Jo had to fight her for control. Being on a bolting thoroughbred was hardly more fun than being surrounded by chanting mooki on a lonely ridgetop. Denied her gallop, Athena jigged sideways in uncomfortable rebellion, throwing Jo roughly around in the saddle. The horse's agitation took hold and stuck until, finally, after ten minutes of painful struggle, Jo lost her temper with the mare. Swearing loudly and leaning far forward, she smacked Athena's neck hard with the flat of her right hand. The horse jerked away violently, showing the whites of her eyes, and half-rearing. The dogs slunk near Athena's hocks with their tails tucked low, sensing that they, too, were only moments away from assault. For a brief minute, Jo hated herself and Athena equally. Then, as they jigged towards the final creek crossing before home, and as the road narrowed to one lane for the last time, Jo heard a car coming up fast from behind her.

'Get off the road,' she yelled in fury at Daisy and Warrigal, 'you stupid fucking dogs.' She reefed at the reins again and Athena nosed the sky in protest. Jo pulled her roughly onto the skerrick of footpath away from the vehicle – which was, thankfully, slowing as it drew near. Don't rear, Jo prayed, for Christ's sake don't rear up with a car right on top of us.

She glanced anxiously around and discovered Rob Starr's yellow ute drawing near, with young Sam Nurrung in the passenger seat, and a chainsaw sliding noisily forward in the tray as Starr hit the skids. Hearing the racket of metal scraping on metal, Jo was momentarily grateful to be on Athena and not on Comet, who would definitely have freaked.

Slowing some more, Starr lifted his right forefinger to Jo in the classic country salute. As she fought to keep Athena and both dogs off the bitumen, and hoping desperately that Starr hadn't seen her slap the mare's neck, Jo didn't respond – she couldn't have responded if she had wanted to.

Later, dismounting at home, stroking Athena's neck in a useless gesture of guilt and regret, Jo slowly put two and two together.

By going up the fire trail directly opposite Chris's place, Jo realised, she must have strayed over near the far top corner of Starr's property. There had been cut timber in the back of his ute. Fresh cut branches and an orange Stihl chainsaw, yellow sawdust on the tray. He had clearly been cutting wood at the top of the hill, not far from where she'd halted Athena on the trail. Either that, or the arsehole was illegally harvesting rainforest timber out of the World Heritage. Either way, that orange Stihl chainsaw was almost certainly the sound that she'd heard.

There was no need, after all, for superstitious panic about mooki and ridge singers.

The relief Jo got from this revelation was huge. She unsaddled Athena with a far easier mind, putting extra molasses in her feed, and brushing her gently until the mare eventually settled.

Losing your temper's not the end of the world, Jo told herself guiltily as she went inside. Horses in the wild have violent, fear-ridden lives. Mares regularly fight each other for dominance, not just the stallions, and a boss mare constantly has to prove her position to the lesser members of the herd. Athena probably just thinks I'm showing her who's in charge. And anyway, horses live in the moment. You haven't forgotten about hitting her, but she has.

'How's Aunty Chris?' Ellen asked from in front of World of Warcraft. Telstra must be having a rare good day, Jo observed.

'Dunno. I got distracted and ended up on the other ridge,' she said slowly. 'And is your homework done?'

'Yep,' Ellen lied cheerfully. 'Annie Bowden rang to see if you're still coming over.'

'She must really want to sell me a stockhorse,' Jo answered, buttering slices of bread with the last scrapings of the margarine container. 'Maybe she's taking lay-by. Fifty cents a week for the rest of my life.'

'Can I come too?' Ellen asked, looking up. If there were new horses to be bought, she wanted to be there.

'Yeah, but don't get excited. It's not happening.' Jo shot Ellen a look, remembering how desperately hope outweighed rationality at thirteen. She pointed to the bright red rates notice on the fridge. 'That's how much hope there is of me buying a registered stockhorse.'

'My paintings'll sell for megabucks one day,' Ellen promised, making Jo smile sadly. Ah, if only. The jahjam hadn't yet realised that the world didn't want Aboriginal art by pale Goorie girls on the east coast. Buyers wanted exotica, dots and circles, red dust and people of Twoboy's colour – the real Aboriginals, cos they, the dugais, said so.

Sitting in front of the ABC news with a cheese jaffle, Jo suddenly remembered that young Sam had been in Rob Starr's ute. The kid seemed to spend his life hitchhiking around the shire ... Had he simply accepted a lift from Starr? Denied the chance of dancing with DJ's troupe, she mused, a fatherless lad might have latched onto Starr's redneck toughness instead. And if a harsh, judgemental Christianity at home makes for a lonely, wandering teenager, then the uncomfortable question arose: Just what sort of middle-aged farmer wanted to take a young boy out into remote bush paddocks in the late afternoon where there was nobody else around to see or hear?

Jo hoped she was wrong, but there had been something in Rob Starr's bearing as he drove past that spoke to her of a hidden darkness. A shying away from scrutiny. This line of thought, and the difficulty of saying anything useful about it to anyone, had her tossing uneasily again before she slept that night.

Jo wandered around the makeshift art gallery inside the high school hall, and quickly realised why Granny Nurrung and not Aunty Sally Watt was doing the honours on the judging panel. Fully a quarter of the exhibits were signed by Watts, Bullockheads or Browns. Nervous at this unwelcome discovery, Jo looked around for the owners of these dangerous surnames. Yep, there was Oscar's missus, sitting with Johnny and a scattering of teenagers she didn't know, Byron and Piccabeen High kids no doubt, over on the far side of the basketball court. No sign of Sally yet, though, nor of Uncle Oscar himself. Maybe an art show inside a dugai institution was too much of an ask for the big culture man. It had certainly been too much for Twoboy, who reacted to any mention of mainstream schools as though Jo was pressing him to pick up a brown snake and begin a polite conversation with it.

Jo felt that the pivoting heads and low unimpressed mutterings of the seated Bullockhead mob probably had something to do with her. She turned her back on them coldly, and went in the opposite direction to where Ellen, Chris and Uncle Pat were parked next to a barefoot DJ. A high school auditorium jam-packed with dugais wasn't somewhere that trouble was likely to start – but then again, with a mob who carried weapons in their cars, who knew? Jo felt a lot less vulnerable standing beside the calmly neutral Wiradjuri presence that was DJ.

'What's the verdict?' Chris asked as Jo came up.

'Some of them are really good, eh.' Jo nodded in affirmation. Ellen's eagle was the standout, but a few of the other students were talented as well. There were the inevitable black hands grasping white ones in friendship, but there were also several excellent renditions of Chincogan in oils and in charcoal. One older boy had produced a fine painting that drew heavily upon his Yamatji ancestry on the far side of the continent, and this framed picture already bore a bright red dot of success. Ellen's painting bore a sign saying Not For Sale, and Jo had proudly heard more than one punter stop and wish that it was.

'You've done well with em, brother,' Jo told DJ as she kissed him hello. 'We all know how much work you do with our jahjams,' she added – then he was mobbed by his adoring dancers and dragged away to perform the opening.

'Lot of the blokes are real jealous of him, eh,' Chris told Jo, 'cos he actually lifts a finger to help the boys.'

'Typical,' Jo said. 'It's a lot easier to run other Goories down than to get off your arse and do something. I wish we could clone him, we need about fifty DJs.'

The mike squealed and squawked from the stage, demanding attention. Jo, Chris and Ellen turned to face the head, who stood alongside the three judges. DJ's boys danced, uncertain at first but finishing stronger, to loud applause from the parochial crowd of two hundred. Then Granny Nurrung stepped up to do the welcome to country.

Behind her, DJ and his boys stood semi-naked, painted in white ochre, and with bright scarlet lap-laps around their hips. Most of the boys had scarlet headbands on, proudly stating that they were youths on the way to manhood, and several had bright red, black and yellow beads on arms or neck, too.

'Geez, get some jumpers on them boys,' Jo whispered to Chris, 'before they all catch bloody pneumonia. And if that old lady makes us pray for the Lord's guidance, or tells us that the fucking children are our fucking future, I'll scream out loud right here on the spot.'

Chris stifled an irreverent giggle.

'Welcome, everybody,' said Granny Nurrung in a high strong voice that made Jo wonder if she was a lay-preacher. 'I'd like to welcome you all here to the combined art show, by our very talented Goorie children. I want to begin by acknowledging that we are on Bundjalung land here today, and I really do also want to thank our Lord Christ Jesus for bringing us together here on this occasion. I'm sure you'll all agree that our young ones have been blessed with a great lot of talent, as you can see. I'd like you to give them all a big round of applause, one and all, whether they've won a prize for their art tonight or not. God bless.'

Duty done, Granny Nurrung stepped back into the line of dignitaries. There had been no direct praise of the heathen DJ, Jo noticed. The entire speech was brief and low-key, she thought as she clapped, very modest, just like the conservative clothes the old lady had chosen for the event. In stark contrast to the dancers, and to most of the Aboriginal people in the crowd, Granny Nurrung wore no red, black or yellow. A paisley scarf in brown ochres was draped around her shoulders in a kind of gesture towards the occasion, but her skirt and jacket were bottle green with a blue trim, suitable for any CWA meeting in the land, and the silver cross around her neck was easily visible from the floor of the hall. As the old lady stepped back out of the limelight, her trim black court shoes stepped on tiny lumps of white ochre which had fallen from the dancers, grinding them into the floorboards. Not for the first time, Jo reflected on the different paths that Goories had taken over the years, the different strategies for survival that individuals and families had found.

'At least she didn't say the bloody Lord's Prayer to kick off,' she told Chris, 'cos I would have walked out, truegod, and probably the Singhs would have come with me. You couldn't blame them.'

'Shush,' said Chris, 'the prizes.'

Participation certificates were distributed, and then the two highly commended awards were given out. Jo began to feel a thrill of jangling nerves, and shifted anxiously where she stood.

Third went to the charcoal drawing of Chincogan. A shy pale girl with a big smile split off from the Bullockhead table and walked up to receive her fifty-dollar voucher, beaming at the floor.

'Sally's granddaughter,' Chris whispered.

Second prize went to the Yamatji boy and his boab trees. Holy crap, thought Jo, meeting Ellen's anxious eyes.

'And first prize,' announced the head to the hushed crowd, pausing for full dramatic effect, 'goes to Ellen Breen, for her painting, *Goorie Life.*'

Jo, Chris and Uncle Pat erupted in cheers, holding each other in a triangle as they bounced up and down for joy.

Filthy looks and a hastily quietened boo from the Bullockheads couldn't spoil the moment. When the head handed Ellen her art-supplies voucher worth three hundred dollars, one of the white teachers leaned over and told her she was the most promising young artist in the northern rivers and not to stop painting, whatever she did. So that's it then, thought Jo later, when Ellen reported this. The dice is thrown and my daughter's future is sealed.

'Talent will out,' Chris said happily on the way home, coasting down the tunnel road to save juice and because the Econovan rolled faster than it drove.

'Just don't think you'll make a living out of art,' Jo lectured Ellen sternly, 'cos in this philistine country you have to be able to kick a football or run like Cathy Freeman to make any real money.'

'Uh-huh,' Ellen contradicted, waving her voucher joyfully in her mother's face till Jo batted it away in proud irritation. Be good, she reflected, if it was a voucher for Fred Henry's garage in Billinudgel and not for the Lismore art supply shop. Having a three-hundred-dollar voucher was one thing, having the petrol to get over and redeem the bloody thing was quite another.

'You done good,' Jo smiled at Ellen. 'Real good, bub.'

'Well, I don't need to ask who won!' Twoboy laughed when they ran inside, Ellen literally bouncing for joy as she showed him her voucher.

Jo kissed the man in front of Ellen and Chris, delighted that he had turned up without warning on a weeknight. The sight of the Commodore parked in the drive still thrilled her as much as it had the first time. It had her singing as she threw her bag into the bedroom. Maybe it really was *love, love, love . . . luh-huv . . .*

'Hers was the best by about a country mile,' Jo skited, opening the fridge. A fresh carton of Tooheys stashed there. She ripped three stubbies out.

'Want a drink?' Jo asked Ellen, awarding Twoboy another brownie point because he'd thought to bring soft drink for the kid.

'Shoulda heard how many people wanted to buy it,' Chris added proudly, winking at Ellen.

'You can get some really good paints with that,' Twoboy told her, handing the voucher back. 'Canvasses, too.'

'Don't want paint,' Ellen disagreed, 'I'm concentrating on drawing and pastels. Can I have a beer, Mum?'

'No bloody way. Have a coke or a cuppa tea.' Jo frowned. Now she'd need to keep a closer eye on how many stubbies were left in the fridge in the mornings. 'Your brain's still growing and it don't need grog.'

'Whereas yours is shrinking and it no longer matters?' asked Ellen. Jo raised her palm and gammoned she was about to slap the child to the ground.

'Was old goonah guts there?' Twoboy asked, draining two-thirds of his beer in one long draw and, winking at Jo, surreptitiously backhanding the remainder to the kid. Ellen quickly disappeared with it to her room. Chris grinned while Jo pursed her lips. Grog was for adults, not kids.

'No,' Jo answered, 'but there was a dozen Bullockheads. None of them too happy when they realised who Ellen was and that she'd done them out of three hundred bucks.'

'They try anything on?' Twoboy asked, suddenly tense. Jo shook her head.

'Nah, just a few dirty looks. The joint was packed fulla white parents, anyway. But I was glad Chris was with us when we walked out.'

Jo ran a finger around the mouth of her stubby. It was difficult to know just how worried to be about the Bullockheads. Whether to accept Twoboy's analysis that they were basically all talk, or, alternatively, keep in mind the memory of Oscar and Johnny on the Devine bridge, approaching with a blunt instrument and only too happy to use it. Sally Watt, Twoboy then revealed, hadn't been at the art show because she'd been in Brisbane that morning, fronting the tribunal with her concoction of half-truths about her family tree.

'*Half*-truths?' Jo asked. She was weary of multiple barely understood family trees, and the suspicions that they aroused. 'How do ya mean, half-truths? Have they got a claim or haven't they?'

'Sally's Oscar's second cousin, right?' Twoboy said, as he ripped the scab off another stubby and threw it into the recycling bucket. His look said he'd been through this a million times before – why couldn't Jo seem to keep it straight in her mind?

'Only second?' Jo asked, surprised. Yes, Twoboy sighed.

'According to Mum, Sally's great-great-grandmother Mary Mullet was born in Piccabeen, but her great-grandfather on the other side, Albert Watt – who's Oscar's great-grandfather too, of course, and Steve's and Patti's and Shane's and all them lot – he was from Newcastle or Sydney or somewhere else way the hell down south. He might even have been from Westown, the lawyer told me today. So Sally might – *might* – have a real claim through her maternal line, but for some fucking reason she's saying her links coming from the great-grandfather Albert. Same bloke Oscar's claiming through, but it's all bullshit.'

'Why would she do that?' Jo asked, deciding that she liked the effect of the beer far too much to stop at one or two. Fuck it, she was going to get bombed on the windfall of Twoboy's carton. She'd gone to work with a hangover before. 'Why not just go it alone on the great-great-grandmother line and not have to deal with Oscar's mob at all?'

'She's running scared,' Chris interjected. 'Oscar's got all them mad cousins that are forever in and out of jail, and he's a bully from way back, always has been. Even as a teenager he was a bloody prick. I remember him bashing the tourist kids one Christmas at the Piccabeen pool. He's standing over Sally to lie for him in court, I betcha anything.'

Jo opened a packet of two minute noodles, and considered this idea. It made a lot of sense. Aunt Sally had always struck her as a decent woman, someone who genuinely wanted to hold the community together with the scant resources she had at her disposal. But good intentions were no match for the brute force of Uncle Oscar. Sally, Jo reflected, had little more than her white husband and her own straight Goorie backbone to rely on when it came to countering the nephews and poly pipes that Oscar could summon with a snap of his fingers. Maybe, given the choice of going Oscar's way or getting nothing at all, Sally had decided to trust the thin trail of blood that they shared, and treat it as the path of least resistance. Jo upturned the Mi Goreng into a bowl and broke the hard wavy mass apart with her fingers before putting it on the bench.

'Yeah, you're probably right,' Twoboy agreed, crunching noodles. 'I used to like Sally alright, before all this shit came along. But she's picked her side. Just bad luck for her she's gone and listened to old goonah guts and jumped onto the wrong team. Cos he ain't winning jack shit at the tribunal with his lies, I'll tell you that for free.'

'I dunno . . .' Jo tossed her empty stubby into the recycling. 'Have you seen his birth certificates and everything?'

'I seen enough,' Twoboy responded tartly. 'He was born here, more's the pity, and so he reckons this his country! But that fat old prick's from freshwater mob, ya can see it in his ugly mug. He wouldn't know how to find the beach with a fucken GPS. Put him up on the hill at Ocean and he'd go, oh daw, what's the big blue wet thing? Yeah, the fucken jang can flap, but he got any story for this country? He's gammon, he got nothing!'

'Well, I hope the tribunal sees it that way,' Jo said, finally convinced that Twoboy knew what he was talking about when it came to the Bullockheads and their scorched earth campaign. With a new beer open, she put it to Twoboy that, really, if you looked at it objectively, Sally Watt was being shafted, the same as he and Laz and Mum Jackson were: cos if Oscar managed to convince the tribunal to hand him the powers of a traditional owner, there'd be no way in hell Sally would share in whatever bounty followed – she'd quickly find herself *persona non grata* in Oscar's stronghold of Piccabeen, and might would once again have been made right, the same as it always had been when it came to blackfellas and the dugai law.

'Are you asking me to feel sorry for Sally Watt?' Twoboy asked, folding his arms and drilling Jo with his black-eyed stare. 'Christ almighty.'

'Maybe.' Jo felt like being stubborn. 'She always had time for me, before you came along. We got along pretty good.'

'She's worked her ring off for years to keep the blackfellas around here at peace,' added Chris.

Twoboy ignored this, and addressed Jo instead.

'Listen, pollyanna, this might look like a fight with lawyers in a fancy courtroom, but really it's a *war*. You got that? A war, not a game, over the same thing that war's always been over anywhere in the world – country. And the sooner you realise that, the sooner you'll work out where I stand, and why.'

It sounded like he was saying, *where you stand too*. 'Like there's ever going to be perfect justice come out of a white man's court. Us mob are at war over the scraps off the white man's table, and once you decide to play that game, it's no holds barred –'

But Jo still couldn't get the picture of Johnny and Oscar on the bridge out of her mind. Something had been bothering her about that day, something that didn't quite fit with Twoboy's avowals of war. She suddenly remembered what it was.

'Well, if it's all a war, if real justice doesn't come into it, then why'd ya chuck Johnny's pipe in the river that day, instead of just smashing him with it?' she countered, before adding tartly, 'and don't fucking call me pollyanna, thanks. I've been around the block a couple of times.'

'Assault with a weapon,' Twoboy told her, 'gets you double the jail time as ordinary assault. Johnny Bullockhead might be fucken stupid enough to go down for a three-year stretch in the middle of a Native Title case, but I'm not. I'm playing the long game, girl.'

'You really thought of that, with him standing there ready to smash you?' Jo asked, disbelieving that anyone could be so cool, half-completed law degree or not.

Twoboy looked away briefly. Then he unfolded his arms and braced his hands on the top of the kitchen bench. Chris and Jo watched him.

'Listen. Strength lies in unity, not in numbers. Oscar thinks cos he's got a big mob of family, all them hardheaded nephews, he's got the advantage, and to an extent that's true, especially right now. But Oscar's really just a fat old cunt who's got where he is with pure rat cunning, not strategic intelligence. And come one week, two weeks, three weeks time, Johnny – who's no fucken rocket scientist, mind you – he's gonna be sitting in front of the telly, or driving the kids to school, or on the bog having a shit, and he's suddenly gonna go: *Hey! Uncle Oscar wanted me to go up against Twoboy on the bridge that day, when he had the weapon, and I had seven-eights of fuck all.*'

Twoboy's eyes gleamed with the pleasure of anticipating this revelation on Johnny's part.

'And at that second, at that exact moment, Oscar's biggest advantage is gonna flip, and become his weakness. Cos Johnny's a fucken dickhead, but he's not so dumb that he'll put his arse on the line for Oscar time and time again once he realises he's expendable. Won't be long, Oscar's gonna be spending more time keeping them boys of his in line, than thinking about how to win the case. And then,' Twoboy concluded with a small grim smile, 'I'll have him.'

'Divide and rule,' Jo mused.

'An army's opportunities come from exploiting the openings in the environment caused by the enemy's weakness in a given area,' Twoboy recited. 'Sun Tzu. Han Dynasty. If Oscar had read it, I might be worried, but he hasn't, or if he did he didn't pay much fucking attention. So when we win in court, it'll be all over red rover for Oscar and every other Bullockhead. The whole mob of em can go and rot in hell, for all I care.'

'Hang on,' Jo said slowly, looking at Chris and aware that now she perhaps *was* being a little bit of a pollyanna. 'I thought you Lawmen were supposed to take care of everything on your country. No exceptions.'

'And?' Twoboy looked blank. The idea that the Bullockheads were a part of his country had never once entered his head.

'Aunty Barb always told me Law meant taking responsibility for the whole bloody lot.' Jo went on, remembering how adamant the old girl had been on this point. Chris nodded. Everything was connected, and nothing could be ignored, however inconvenient.

It finally dawned on Twoboy what his woman was on about.

'Shit. You looking for Saint Twoboy again, are you?' he asked sarcastically.

'I'm just looking for a bit of consistency,' Jo argued, digging in. 'Either everything on country's connected, or nothing is.'

'Well, once they lose the case and fuck off, they won't be on my country,' Twoboy said breezily. 'So the problem won't exist.'

'But you just said Sally might have a legitimate claim!' Jo retorted as she opened the fridge door.

A momentary pause.

'So, I contain multitudes,' Twoboy threw at her with a boyish grin. 'Sue me.'

You charming handsome bastard, thought Jo, softening. You get me on that jag hook every time.

As Chris's old bomb sputtered and backfired into life in the driveway a few minutes later, Jo opened another stubby and looked at Twoboy through frosted beer goggles.

'I might be a little bit drunk,' she confessed.

'I think you might be right,' he twinkled.

Jo decided that standing in front of her was absolutely the most gorgeous man she'd ever seen, let alone kissed. She told him so, and Twoboy laughingly agreed. He scooped Jo up and into the bedroom, where they proceeded to make a great deal of noise. Lying in the rumpled bedclothes, Jo reminded Twoboy of what he'd said earlier in the week.

'You know how you said you're big and black and educated, and nobody thinks you're a good idea?' she asked.

'Mmm,' he responded, half-asleep with his arm around her neck and his dreads spilling chaotically over both pillows.

'Well, I think you're a good idea,' Jo told him, curling into his shoulder. 'I think you're a bloody good idea.'

Twoboy smiled gently, and promptly lost consciousness. Soft snoring filled the room.

'I love you,' Jo whispered anyway.

'So we finally gotcha over to the wilds of Burringbar,' Annie teased. Jo stood on the dusty concrete apron of the Produce Store at the End of the World. Outside the huge metal shed, Ellen was making a noisy fuss of Annie's Irish wolfhound, Doofus. Annie clambered down from her antediluvian forklift, which stank of burning brake pads, tossed her cowboy hat onto the counter, and hugged her visitors. From his reclining lounge chair in the depths of the shed, Dicko boomed a greeting. Nothing new there then, thought Jo drily, Annie doing all the hard yakka while Dicko nurses his depression and talks shit to the few customers he can actually stand.

'How's business?' she asked, comparing Annie's prices on the wall to those at the Co-op. Slightly cheaper. They'd want to be, since the Produce Store really was at the end of the world, out along a beautiful but isolated bush road dead-ending at the western foot of Bottlebrush. If it wasn't for Annie, Jo often thought, nary a soul would make the trip to this out-of-the-way valley. Personally, she wouldn't have gone to the end of her driveway to buy feed off Dicko.

'Yeah, not too bad. The salt-licks are flying out the door, they keep us going.' Annie nodded at the salt-licks custom-made onsite that she sold all over the east coast to the owners of glossy show horses desperate for an edge in the ring.

'Remind me to grab one when I go,' Jo offered. It was payday, her petrol tank was full, and the rates were finally taken care of. She'd have thirty dollars spending money this fortnight, after the indulgence of the salt-lick.

'Well come and see me nags.'

Annie opened the five-bar gate to her stables, carefully back-heeling a Scotch thistle into oblivion. Ellen and Jo followed her through a narrow lane to the stalls, where six handsome equine heads were looking out eagerly for their dinners. Three of the nickering horses were good-looking chestnuts, yearlings out of Annie's foundation broodmares, which grazed, fat-bellied with this season's foals yet to drop, beside the stables.

'Your mares throw true to type, eh,' Jo noted.

Annie nodded at the yearling carbon copies.

Another pair of stabled heads were bay fillies, reeking of quality. They had just been trucked back from the home of a prize-winning stallion down south.

'Remember this one?' Annie said, removing the hood from the taller of the two fillies. 'You liked her blaze. We registered her as Burringbar Whatnot.'

Jo remembered seeing the horse almost two years ago. She'd liked the question mark crescent that curved down the middle of the filly's forehead before dribbling to an end just short of her nostrils. Jo put a hand out for the horse to smell.

'She's beautiful,' Ellen said wistfully.

'Yeah, she's a cutey alright.' Annie's gruff manner did not quite mask how proud she was of the horses she bred.

Jo stroked Whatnot's neck, noticing how quiet all Annie's

yarraman were. Being a two-year-old, Jo estimated, Whatnot had already had a couple of thousand dollars work put into her, on top of the stallion's service fee of about a grand. Plus a fair whack for Annie's profit. Ah, wish. She's lovely, Jo told herself in a feeble attempt at consolation, but she's no Comet.

'And now for the piece of resistance,' Annie announced, opening the door of the last stall. Jo's heart flew up into her throat and she heard Ellen's sharp intake of breath. Standing in the bright yellow straw of the stall was the taffy she had been ordered to come to see. The filly was stunning, with a fine classic head, small ears and clean straight legs ending in four black hooves. When she matures, Jo judged, she'll muscle up and really turn into something out of the box. And that *colour*. The horse's coat shone with the soft bronze of a stingray seen through shallow water in afternoon light.

'Hooley dooley,' Jo turned to her friend, rapt. 'She's something like a racehorse undersized!'

'Yeah, we must've done something right,' Annie said with a small smile of pride, sliding the rugs off to reveal the horse's sculptured lines. The filly flicked her creamy tail at an imaginary insect on her flank, then rubbed her dark nose against a foreleg. Her large eyes held a haughty expression, not caring whether or not the humans watched her. She was a princess holding court before her inferiors.

'Far fucking out. What's her name?' said Jo, entranced.

'We registered her as Burringbar Hotrod, because she's a Hot Cat granddaughter, but her stable name's Gift.'

'Wow. You gonna start her before you sell her?' Jo asked. The taffy let out a loud whinny to one of the broodmares outside, and shifted nervously in the stall, her tail swishing with mild anxiety. Not yet settled from her trip up, Jo thought, still working out where in the new herd she belonged.

'Steady on, love. Who said I'm selling her?' Annie said. Of course, Jo chided herself. A filly like this didn't come along every season; Annie would keep her to breed from, try and get more of the taffy colour into her herd, and the height and that fine-boned head, too.

Maybe by the time Gift was dropping foals in a few years, Jo'd be in a position to buy one. She should get Annie to stick her on the list of people lining up to buy the colt foals. Jo dreamed of rounding up cattle in the Big Paddock aboard a leggy taffy gelding that could turn on a dime.

'How did she end up taffy?' Jo asked with a wrinkled brow, suddenly curious. Taffy was a genetic variant of black, and neither Annie's stallion nor the father of the bays was black.

Annie laughed. 'Ah, now there's a story. Her mum's an escape artist from way back – that little bay Hot Cat mare, remember her? Well, when she was down south last year – having been trucked there, mind you, at great bloody expense, to have a dirty weekend with Jagged Edge – she decided she liked the look of the thorough-bred across the road better. Big, black mother of a thing that placed in two Caulfield Cups. Mum jumped the fence and here's the result. She should make sixteen hands, I reckon.'

Jo laughed, too. That adventure meant the filly was a first cross stockhorse, not a pure blood. That would bring the price down a little. Say four thousand. Still unimaginably out of reach.

'So you like her, eh?' Annie was squinting into the stall.

'Yeah,' replied Jo, 'of course I do. She's bloody beautiful.'

'Well, mate, there's a reason we called her Gift,' Annie said.

Jo looked across, not understanding. Doofus nudged her leg, and Jo reached down and patted the dog without taking her eyes off Annie. She waited for an explanation.

'She's yours. We registered you as the new owner,' Annie said, sticking her hands in her jeans pockets and leaning back against the stable wall. Ellen let out a squeal of delight that made several sets of ears swivel her way.

Jo instantly shook her head, ignoring the childish voice inside her that was screaming to say yes. She didn't want charity off Annie. Off anyone. Land, yes. Justice, yes. But not bloody charity. The awful loss of Comet wasn't for Annie to try and fix; she wasn't responsible for that. She wasn't even a dugai. That tragedy had nothing to do with her.

'I don't accept charity off friends, mate. Thanks anyway.'

'Hang on a minute. It's not charity, exactly,' said Annie, watching the filly, who was now rubbing her nose on the steel mesh partition of the stall. 'I'm not losing anything on her, put it like that. Just accept that the horse is yours – that she's meant for you. And don't go looking her in the mouth too hard.'

'Take her, Mum!' Ellen urged, horrified at the idea of the filly being lost because of her mother's stupid pride. 'Don't be an idiot. How else are you ever gonna get a horse like that?'

Jo shot Annie a curious look. Not losing anything on her?

'I'm serious,' Annie said, beginning to smile because she could tell Jo was about to give in. 'Accept her gracefully, and don't ask too many questions. She's yours. It's really very simple.'

'She's not stolen, is she?' Jo probed, chewing on her bottom lip.

Annie laughed and said she would show Jo the papers back at the shed. *Therese*, thought Jo suddenly, tears accumulating hotly behind her eyes. This is Therese's doing, with some of that ten grand from the scratchie. She looked at the filly and began to imagine owning her. Riding her. Putting her in foal, eventually, and breeding more taffies. Watching newborn golden colts and fillies cantering in her paddocks beside their mother.

'I'll truck her over for you today, if you want,' Annie added with a huge grin.

'You've made me cry now, you bloody beeyatch.' Jo blew her nose.

'Stand next to her,' Ellen instructed, raising her mobile phone. She took Jo's picture with Gift looking over her shoulder at the camera.

'Its a crap photo,' she informed her mother. 'Your face looks all blurry. She looks good, but. See.'

'My face *is* all blurry,' Jo said, wiping her streaming eyes and going into the stall to introduce herself.

CHAPTER TWELVE

'I'm heading up the top now,' Twoboy rumbled. 'You coming, or what?'

Jo briefly took her eyes from the wonder of Gift, grazing right there in her paddock, to look at her lover stowing an MP3 player into his backpack. His question was pregnant with meaning. Whose side are you on, it asked, mine – or the rest of the world? The man had spent half the afternoon testing the device, readying it for this latest excursion to the ridge. As he waited for her answer, Twoboy squirted white insect repellent onto his hands and smeared it thickly over his neck and ears, readying himself for the long hours of searching. Its chemical stench filled the kitchen, overpowering the incense that Jo had just burned in an attempt to drive out the lingering smell of the mould the big rain had left behind.

'I said no,' Jo flared. 'Which part of no are you having trouble with, exactly?'

There were a million things she'd rather do than go up on the ridge and seek out the talga of the dead, full moon or no full moon. If she thought it would make any difference to the case, then maybe – *maybe* – she would have agreed to go along with his crazy obsession, stepping by his side onto that dangerous ground. But her man was living in cloud cuckoo land, chasing after songs and meanings that no dugai in Australia would ever consider important, or even admit were real. Maybe a wild-eyed anthro or two might agree that the ancestors were talking to him. Everybody else would sling him in the Lismore clinic onetime, and throw away the key. Same as they'd lock her up if she went around telling everybody about what she'd heard beside the fallen gum. They'd be whipping out the Melleril before she had time to say *audio–visual psychosis* or *schizophrenic tendencies*. It was lose–lose, and this little black duck was staying right at home where she belonged, thank you very much.

'Then I'll go by meself,' he answered, turning abruptly on his heel and heading across the Big Paddock. 'Thanks for nothing.'

'Ah, get over yaself, ya womba prick,' Jo muttered, and turned her back on Twoboy and the ineffable mysteries of the ridge. She eyed, instead, the infant walking-stick palms that she had uprooted at work and brought home to replant around Comet's grave. The half-dozen seedlings were clustered in a muddy bundle against the side of the feed shed, and she had plenty of light left to get them in the ground if she hurried. Then maybe time to do another session on the lunge with Gift. Jo's face softened.

She wondered for the thousandth time how she should best respond to Therese, who consistently denied, grinning and shaking her head, that she had anything to do with the horse's sudden appearance in her life.

'I'm gonna go whack these in near the dam,' Jo called to Kym.

Her sister, along with Ellen and the boys, was standing at the ute, which was now newly decorated with an assortment of stars, handprints, and stylised local wildlife. The cheerful art reminded her of Rover Thomas but with a distinctly east-coast flavour. On paper last night Jo hadn't been convinced, but she was proved wrong now. Splashed over the doors and bonnet of the car, their bold, simple Goorie designs in red, black and yellow looked exactly right.

'Good eagle!' Jo praised their efforts with a tiny pang of misgiving. She and Ellen would be conspicuous everywhere they drove now; no more hiding away in the anonymity of just another white Toyota. The car proudly proclaimed that here were Goories driving around, coming soon, alive and deadly, to a town near yufla.

Jo hoped that the Bullockheads were planning on keeping to the south of the shire; they certainly wouldn't have any trouble finding her on this side of the river if they came north. Maybe it was time she, too, started carrying a pipe or a baseball bat behind the driver's seat. Ah, lordy. What *would* Buddha do?

'She's pretty flash, eh?' Kym said proudly, putting a finishing touch to a purple platypus swimming towards the ute's rear wheel, which now stood for a waterhole.

With her passenger door complete, Ellen suddenly dumped her brushes in a vegemite jar of water, roared a mock threat and broke away. She chased Jarvis and Kai, trying to smear her paint-reddened hand across their faces. The boys shrieked happily as they did dust-spurting laps of the house. Daisy and Warrigal barked and bounded alongside the kids, tails wagging sixteen to the dozen. As Ellen ran out of puff, the boys and dogs collapsed in a pile of giggles beside the car – where Timbo was intently using a mango twig to scrape a delicate pattern in the yellow paint of his turtle.

The lad's pretending to write his name, Jo noted in amusement. Well, we've got a muso and a couple of decent artists in the family now, must be about time we had a writer.

A perfect day. Jo grinned some more and fought the temptation to turn a hose on the tangled pile of boyish limbs in front of her. She longed to hear her nephews scream and laugh all day – the sound that had echoed through this valley for thousands of years. Happy blackfella kids, *jahjam minjehleyni*. The tanks weren't big enough to squander the water though, so Jo went, instead, to put her trees in the ground.

'Come and slap ya hand on ere first, tidda,' Kym called. 'It's your car.' Jo obediently came back, to place a yellow palm on the driver's side door where a space had been left below the Milky Way for just this purpose. Twoboy wasn't here to add his print, she said then – he'd gone up to begin his crazy vigil on the ridge again.

'Tilting at windmills, eh? What that fella reckon he's gonna find up there?' Kym asked, beginning to tidy the paint and rinse the brushes under the outside tap, turning the muddy puddle beneath it into a watery rainbow.

'Enlightenment, maybe,' Jo said. 'Christ only knows. Who knows what men think?'

'It's for court, but, hey?' Kym pressed.

Last night Jo had finally told Kym about hearing the talga. Jason had enough similar tales from Waka Waka country to make Kym listen and nod thoughtfully. It was a shame, the sisters agreed, that Aunty Barb had passed, since their old aunt would have known exactly what to make of the talga, or at least what to do next. Jo told Kym that, since asking Aunty Sally Watt obviously wasn't an option any more, she intended to look for Uncle Humbug and get his opinion. That's if he would agree to yarn. Some weeks only Slim was privy to Humbug's communications, and besides, the old man had been keeping a low profile lately. Someone said he'd been locked up again, poorfella.

'Can't Twoboy just ask his mum?' Kym looked up from her dripping brushes to the ridge.

Mum Jackson was pretty vague to start with, Jo explained, and a minor stroke a month earlier had disabled her even more. Laz had been at his wits' end trying to keep on top of his son's misdemeanours, keep Mum Jackson out of hospital, and do the Native Title research as well.

'That's the thing about elders, eh?' Kym responded wryly, flicking her brushes dry. 'They're *old*.'

'Yep. But Twoboy thinks he's the man, and can short-circuit the process,' Jo said. 'Go bush and talk to the ancestors, straight up. I keep expecting him to come back down and say yeah he found em, and they told him to get a haircut and get a real job.'

Kym laughed, then grew more thoughtful.

'It's a fulltime job, Native Title, eh?' she said. 'It's driving Jason's family mad too. Shitfights everywhere you look. First cousins not talking after fifty years, brothers bashing brothers, it's Colonisation 4.0. The dugai don't have to lift a finger anymore – they've outsourced it to us.'

'Yeah, you're right. I really think Twoboy's finally lost the plot, too,' Jo said. 'He thinks if he can just get them old fellas singing on his little recorder, he can learn it and sing it in language at the tribunal, and that'll prove the connection he needs. But, I mean . . .'

She opened her palms and shrugged in mute frustration. It was madness.

'That doesn't make sense,' Kym agreed, narrowing her eyes. 'Not unless it's been written down somewhere already by anthros. Even then.'

'I tried to get Laz and Uncle Cheezel to talk sense into him, but no good,' Jo went on. 'The stress is pushing him right over the edge, I reckon.' She sighed mournfully and walked away to the dam.

Half an hour later, with dusk falling, the spindly palms had been planted in a circle around Comet's cairn. Come next summer, she told the colt, there's gonna be red berries fruiting all around you, lad. That'll bring bilin bilin for sure. Jo went to the fringe of the pine grove and checked the she-oaks. Each of the two dozen saplings she'd planted in May looked to have survived the worst of winter. Most were now beginning to poke their dark green tips out of the tops of their plastic bags, Jo noted with approval, as she ripped crofton and billygoat weed from around their bases.

Finally she stood tall and stretched her tight back muscles to either side, then washed her hands with a bucket of dam water. Jo whistled for Gift, banging on the plastic of the empty bucket.

The filly immediately came trotting over from where she'd been grazing beside Athena, neck arched and tail high. You are so bloody beautiful, Jo thought, putting a moist hand on the soft dark velvet of Gift's muzzle. She couldn't even look out her kitchen window at the filly without a big silly grin on her face. Horses were so easy to love.

'Can one of you blokes grab that esky?' Jo asked the next day, staggering to the ute with her backpack, a long length of dog chain, assorted towels and jumpers, and a three-litre bottle of orange cordial.

Jason shouldered the blue and white esky and eased it down into the tray of the ute where dogs and kids milled in noisy chaos, fighting for space and vantage points. The big boys and Ellen were standing with their arms looped under the bar that ran across the top of the cabin. Twoboy and Jason both sat beneath, their backs against the cabin, looking at the tailgate. Timbo was firmly wedged on his father's lap with strong tan arms lacing him where he belonged. The dogs resigned themselves to being lowest on the pecking order, standing at the men's feet with their tongues lolling.

'Youse wanna hang on tight,' Jason warned Kai and Jarvis before calling, 'Drive nice 'n' slow, sis, we don't want any of these lads sailing over the top.' He stubbed his durrie out on the scoured white paint of the tray and redoubled his grip on Timbo.

'Nah, foot it, darl. They'll bounce,' Twoboy joked, then he instructed the boys on how to stand, with legs spread wide and their knees bent to absorb the shock of the rough roads. Despite hearing nothing the previous night on the ridge, his mood this morning was buoyant. Perhaps today, at the lake, far from prying white eyes and the interference of mobile phone signals and satellite TV waves, he would at last receive the ancient messages he was waiting for.

'Yeah, I know,' Jo called back, with a dubious glance in the rear-view mirror. The boys were safe enough at low speeds, but she doubted they'd have the stamina to stand and cling for the forty minutes of dirt track it would to take to get to the lake. After checking once again with Kym that she didn't want to take two cars, Jo slowly reversed out of the drive. Beneath the lychees, Athena and Gift briefly raised their heads to check on the movement of vehicle and humans, and then returned, satisfied, to their endless munching. The outline of Gift silhouetted against the backdrop of green hills stayed with Jo as she drove south into Billinudgel; the creamy contrast of the filly's mane and tail to the bronzed slate of her body, her delicate nostrils, the sharp ridges of her cheekbones running beneath satin skin. That darkest brown of her wise eyes.

I think I could stand and look at them long and long . . .

'You're miles away, aren't ya?' commented Kym, bringing Jo back to the cabin. A carful of Murries in the other lane of the Pacific Highway suddenly tooted and yelled in appreciation of yesterday's art. Yep, this automatic visibility, thought Jo, tooting and waving back, was going to be the future. Oh well. Probably do Ellen good to have a bit more recognition, help her feel okay about living in that lily-white skin.

'Ah, look at this bloody dickhead, will ya,' Jo sneered, as a buttercup yellow Hummer roared past them in the right-hand lane at a hundred and forty kays. On its rear window was a large Australian flag inscribed with the legend: *Support Our Troops*.

'They support the troops alright,' Kym replied, 'till they come home foaming at the mouth with PTSD. Who else is gonna die to fill their petrol tank?'

'You reckon they've thought it through that far?' Jo asked sceptically.

'Nah, probably not. But did you hear they've brought out a more affordable version of the Hummer? It's a car sticker that says *I'm a complete fucktard*. Fits any model, apparently.'

Jo laughed.

Then the Burringbar exit came into view, and she pulled off into the hinterland, where boolimen were scarce, and wouldn't be magnetically attracted by the art and the dark bodies in the tray. The busy clamour of highway traffic was replaced by a Kev Carmody CD and by the wind rushing past Jo's right ear. As they hit the first stretch of dirt and heard the kids shriek with excitement at the potholes, she slowed even more, and realised that the drive was going to take a lot longer than they planned.

'Crap,' said Jo vehemently to the steering wheel, 'I forgot to bring matches. And the bloody insect repellent.'

'Nah, it's all good. Jason's got his lighter,' Kym reassured her. 'And there shouldn't be many mozzies at this time of year, eh, not during the day.'

'Real good blackfellas, eh,' Jo mocked herself. 'Can't go bush without a carload of crap. Not like the old days.'

'Yeah, I remember when we was littles, eh,' Kym agreed, 'Mum'd give us a box of matches and a spud to put in our pocket, and say gorn, get, I don't wanna see yez till its dark.'

'I meant way back when, but yeah, I remember . . .' The tallow-wood trees beside the road were in heavy blossom. The delicate creamy flowers reminded Jo of the gum blossom that had decorated their parents' coffins in the Ballina funeral home. Aunty Barb had insisted on native Australian flowers; a white neighbour, Mrs Epstein (Jo suddenly remembered this for the first time in nearly thirty years), came bearing a beautiful bouquet of yellow and orange gladioli, and had to leave them in the foyer. Only gum blossom was allowed to go to the fires with Mum and Dad. Shit, Jo thought, why think of that horror today? It was going to be a good day, a family day at the lake, and there was no need to dwell on morbid things. She hadn't gone to counselling for two years to be dragged backwards to childhood misery, not after all this time.

'You've gone walkabout again.' Kym looked across at her.

'Just thinking bout Mum and Dad,' Jo said. 'Dunno why. I can go a week at a time, these days. Longer even.'

Kym nodded and put her hand gently on Jo's shoulder.

'What's this you've got?' she asked curiously, rubbing at the raised weal on Jo's arm with the ball of her thumb.

Jo told her about falling on the vase.

'You know that's how some blackfellas get married? With a scar there, just like that?'

Jo laughed and looked in the rear-view mirror at Twoboy. My husband? My *crazy* husband. Not that he's Robinson Crusoe there.

'Remember Mrs Epstein at Mum and Dad's funeral with the gladioli?' Jo asked. To her relief, Kym nodded at the same memory. It had really happened. 'Thank Christ Aunty Barb was there for us, eh. I haven't been to visit her grave for the longest time. And after all we put her through.'

It was nine months or more since Jo's last visit. The trip to the Piccabeen cemetery, on the far outskirts of the inland town, was one of those out-of-the-way journeys that Jo just never seemed to make without deliberate planning. She would go soon, she decided. Pay her respects in person. Take Twoboy along, and introduce him as her man – she should have done that weeks ago, even if it was deep in the heart of Bullockhead territory.

'Speak for yourself,' Kym retorted, diving into her handbag for chewies. 'I was an angel, you were the bloody ratbag, always taking off. Well, you and Stevo.' She wound the ute window down and held the chewies out and back for Kai. 'How is he, anyway, you talk to him lately?'

'Yeah, last week. They're talking about going to live in Mumbai, now. New business opportunities springing up there, he reckons.'

'I bet the gunjies chasing him over Devine's Hill when he was eleven never saw that in his future.' Kym shook her head at how their little brother had turned out.

'All's well that ends well.' Jo had slowed until Kai got both hands firmly on the bar again. She looked pensively in the rear-view. The dogs were milling happily at the far end of the tray. She could only glimpse them through a forest of brown legs, and Ellen's jeans.

'Eh, look out!' Kym cried as a pair of wedgetails came into view, riding the thermals far overhead. Jo leaned forward and peered up, focusing on the distinct diamond of each bird's tail and the massive span of their black-brown wings. Little wonder the Yanks took an eagle for their national totem, she thought. Blind Freddy could see it was the king of birds.

'That's Twoboy's meat,' she told Kym, still craning her neck and slowing. 'And Laz too – all the Jackson men are eagles.' Kym turned and banged on the back window to make sure the crew in the tray had seen. Six upturned faces told her that they had. The wind whipped his words away, but Jo could see in the side mirror Twoboy's mouth moving as he greeted his bird. He'll be pretty happy, Jo thought, now that the eagles had come to give him safe passage onto the country they were about to enter.

After several minutes of driving on corrugated dirt, Jo began to take note of the sparse road signs on the tracks forking off the main road. It had been a very long time since she'd been to the lake, and she was wondering if she'd missed the turn when a familiar derelict cattle dip told her she hadn't. They bumped down a sandy anonymous trail for two more songs, to eventually find a large clearing in the tea-tree scrub. The lake stretched out, smooth and blue and beautiful, in front of them. The clearing, they were delighted to see, was empty of other people, decorated only with a National Parks list of exhortations in a plastic sleeve pinned to a fencepost, telling the world not to light fires, leave rubbish, bring dogs, nor to kill anything in the area. I'll chain the dogs, Jo thought, but bugger not having a fire. And any pooning that wanders in will just have to take its chances. She couldn't see Twoboy and Jason letting a fat porky wander off uneaten, and fair enough too. Not like they were an endangered species.

'It's not a total fire ban, is it?' she asked Twoboy, who had no idea.

'Last one in's a rotten egg!' yelled Jarvis, as he leapt from the tray, ripped his shirt off and bolted towards the water. Jason flung the esky down and sprinted after his middle son. It was Kai who got to him first though, catching his brother by the waistband of his shorts and hurling him in a wide flailing semicircle away from the water.

'You gone and lost ya fucken marbles, boy!' Jason asked, looking down at Jarvis sprawled on the fine white sand. 'Don't you know you never jump in strange water straight up? This place don't know you! Crikey!'

Jarvis shrugged, suddenly shamed. He looked away and feigned interest in the freshwater reeds at the water's edge. Jason shook his head, then squatted on his haunches and introduced his family to the water. Twoboy and Jo joined him, performing the necessary steps to ensure they could swim there unharmed.

Two hours later the boys were shivering with cold around Jo's illicit campfire, despite the warm sun and bellies full of burnt sausages.

'These jahjams need some exercise to warm them up,' announced Twoboy with an evil grin.

He and Jason led the kids into the bush, trekking around the eastern edge of the lake to where a rocky hill overlooked a tiny hidden gully filled with tree ferns and orchids. From the lake shore, Jo and Kym saw the boys scatter into the undergrowth, chasing goannas. There was yelling, laughter, and no success. Lucky we're not relying on you lot for a feed, their father observed drily.

Twoboy announced soon after that he was leaving them, to head into the bush alone, Kai and Jervis found a thousand different ways to ask him what he'd be doing by himself in this strange country. Their uncle had only one infuriating answer for them: silence. Jason flicked a hand up in salute, and led the boys back to the lake, where Jo, Kym and Ellen were sprawled at ease on the sandy edge of the water, listening.

'C'mere bub,' Kym said to her youngest later in the afternoon. Timbo was poking at the coals with a piece of driftwood, trying to turn its tip to a glowing orange coal. She put down her sudoku book and brushed white grains of sand off his arms. 'Had enough to eat?' The child shook his head, and Kym found him the last boiled egg from the bottom of the esky. Jo took the egg and displayed it between her thumb and forefinger.

'Who disfla?' Jo asked. Timbo screwed his face up.

'Bilin?' he guessed. Everybody laughed.

'No, not bilin, bub. Jugi jugi,' Jo taught, as she peeled the egg for him. 'Got that?'

'Not bilin,' the child repeated uncertainly, the large white ovoid cradled in his tiny brown hand. Kym and Jo both laughed again.

'No, it's a bit big for that mate. And we don't eat bilin eggs anyway, not these days,' his mother told him, 'they're too pretty for that. Not enough of them to be eating their eggs just for fun.'

'I seen two bilin before,' Timbo said, taking a careful bite out of the white egg, exposing its crumbly yellow core. 'When the mibun flew up high, high, high in the sky.'

Jo pricked her ears. So, when the eagles were soaring and wheeling overhead that morning, Timbo had noticed two bilin, hiding in a treetop, beside the road. 'Like this,' he said now, lowering his head and freezing with his little legs tucked beneath him, the very picture of a king parrot making itself the smallest possible target. Jo and Kym glanced at each other. Nobody else had seen the brilliant scarlet and green parrots, or even suspected them.

'He doesn't miss much,' Jo said, approving. *Baugul mil.*

'The thing is how much there is to miss,' agreed Kym thoughtfully. 'I mean most of the time, by definition, we think we *have* seen everything. Because how do you even begin to know what you haven't seen?'

'Sounds like Schrödinger's cat. That shit can really make your head hurt if you think about it too much,' Jo answered. Right then she was more worried about what she definitely hadn't seen – Twoboy, who was still not back from his quest with the sun now getting alarmingly close to the top of the hill on the other side of the lake. The largest trees, eucalypts and quandongs, were already throwing long slanting shadows across the lake's rippled surface. The water that had looked a bright appealing blue to Jervis beneath the mid-morning sun as they arrived was now closer to black.

'Ellen,' Jo urged in an attempt to take her mind off this problem, 'give us a hand to put this stuff away, eh?' Ellen groaned, and mimed creeping away, with exaggerated raising of her knees and shoulders. 'It won't take long,' Jo insisted.

Ten minutes later the camp was clear and the ute packed. Everything and everybody was ready to go – except for the one missing ingredient: Twoboy.

'I'm freezing,' complained Jarvis. Behind him, Kai sneezed.

Crap, thought Jo, seeing the first bat of the evening flying overhead. She grimaced at the idea of navigating the forking sandy trails at night.

'We'll end up lost in the hills near bloody Murbah, if we're not careful,' she told Kym. 'Bugger that for a joke. Be better off camping here for the night and braving the mozzies.'

'I'll check if any of these tracks show up in the UBD,' Kym offered.

'Yeah, well, good luck,' replied Jo glumly, wondering if Jason could navigate by the stars. Bored with waiting, Ellen picked up Timbo's driftwood firestick from the coals and began tossing it end over end at the water's edge. Its reddened tip made narrow ellipses of fire in the grainy air.

'You get another one, bub,' she encouraged her cousin. Before long all four kids had glowing throw-sticks and were making patterns against the dusk, laughing and yelling, writing their names and miscellaneous insults for each other in the dark.

'Do you remember how to tell how much light's left?' Jo asked Jason, who wrinkled his nose and shook his head. It had something to do with how many fingers you could hold between the setting sun and the horizon, but what length of time the fingers equalled nobody knew. He held his right hand up. Two fingers. No, not really two, closer to one and a half.

'Real good blackfellas we are,' mourned Kym.

'Get a jumper on, Jarvis,' Jason reminded his son. 'It's in the black bag.'

'Oh, fuck Twoboy!' Jo suddenly erupted, slamming an open hand loudly against the car. 'Where the bloody hell has he got to?'

'Nothing here,' Kym said, closing the street directory, with its useless maps of suburban roads and major highways. 'We'se waaay too far off the beaten track.' She let the UBD fall heavily onto the passenger seat, and sighed.

'Try that topo map,' Jason suggested with a hint of smugness. 'I stuck it in the backpack last night.'

'Aunty Barb would know about the fingers,' Jo said.

Jason strode to the water's edge and let fly a series of loud cooees that sounded through the clearing and across the lake. There was no reply, and Jo felt a spasm of alarm run through her. Sounds carry a long way over water. Was Twoboy safe, somewhere – or had he finally strayed too far, and too dangerously for the ancestors to overlook his transgressions? Was he lying bitten by a brown snake, or sweating in agony with a snapped leg in some distant gorge? She let out her own cooee, but the only answers came from frogs and cicadas. Then a trio of kookaburras on the ridge sang out, chuckling. Great, thought Jo, that's all we bloody need – rain. Now we can get bogged as well as lost. She saw a bank of thick cloud building over the hilltop; any faint hope of navigating their way home by the stars faded.

'Everything alright?' Ellen asked, returning to the car trailed by a petulant Timbo. The boys had thrown his firestick into the lake just to hear its angry hissing.

'Yeah. Probably,' said Jo, causing Ellen's forehead to crease with worry. She promptly picked Timbo up and rested him on her skinny hip, where he had scarcely been since he was a toddler.

'Here,' said Kym, as she closed the car door and waved the topo map at Jo, 'if the tracks aren't on this they're not gonna be on anything.'

She spread the much-folded paper across the bonnet of the ute. Five concerned faces peered down. What had infuriatingly been called 'limit of maps' in the street directory was, on the topo, a finely detailed area full of whorled contour lines, clearly marked minor roads and symbols indicating landmarks large and small. With her index finger, Jo traced the morning's route from the Burringbar turnoff, south-east through the valley and onto the dirt backroads that had led through the thick bush to the lake. Even the old cattle dip was marked. Kym and Ellen both yelped when Jo's finger ran off the edge: the map ended well before the much-forking track they had taken arrived at the water. Jo twisted her mouth ruefully and looked up. It would still be a risk to drive out in the dark. She found herself thinking about that last boiled egg, and wondering if the thermos was really completely empty of coffee.

'Well, if we're careful we should be right, eh,' Kym said, finally. Not a statement, but a question. Maybe, thought Jo. Accentuate the positive, unless it means a cold night in the ute tray with four young kids and no fucking dinner.

'How much petrol you got?' Kym asked, wrapping a damp towel around Timbo, who was starting to shiver in Ellen's arms.

'Half a tank. It's not that, it's the idea of buggerising around getting lost on these tracks in the dark,' said Jo. 'And maybe bogged.'

'We better see if Twoboy turns up, first,' Jason chimed in. 'How dirty will he be if he turns up and we've gone?'

Let him find the dig tree, thought Jo. Serve him right for pissing off and not coming back, not even thinking of the kids, looking for unfindable answers to questions nobody else is even asking. Who does he think he is, Bilbo fucken Baggins?

'Mmm,' she answered, throwing another futile cooee towards the water and hearing the sound fade to nothing.

'Good thing Jase thought to chuck the topo map in, eh,' Kym said to nobody in particular, slapping at the first blood-engorged mozzie of the evening.

'I got sick of doing unplanned overnighters when I was about twenty,' Jason told Jo, 'I'm a proper little boy scout these days.'

As he spoke, a loud cooee trumpeted from the bush behind them. They swung around, relieved and singing out in response. A minute later, Twoboy emerged from the scrub, grinning and unharmed.

He hadn't been lost, he claimed, sucking great gulps of orange cordial, he just hadn't been in any great hurry to get back to the car. No worries.

'Ah, gammon not lost! You reckoned you'd be back well before dark,' Jason mocked, as the women rolled their eyes at each other.

'Well, look la – sun not gorn yet!' Twoboy climbed up into the ute, plopped himself down in the tray and pointed scornfully to the last tiny hint of gold that was lowering itself behind the ridge. 'You Wakas too scared from the hairy man, are ya? Or are youse like dugais – scared of the bush?!'

'I wouldn't be joking about dugais if I'd just been walking in circles for three hours, bruz,' Jason retorted.

'If you've *quite* finished, let's just hit the road, eh?' Jo announced. 'Get these jahjams home.' There was no time to be standing around swapping insults as the dark fell.

'Don't go overestimating the charms of your company, brother,' Twoboy asserted. 'I knew exactly where I was the whole time.'

'It's the same,' Timbo said to his mother's back as she rearranged the bags in the cabin to make room for her feet. He was crouched over the topo map, which had fallen onto the white sand beside the ute.

'Yeah, I believe you,' said Kym to Twoboy over her shoulder. 'Millions wouldn't. Give that map here, bub, time to shoot through now. Get a jumper on Timbo, will ya Kai, or he'll freeze.'

'Mum. It's the same,' Timbo repeated, to no avail.

'Jump in the back, lad,' she repeated, lowering herself with some delicacy around the carefully positioned bags. Jason vaulted into the tray beside Twoboy and began extracting the jumpers the boys would need for the ride home in the cool night air. He beckoned Timbo towards him.

'Look, Arnie Jo,' Timbo whinged, pushing the creased and folded topo towards his aunt.

'Just make sure that fire's right out will you?' Jo asked Ellen, looking around to check that nothing got forgotten. She tapped the tailgate, causing both dogs to leap wetly into the tray. To her amusement, they shook copious amounts of lake water over the unrepentant Twoboy. He kicked out at them and growled in cranky protest. Jo laughed.

Baugul warrigal.

'Hurry up, Timbo, we wanna hook it,' Kai moaned from the tray, squeezing Jervis aside to claim the central spot on the bar. A war of elbows ensued. Finally noticing Timbo's frustration at being ignored, Jo squatted down beside him in the circle of yellow thrown by the cabin light.

'What's wrong, bub?' she asked impatiently. The child pointed at the passenger door where Ellen had pressed her red hand the previous afternoon.

'It's the same,' he repeated, pointing at the topo. 'See?'

It took Jo several moments to understand what he was talking about. When she did get the sense of what the child was saying, the noise of the others instantly fell away. What had been idle chatter at the end of a long and happy day, was replaced abruptly by a kind of roaring blankness in her head. The world shrank in a split second to what lay inside the circle of yellow light: herself, the intricate whorls of the map, Timbo's tiny brown fingers curled over the edge of the paper, Ellen's red handprints.

'Sweet Christ Jesus,' Jo whispered. She stared from the car door, to the map, and back again.

Everything was there.

The contour lines, roads and watercourses of the country shown by the map were marked in exact replica by Ellen's red palm print. Starting just below her daughter's fingers, the artery of the Brunswick River wound its ancient way through the valley. The major roads snaked over the land, with smaller gravel offshoots falling away to either side in the hills. There, mutely represented in clear red traces on the white car door, were the bitumen roads, built on bullock trails, that were built on the paths that the Bundjalung had made with their bare jinung before Rome was thought of, before Christ walked or Mohammed breathed. Before almost anything. Ellen's been carrying the entire valley around with her for thirteen years, unknowing, Jo thought wildly. *I gave birth to the valley.* Wordlessly she reached out for Ellen's right wrist. She turned the child's hand over so that her palm was clearly visible under the cabin light.

Everybody had fallen silent.

'Gimme that pen you had,' Jo finally said to Kym, without taking her wary eyes off Ellen. She held her breath as she traced each line of her daughter's palm in black ink. When she was finished there was no need to compare it against the topo. The map of flesh staring back at them was exactly correct.

Jo dropped Ellen's wrist, and stepped back, staring at her from the edge of the circle of light. She felt blood thrumming in her ears. Kookaburras laughed loudly on the ridge, but Jo didn't hear a thing.

'What's it mean?' Ellen asked in a tiny voice.

'I don't know,' Jo told her. 'I don't know. But it'll be alright. If it's there today, it's always been there.'

I hope it'll be alright. I hope it's always been there.

'Do yours,' said Ellen shakily. But when Kym used the pen on Jo's hands, a random assortment of unfamiliar lines appeared, telling them nothing, just as they did on her own, and on Twoboy, and on the boys. Night fell, and in the darkness it seemed clear that this business belonged to Ellen, and nobody else.

Jo drove away from the lake feeling as though a thick fog had risen to separate her and Ellen from the rest of the world. Her daughter sat trembling beside her in the front seat, her face tense and pale, eyes fixed on the dashboard and her hands pressed down hard against her thighs in denial. Jo craned forward as she drove, headlights piercing the night, as she tried to make some distinction between the forking paths the road presented her with. After four or five uncertain guesses that proved correct, she eventually recognised a particular burnt-out tree, and swung the steering wheel hard left with a great sigh of relief. A couple of minutes later they passed the cattle dip. With the others yelling and hammering on the cabin roof in triumph, Jo reached out and took Ellen's right hand. She held it to her shirt just above her heart, and said the only thing that seemed to make any sense.

'You're safe with me, Elle. So don't panic, not yet.'

'But what's it *mean*? Why's it on me, not on you or Aunty Kym? Or Twoboy?'

'I don't know,' Jo said truthfully. 'But if it's there now, it's always been there. The only difference is we know about it now.'

'I hate this stuff,' said Ellen vehemently, on the verge of tears. 'I *hate* it!'

'I know, but it's part of you, Elle,' Jo said carefully. 'We're gonna have to find a way to live with it. Together. We all are.'

Jo squeezed the jahjam's hand hard, then started to put her own hand back on the steering wheel, but Ellen laced her pale fingers through her mother's, and stubbornly refused to let go. As they drove the dirt tracks back to the Burringbah turnoff, Jo swallowed the claustrophobia that surged through her at Ellen's clinging. With a deliberate effort, she fought down the almost overwhelming urge to reef her hand away to freedom. At fourteen, when she was running wild, looking for trouble anywhere she was likely to find it, Aunty Barb had held her close and had loved her. That old lady had wound herself around the child that Jo had been with the soft words and tenderness that a hurting teenager craved. Now, however difficult it was, however much it felt to Jo like her hand was locked in a slowly tightening vice, she knew she had to keep holding on. She would become Aunty Barb, keep Ellen close in her turn, and in that way, her terrified daughter's world would be kept from splintering further into chaos.

Later that night Jo sat frozen into immobility at the kitchen table. Ellen was perched on a wooden chair beside her, bony knees drawn up to her chest, as Twoboy talked on and on, intent on making his case. It is really very important, Jo thought in a hazy, disconnected way, that all I do now, for this minute, is continue to breathe. Don't speak. Don't argue. Don't, above all, raise your eyes to the man standing there and start screaming at him, because once you do ... once you do ... Beneath the endless words streaming from Twoboy, a part of Jo was dimly aware of the kitchen knives, resting in the slotted knife box on the other side of the room. If I just sit still, and breathe, and don't scream at him, and *definitely* don't move towards the knives, it might all be okay. If only he would just shut up; shut up and go away so that my head could begin to work again.

'But can't you see it's why we had to go to the lake?' Twoboy urged. His black eyes were alight with triumph, for he knew that his quest was over at last. 'The song on the ridge was a red herring. Or only meant for you, Jo. But this is different, this is Proof. We can show them her hands and then there's no arguing with it, because it's right there staring them in the face! They *can't* deny it!'

'She said no way,' Jo answered in a dead voice, wishing Twoboy would just get in his car and go, as Kym and Jason eventually, reluctantly, had gone. Like any tribunal judge would care about Ellen's hands. *If it pleases Your Honour, come and have a dorrie at this.*

'But it's the key to the whole bloody thing!' Twoboy argued, losing his last fragment of patience after more than an hour of fruitless back and forth. 'It's the last piece of the puzzle, Jo! It's the proof we've been after for five fucking years!' He stood squarely on the other side of the table, clenching and unclenching his fists on the back of the chair in frustration. Ellen shrank further into herself, lowering her face onto her knees so that she became invisible behind a curtain of brown curls.

'Your binung painted on or what?' Jo repeated wearily. 'She said no an hour ago,'

Ellen began silently crying. When Jo turned, it was to glimpse a single fat tear sliding down her daughter's face, hovering at her pale jawline before dripping onto the leg of her jeans, darkening the sky blue denim to cobalt. Ellen once again had her mother's left hand in a vice-like grip, and all of a sudden Jo didn't find this terrified clutching to be claustrophobic at all. Hot rage at Twoboy boiled up in her like lava. Jo knew that she was on the verge of becoming somebody very dangerous indeed.

'She doesn't get the legal implications,' Twoboy ploughed on, not seeing Ellen's tears. 'That's why she's saying no. But Elle, if you just knew what it could mean for us, for Mum and Uncle Laz and –'

Jo looked up and locked eyes with the tall man. She realised, as though from somewhere outside of her body, that she no longer really cared if she started screaming at him. Whatever it took to make Ellen stop crying and shaking. That was what she would do. Talking wasn't working, therefore it was time for Twoboy to leave the house. That would make space for something else to happen. When Jo spoke again, it was in a very clear and deliberate tone.

'She's not fucking stupid. But she's a kid, she's *thirteen*. And she said no. So you need to go now, and let us sort this out on our own.'

'You wanna think about what you're doing, Jo,' Twoboy warned grimly as her words sank in. He folded his arms and glared across the kitchen. 'It's no time to be sittin on the fence, here. You're part of this case. You wanna give that up? Let the dugais win? Let Oscar steal this country from under us?'

Christ, can you even see this jahjam shaking in front of you? Jo thought. She stood and put her hands firmly on Ellen's narrow shoulders. Can you see the prison of fear she's locked in? Or is she suddenly invisible to you? Jo felt the lava rise higher, almost into her throat. Her eyes flicked to the knife box and back.

'Listen. You're way off tap if you think any white court's gonna give two shits about her hands. But even if they did then I'd give it up like that,' said Jo, snapping her fingers. 'Let Oscar fucking have it. Let them win. How can anything be *winning* if it hurts her this bad?'

Twoboy gave a short astonished laugh.

'*Let them win.* Well, that just says it all, doesn't it?' he answered bitterly, staring at Jo.

Jo knew now that she wouldn't go to the knives. Somehow, the instant she had uttered the words *let Oscar fucking have it,* her body had begun to change. Jo now felt the fleshy boundaries of her skin weirdly dissolving. She became tremendously heavy and solid. There was no need for knives, nor even for argument, for she was as massive as a mountain, as heavy and immovable as Chincogan or Bottlebrush. Standing in her kitchen with her hands on her daughter's quaking shoulders, she had somehow grown large enough to contain every Bundjalung woman who had ever stood near the place she stood. With her palms on Ellen's shoulders, she was a thousand black women, ten thousand black women, a mighty army of Goorie women who had been holding their jahjams safely on this same spot for tens of thousands of years. As her body swelled and rippled with this army's massive strength, Jo came to understand that she was no more alone than the stones in the creek were alone, or the blades of grass in the paddocks.

'That's it, bub,' said Aunty Barb, carefully rolling a smoke in the corner of the kitchen. 'That's the way.'

'You know what you remind me of?' Jo said to Twoboy, danger-ously quiet. 'Those people that go I'm not racist *but*. I'm not sexist, *but*. I'll tell you this onetime, Twoboy Jackson – if you love me, you'll drop this crap right now. Cos there's more to Law than some bullshit dugai court will ever know, and there's more to life than politics. And if you can stand there in front of me and talk about making this jahjam go to court, and not see her crying, not hear her saying it's too bloody hard for her, then . . .' Jo shook her head in utter disgust.

'But you're asking me to give up my *land*,' Twoboy cried. 'My budheram jagan! It's too much, Jo! How many times we gotta lose our country? How many times?'

'I'm not asking you for anything,' Jo said, refusing to be seduced into yelling. 'I'm just telling you – this jahjam's not gonna front any court. It's my job to keep her safe, not to put her up in front of some white court to be shamed and picked apart. I love you, man, but you've got to believe me: this kid comes first.'

'So that's it?' Twoboy asked, sinking back against the kitchen bench and clutching at his temples in disbelief. 'You're gonna sit here on ya twenty acres and let us lose our Native Title? Just sit back and watch it all happen?'

Jo hesitated, knowing Twoboy's huge anguish, his years of des-perate hoping. She measured the man's pain, and put it in her mind against Ellen's silent racking sobs, the folded agony of the child in front of her. She felt the pressure of the child's fingers reaching for hers, and she thought of the ink-blackened lines on Ellen's palms, the mystery and wonder of them. The country is pressing tight upon me, Jo thought as she grasped Ellen's hand hard in return. The coun-try is holding us together, me and my girl.

'It'd only be one single day in court,' Twoboy went on hammer-ing, sensing a tiny change in Jo. 'Just a few hours. Our mob have *died* for this jagan, Jo, you know that. How bad can one single day be, Ellie, just one day – with us there beside you?'

Without looking up, Ellen shook her head violently. Jo gazed down at her brown curls, seeing the single matted dreadlock that Ellen had grown. She let herself imagine how bad *one day* of standing in a dugai court might be for a thirteen-year-old child. She thought about the look on Ellen's face on that one day, and on the day after that, and the day after that. The army of women clustered close around her. She could feel them softly breathing.

'You can do it, bub. Talk straight, now,' said Aunty Barb, putting a flame to her durrie and drawing back on it to make a bright red coal in the far corner of the room.

'I'd rather sink that blade in your neck,' Jo said quietly, pointing at the knife box. 'Now go, and don't bother coming back till you've changed your tune.'

Chapter Thirteen

In the wee small hours of the night that followed, Ellen slept beside her mother, her tear-stained face resting on a ragged pillow with synthetic fluff spilling from its end. Jo tossed and turned for hours before finally, as the red numerals of the clock read three a.m., falling into a deep slumber. She dreamed, then, that she was standing in the backyard as a tremendous storm raged. Huge purple thunderheads surged across the valley and came towards her over the ridge; the whole sky boiled with water and fury. When the howling wind peeled the tin roof off the farmhouse and took it sailing eastward, Ellen was revealed standing exposed in the kitchen. Thunder rippled around the hills, echoing in the roofless house. Lightning snapped down like great silver flashing knives and found the mango tree, exploding it in a shower of flame. Then, to Jo's horror, a second bolt struck Ellen. She sprinted to her daughter's rescue but when she arrived inside the roofless walls she discovered the child standing there unharmed. Ellen laughed joyfully, holding both her bare wet palms up to the purple sky as she waited for another strike to arrive.

I am jalgani, she told her mother. *I am the lightning; nothing can hurt me now.*

Jo woke from the dream gulping for air, her heart drumming madly in her chest. For a long moment she had no idea where she was. It took minutes for her to realise that she was inside her house, safe in her own bed, and that the dream wasn't real. Ellen was still fast asleep beside her, faintly snoring. Jo threw herself flat onto her back and stared into the darkness in bewilderment. What did the dream mean? Who in the world could she ask about Ellen's hands? Had she made the right decision to send Twoboy away, and, above all, what on God's green earth was she supposed to *do*?

The army of women had dissipated as she slept. Jo was once again lying alone in the dark, clueless. Somewhere there had to be answers to the impossible questions of her life, but she didn't know where to even begin looking for them. Unless.

'Help me, Aunty Barb,' she called tentatively, not wanting to wake Ellen, 'which way?'

The silence grew thicker, and the night darker.

'Aunty Barb!' Jo repeated in growing desperation. 'What do I do now?'

There was no reply, only the hint of a feeling – but this sensation gradually grew stronger and more insistent as she lay looking upwards. Beyond the ceiling the Emu was wheeling in the Milky Way, a billion miles above the farmhouse. The growing feeling had no voice, no face and no name, but it brought an irresistible message:

Get up. Stand up. Start walking.
Go west.

Jo left the house in bare feet, ignoring the soft whickering of the horses when they saw her looming in the starlight. Daisy and Warrigal padded in her wake, but she didn't see them. In the sheen of the waning three-quarter moon, she clambered through the barbed wire gate at the back of the Big Paddock and headed up along the trail she'd ridden on the day of the talga. She padded steadily higher, until she reached the fallen gum.

Jo stood there, listening to the night sounds. The urge to keep going remained. She clambered over the high white trunk and kept on walking, growing breathless from the steepness of the trail. She hoped that Ellen was still sleeping in the house below. Anxious as she was about this, the sensation dragging her to the top of the ridge was far too strong to disobey. It felt, now that she was out of the house and actually walking westward, as though the pulling was a kind of long unsung music inside her, growing ever louder, demanding to be voiced when she reached her destination. As she drew closer to the summit, Jo felt the blood in her veins becoming richer, turning to a mingling of many bloods and of many stories. She felt a strange and ancient current springing from the jagan to course through her body and her brain. Walking the trail as it rose through the folded hills, Jo knew that nothing else in her life mattered as much as this. She had been born to walk to the top of this ridge, and put on earth to look, at this particular time, from its summit to the western horizon, where Mullumbimby slumbered. She could no more have turned around to check on Ellen than she could have leapt from the hilltop and flown.

At last, mud-streaked and grazed from a myriad of tiny lantana scratches, she was finally there. She stood atop the spur of Chincogan, her right hand resting on the trunk of a huge mountain ash. She breathed hard as she looked down into the crease of land below. A dozen patchwork farms, Rob Starr's among them, lay sprawled between her and the distant silvery curve of the river. In the far distance, the shops and houses of Mullum were faint, lit squares in the misty pre-dawn light. Chincogan squatted fatly to the side of the town, its high, curved, saddle peaks rising up against the still-starry sky. The Southern Cross hung directly over the town, and Bottlebrush Hill was a dark bulge behind her, surveying her as she stood and waited. Jo could hear the distant pounding of the surf hitting the beach at South Golden; gradually she became aware that the regular thudding of the waves on the hard sand exactly matched the metronome of her own insistent pulse.

Well I'm here, she thought, listening, her nerves wildly alive with expectation.

Nothing happened for a long, pregnant minute. Then, as the first touch of dawn began to break far in the east, she became aware of small rapid movements in the bushes around her. She heard familiar twitters. Fairy-wrens, a dozen or more, were lining the low branches she stood among. The birds flicked their tails upward, popping from branch to branch. They chirped severely at her. As she watched, more and more of the tiny birds arrived. After five minutes there were two dozen, three dozen, fifty, a hundred fairy-wrens, chirping and scolding in the trees surrounding her.

The hair on the back of Jo's neck slowly rose as she understood that every single wren was looking straight at her. She swallowed.

Jingawahlu nyawarnibil, she offered nervously. *Hello little birds.*

In response, the birds rose as one body. For a crazy moment, Jo thought they meant to attack her. She flinched, and went to protect her face with her hands. But instead, the mass of tiny feathered souls flashed past so close that they brushed her arms and her hair. She felt a small grey wingtip against her cheek. Then as she stood and watched, the flock hugged the curve of the hillside, diving down through an ocean of crisp morning air until they reached the bottom of the western slope, where Rob Starr was squatting beside a rocky waterhole, facing a shirtless Sam Nurrung.

Jo couldn't find the air to breathe.

The black boy had his back to her. He stood facing west with his arms outstretched, a crucifix backlit by the emerging dawn. From her vantage point, half a kilometre above, Jo couldn't see Sam's face. Nor could she make out the expression on Rob Starr's. Fearful, and with a sense of growing disbelief, Jo watched as the wrens wheeled in unison above the distant figures, to land on the spreadeagled arms of the boy. Sam Nurrung didn't move, but stood in front of Starr unflinching. A low hum rose through the air and Jo knew that she was hearing the talga again. The song was making its way up the face of the ridge to where she stood, invisible and trembling. She let out a small moan.

Ah, no. Nothing makes sense. It's too much.

She wanted desperately to turn away and bolt home, back to the safety of her own house, her own bed. But something in the song caught her. The talga held her, trapped beside the ancient mountain ash, as the sound reverberated through the valley. Far below, Starr spoke to Sam, who spun around and faced the ridge. Starr pointed directly at Jo. Horrified, she lunged a couple of panicky steps backward into the bush. Starr couldn't have seen her so far away and so shrouded in forest, she told herself.

Sam shaded his eyes, searching, staring. The movement of his arm made the wrens flutter and wheel above his head, protesting and looking for another perch. Then the boy let out a stark cry in words that Jo didn't recognise.

The birds reformed themselves into a squadron, and flew like bullets back up the slope. They found Jo easily where she crouched among wattle branches in fear. They danced in the air around her, circling her, pirouetting from branch to air and back again to the trees. They followed her escape downhill, chittering in annoyance all the way, until, dew-soaked and sobbing for breath, she reached the fenceline. Jo flung herself through the wire and bolted across the Big Paddock, back to safety and home, back to some semblance of normality, where she could hear the phone ringing off the hook as she arrived at the back door.

Jo stepped out of the shower and towelled herself dry. Hot water pounding on her head for half an hour had helped push down the sight of Rob Starr and Sam Nurrung. It was now time to think about Ellen. From the doorway of the big bedroom Jo looked at her daughter still lying in the foetal position beneath the warm blue doona. The child absolutely refused to entertain the idea of going to school, or even of leaving the farm with Jo to seek answers. She refused to do anything but lie still, and hope that everything inexplicable in her life would simply go away. That she might wake up, the next time, with nothing at all unusual on the reddened, black-lined hands she constantly scraped at as Jo talked.

'Well, will you come with me and see Uncle Humbug?' Jo

urged gently. 'He might know. It might have happened before, to someone else.'

Ellen shook her head, obstinate with incomprehension and fear. Nobody could explain her, let alone help her. She was a freak of nature, and she was staying put in the hope that nothing even worse would go wrong.

Jo rubbed hard at her face in frustration, trapped by impulses that tore at her in different directions. The solace of the shower had told her that she needed to go to water now, to be beside the healing ocean until she found some direction, but at the same time Ellen clearly needed her here at home. Chris was sick again. Therese couldn't help either, for she was in Brisbane where Amanda's mother was now in intensive care. Jo gazed at her daughter, wondering how her life had come to this pass. It seemed such a short time ago that the biggest mystery she faced had been the old headstones at work, and who they belonged to; a question, and a state of being, that now seemed pathetically simple.

At the other end of the house, the phone rang on and on. Caller ID said it was Twoboy. Jo blocked out the clamouring, then finally threw the phone onto the kitchen bench, disconnected. The man could wait, along with his stupid blokey blindness and his mad demands upon Ellen. There were no good answers to be had in his phone calls, nor in the Native Title Tribunal either.

'I just feel like Uncle Humbug might be able to help,' Jo said tiredly, sitting down on the bed and holding Ellen's soft white wrists that were black where the Nikko pen had smeared during the night. Hadn't the old man claimed to be *the one true blackfella* for this country? In the absence of her parents and her darling Aunty Barb, in the absence of other elders, Jo would take what was on offer. She had to look for Humbug.

'You go,' Ellen said, roughly shrugging Jo's hands away and pulling the doona high around her ears. 'Holly's coming round. She'll be here by one.' Jo breathed out, closed her eyes, and assessed this idea. Was Ellen waiting to see if she was going to abandon her? Or would she really be alright if Jo went seeking the old man in the park, if she went and spilled her tales to him of mapped hands and enchanted wrens, of the signs and wonders of the Mullum ridge?

'I'll wait till she gets here.' It was too risky to leave the kid alone, and, anyway, Humbug might take some finding. Ellen rolled over in the bed and squeezed her eyes tight in obvious relief. *Good call*, Jo thought, as she lay down beside her child and held her tight, all the while trying to find some way to put a squatting Rob Starr together with a cruci-fied Sam Nurrung in her head and not go stark raving mad.

Jo pulled up in Bruns and switched off the clattering ute. The river beyond the massive Norfolk Island pines was a mere skin of water on the land. Long fingers of exposed sandbank had dried to yellow in the midday sun, and the pirate ship loomed menacingly out of the river, marooned there until the turning tide came and floated it again. Now that school holidays were over, a mere handful of locals were sprinkled throughout town. Jo was the only person standing on the pub side of the river. She walked across Torakina Bridge, peering beneath the heavy timbers, and wondering where Slim and Humbug might be found.

'I brought Slim home,' DJ told her from where he sat fishing on the rocky seawall beneath the casuarinas, 'but Uncle Humbug's in the lockup again. That prick of a copper in Mullum booked him for drunk and disorderly.' He raised his bushy eyebrows at Jo: *It sucks, but what can you do.* Jo grimaced in return, seeing her chances of easy enlightenment collapsing. On the beach behind them, DJ's kids played sandcastles. The toddler was learning how to count using the half shells of ugari which the full moon had left in its wake.

'Least he'll get a feed, I suppose,' she said.

DJ grimaced.

'Feed of shoe leather maybe. The dogs flogged him up real good, from what I heard. Palm Island all over again, except you've gotta die to make the news – or no, you need a riot to make the papers,' he corrected himself. 'Nobody gives a shit if you just die.'

'How can they do that to an old bloke?' Jo curled her lip in disgust. She imagined the outcry if a blackfella had belted into one of the grey-haired pensioners who sat gossiping each morning outside the newsagent. The Goories would never hear the end of it, but because Humbug had shown the terrible judgement to be both homeless *and* black, well, that was an entirely different kettle of jalum.

'How ya doing, anyway, tidda? You look tired,' DJ asked.

Jo muttered something dismissive. Instinct told her that no Wiradjuri man, however decent, would have the answers to her Bundjalung problems. Defeated by his news, she turned back towards the other side of the river – but then stopped dead in the middle of the sandy track.

'You sure Slim's alright?' she called back. Bad enough that Humbug had been bashed, without his brother going missing as well. If she was in the lockup she'd want someone looking out for her family.

'Yeah,' DJ replied in easy reassurance. 'Big lump in him, too! I reckon he mighta grabbed somebody's budigan for feed last night.' They laughed at the idea of a domestic puss coming face to face with a hungry ten-foot python: Humbug's revenge.

As she walked back towards the ute, Jo reached a decision. If Humbug was locked up in Grafton jail, and if, at the same time, Ellen refused to leave her bedroom to go and see the old man, then whatever wisdom Humbug could have offered was unavailable. She had no other option, then, but to go to the water for answers.

Halfway across Torakina Bridge, Jo stopped and gazed down at the steadily rising current. It reached around the massive barnacled posts beneath her and flowed smoothly on either side, shining and rippling as it took the path of least resistance, heading upriver towards the mangroves. A few dark shapes hovered below her, waiting motionless in the deep pools low tide had left. Jalum, holding steady in a world of change. Downriver, just past the caravan park, a brahminy kite circled, ready to drop and snatch a meal. Jo knew that the water she watched was endlessly cycling upriver and down, travelling constantly between the saltwater and the fresh. It struck her, as she watched the flow dividing around the bridge posts, that the Buddhists were right. Change *was* never-ending. Nothing in the world stood still for long, and to be alive was to move. They were right, but they had perhaps missed something, too, something key about the Bundjalung world of water and trees and jagan which surrounded her. Everything changes, Jo thought, as the current carried her mentally upriver to the fresh water, but not at random. There's a deep system and order to it, because everything is forever turning into its own opposite. Swimming fish becoming flying hawk. Swift hawk dying and decaying into solid earth. Earth reaching skyward as trees, turning to fruits and honey and flowers, falling back down again as leaves. Everything in the world was shapeshifting around her, every moment of every day. Nothing remained as it was.

Aunty Barb had gone in, the same as her parents had. Sally Watt and Uncle Oscar were unreachable, and Uncle Humbug was grasped powerfully tight in the grip of the dugai law. Jo looked down at the flowing path of the river and she set her jaw against these realities. If she really wanted answers, there was only one road open to her. She would have to do what Aunty Barb had always taught. She would sit and enter dadirri; she would watch and listen to the roll of the endless waves until some flash of enlightenment came, some message on how to respond to the rusted barbed wire nest of her life. She would go sit on high ground and find some way to help her suffering firstborn. There was nobody else left to ask. She, Jo Breen, would have to become her own elder.

If Bruns had been quiet, Ocean Shores was a ghost town. All the kids were in school, all the adults gainfully employed, and the tourists departed for points south and north. Jo sat cross-legged on the crest of the hill. She was resting her back against the granite and bronze directional marker that was the last material evidence of humanity between Ocean Shores and New Zealand. She gazed out over the saltwater, where a distant late-season whale was spouting. A crow perched in the nearby lemon-scented gums, directly above a plaque proclaiming that somebody Devine had discovered this place. Jo would normally have been delighted to see that the crow had crapped purple fig-seeded birdshit all over this spurious claim. Today, though, she barely noticed it, nor the whale either. Her mind was boiling with other matters. It took all her composure simply to sit quietly in dadirri. To do nothing, with Ellen lost and afraid at home.

Sit still, Jo.

But, her mind argued endlessly. *But*. But Ellen's terrified, and I'm confused, and Twoboy's gone, maybe for good, and what about Rob Starr and Sam Nurrung and –

Knock off yabbering! Jus sit ning. The answers are all there.

Jo sat, following the movement of her breath carefully and deliberately. Five minutes passed, ten minutes, a quarter-hour. She closed her eyes and became aware, beneath the jangling of her nerves, that she had only had two hours sleep. As she sat and stilled herself, though, silence wrapped itself around her, thread by thread. And in time, as she sat more intently, what had seemed to be silence then splintered, as she knew it would, into a myriad of small, discrete sounds. A motorboat chugged slowly upriver from the caravan park towards Mullum. An occasional cry of glee or despair made its way over from the golf course. Cars murmured along the highway. The seagulls at the Co-op a kilometre away squarked and squabbled over the scraps the fishermen allowed them.

Then Jo opened her eyes, for she had once more heard the distinctive chittering of fairy-wrens. *You again, you buggers. What now?* She shifted her weight nervously and waited to be inundated, but the mass of birds from the ridge didn't materialise. Instead, a single pair, a blue-backed male and his drab grey-brown wife, chirped at her from a red-flowering bush on the hillside. Jo looked steadily back, waiting to see what kind of spectacle she would be presented with this time. Encouraged, the male darted up onto the directional marker at her back. The massiveness of the granite and bronze plinth served to underline that, for all his beauty, the wren was little more than a few dozen feathers and a voicebox. The bird trilled loudly at Jo, and then rose in a kind of arabesque before returning to the flat circle of the bronze disc. His wife joined him and did the same midair dance. Over and over again, as Jo looked up at them, the two birds fluttered in their repetitive pattern above the marker plinth. The movements reminded her of something, but exactly what the *something* was eluded her.

Jo puzzled over it, and then, as she failed to extract any purpose from the birds' flight, her eyelids sagged wearily. She let her head fall back; twisting herself around to watch them was making her neck ache. She no longer watched the dancing, but she saw it instead in her mind's eye, the landing and lifting, the pattern of the birds' movements in the salty air. She ached to understand. Almost certainly it was connected to something important she had seen recently, but her head was a fog of sleeplessness and confusion. Jo groaned aloud, exhausted by her ignorance and the unending demands being made on her to exceed it. The temptation to fall asleep in the sun, and leave these demands far behind, began to take her over.

No. We need answers.

With a tremendous effort of will, Jo forced her eyes open and turned around. As she did so, a fat cloud blew across the face of the sun. Momentarily the wrens became, not birds, but mere dark movement, silhouettes against the looming grey mass of water vapour. For a split second, in the changed light, Jo stopped noticing the birds' feathers, their chittering, and their contrasting colours. She saw only the path they tracked though space, the great looping shapes they were making in the air above the plinth. And then she realised what it resembled. The birds' dancing curlicues looked like the curves the kids had made when dusk fell at the lake, the insults and names that they had written in the air with their glowing firesticks.

The hairs on Jo's arms goosepimpled. Her breathing grew fast. These two wrens weren't flying aimlessly, any more than the flock at dawn had been. The birds were messengers, talking to her in the only language they could share, dancing their message in the air. Jo had watched their kin on the farm, flitting between trees and bushes time and time again. She had listened to them chirping there, had spoken to the wrens often, at home, at work and this morning upon the ridge. She had even grown to love the tiny birds, but, she now realised with an unspoken curse for her own obtuseness, she had never before really paid attention. Sitting bolt upright with all thoughts of sleep forgotten, she looked at the male with new eyes. Sensing a change, it gave a long, excited trill, then started from the bronze marker and flew west–south–west to its red-flowering shrub. It trilled anxiously at her before it flew back to land where it had begun.

The female went next. By the time the birds had darted west–south–west and then returned twice more, Jo was on her feet and ready to resume her search for the old man, even if meant a six-hour return trip, west–south–west to the Grafton jail. She'd drag Ellen there, if need be.

Jo shouted her thanks to the wrens as she bolted along the hilltop to the ute and hurled herself inside. Screeching to a halt at the stop sign at the bottom of the hill, she turned her mobile back on: eleven missed calls. The first eight were from Twoboy, and were ignored, but the last three were from home. Fear seized Jo.

Then the phone rang in her hand.

'Come back, come back home now!' Holly sobbed over the screaming in the background. 'I went to the toilet and Ellen stuck her hands in the fire –'

Jo's right foot hit the accelerator and didn't lift.

The animal screaming had stopped, finally, with the morphine in the ambulance. Now Jo sat beside Ellen's stretcher at Lismore Base Hospital telling Paul to get himself on a flight that afternoon, the earlier the better. Surgery was at seven o'clock. Then she turned the phone off again. She didn't need any more texts from Twoboy on top of the fifteen already unread in her inbox.

Jo leaned back and closed her eyes, giddy with exhaustion and remorse. What had she been thinking, leaving a fragile thirteen-year-old in the care of another *child*? A wave of revulsion ran through her at what Ellen had done. She shivered at the picture of her daughter turning the stove burners on high and thrusting her two hands into the flames, trying to burn away the evidence on her palms. Oh Ellen, my jahjam, my darling girl, what is it we've done?

'Miz Breen, has Ellen tried to hurt herself before, to your knowledge?' asked a mental health nurse. Jo opened her eyes and tried to focus. Christ. Now it begins.

'No. Never.'

'And she wasn't at school. You say you weren't at home with her . . .' A meaningful pause.

'Clearly not,' Jo said wearily.

'Well, when she gets out of surgery, we're going to ask you and her father to come and meet with the mental health team, so we can talk about what to do next –'

'She's not crazy –' Jo began, then quickly stopped when she saw the nurse's face. There had been blood, and pain, and screaming. And Ellen – the fact made choking tears rise in Jo's throat – had done this to herself. A different tack was required. She swallowed the tears.

'Is there a Koori liaison?'

'Are you part-Aboriginal?' The nurse seemed surprised.

Are you part-fuckwit?

'I'm Goorie.'

'She's on sick leave, sorry. I could try and find someone from the health service to come over, if you like, but there's a lot of people away at a funeral . . .'

Ambulance sirens sounded on the road outside, and the normal commotion of a hospital went on all around them. Patients wheeled and crutched past. A man with a face like a smashed crab was hurried past by orderlies; his gay partner trailed, inconsolable, behind them. Lifts rose and fell beyond the glass doors that separated Emergency from the other wards. Forms were thrust at people, to be filled out, then taken away again. The nurse standing in front of her wasn't unsympathetic, but Jo could feel Ellen being dragged inexorably in the direction of the psych ward or DOCS or both, if she couldn't find a Goorie in a uniform who understood that you might have certain inexplicable reasons to stick both your hands into an open flame and still not be exactly mad. And that, far from neglecting Ellen, she had been trying to find her some help.

'Can you? I need to talk to a Goorie . . .' Jo said, as she leant forward to rest her head momentarily on the wall, and fell asleep in mid sentence.

When she woke, Ellen was in theatre. The distance between herself and her damaged child – Ellen, badly hurt on another floor of the hospital, being stitched by dugais she'd never even met – struck Jo fully then. She wept helplessly into the white bedsheets beside her, bent over by great racking sobs of sorrow and failure.

When the storm eased, she blew her nose and got up. She wandered unfamiliar corridors, found some espresso in a cafe, and after a call to Kym that brought more tears and fresh questions, made her way back up to Emergency. She had no desire to share the second-hand smoke and misery of the others waiting around outside; she wanted to be exactly where Ellen would be when she woke up. Through there, the nurse pointed with a clean bedpan, Ward Three. But you'll be waiting a while, she warned.

Jo called Therese, trying not to sound as desperate as she felt, and then briefly considered ringing Twoboy. But she was dirtier on him now than she had been the night before, since if he hadn't pressured them in the kitchen for that agonising hour . . . who knew? Her head still swirled with the horror of Ellen's bleeding, crippled hands. No, she'd talk to Twoboy when she was good and ready.

Inside Ward Three, Jo kicked her shoes off and collapsed onto a vacant bed. She pulled the clean sheet up over her head and lay there, hoping to be invisible to the world, or at least unmolested by it. Her mind raced between the image of Ellen's meat-raw fingers, curled in agony as Holly ran the kitchen tap water over them, and what she'd seen from the top of the ridge at dawn. I'm not mad, she thought suddenly, beneath the hospital sheet, but this must surely be what going mad feels like.

The ten p.m. news scrolled silently on a TV screen, showing a single-fatality accident on the Piccabeen bypass and a grassfire being brought under control at The Pocket. Texts arrived in Jo's phone, and sirens and trolleys came and went as she dozed, but it was a different sound that woke her in the end.

'Miz Breen, Miz Breen, your daughter's out of surgery. She'll be waking up in Recovery soon.' The nurse smiled as she shook Jo's shoulder. 'This way.'

Jo sprang up and followed, to find Ellen asleep in yet another part of the hospital. The grafts had been completed. And now, the doctor said, it was a matter of being sure that that they took, and that infection could be kept at bay.

Seeing Ellen lying there in the hospital cot, pale and vulnerable, with her hands transformed into great white bandaged clubs, Jo could barely speak. She nodded like a bobble doll at everything the uniforms said, then sank into a chair, clutching sheafs of paperwork. She was too drained to cry or ask questions, too tired to do anything but sit and look at the still lightly sleeping child, and follow numbly as they were taken back to Ward Three. When her mobile rang she lifted it dully to her ear without thinking.

'Jo! Where in Christ's name have you *been*? I've been trying to get onto you –'

'I'm at Lismore hospital with Ellen,' she told Twoboy, who screeched to a halt in the middle of his questions. Jo told him the saga, and there was a long, ticking silence between them. She waited for him to ask the one unforgivable question, to ask if Ellen had succeeded in destroying the map on her hands.

'So she's outta surgery?' Twoboy asked. 'Is she gonna be alright?'

'They reckon. No thanks to you.'

'How about you – are you alright?'

Jo laughed, a slightly hysterical laugh. A map of the valley had appeared unbidden on Ellen's hands. Birds were telling her where to go and what to do. Rob Starr and Sam Nurrung had been doing God knows what in the early light of dawn. Her daughter – her daughter *the artist* – was lying in front of her with hands like raw beef sausages. And the only possible avenue Jo could think of for answers was Uncle Humbug, locked away behind blocks of sand-stone and razor wire in Grafton jail.

'Am I *alright?*' she choked. 'Am I *alright?*'

'Yeah,' said Twoboy, sounding alarmed, 'are you with someone, Jo? Who's with ya? Is there a nurse or someone I can talk to –'

Jo turned her phone off. Fuck him and the horse he rode in on. She sat, turning around in her head the question of whether or not she was in any way *alright*. As she considered this, two nurses pushed a trolley bearing a car accident through the swinging doors at the end of the ward. Down the gleaming lino they came towards her in their starched blue uniforms, looking like a royal procession. Their rubber shoes were soft and silent, and apart from the faint squeaking of the trolley wheels, the entire immaculate parade made no sound. When it arrived next to her, Jo stopped laughing. She simply stared. The stretcher was not a car accident at all.

The nurses had delivered to the bed next to Ellen the swollen, battered and yet apparently indestructible person of Uncle Humbug.

The nurses manoeuvred the old man into bed and carefully positioned his drip out of harm's way. Humbug's cop-blackened eyes glittered with rage above the tubes pumping oxygen into his nostrils. Then the nurses shifted, blocking Jo's view. Indistinct muttering reached her ears.

'Still waking up,' one nurse told the other, 'hallucinating about pythons, the poor old bugger.'

When they had left, Humbug turned his head slightly to face Jo. The tiny movement made him groan aloud.

'You, girl,' he rasped through what remained of his teeth, 'get me outta here. I gotta find my brother.'

Jo scraped her chair over to the old man and told him that Slim was safe back at home in Bruns.

Then, 'You gotta help me, Uncle,' she started. 'I got some problems – big problems I need to ask you about.'

The old man smiled weakly. He did more than smile – he wheezed with quiet, agonised laughter. Then he gave Jo his considered opinion, that at this particular moment, he, Uncle Humbug – the homeless, diabetic bearer of seven fractured ribs, a broken nose, a fractured arm, two severely blackened eyes and a swollen mouth with thirty stitches in it – was the one who had *big problems*.

'I know you do.' Jo grasped his good arm. 'But you can see my girl lying here hurt bad, eh. And you *told* me Bruns is your country. So, Uncle, tell me what you make of this –'

Jo sat by the old man and unfolded the story of the strangeness that she had lately seen and heard. She told him about hearing the talga the first time, and how she had run from hearing it ever since. She described Twoboy's fruitless striving to capture the song for himself. She spoke of the trip to the lake, and the revelation of Ellen's hands. The vision – or had it perhaps been a hallucination, Jo now wondered – of Rob Starr and Sam Nurrung, the boy standing covered in fairy-wrens on the western slope of the ridge. And last of all, the birds on the hill at Ocean Shores who had sent her to find him, before she was interrupted by the terrible phone call from Holly.

When Jo finished, she sat and humbly waited. The old man hadn't responded at all as she recounted her story. He had looked straight ahead at the ceiling, avoiding her gaze. If his eyes hadn't been open she might have thought he was asleep, or even dead. Jo was patient, as the seconds stretched out into minutes of waiting. But she was reaching the limit of her endurance when Humbug finally answered.

'I dunno nothing bout any of that,' he muttered. 'My head hurting, anyways.'

'Ah, how can you not know something?' said Jo, shattered. 'You said you were the one true owner for Bruns!'

Humbug lay very still in his cot. Shame and fear mingled in his mind as he tried to think through the fog of pain that was enveloping him. It was less than twenty-four hours since the dugai's right boot had landed squarely in his jang, the same dugai's boot that had been stomping on his face forever. This young woman sitting here beside him needed somebody, yes, but Humbug wasn't the one to give that kind of help. Talga in the hills was nothing. Everyone with any sense knew that the old mooki were still in there, still singing up the country. But the mountains appearing mapped on the palms of her daughter's hands?

Fuck that, thought Humbug. *Gonna leave that kind of shit well alone.*

'Nuns bin raise me in the Home, girl,' he told Jo. 'Ya gotta look somewhere else.'

'But you have to know!'

Jo felt like throttling the old liar. There could be no mistake. The wrens had sent her towards Humbug, who had claimed to be the one true blackfella for the valley. Jo *knew* he had the answers she craved, the answers that would ease Ellen's troubled mind and take away the terror in her eyes. Every cell in her body was screaming it.

'Go ask someone else. Go to the old mission, ask themfla.' Humbug closed his eyes in dismissal. He really did have a splitting headache. That arsehole copper needed singing onetime.

'Who? Who do I ask?'

Jo fumed, but Humbug ignored her, feigning sleep. She swore under her breath, casting a helpless sideways look at Ellen who lay oblivious in the next cot.

'Please, Uncle Humbug, please!' Jo found she was begging. 'I'll help you. I'll get you outta here, I swear I will.'

Humbug opened his eyes. Now she was talking.

'I'll take you home to Slim,' Jo promised wildly, hope building inside her. 'Just *please* tell me who to talk to. *Please.* I gotta help my girl, Uncle, look at her. She's only thirteen. I gotta look after her.'

Humbug glanced at Ellen and swallowed. His bruised and blood-shot eyes narrowed as he examined Jo's face. Even though his head was throbbing, he could see the woman's anguish and her fierce determination. This jalgani wasn't going to give up her fight anytime soon. Uh-huh. She was ready to kill somebody if she had to, to protect her jahjam. Nobody, Humbug reflected bitterly, had been prepared to help him when he was thirteen and in the Home. Thirteen was an age that he remembered certain parts of all too well. Other parts of thirteen, even worse, had been locked away forever in the dark caverns of his memory. Humbug had spent his adult life knowing that none of his ancient shame would ever alter or disappear – but now, lying in Ward Three of Lismore Base Hospital, he discovered that he had been wrong. To his astonishment, watching Jo sitting there fighting to protect her daughter, the old man felt something shift inside his chest. Something that had been badly broken, that had been jammed in exactly the wrong spot for over forty years, clicked then, into its proper place. Humbug blinked with surprise. His headache had vanished.

'Well,' he said reluctantly, 'my big tidda. She really the one ya want. Not me.'

Jo's heart leapt with sudden hope. She flashed a dazzling smile at Humbug. At last, someone with a direction to point her in; someone with something useful to say about this whole mess and confusion. Someone older, someone wiser, to tell her what the fuck to *do*.

'Oh! Thank you, thank you so much, Uncle. Where can I find her?' Jo asked, feeling the impossible load of responsibility already begin to lift from her shoulders. Humbug painfully raised a with-ered finger, lowered his gaze along its trajectory, and pointed to the swinging doors – just as, through them and into the ward, walked the surgeon, two green-clad nurses, and Granny Nurrung.

'That's er.'

Granny Nurrung looked hard at Jo, then at Ellen, and lastly at Humbug.

'You best close your jang, girl,' she advised Jo, whose jaw hung open in amazement, 'afore a big snake crawls in and makes his yumba there.'

At midnight, Jo turned her phone back on and gave Kym an update. Two minutes later, Twoboy rang.

'How is she?' he said immediately. 'Is she okay?'

'She's awake, and pretty sore and groggy,' Jo replied tightly. 'But she'll survive.'

'How are you?'

'Yeah.'

'You hear about Oscar?' Twoboy asked cautiously. Jo sighed. He was in that other world still, and she was in this one.

'Yep. I heard.'

'Aunt Sally mob wants to meet up here for mediation. But if you want me down there with you, I'll –'

'No.' Jo said instantly.

'Alright. I'll stay away. If that's what you want.' A hundred miles to the north, Twoboy shut his eyes, wondering what he had broken, and all for nothing.

'I don't want you here,' Jo told him.

'I hear ya,' he answered in a smaller, sadder voice.

'Not yet.'

Twoboy's heart lifted. He threw his head back in relief, and tears pricked at his eyes. 'Okay. Okay. I'll call you first thing in the morning, darlin, alright?'

'If you want.'

Jo snapped her phone shut and went back to the ward.

Three days later Ellen had been moved to the Mullum hospital, into a room with a window looking out on the lush lawns of the cemetery. It was here that Granny Nurrung sat outside on a blue plastic deckchair, holding court beneath a stand of Piccabeen palms, which had dropped an avalanche of red berries onto the square pavers at her feet. Jo sat stiffly to one side of the old lady, holding a soft drink in her lap like it was her only friend in the world. Rob Starr and Sam both sat on the concrete kerb on the other side of Granny, next to Humbug's wheelchair. Ellen was inside on the ward, recuperating. She had had her own personal audience with Granny Nurrung the night after the surgery, a conversation that Jo hadn't been privy to, and which Ellen refused to talk much about. It had taken only ten minutes, but it left the child smiling, and that was enough for Jo. The wrens hadn't lied. But now it was her turn.

'Robbie here says you seen some things. Reckons you need some answers,' Granny Nurrung told Jo in a voice that suggested she felt very differently. Far from gratitude, Jo felt irritation flare at the very idea of Rob Starr discussing her needs with anyone. She said nothing about this lingering resentment, but Granny Nurrung saw it.

'Robbie's a good man. And he bin a good friend to our family.'

'He threatened to kill my dog,' Jo blurted. *And that was just for starters —*

'I'd never really hurt a dingo,' Rob Starr told her quietly from the other side of the small courtyard.

'— and then he murdered my best horse!' Jo added, shooting him a hostile glance.

'And apologised for it,' Granny countered.

Jo shrugged at the pavers. An apology. So bloody what.

'And then replaced him, with another yarraman,' Granny Nurrung went on. Jo's head snapped up at that. It had been Rob Starr all along.

Jo shifted in her plastic chair as she processed this information. She gazed across at the man sitting opposite, seeing him morph for the first time into something more complicated than a killer.

'But why put that rotten fence there at all?' she demanded. 'You knew it blocked the fire trail! You knew it was public land.' Rob Starr nodded, then looked to Granny.

'Fire trail in the wrong blooming place, that's why,' Granny answered for him, 'Old Jimmy Mooney went and built that track in the wrong place altogether. I *told* Robbie to put that fence up. Cos we don't want strangers traipsing all over the place. Going where they don't belong. Seeing things they shouldn't see.'

'Seeing things they shouldn't . . .' Jo repeated uneasily. She had *traipsed about*, gone up the ridge at dawn. Seen things.

'Mmm. Special things.' Granny glared at the entire assembly, then paused. 'I wouldn't say. I wouldn't say it – except for your girl. Her hands. We bin waiting for her, see. For ceremony.'

Jo folded her arms and leaned back in the chair, staring hard at the red berries dotted on the ground before her. Her heart pounded in her chest. She felt as though she was sitting inside a kaleidoscope, a kaleidoscope that had just been shaken by a great dark hand. She had attributed greed to Rob Starr, and stupidity, and malice. Had judged the man an ignorant redneck and probably a paedophile. But the real explanation was one she couldn't possibly have arrived at on her own. The blunt dugai farmer with his barbed wire atrocity and his three-hundred-dollar boots was doing Granny Nurrung's bidding all along, protecting the Goorie Law. Looking after the place that Granny now spoke of in a hushed and reluctant voice.

'The waterhole,' Jo whispered. 'At the base of the ridge.'

'Yowai,' Granny agreed. 'It needs looking after. It needs my Sammy here, and it needs your girl, too. She the next one.'

Jo shook her head in wonder, frowning.

'You could have just said. I would have stayed away.'

'Yeah. You mighta stayed away. Or maybe not. And then how about your man Twoboy?' Granny Nurrung asked, her tone hardening. 'He pretty good at staying away, is he?'

Jo locked eyes with the old woman. So she knew Twoboy, and somehow knew as well how far the man was prepared to go for his Native Title. She bit her lip hard.

'Mmm. Didn't think so. Looks like he'll be getting his Native Title now after all, but my young cousin's still got a lot to learn.'

'Your *cousin!*' Jo blurted, dropping her drink on to the pavers where it fizzed and leaked unheeded in a large brown puddle. She stared in disbelief. Yes, Granny nodded. Her second cousin. And Humbug's too, of course.

'But why didn't you tell him?' Jo asked in amazement. All the time Granny had known who Twoboy was . . . All this time, all those hundreds of hours the Jacksons had spent trawling through archives and records, searching for evidence to make up for the lack of bodies, the lack of stories, the lack of proof. All Twoboy's madness about recording the talga. The fight over Ellen's hands. The agony of not being able to pinpoint Grandad Tommy and claim his Native Title the way the white court wanted, and all this time Granny and Humbug had *known*?

'We never grew him up,' Granny Nurrung said bluntly. 'We don't know him. He our blood, yeah, but he don't know this place. Not like we do. And he's a proppa cheeky bugger, too, stirring up all that trouble with Aunt Sally. For Native Title! We're not interested in blooming Native Title! What's the good of Native Title? A bitta paper from the government if you're lucky. And a punch on the jaw on the Durrumbil bridge if ya not,' she added, making Jo suddenly stare.

Granny Nurrung laughed sardonically, and went on.

'I'm on the pension. And this one –' a nod here at Humbug – 'he nearly sixty. He gonna go get a government job? Wear a nice ironed shirt every day, and use a computer? No, I don't think so. We all looking after the country the proper way, and when Sammy big enough, then it'll be his turn. More better when there's a jalgani and a man both, but anyways, he'll look after that rockhole when the Lord takes me home.'

'But what if Rob had to sell up or something?' Jo was deeply sceptical. 'The new owners can just lock you out. Who'll look after the rockhole then?'

The old lady glanced over at Rob Starr, who was smiling gently, and examining the tops of his R.M. Williams as he listened.

'Robbie, now,' said Granny. The man lifted his grey-eyed gaze to the others. The old woman pursed her lips and tilted her chin at Jo.

'You reckon this one needs answers. You tell her.'

'It's not my farm,' Rob Starr said quietly to Jo. 'I still live there, but I haven't got any kids of my own, so I signed it over to Sam a few years back. The papers are in the bank in Mullum.'

Astounded, Jo looked over at fifteen-year-old Sam Nurrung, sitting there patiently while the adults talked about him and anticipated his future. No wonder he's got that straight back. He's a young Bundjalung noble, she breathed to herself. *Landed fucken gentry.*

'What about the singing, though, and Ellen's hands?' Jo went on after a minute. 'What's that all about?' The old lady laughed, but didn't answer. Rob Starr and Sam Nurrung both smiled at the ground. Jo realised with a flash of anger that she wasn't going to be told everything. Some things would always remain unknowable unless she figured them out for herself. As she wondered how to reconcile herself to ignorance, Granny surprised her.

'Her hands? Well, that's just the Lord's way of bringing your girl home to country.' Granny looked hard into her own palms as she spoke. 'You might call it a miracle, I suppose. As for the talga, that high country is proper strong kalwunybah, girl. You got any lingo, you know what that is?'

Jo frowned and shook her head. She didn't care very much any-more how ignorant she seemed. It was becoming obvious, anyway, that she had lived for years on land she had barely known, barely even *seen*, for all that she was local and had title deeds that bore her name. For all that Ellen had worn the country on her hands all her young life, until three days ago.

'Place of something,' she answered, ashamed of the few pathetic scraps she knew.

'Kalwunybah. Liarbird place,' said Granny Nurrung softly. 'That talga you bin hearing, that's the liarbird singing out to you, calling you. He telling you that you found the right jagan there, you and your girl. Telling you you're home.'

Jo gasped with relief as her mind flew to the small earthen clear-ing that she had lain in after her fall. Of course. A lyrebird's dancing ground. She felt the hard burden of superstitious fear inside her evaporating. Tin Wagon Road was *the right place*. After all this time, finally, she'd found something like a home.

'So it's not mooki!' She laughed joyfully. 'Just lyrebirds! Jesus Christ, I was so scared of that talga for so long.'

Sam snorted, and shot her a scornful look, as though she had said something silly.

'What?' Jo asked, confused.

'Who do you think taught them liarbirds that song?' Granny Nurrung quizzed Jo. Oh my God, Jo realised. The hair on the back of her neck stood stiffly to attention. The old people. Singing beside the rockhole, doing ceremony, the same ceremony Rob and Sam had been doing at dawn. The lyrebirds were repeating the song they had heard, and passing it down through hundreds of generations.

'That talga been sung there forever and always,' Granny Nurrung went on. 'Protection for the water, see. Then, Captain Cook time. Our old people seen the dugai come in, seen the way they were. Greedy. Breaking their own law, the ten commandments of the Lord God himself. Went too wild, shooting us mob. Chopping jali jali, killing the rivers. Stealing the jahjams away. Our old people saw the dugai couldn't be stopped, and they knew what they had to do. Our mob mighta started wearing trousers, and working for the white man, yeah, but first they made sure they left their talga in a safe place where no dugai could ever take it away.'

For the first time that day, Granny Nurrung smiled a smile of real happiness.

'See, it looks to all the dugai like only one thing happened here, on our budheram jagan,' she told Jo. 'But no. Something else happened too. Cos lotta Goorie mob dead now, or taken far away, but our little family still here. We still singing our special place. And Sammy boy, he gonna be manager for that country both ways. Dugai way *and* Goorie way.'

Jo sat, stunned into silence, assimilating the old woman's story. There had been generations of resistance to bring them to this point, sitting outside the hospital in the shadow of Chincogan, with Ellen inside slowly healing, waiting to take up her part in a long, unbroken chain. Looking at Granny Nurrung, and Humbug, and Sam, it gradually dawned upon Jo that to destroy the talga of the rockhole, the dugai would have to kill every last Goorie who knew it. They would have to clear the World Heritage forest, and then they would need to destroy every lyrebird in the valley as well, probably every lyrebird for hundreds of miles around. But unless they did that, unless they went so far in their savagery and their madness, then the talga would always be sung in the nooks and crannies of the bush where it seemed like nobody at all was listening. And the ancient song would always be heard on the other side of the ridge, now, too, on Rob Starr's farm that was really Sam Nurrung's. And she herself had come home, just as the rockhole had found its second keeper. They would all live, now, with the knowledge of their sacred story place, *budharam kalwunybah*. Just as the old people had wanted.

Two weeks later Twoboy parked on the footpath outside 287 Tin Wagon Road. He looked sick with anxiety as he walked up the drive to where Jo was sprawled eating her lunch in the backyard.

A few paces away, Gift and Athena tore gleefully in unison at the short sweet grass beneath the clothes line. First one yarraman ripped and chomped at the overgrown lawn, then the other quickly echoed it. Together, their eating made a double syncopation that reminded Jo of her own heartbeat.

Oh my baugul yarraman, you're the heart of me and you always were.

'That's the way to mow a lawn,' Twoboy called bravely as he reached the mango tree. Jo looked up.

'Well, look what the cat dragged in.'

His heart in his mouth, Twoboy came over to her. He bent and took Jo's face in both hands as he kissed her. Jo smiled as she kissed him back.

'How's tricks?' she asked, tossing last fortnight's *Echo* aside. She had read the front page story of Uncle Oscar's death a dozen times, and was no closer to deciding if the prang had been an accident.

Rumour had it that Oscar was being investigated for child abuse when his XR6 left the highway at Piccabeen and ploughed into a large casuarina grove. In the days beforehand, half-a-dozen victims had come forward. His own niece was going to stand up in court and testify against him.

What goes around, thought Jo grimly, comes around, sure enough.

'Yeah, it's all good. Mediation's done the trick. Sally mob and us mob are now officially co-claimants!' Twoboy produced a bottle of champagne and two glasses from his backpack. 'Mum's happy, I'm happy, and Laz and Uncle Cheezel reckon they can both live with it.'

'At last,' Jo said, relaxing into a grin, 'I'm just glad your Mum's still around to see it.'

'Yeah,' agreed Twoboy. 'Funny thing, though. She's been tuning in and out a lot. Last night she was pretty sharp, hey, and she told us about a conversation she overheard as a kid. She reckons she heard the adults whispering, saying there was a sacred site along this road. A cave, or a spring or something – and they were talking about who should look after it when they were gone. They all shut up real quick when they saw she was listening. And she never remembered a bloody thing about it till yesterday.'

A curious smile played over Jo's lips.

'True?' she asked. 'Just as well your Native Title wasn't riding on it, then, eh.'

'I reckon!' Twoboy widened his eyes in alarm at what might have been lost. 'So we still going to this barbie?'

'Yeah. But can ya show me those chords first? I want to play something for the guest of honour. Granny Nurrung.'

'You might wanna start with something a bit easier,' said Twoboy doubtfully.

'Oh,' said Jo, hiding her mirth, 'I reckon I'll pick it up.'

'Grab the git then,' Twoboy said, easing himself down onto the grass beneath the clothes line and gazing up thoughtfully at the ridge. Native Title was on its way at long last. Sally mob had agreed to stick south of Tin Wagon Road. As the oldest Jackson, he,

Twoboy, would become the recognised blackfella owner for the valley between Middle Pocket and Crabbes Creek. Yet there was still a song up in the high country there that he hadn't heard even once; a song that still waited for him. Twoboy sighed. Patience was needed, a lot of patience. Until the ancestors were ready to reveal themselves, *Redemption Song* would have to do.

Jo stood up. As she went inside she noticed a blue-grey flash over by the young jali jali billa. Bluey was building a nest in the big camphor laurel which overhung the dam. Jo had noticed mulanyin flying to the scrub on the ridge and returning often, lately, with a suitable stick in its beak. Her face softened as she went inside to the kitchen, where Ellen bent with gauze-covered fingers over her sketchbook. The girl was drawing a set of Babushka dolls which began on the outside fair-skinned and blue-eyed but grew darker and more Goorie-looking the deeper you got.

'Wanna see something funny?' Jo asked on her way back outside, holding the Maton aloft. 'I'm gonna let Twoboy teach me to play this.'

Ellen grinned an evil grin.

'I'll be there in a sec.'

The child clasped a fine-tipped ink pen in her damaged hands, ignoring the pain in her quest to make something of beauty and meaning where none had been before. Then Ellen remembered.

'Mum! Danny from the Co-op said to ring Farmcare. Something about a muffler.'

Jo burst out laughing. She rested her hands on Ellen's shoulders and wound a strand of the girl's dark hair around her finger before tucking it behind her ear. It is a fact universally acknowledged, she thought, bending to kiss the top of Ellen's head, that a teenager armed with a Nikko pen is a wonder to behold, a precious, precious thing that we all must keep close to our hearts, and protect by any means necessary. And if it isn't, then it fucken well oughta be.

Glossary

In this novel, Jo speaks a mixture of Bundjalung and Yugambeh languages, interspersed with a variety of Aboriginal English terms. Readers wanting to learn more may refer to *A Dictionary of Yugambeh and Related Languages*, or the several dictionaries of Bundjalung, all of which were compiled by Dr Margaret Sharpe with the guidance of Aboriginal informants.

anthro   anthropologist (Aboriginal English, widespread)
baugal   good
bilin bilin   king parrot, associated with Billinudgel area
billa   casuarina tree (she-oak)
binung   ear (widespread)
binung goonj   ear not good (deaf or, less often, mad/stupid)
blackfella   Aboriginal man or woman. Does not refer in Aboriginal English to other black people.
booliman   policeman (widespread)
budgeree   good (Aboriginal English, widespread)
budheram   a) very good, or b) sacred
budigan   pussycat
bullang   cattle
bungoo   money
bunji   friend or partner
coochin   red earth

dadirri   form of Aboriginal meditation

disfla   this one (Aboriginal English, widespread)

dorrie   a look (Aboriginal English, widespread)

dreckly   soon (Aboriginal English, widespread)

dugai   white Australian/white person generally

durrie   cigarette (widespread)

gammon   a) rubbish b) joking, fake (widespread)

geeyahn   possum

gin   woman (offensive)

gone in   died, returned to one's country (widespread)

goonah   shit

Goorie   Aboriginal person from far northern New South Wales or south-eastern Queensland

gunjies   white police

gwong   rain

jagan   land

jahjam   child (pronounced *jar jum*)

jahlela   eating

jalgani   woman. Also the word for lightning.

jali jali   tree or trees

jalum   fish

jalum bira   fishing

jang   mouth

jingawahlu   greetings

jinung   foot

jinungalehla   standing

jiraman   kangaroo

jugi jugi   domestic chook

juhm   cigarette/smoke

julabai   piss

kalwunybah   place of lyrebirds

kanakas   Pacific Islander labourers (offensive)

kibum   moon

kipper   young, youthful (as in young initiates)

koruhmburuhm magpie

kubbil carpet snake

mibun wedgetail eagle

mil eye

milbong eye gone (blind)

minjehleyni laughing, happy

minya meat

mooki ghosts

mulanyin blue heron

Murbah short for Murwillumbah

Murri/Murrie Aboriginal person from most of southern Queensland

muttika motor car

ning quiet, silent

Njuruyn emu

nurrung the colour blue, here implying sky

Old People ancestors (widespread)

onetime a) soon, promptly or b) used for emphasis

oodgeroo paperbark tree

pooning echidna

porky porcupine

talga music

taran frog

themfla those people (Aboriginal English, widespread)

ugari shellfish, 'pipi'

warrigal dingo or domestic dog (Aboriginal English, widespread)

wirringin winter

womba insane or very silly

yanbillilla walking or going home

yarndi marijuana

yarraman horse (Aboriginal English, widespread)

yufla people being addressed (Aboriginal English, widespread)

yumba home or house